Book One

To Face the World

Runners

Book One

To Face the World

By

John C Pelkey

Runners

Book One: To Face the World
Book Two: A Time for Icebergs -- Coming Soon
Book Three: The Last Day Lily -- Coming Soon

Desert Breeze Publishing, Inc.
27305 W. Live Oak Rd #424
Castaic, CA 91384

http://www.DesertBreezePublishing.com

Copyright © 2014 by John C. Pelkey
ISBN 10: 1-61252-622-5
ISBN 13: 978-1-61252-622-5

Published in the United States of America
eBook Publish Date: December 2014
Print Publish Date: December 2014

Editor-In-Chief: Gail R. Delaney
Editor: Lysa Demorest
Marketing Director: Jenifer Ranieri
Cover Artist: Debbie Taylor

Cover Art Copyright by Desert Breeze Publishing, Inc © 2014

All rights reserved. No portion of this book may be reproduced or
transmitted in any form or by any electronic or mechanical means,
including photocopying, recording or by any information retrieval and
storage system without permission of the publisher.

Names, characters and incidents depicted in this book are products of
the author's imagination, or are used in a fictitious situation. Any
resemblances to actual events, locations, organizations, incidents or
persons -- living or dead -- are coincidental and beyond the intent of the
author.

Dedication and Acknowledgment

Dedicated to my former critique group, who saw Runners every week through eight months and thirty chapters, and never let me get away with anything. Anya, Eryn, Gary, and Kristi. You were the best. Thanks.

Prologue

July 28, 1996

Brrringgg!
What is it? Alarm clock. It sounds terrible, complaining extra loud for working on its day off.
I thunk it into silence as it's about to quit.
Sunday, five a.m., today is the day. I'm awake.
And up. I try to stuff my legs into jeans, but keep missing. Too much excitement coupled with too much tired and even more tension. Finally, I win and the jeans are on, along with a sweatshirt that didn't dare fight for fear of losing an arm.
I sneak downstairs to the family room, missing the last three steps and creating a two hundred decibel thud.
So much for me being quiet.
I hear my misnamed collie Rex throw out an exploratory *woof,* soon joined by a dozen more.
Some watch dog. She would watch a burglar steal her precious doghouse off the porch without as much as a growl, but one peep inside and it's bark city.
"Shut up, Rex," I yell out the back door. She doesn't stop, but her bark tone changes from *intruder* to *feed me.*
As I shoot on the TV with the remote, Dad emerges from the master bedroom in his red-plaid pajamas. "Why are you up?" he asks.
"It's today," I say. "She runs today. It's now."
"Well, quiet your dog. We don't want to wake the neighbors."
We have no neighbors.
Bob and Jim, the commentators, pop in after a commercial with, "Good morning, Atlanta." They yawn and stretch, even while on the air, making a big deal of how tired they are at eight a.m. their time. I managed about two hours, and they act like they slept about the same, but we have different reasons. I fretted; they partied.
Mom, taking the time to put on a robe, wanders out after Dad. She tosses Dad his.
"...one hundred five degrees in Atlanta today, and over ninety-five percent humidity again..."
Rex's barking continues. *Dumb dog.* I go out on the porch, and, instead of admonitions, I pick her up and bring her inside. At eighty pounds, Rex is fat to go with old. "You need more exercise."
"No dogs in the house," Dad mutters, unconvincingly.

John C. Pelkey

"Nobody gets to interrupt this," I reply. I'm not going to miss her moment.

"...the women's 3000-meter final is next. Seven and a half laps around a four hundred meter track..."

The phone rings. I put Rex down to answer. She scrambles for the back door. "Sit," I command as I pick up the phone.

"I'm already sitting, but thank you for thinking of me."

Beth.

"This is it, Jon Boy. We are all up watching. You have the recorder going yet?"

"No!" I hand the phone to Mom, who adds, "Bye, Sweetie," and hangs up.

I set the VCR on record. "...Trina Marlov. At twenty-six, she is the favorite and the world record holder with a time of 7:59:33. She was the first runner to shatter the mythical eight-minute barrier. Last year she won the woman's 3000-meter run in Oslo..."

Trina is a big woman, impressive, her coach, confident.

The phone rings again. Dad and Mom have set themselves in glue in front of the TV and point.

"Are you ready, LB?"

Dave, stationed at Fort Benning and less than a two-hour drive to Atlanta. If only I could be there.

"Hey, I did eight this morning. You would have been proud. You should try it with a sixty pound pack."

"No thanks, but if you want to run with me next time you're home."

"No thanks back. I said I did it, I didn't say how fast. I'm not in your league."

Coming from you, this is a top-end compliment.

"I want you to know I'm pulling for you two," he says. "Bye."

As I turn back to the TV, I smile inside.

"Jon Boy" and "LB." They've used those silly nicknames for me all my life. I hope they never change.

The TV pans across the runners. My favorite, the American upstart, has the fourth fastest qualifying time and stands next to Trina.

She doesn't look like a runner. She looks like a little kid. Blond, small, barely over five feet tall. Young, barely nineteen, looks thirteen. Slight build, barely there. Great legs though. No "barely" about them. A runner's legs.

She spots the camera, waves, and blows a kiss.

I can almost feel it hitting me.

Bob and Jim profile her. "...They call her the 'Pocket Rocket' because of her small size and tremendous acceleration..."

A nickname Lisa created. I wonder if she's watching. Yeah, she is.

"...and last year, she won the 3000-meter run in St. Petersburg, Trina's hometown. In a slow race, she and Trina stayed in the pack. Trina underestimated the American, who blew her away in the final fifty

2

To Face The World

meters. A month later, at a much-ballyhooed rematch in Oslo, our little runner didn't stay for the final. Someone in her life died. After missing Trina's world record in the preliminaries with time of a 7:59:49, she left to attend his funeral..."

Priorities.

More chitchat. "...She won her 3000-meter preliminary two days ago. In a textbook run, she stayed in the pack, caught, and passed the leader at the finish to win by an eyelash..."

Someone has to slip in a commercial, preceded by the *Tum, tum, tadum, dum, tum* melody they have to play every five minutes. Finally, the screen returns to the race and to Jim and Bob. It shows the mandatory standing around and getting ready.

"What's your prediction, Bob?"

"Jim, I don't think Trina will let anyone stay close this time. They don't call our girl the 'Pocket Rocket' for nothing, you know."

"Then, Bob, you agree Trina has to build up and maintain a substantial lead to win this race?"

"Of course, Jim, she will have to grind down the competition. If they are close, say in the last two hundred meters, it won't be close at the finish."

"Well, Bob, I'm sticking with our girl. She's nineteen now, and much wiser than last year. I think our runner will stick close, and blow Trina away at the finish."

"Anyone else to consider, Jim?"

"Always the Chinese, Bob. However, if our little runner and Trina don't finish one-two, it would be one of the larger upsets of these games. Any chance at a record?"

"Jim, the fastest time here so far is 8:28, and neither of the favorites produced it. Although we have the two fastest runners ever at this distance, it doesn't appear the pack is going to push it hard enough in the stifling heat. My prediction: No record will fall."

Bob and Jim blur out as the camera transitions back to the track.

The phone rings again. I grab it and try not to snap out my "Hello?"

"It's me."

Cindy.

"May I share the moment on the phone? You don't have to talk."

"Sure." We lapse into silence.

The starter's hands are up. *Bang!* They're off!

The American bursts off the line ahead of Trina and the rest before the first turn, and she steadily pulls away. The camera focuses on her personal coach, who is gaping at her in obvious disbelief. The "expert" people in the stands groan.

Bob wonders aloud, "What is going on? She can't keep up her pace."

Cindy echoes it. "Jon, what is she doing?"

As she completes the first lap, four hundred meters, she is twenty

3

John C. Pelkey

meters ahead of the next competitor. The sideliners yell conflicting instructions at her. She watches the electric timer at the split and ignores the people. The American coach flings his clipboard and turns away. The Russian coach isn't smiling either as she checks the times; the rest of the runners are slow.

The camera focuses on the American runner, zooming in close. She maintains a steady pace and her head nods in rhythm as she breathes, completely imperceptible to anyone not looking for it.

She's counting! She is timing her laps the way we taught ourselves so long ago.

To Face The World

Hi.

My name is Jon Perone, pronounced Pear-Ron. I'm a runner. A runner is a person who runs often and for long distances. I grew up a runner, sports wise; wasn't much else I could do. I had green eyes hidden behind wire-rimmed glasses, a ski jump for a nose, narrow shoulders, long, skinny arms, and small hands. I wasn't what you would have called macho. Great legs though, even then. A runner's legs. I won "Best Looking Legs" my senior year in high school, along with "Most Likely to be a Corporate Executive."

And now? Well, I still have green eyes. Thankfully, except from Jen, the rest of me grew.

This is my story, but it's not only about me. I mean it is my life and all, but so much more to life lies beyond the effort it takes to show up for it each day.

Life is about loving, and about someone loving back.

Life is about learning more than what seems to unfold the minute it happens to unfold.

Life is about believing in something or someone, especially when no one else does.

Life means the loving, unfolding, and believing happen for a reason and have some purpose.

Sometimes, finally figuring out even a little bitty part is worth all the trouble.

*****

On to my story. The first part begins on the playground back in March 1987, during recess in fourth grade.

*****

"Hey, batter, batter. Hey, batter, batter. Saaawwwiiing!"

Ed, our designated short stop, again distracted me with his best Cameron Frye imitation. I dribbled the ball foul toward first base and give Tommy his second strike. Even without Ed's distractions, I couldn't hit Tommy. A foul was a hit in my book.

Sandlot softball wasn't my favorite. Since I seldom got the chance to bat, I wasn't about to give up. One more strike.

The bell rang, but Tommy waved at me to stay put. "I want the last out."

I was the last out. Since we had no catcher, the batter had to chase the ball to the backstop if he missed. I missed. Tommy's pitch came fast and high, and I could only wave at it with the bat as it went by. The ball bounced once and stuck in the backstop screen.

"Stee-ri-ka Tha-ree!" As usual, Ed overdid everything. "Mark Langston strikes out Gorman Thomas for the third time tonight."

"Hey, you don't strike out your own teammates," Dan countered.

John C. Pelkey

Although almost sticking up for me, he wasn't about to help me get the ball dislodged. I watched Tommy's victory dance as I pulled on the ball, but it wouldn't budge. When I hit it with the bat, it came loose and squiggled away.

The principal appeared on the school steps, waving a bullhorn. "You have one minute to reach the door or you get detention."

Everyone took off as fast as they could go, leaving me behind. We had a thousand feet to run, no hope. Fighting back tears, I decided to give it my best shot, even with the bat and the late start after chasing down the ball. Halfway to the school building, I caught the slowest kids, and I passed the fastest kid, Tommy, right before reaching the door. I saw the surprise on his face as I passed him. I had never run as fast before. I had never even tried. My first real try, it seemed easy.

The principal grabbed me.

"I made it on time, didn't I?" I blurted out at him, dropping the bat and ball. He had me by my arm, which scared me.

"Yeah, you made it fine," he said, gasping, as if he had done all the running. "Five seconds to spare. But you shouldn't have. You're too young to run so fast."

As the rest of the group straggled in, he addressed them, still hanging on to me. "Fellows, this young man's speed and dedication have saved you. I hope you appreciate him."

I got a high five from Tommy, my first one ever.

"Go to your class."

They didn't argue. Someone grabbed the bat and ball, and they all disappeared in an instant, leaving me alone with the principal.

He let go, squatted down next to me, straightened out my shirt, gave me a warm smile, and said, "You're a runner, Jon Perone, a real runner."

*****

Okay, so much for the warm up. The main part with the girl begins almost two years later.

Chapter One

January 1989

"So you think looking like a dork will snag you a girl."

Never, ever try to comb semi-dry, unruly hair with the bathroom door wide open.

Along with the door, I left myself wide open for verbal sniping from my older and wiser brother, Dave. It didn't help watching him stand in front of me in a towel while modeling muscles I only dreamed of possessing.

Pumping up his chest, he displaced half the oxygen in the hall. For my chest, no one could tell the difference between when I pumped it and when I didn't.

"I mean, look at yourself. You're skinny, you wear glasses, and you have no arms." He flexed his arm muscles. "I do sixty chin-ups every day," he boasted. "Face it; no bodacious babe is going to give you a second glance. Now, you could get some homely, bookworm skag, maybe, but who wants one of those. So give it up, LB, and let me have my turn."

Little Brother. Dave didn't even call me by my name. Worse, he was correct. No girl would notice me based on my appearance. In all of my twelve years, none had.

In contrast, every girl noticed Dave. At sixteen, he had long since passed six feet and weighed over two hundred pounds. A three-sport letterman in football, wrestling, and track, he threw bodies in the fall and winter, and threw stuff in the spring, all muscle sports.

"Scramble, Egg," his other nickname for me, used when he wanted me to move. "This is a new year. Don't begin it on my bad side."

I gave up on my hair and moved out the door and into the hall, the same daily routine. I went first, my sister Beth followed me and took forever, and Dave began his day last. If lucky, I got a minute between Beth and Dave to brush my teeth and try to comb my hair.

As I trudged back toward my room, he said, "Wait a second, LB." I turned to face him. "It's more than building muscles. You can't become a babe magnet while sitting at home reading books, or by running through the forest and up and down our street. You have to get beyond your tree at the corner. You have to face the world."

Bummer. You've crushed my entire existence, reading and running, in a single sentence. Not to mention my tree. Life isn't fair.

"I'll show you," I muttered to myself, slamming my door. "Someday,

John C. Pelkey

I'll go beyond our street and find the best girl out there. And someday, BB, you'll have dirt." I made a hands-folded prayer signal and stared up at the ceiling. "You listening?" I asked.

Not likely, huh, God. I'm sure you have better things to do. You've given Dave's two yummies in two years. His current flame, tall, blond, curvy, and available, only reminds me of my own inadequacies. Plus she is in as good a shape as he is. With her muscles, even she can take me.

After feeding Rex and our cats, I tried to reach Dave's chin bar in the barn while Beth fed her two horses and our three cows. Beth was halfway between Dave and me. She spent more time focused on trying to grow her boobs to please guys than anything to do with a younger brother. I didn't mind. At least on the rare occasion when she did speak to me, she was civil.

This must have been such an occasion. When I couldn't even reach the bar jumping, she laughed and grabbed me from behind. "On three. One... two... three."

Between her boost and my jump, I reached it. I managed two good chin-ups and one not so good before my arms told me they were ready to strike. "Three this week," I told her. "Four next week."

"You better find something to climb on, because I'm not boosting you up every day." Despite her comment, she helped me back down. "Why the sudden interest in chip ups?"

"Dave says he does sixty every day."

"Dave says a lot of things, although he does do something to keep those muscles." She glazed off for a second.

What do girls think about when they go into glaze mode?

"Is he a hunk?" I asked.

"Yeah, I guess; all my friends think he is. Dumber than a brick, though. I'm not much smarter." She swished my hair. "You got the brains, Jon."

I thought Beth was kind of cute for a sister, but a bit too skinny like me. "What did you get?" I asked.

"Looks," she replied. "Like Mom's. Someday maybe her boobs, too. Soon, I hope."

"Is it why you push on the pumpy thing we saw advertised on the TV?" I asked.

"Hey, have you been peeking in my room?" she snapped.

"It makes a noise," I replied, a rather lame explanation.

"I wondered about the dumb squeak sound," she said, softening her glare to a smile. "Hey, a girl has to improve her assets. Don't tell anyone."

"I won't, promise," I said, shaking my head.

I have no one to tell.

"I have to look good. I'm not going to be a rocket scientist like you."

I don't want to be a rocket scientist, but I don't want to get a B either.

Deciding not to think about it, I left for the half-mile walk down to the end of Notch Hill Road, where I caught the bus for the eight-mile ride to South Valley Middle School. Birds chirped in the trees. I heard the occasional thwack of a golfer hitting his ball on the golf course beyond the thicket bordering our road on the west side. Some people golfed every day, even in the winter, although Washington winters were more wet than cold. Today wasn't either.

Each of the other four residences on the east side of Notch Hill Road had pastures like ours, but we were the only ones left with horses and cows. The rest grew grass and mice. They gave our barn cats something to do if they got tired of dry cat food.

Shortly before reaching the bus stop, I jumped up and rapped the weathered and leaning "Welcome to Aurora Valley" city limit sign, as I did every day. No one understood why our road needed a sign coming back from a dead end. Everyone had to leave Aurora Valley to drive up the road in the first place. Of course, they had put up a sign facing the other way, reminding people they were leaving. One day when it fell over, they just took it away. Maybe they had a more important road needing a going-away sign.

The sign marked the separation of our country road and the city streets. Aurora Valley began just before Notch Hill Road reached De Soto Avenue. On the right, an enormous maple tree dominated the intersection. It was larger than every other tree lining our road.

Mere seconds before the bus arrived, Dave dropped Beth off next to me while on his way to the high school. He had to throw out some smart remark like, "Doing a good job there holding up your tree."

It is my tree.

Someday, after I grew up, maybe I'd buy the land and save the tree. The lot was large enough to build a house up on the hill behind it, and far enough away from my maple tree to save it. I was certain, though, with the amount of leaves it dumped, no one would.

Occasionally, Beth and I shared the tree in the rain, waiting for the bus. No other kids lived on Notch Hill Road. We stopped being big sister and little brother when the bus came. She went first and always sat in the back; I sat in the front. She didn't ride the bus home, too many after-school activities, so I had my tree and the walk to myself.

Once on the bus, I continued to transition into my daily routine for school, disappearing mode. My third and fourth "skills," singing and math, had placed me in the advanced math class and the middle school choir, one of only two kids from sixth grade. To make it easier, for them anyway, they stuck me in a locker right in the middle of the older kid wing, far away from my peers, whoever they were. Not like anyone noticed.

Life really isn't fair.

At school, I blended in as invisible. No touching. No eye contact. Lots of direction reverses. Keep moving. Say nothing. If unlucky, which

John C. Pelkey

happened too often, I encountered the girl in the next locker.

Meredith, a colossal eighth grader, had the size to play linebacker for the Chicago Bears. She had the disposition of a Bear linebacker, too. When in a good mood, she called me "Larry La La" for my singing. When in a bad mood, she called me worse things.

Meredith jammed her locker, so, instead of responding to the combination, it opened when she slugged it. It closed when she slugged it, too.

Some days she slugged me hello, some days gave me a hug, which wasn't better. Much taller than I was, she crushed me against her "growing concerns" as she called her top, and whispered, "I want some tongue," loud enough for everyone to hear. I wasn't certain what she meant, but as far as I could tell, I had never given her any.

This day she muttered, "I hate school," and slammed her fist into the locker a second time. To my surprise, she gave me a non-crushing hug and added, "Happy New Year, Jon," as she stomped off. Her scowl, more cruel than normal, told me someone had ticked her off. I didn't know who did, but I had a thrill about who didn't. Me.

The next day, Meredith was gone.

"Hey, Perone, your babe got booted for writing a paper full of obscenities." The kid in the locker next to Meredith spoke to me for the first time.

Falling for the bait, I mumbled, "Writing a paper got her kicked out of school?"

"Na, swearing got your sweetie an F. Slugging Ms. Hargrove for the F got her kicked out."

I felt good for about one second, until he added, "You know you liked her, Perone. I saw you squeezing her tits."

Yeah, but squeezing them with my nose doesn't count.

"No more tongue, Perone; you're gonna miss it."

I realized I was going to miss Meredith. As long as she had been there, no one else bothered me.

Beth, surprise, rode the bus home. I took off ahead, but she caught me.

"Heard you lost your girlfriend today, Jon Boy."

"Don't call me Jon Boy," I snapped.

"So you did."

"She wasn't my girlfriend, but she was my friend. She was nicer to me than the rest of you eighth graders."

"Did you slip her some tongue?"

"No."

"Do you know what it means?"

I took off running. Beth couldn't even remotely keep up and didn't try. Instead, she yelled, "It means you stick your tongue in her mouth when you kiss her. You should have tried it; you would have liked it, Jon

To Face The World

Boy."

I shouted back. "You call me 'Jon Boy' one more time and I'll tell everyone what your real name is, Bathsheba."

Beth fell silent, but I saw a rock skip up the pavement next to me.
Point taken.

*****

Everything changed two days after Dave's kind remarks and the day after Meredith's departure. It began normal, as I made my way to my locker before school started, counting the floor tiles, something I did regularly in the eighth grade wing.

When I glanced up, I saw a girl. Not just any girl, *the girl.* She was almost my height, slender, shoulder-length blond hair, with a slightly turned up nose, and a slightly turned down mouth. Her high cheekbones curved into tiny, matching dimples. She had an aura flowing around her, which absorbed and radiated all the light in the hallway. Her face, angelic, a face a twelve-year-old male, *me,* could forever get lost in. She shined without even noticing me. Or maybe she shined because she didn't notice me.

She wore an enormous emerald green sweatshirt, which stretched halfway to her knees. It said "Sugar Bay Plantation" under a sailboat, sunset, and bent palm tree.
Sugar Bay Plantation, where is it?

A white, pleated skirt barely appeared below the sweatshirt. Her sweatshirt color matched her green knee socks and her skirt matched her sparkling white running shoes, properly laced.

She had great legs, even as a sixth grader. Not the skinny, stick kind the rest of the girls had. Not fat either. Her knees didn't have knobs like everyone else, including me. Her skin seemed more light golden than white, indicating she had more sun than we got in Western Washington. She seemed older than I was from her skirt down, but younger otherwise. She didn't appear to have any discernible figure under the sweatshirt, only lots of extra space unfilled.

I realized I had gone from her hair to her feet and back again, in the short time I watched her. As she hadn't noticed me yet, I had ample opportunity to do a complete review, top to bottom.
Her bottom seems as lost in the sweatshirt as her top.
Oops. It's not like I'm standing here ogling her. Yes, I am!

She was in Meredith's locker, or at least trying to get in. Her backpack leaned against my locker, with her coat on top.

Holding a paper, she spun the combination again, with the same result. The handle didn't move. I stood stupidly to one side of her, watching and waiting, for what I didn't know.

Finally, she noticed me, her emerald green eyes connecting with

John C. Pelkey

mine. I thought my being quiet would startle or upset her, but I didn't appear to. Instead, she gave me a shy smile, lighting me up, along with the whole hallway behind me, maybe the whole school building. She hooked me for life from the very first second of her very first smile.

"It won't open," she breathed at me.

She spoke! To me!

She had a slight accent, which made her speech sound as lovely as the rest of her. She smelled good, too, something like cocoa butter, a fancy shampoo like what Beth tried on occasion.

You are so beautiful.

I thought-whispered more compliments to her in my mind, hoping she could hear them. When she couldn't, I realized I had to say something aloud, so I calmly responded, "The girl who had your locker until yesterday, well, she jammed it. So um... er... uh, you have to hit it, uh... sort of... um, like this."

I can't believe it. I'm speaking to her and she's listening.

I gave the locker my best shot, a blow sending pain shooting past my elbow, past my shoulder, clear to my feet. The locker remembered, and opened.

"Oh, thank you," she trilled, while stuffing in her coat.

"Um, you're new here." I deducted things well. "If you need help with anything at all, ever, please ask. I would be happy to help you in any way people... can help... other people... in need." I babbled and stumbled at the same time.

"Oh, thank you," she trilled again, proving my point.

"Jon," I replied as an introduction, and added, "Three letters," to separate me from the four letter Johns. "Perone. Jon Perone."

"Oh, thank you, Jon. J... O... N?" I nodded. "Jon." She kind of rolled it around with her tongue, as if tasting it. "Okay, got it, Jon. Bye." She dismissed herself with a smile.

So this is heaven! I love it!

Leaning against her locker and ignoring the ringing bell, I pictured our future together.

She is going to be here every day, many times every day. I am going to be here to open her locker for her. I am going to bash my hand every day, many times every day for her. She is going to say, "Oh, thank you," many times every day for me.

If I survive, maybe we could be friends and I can ask her to...

I stopped, a sickening feeling enveloping my stomach.

I could ask her to do what? Run? Read? Sing? Make up math story problems?

Ouch!

I had nothing to ask her to do, nothing to include me in, anyway. I resolved to expand my horizons.

"Mr. Perone, this is school and you are a student here. Aren't you

To Face The World

supposed to be somewhere?" An obnoxious and uncaring hall monitor broke my reverie.

*****

When I reached my hall the next morning, she stood there, waiting for me to open her locker. I walked the final twenty feet, studying her as she studied me back. She wore jeans and another sweatshirt, this one from Poipu Beach, Kauai, Hawaii. I was certain she would fit in on any Hawaiian beach.

Maybe we could honeymoon there.

My arm groaned, but the rest of me sang as I set my backpack down and prepared to do battle with the locker again.

It's a painful job, but somebody has to do it. Today, I'm the somebody.

Pride does go before a fall.

It was a big fall.

She raised one small hand and sighed. At least I think she sighed. "I'm only a sixth grader, so I've moved to the sixth grade wing. I wanted to tell you so you wouldn't hit my locker and hurt yourself for nothing. You must be older. Thanks for your help, Jon. Bye."

"Oh, I'm not older," I croaked. "I'm in the older choir, I mean the middle school choir. It's why my locker is here, in the older section." I charmed her right off her feet.

"Oh," she said. She walked a few feet, stopped, turned around, and gazed at me in an odd sort of way, with the same shy smile, which drew itself up into a question, complete with a crinkle between her eyes. Her smile imprinted onto my brain cells forever.

"I hope to be in choir next year," she remarked, mostly to herself as she stared at the floor. She raised her eyes and smiled again. "We could have a class together."

I saw the sparkle in her eyes as she locked them to mine as she backed away.

Still, you're leaving, slowly, but surely, leaving... me.

"What's your name?" I asked, trying to get her to stop.

"Oh, I'm sorry, Jon. My name is Jennifer, or Jenni, spelled with an 'I' on the end. Jenni... Carling." She returned to me, reached out, and took my hand, sort of a shake without moving up and down. "Pleased to meet you, Jon Perone."

She's touching me!

Every nerve in my body concentrated on her touch. Her hand felt warm, as if I had touched Mom's electric blanket set on low. Her fingers were soft, but strong, with a guy grip. I wanted to keep her hand forever, but she took it back.

"Bye, Jon."

I tried to think of something to make her stay.

John C. Pelkey

What to say? Jenni, you are beautiful. No, stupid. Think of something, anything. I love your name. No, I would love it no matter what it was.

In total disarray, I blurted out, "Where is Sugar Bay?"

She turned and considered me, clearly confused.

"Your sweatshirt, from yesterday."

"Oh, the Sugar Bay on my sweatshirt. I don't know where or even if it exists. It's something my dad pours money into for a tax break."

Jennifer's eyes glazed over and I could feel her anger, although not directed at me. It didn't matter. I had done it. I had squashed our budding relationship with a single dumb question.

She left me, dragging my dreams along in her wake. Crushed, I watched her walk out of my world. My heart slipped into my stomach, giving me a terrible case of indigestion, or so I felt.

Only twelve years old, my life is over.

Chapter Two

My world went back to the normal routine it was before I met Jennifer. I had no classes with her, no lunch period. Her mother brought her to school and picked her up, dropping her off from the street, not the parking lot, and making her walk farther. Her mother drove a fantastic, deep green-colored car I recognized as a Mercedes. She must not have wanted to get it dented mixing with the common-place other cars.

If I saw Jennifer, she was off in the distance talking to someone else. If she passed me in the hall and noticed, she would say "Hi." If she said "Hi," I said "Hi." This gave her new girlfriends the opportunity to scrutinize me. Once I said "Hi," first, kind of to her back. Either she didn't hear me, or she didn't want to. I managed to complete the entire school year without any conversations of two or more words with her. Our relationship was progressing well.

My relationship with my brother was progressing well, too. One morning he caught me in front of the bathroom mirror, searching for an arm muscle. "Here, let me check," he said, grabbing my arm. After crushing my muscle between two fingers, he pronounced judgment.

"How could a man as strong as Dad and a woman as attractive as Mom ever produce you? Somebody must have switched you at the hospital."

For the difference it made, better had he punched me. A punch I could get over. I was certain why Jennifer confined her conversation with me to one or less words. I congratulated myself for my failure to attempt any kind of conversation with her.

With nothing going for me, why would she bother? Why should I?

My only satisfaction in life came when Dave's second girlfriend dumped him for a skinny guy with glasses and a permanent Honor Society reservation. Dave's grade point average hovered in the low twos on a good day. Not things he appeared to worry over, either about her or his grades.

A week after I won the Knowledge Bowl Team's MVP award, he won Aurora Valley's Athlete of the Year award, a first for a sophomore. I got a two-square-inch blurb in the paper's "Other Events" section; he got a front-page photo and full sports page write up.

With a single night of mourning the loss of the blonde under his belt, he went fishing for another girl. "Plenty out there looking for love. And I got plenty of love for them to look for."

He took up with a willowy, exotic Hawaiian girl, who made the blonde seem average. She had the most beautiful eyes -- when she

15

John C. Pelkey

smiled, they sparkled almost as much as Jen's -- and the shiniest black hair I had ever seen, all the way down past her seat. Plus she could stand on one hand. Dave was moving up. I had yet to move.

*****

During the following summer, I found out where Jennifer lived, purely by accident. One Saturday, while running to my mom's shop next to the high school, I spotted the green Mercedes. To my surprise, it turned into a driveway across the street opposite me. I was in the well-to-do section of town, about a mile from my house, with a mile to the high school beyond.

Future reference. Some day we will attend high school. I can run to her house and walk her to school. Ha, ha.

Even my mind thought I was a joke.

Not to be conspicuous, I ducked behind the picket fence of the house I was next to, and fiddled with a weed I found in the bark dust, pulling it out. As I watched, I found a couple of others and pulled them, too.

A silver-haired man, no doubt her father, got out, repeatedly pushing a device, most likely the garage door opener.

"Darn thing doesn't work."

"Well, don't sit there; get the key," came from inside the car, maybe from Jennifer's mom. With tinted windows, I couldn't see her.

The car door behind her father opened and Jennifer popped out. She trotted toward a hedge growing out from their house and disappeared, as if she went right through it. Her dad got back into the car. Thirty seconds later, the garage door opened.

A shadow appeared, attached to a man towering above me.

"You do yards?" he asked.

"I can do yours," I said. *For free,* I added to myself.

"Funny way of applying, pulling my weeds, but, obviously, they need some pulling."

"Great, sir. When can I start?"

"I think you already have, young man."

Young man.

My first ever adult reference and my first gainful employment. The homeowner, Mr. Dunlap, was one of the many people who worked in Seattle. He didn't want to spend his days off recovering from regular work by trying to do yard work. When I thinned out the dead blooms on his flowers and trimmed his hedge, he paid me more than I expected, and set me up for every Saturday.

Thus, I had discovered a new branch on my narrow horizon, only six months later. More important, it was right across the street from Jennifer Carling.

To Face The World

"You did what?" Dave muttered, after I surprised my family with the good news at dinner.

"I have a job," I repeated. "I'm going to take care of Mr. Dunlap's yard."

"Yard work isn't a real job," Dave retorted. "I got a job."

Yeah, you got a job digging ditches for Dad, with a career path to operating a backhoe. I have gained outside employment. Unlike you, my wages come into the family instead of across it.

Alone in my room, I compared our recent accomplishments. The high water mark, I had a four-point average, double Dave's two.

In middle school, I had a letter in Knowledge Bowl, two math competition trophies, and an annual choir participation certificate.

Dave had been a two-way starter on the football team from his first game as a freshman. He won his last ten matches in wrestling, and held the league records throwing the javelin and the discus. In two years, he had six high school letters and an MVP in football.

Dad and Mom went to Dave's football games, Dad, alone, to his wrestling matches and track meets. Mom went to my Knowledge Bowl tournaments and math competitions. Dad and Mom listened to me sing. I guessed it made us even, at least one parent each, but somehow I felt slighted.

It wasn't like my parents intentionally played favorites. Dad had football, wrestling, and throwing stuff in track to talk about with Dave, the same things he had done in school. Mom had Art Club, Journalism Club, and Year Book staff activities to talk about with Beth, the same things she had done in school. Neither had a lot of math and singing to talk about with me. At least Mom tried, although less as time went on.

I still harbored hope. Someday I would be taller and stronger, if not more handsome, and then Dad would notice me. I continued to use Dave's chin bar, jumping from a bucket to reach it. By the end of summer, I had added four more for a total of seven, twice a day. Breaking Dave's sixty seemed impossible, unless I tried ten times a day.

Maybe Dave splits it up, like thirty, twice a day. Who am I kidding? I know he doesn't. He's massive; I'm skinny. He has real live girls in his life; I have dreams of one girl, Jennifer Carling, not remotely in my life. Not much of a comparison.

I decided to call her Jen, in my mind, anyway, because everyone else called her Jennifer or Jenni. Calling her Jen made her special. I made up Jen songs as I mowed, the noise of the mower drowning me out when I sang them. However, my mowing and singing in Mr. Dunlap's yard didn't provide any opportunity to see Jen, even though she lived across the street. She was busy Saturdays and never home.

Not to be discouraged, I read up on how to garden, about twenty books, and practiced on his yard. It must have paid off. He recommended me to his friend, Dr. Canfield, who lived on the north side

John C. Pelkey

of the Aurora Valley Golf Course.

Dr. Canfield had a beautiful home. The road narrowed in the front and looped around and down in the back, following the curve of the golf course. He viewed a green out the front, and a tee, a fairway, and a green out the back. He had only one neighbor, whose property also extended from the upper road in the front to the lower road in the back. Dr. Canfield had a huge deck with a hot tub. Mostly, he had lawn, lots of lawn. It followed the road and dropped from the front to the back, well over half an acre. It had tree islands, with flowers around the huge evergreen trees, which someone had trimmed up high so not to ruin the view.

I had to mow with his electric mower, around the trees, up the hill, down the hill, always keeping the cord safe, and always having to backtrack around each tree, each pass. It took two hours to mow and another hour to edge, rake, and weed. It was worth the effort when he paid me twenty-five dollars a week. I practiced every concept I learned to make Dr. Canfield's yard the most beautiful in town.

*****

While walking home after mowing Dr. Canfield's lawn, I made a startling discovery across the road from our driveway, a golf ball half buried in the ditch. I searched along the road and through the bushes, finding two more. They were all the same brand, Clover, one I had never heard of or seen advertised on TV. I found the fourth one on our side of the road. I surprised Dad when I told him where I found them, over one hundred yards from the golf course and not in the direction between any tee and green.

"Someone must not have been entirely pleased by his golf game," Dad observed. "Good thing they didn't hit anyone. Why don't you take them to the pro shop at the golf course and see if they will buy them? While you're at it, ask them to remind their players to hit down the fairway, not across it."

I thought he was joking. However, Sunday evening I decided to see what would happen. I struggled through the sticker bushes and swamp into some tall grass next to a lake. I couldn't believe what I found. There were golf balls all over the place. It was like hunting Easter eggs, only easier. I took off my shirt and filled it full of golf balls. After easily wading across a narrow part of the lake, which turned out to be about a foot deep, I found the pro shop as it was about to close.

"Would you like to buy some golf balls?" I asked the man locking the front door, whose tag said "Melvin Hernandez." I liked talking to him. Even though I was twelve, he was my size.

"Let us see what you brought me," he said, not sounding entirely pleased.

To Face The World

I dumped them out on to the ground.

"Where did you find them?" he asked, apparently surprised at the size of my stash.

"Over by the lake." I pointed.

"You found them on the golf course next to the lake?" He didn't sound like he believed me, and maybe I was in trouble.

"Not on the golf course side, on the other side. On the corner where the lake is narrow."

"How did you get there?" he asked.

"I live there, on the other side of the lake, through the trees, across the road."

He fingered through my stash, dismissing it, until he found something he wanted. One after another, he picked out the four golf balls I'd found by the road. Each time he found one, his frown lessened. He carefully checked each one of the rest, searching for a fifth one.

"These are rare," he said. "I will take these. How much you want for the lot?" He smiled as he said it, so things were okay.

"Don't know." I bargained well.

"I tell you what. I do not buy them, because you do not sell them. Not to worry; no one else will go to there. So hear the deal. You bring me the golf balls, I teach you to play the golf. You want to learn?"

Mr. Hernandez had used a word I had only heard once before in the same way. "He who has ears, let him hear," came from a sermon. When Mr. Hernandez talked, he sounded like a minister, standing high up in his box.

After thinking about it, I replied with, "Sure. Why not?" Other than mowing lawns, running, and reading, I hadn't packed my summer schedule full of activities. Golf could expand my horizons even more, something else Jen and I could do, if ever.

So we became friends; Mr. Hernandez taught me how to play and I listened to his sermons. He had plenty of sermons. We were two five footers, sixty years apart, playing the game of golf and life together.

We began the next Saturday after lawns. Mr. Hernandez brought out a set of short loaner clubs and tested them on me, watching my swing. After some adjustment, we moved to my first encounter with a golf ball on the putting green.

"You drive for show, but you putt for dough," he said, easily sinking one from about thirty feet. I could sink them from five feet, and further as he showed me how to line up my putts.

"You are one bright boy; am I right?" All I could do was nod.

"Math major?" I nodded again.

"Ninety degree angle, always, your putter to the golf ball. Your ball's route to the cup may or may not be directly at it. Read the green. Listen to it. What is it telling you? Lean left? Lean right? Pay attention. Before you swing, think the ball into the cup. See it going in."

John C. Pelkey

The next week we tried the driving range. This was much tougher as I kept glancing up and missing the ball.

"See this ball, Jon," he said, waving one at me. "It does not go anywhere on its own. It only goes when you hit it. You cannot kill it, so be not afraid to swing. Smoothly. Watch your ball when you swing. Count to two after you hit before you look away. Swing, hit, one, two."

To follow up what he said, he whacked one against the two hundred yard sign, straight and true. Following his teaching, I whacked one, barely missing the one hundred yard sign, but it still felt good.

"How long have you played?" I asked.

"I was younger than you," he replied, drifting off for a minute. Finally, he came back and sat on a bench behind the driving tees.

"Jon, my young friend, I will tell you my story. I was born in Mexico. We had nothing and over here was everything. One day I snuck across the border alone. They didn't have golf carts in those days. I earned my first American dollar caddying on a Southern California golf course."

He fished out his wallet and showed it to me, folded neatly in a corner. It was a silver certificate, dated 1928.

"Jon, I found my life with the golf. I worked at anything around a golf course in exchange for getting to play, sometimes on Sunday nights like now. I did not have an instructor, so I taught myself by watching others at play in the day and copying them at night."

We stopped and whacked some more balls. With concentration, watching the club into the ball and not letting my eyes wander, the ball went somewhere, occasionally rolling past the one hundred yard sign.

"I won some, but never made the big time," he said between swings. "I played the best courses, and never stopped trying to improve. Now, I feel the age in my swing, and in my heart. But I still love it, love the golf."

I focused on my next swing, and it rolled almost to the one hundred fifty sign.

"Good swing, Jon, good finish." He put his club into his bag and I followed. "Here," he said, handing me a tube device about two feet long. "When we practice after closing, we have to pick them up."

I learned to putt, drive, chip, and pick up golf balls. My golf horizon improvement came with chores, but it was still fun. Mr. Hernandez never asked me to do something he didn't do, although practicing at the driving range was more for me than for him.

"You have great concentration, Jon. You can do well. Bring some more balls if you can; we play again next week, maybe on the course."

*****

True to his word, with forty more golf balls in his hamper, we teed

To Face The World

off the next Sunday night. I took twice the shots as he took, not counting misses, but felt something happening to me. Golf, even as bad as I was, I could feel it growing on me. I could do this. Mr. Hernandez could do it, too. What he lacked in distance, he made up with accuracy.

"Good shot," he said on the seventh hole, a par three, when I reached the green on my fourth shot. "When you grow, you will develop more power. You will see."

"Did it bother you not to grow taller?" I asked, wondering if it was a good question.

"Jon, let me tell you how it is good to be short. My Juanita, she is much taller than I am. This is good. Let me explain. Say you are with a girl. You are alone. She put her head on your chest. Nice, huh? I am with my Juanita. I am short. I put my head on her chest. Much nicer. Who has the better deal?"

I told Mr. Hernandez about Jennifer Carling, the only person to whom I spoke her name aloud.

He thought the name Carling was familiar, but he didn't seem to know why. He did offer me some advice. "You only now finished with the sixth grade, not ready for the girl. Let the time go by. When you are ready, you be friends first. When you are good friends, things can happen. Do not be discouraged you are not Mr. Bogart or Mr. Gable yet. You are a great boy, Jon. If it is meant to be, she will find you out. You want to be good at something today, you be good at the golf."

I mulled over what Mr. Hernandez said on my way home. Bogart and Gable weren't great looking men either. I found a wet nose in my hand. Rex had come to greet me. I raced her up the driveway.

John C. Pelkey

Chapter Three

Seventh and half of eighth grade came and went, eighteen months of me alone with me, for the most part anyway. Although I thought about Jen, I slowly stopped thinking about her and me. I made enough semi-close friends in school to get by, and spent the summers reading, running, mowing two lawns, and playing golf in exchange for finding more golf balls. Except for Mr. Hernandez, everything I did, I did with me.

I would run through the forest next to our farm, almost two miles up a curving gradual slope to the top of a hill called The Notch. It was a flat rock formation with a high side and a low side, with a notch cut in the middle. From the other side, The Notch was a sheer cliff. At the top, the high and low sides of The Notch were bare rock and steep, with grass covering the space between them, about ten feet wide. I could peek out over Aurora Valley, or sit and read, with Rex as my only companion. No one in my family went there with me and no one else knew.

*****

In February, our country invaded Iraq. Unlike the Vietnam War, according to my parents, it had no noticeable effect on anything except Dave. It also ended as fast as it began.

"I want to fight, kick some camel jockey butt. This is our country and I want to help defend it."

I wanted him to fight, too, but I wasn't up on how fighting for one country against another ten thousand miles away was defending anything. I did know I was thoroughly tired of defending myself against Dave. He tormented me just enough to stay under our parents' radar. I didn't help my cause by keeping my mouth shut, but at the same time, I didn't want to become the sissified little brother.

"Dave, you need to finish senior year before we talk about it. After you graduate, if you want to join any armed forces branch, you will have my full support."

Dave beamed, for about two seconds.

"Although they live in the desert and worship a different god, they are people, Dave. Most of them have the same hopes, dreams, and feelings you have. Racial slurs are not acceptable in any circumstance. You remember that."

Dad's short directive ended the conversation. Despite Dave's bluster, Dad's word was law.

To Face The World

Beth didn't torment me, other than an occasional "Jon Boy," which I tried to tolerate. I countered with an even rarer "Bathsheba," which she did not try to tolerate.

"You call me Bathsheba in front of any other person and you will regret breathing. I promise."

I kept my mouth shut. She got her way, and I didn't get mine. Same with Dave. Not getting their way was what happened to all younger brothers.

As we got older, Beth's zany personality grew on me in a good way. Sometimes when we fed the animals in the morning, she would practice breaking up speeches.

"Zack, it's been, but it isn't going to be. You are so special, and you will be to someone. You will have to move on because I already have." She cracked a smile. "What do you think?"

"You could say, like, 'goodbye,' maybe," I offered.

"Jon Boy, you are missing the point. I must get it right. I don't want him to catch me in a stutter at a time like this. I want him to remember me, and I want him to remember what could have been. Last impressions are so important."

As I had yet to break up with a girl, or have a girl break up with me, this didn't mean anything. I would have to wait for the event to understand.

Beth grew in other ways, too, both taller and curvier, as she had hoped. I became proud of her being my sister. I wished I could feel the same about Dave, and continued to pray my dirt prayer on occasion when he did something unusually despicable.

I worked up to ten chin-ups, twice a day. I still didn't have much muscle to flex, but mowing lawns became easier. More positive, I didn't need the bucket anymore. I guessed we were all keeping our horizons on the horizon.

*****

Dave's Hawaiian girl went back home, and he lost her. As he had spent so much time at her house, life with him had almost been tolerable. My joy at his failure contrasted with the crush of dealing with him at home again. My joy became short-lived, as with all hunk types, he bounced back.

The next week, he began seeing another girl. With golden brown hair swirling all around her matching brown eyes, Cindy, his senior squeeze, was the best looking of the lot and the nicest, even to me. She didn't exactly flirt with me, but she made me acutely aware she was around. If she bumped into me, she didn't get upset about it. Once, reading over my shoulder from behind, her front brushed against me. She had to notice, but kept reading.

23

John C. Pelkey

"Are you okay, Jon?" she asked without moving. I guessed she felt me tense up.

A complete surprise, I replied with, "You smell good."

What am I saying?

Cindy took it much better than I did and said, "Of course I smell good." Instead of moving away, she wrapped her arms around me and gave me a hug. "It's so sweet of you to say so."

For the first time, I realized how nervous Cindy made me. I wondered what it meant, but had no one to ask.

Dave didn't live at Cindy's house. They had issues over there, so Cindy hung out at our house. This changed things. As Dave couldn't be mean to me and nice to Cindy at the same time, he had to give up his normal behavior and become somewhat human.

In contrast to Dave, once allowed to date, Beth averaged a guy a week, sometimes two. "If I have to go to college, I see no point in wasting my time on one boy in high school. Be like having hamburger every night."

"More like steak," Dave replied. "When you have the best, no point in shopping around."

My dirt prayer had reversed again. Now he had the best girl ever; I had dirt.

*****

Although we had choir together and PE at the same time, I didn't see much of Jen. I was a math and science person; she was not. She was a social person; I was not. The day at the locker became a distant memory, and I moved on with my life. I even had a girlfriend for a while, a math, science, and reader type, who sang soprano two seats from Jen.

In math, Alyssa and I teamed up for an in-class assignment to create story problems. She called me about it after school and we compared academic notes. We both had 4.0 averages, but my Knowledge Bowl MVP trophy put me slightly ahead in her mind. I guessed it made me desirable in some unknown way. Still, it felt nice when someone noticed.

We talked, or she talked and I listened. Although we didn't do anything outside of school beyond her phone calls, it was a leg up on my social status.

Alyssa fit Dave's description of the suitable candidate for my level of value as a male. She was tall and thin, with long, straight hair, and might have been halfway attractive with her huge glasses off, which was never. She was quite pushy, and her pushing me gave us both something to do.

At lunch, I had been a lower-level fringe sitter to Ed and Dan, who were upper-level fringes to Tom. "I'm not sitting with those guys," Alyssa said when I jacked up enough courage to ask her to have lunch

To Face The World

with me. "We're sitting over here."

Unlike me, Alyssa had fringes who sat wherever she sat. Instead of guys, I ate lunch with girls, a step up and worth the pushy, so I hoped.

I soon learned I had overrated the girlfriend part. My single effort at doing a boyfriend-girlfriend thing, trying to take her hand, she met with instant resistance. "Your space," she said, pointing at me. "My space," pointing at herself. "Separate, but equal."

She tried to make it into a joke, but it fell flatter than she was. Tough having a girlfriend who didn't want me to touch her. Worse, she was one-sided, as she didn't have the same issue, her being physically pushy along with emotionally pushy.

Alyssa's single lasting contribution to my life came in late February, two years, and almost two months after I met Jen. When Mr. Dobson, our amazing new music teacher, asked someone to volunteer to direct for a spring competition, the class froze.

"I know this is new for everyone, but some of you may want to be music majors in college. Think of this as an opportunity."

"Opportunity to get our butts kicked." Someone mumbled it, but he heard.

"So what if we get our butts kicked. Has anyone here ever not gotten their butt kicked? It doesn't mean you give up. When you are as old as I am, you regret what you didn't try far more than you regret what you failed at."

Most everyone laughed, which I understood, as Mr. Dobson still had to be in his twenties.

"If no one volunteers, I will volunteer someone. I might volunteer someone anyway. What do you think of that?"

Silence.

When I glanced at Alyssa, she pointed at the podium and waved her fingers in a walking motion, in essence, telling me to go. Pushy, as usual.

No way am I going to volunteer.

Alyssa's motion caught Jen's attention, and she followed Alyssa's eyes, finding me at the other end. Instead of glancing away, which is what I always did, I found myself frozen in an eye lock with her. She flashed what I could only describe as intense anger, and it burned right through me. She pointed at Alyssa and mouthed the single word, "Why?"

I didn't understand her question. Jen was furious at me for watching Alyssa?

"Mr. Perone, what are you doing?" Mr. Dobson forced me back to reality. The entire class had caught me staring at Jen and laughed out their pleasure until he cut them off with a swish of his baton.

"Now choir, let's give Jon the opportunity he so richly deserves," he said. "I'm waiting."

25

John C. Pelkey

"Sir, I guess I'm volunteering."

"Well, thank you so much..." he said, looking at me, "...Miss Carling." The class stared to snicker some more, as he turned to face her. "Jenni, I hope your personal choice for conductor is a good one for us."

The class loved it. If they were laughing before, it was nothing compared to now. I didn't dare peek at Jen or Alyssa, or anyone else. Even the seventh grader sitting behind me in the bass section felt brave enough to whisper a tired, "Smooth move, X-lax," cliché.

"Okay, class, enough. I didn't see anyone else volunteering. I think you should all recognize Jon for taking one for the team."

The class responded with a smattering of applause, which quickly died.

"So, Jon," he said, turning to me. "You're it. Stop after class to get the music and we'll discuss what you need to learn over the weekend. Monday, you direct."

In one swift second, Jen burned me, Mr. Dobson awarded me a leadership role along with a weekend of homework, and Alyssa dumped me. For what reason exactly, I didn't catch on for the last one right away. A tiny hint floated in when I searched for her in the hall after class.

No Alyssa, but I did see Jen watching the door, apparently waiting for me. Our eyes locked again, and I found myself stopped in front of her.

"Sorry," she said, biting her lip.

"Horizon," I replied, the only word I could think of.

"What?" she asked, her face drawn into confusion by my great communication skills.

"Horizon." I made a huge sweeping gesture to the horizon I could see in my mind. "I'm broadening it."

"You're not angry?" she asked.

"At you, no, never."

You are the most fabulous person ever to exist on this planet. I would never be angry with you.

"Thanks," she said. "I didn't mean to... I just... Thanks."

With so much conversation under our belts, we parted, at least smiling. Two conversations in two years. If we were immortal, we could be together in maybe ten thousand years. I completely missed how she may have wanted to say more.

I had been a tenor until my voice changed me into a baritone, now singing with the basses. I never had a reason to pay attention to, much less understand, what the girls sang. Now I had one. To properly direct the choir, I would need a crash course on alto and soprano. Lacking anyone else to confide in, I shared my new assignment with Beth.

"You volunteered for something?" she asked, trying to keep from laughing. "What were you thinking? I know. Straight As isn't enough; you need straight A pluses."

To Face The World

"Beth, you sang girl parts in choir in middle school. Can't you help?"

"Notice I'm not singing in any choir now. There is a reason, like I can't sing. Ask Mom."

This turned out to be great advice. I had a weekend to learn to direct all four parts to a piece of music none of us had ever seen. My plea to Mom gave me an instant jackpot.

"Sure, Jon, I can help. I haven't played much in years, but this appears simple enough."

Simple, with four parts completely unrelated to each other?

After a few scales on our old piano, Mom launched into the piece, playing it with ease after a couple of passes. With her help, by the next day I could sing all four parts and found out their relationships.

"Mom, thanks," I said after we finished Sunday night.

"You are welcome," she replied, smiling.

Instant suspicion. "Why are you smiling?" I asked.

"No reason. Except, this is the first schoolwork I've helped you with since fourth grade."

"Mom, you help me every day."

"How?" she asked.

"By being my mom."

Perhaps I overdid the compliment, but it didn't hurt.

*****

I figured out my life was on a new course when Alyssa didn't sit at "our" table on Monday, where we had been sharing lunches for three weeks. Instead, she and her fringes moved to the far side of the lunchroom. Thus, what I thought would be our first encounter after the magic moment, turned out to be me with me.

Other couples, even ones not as lame as we were, managed to survive disagreements. Plus I had volunteered, as she wanted, worth at least one Brownie point

Instead, sitting alone, I pulled out the orange Mom had packed special for us to share. I thought about rolling it across the lunchroom at her, but played catch with myself instead.

When the orange disappeared, I found Tom, the closest guy I had for a friend, reaching over my head. He flipped it up for me to catch.

"So," he said, plopping down across from me. "Heard the news. No more Alyssa."

"Who told you?" I asked.

"I did." Trish, Tom's girlfriend since birth, settled in next to him. "Alyssa says you have the hots for someone else."

"Did she say who?" I asked Trish.

"No. Who is what we want you to tell us."

I stared across the room at Alyssa, who had moved around the table

27

John C. Pelkey

to face away from me. "I guess I could go ask her so I would know, too."
I could see neither Tom nor Trish bought my self-defeating comment.

"Come on. What happened on Friday?" he asked. "Did you say something to her?"

"What happened? I'm directing choir. Alyssa waved at me to volunteer, and when another girl tried to see who she was looking at, Mr. Dobson noticed and picked me."

"Who was the other girl?"

You nailed the question of the day. No way can Jen looking at me contribute to altering Alyssa's feelings. Although I think about her all the time, I never say or do anything. How can anyone else possibly know?

"Jennifer Carling."

There, I admitted it. Even to myself.

"What did she do?" Tom asked.

"She glared at me."

Trish snickered, but Tom flat-out laughed. "You are trying to tell us Alyssa dumped you because Jennifer Carling glared at you?"

"No, Alyssa dumped me because Alyssa dumped me. Jennifer didn't change anything."

"Don't you think you should make sure?" Trish asked. "You two are the smartest kids in our class. You kind of go together."

I jacked up my courage and approached Alyssa as she stood up from lunch.

"What?" she demanded, even before I opened my mouth.

"I wondered if I was dumped."

"What do you think?" she snapped.

"Yes, I guess." It was more of a mumble than an answer.

"I saw the way you two checked out each other, like you were ready to play doctor. I thought you were over her by now. Obviously, you're not. I think you're butt slime, Jon Perone. The kind that slides down..."

I didn't wait for her to finish, but spun and split, almost a sprint, completely confused.

You think I'm not over Jen? How can I not be over someone with whom nothing has ever happened? Until today, I've never uttered Jen's name aloud to anyone except Mr. Hernandez. Yet you still said it. And doctor? I don't check out people like... Do I?

All through math class, I could feel Alyssa's eyes turning into daggers, trying to carve holes in the back of my head. One more time I was happy I chose to sit in front. No distractions. I did the only thing I could think of; I ignored her.

It's what the dumpee should do to the dumper, so I'm doing it.

Chapter Four

PE was my last class before choir. I knew we were to begin volleyball, which was about the only sport other than running where I was as good as anyone else male. What I didn't realize, it was to be co-ed.

The first time at co-ed anything is always the most interesting. The boy's PE teacher announced, "With thirty boys and three on a team, we get ten teams. We have five courts; fill the courts with three on each side. Leave a space between you. Go!"

This gave us our first clue something different was coming. After a couple of minutes of swarming around, I found myself with Ed and Dan, my pre-Alyssa lunch fringe partners. We spread out; they took the front corners, leaving me the back middle.

The other locker room opened and girls poured out, fanning themselves across the gym next to the shoved-up bleachers. None even considered an approach to the boys, all virtually at attention, watching them.

"Okay, everyone," the boy's PE teacher said. "This is co-ed volleyball, which means boys and girls will co-exist on the same teams. We will play a round robin tournament. Every team plays every other team. The two best teams will play for the championship next Friday."

Unlike the scatter and plop we did, the girls' PE instructor began to randomly read off names, pointing at a spot between two boys for each girl. After she called the tenth name, and no girl left the safety of the bleacher wall, she added, "Move it," to the conversation of names and silence.

Names were only names, until she pointed at the space between Ed and me. The next name changed my entire perception of life, both here and in the hereafter.

"Jennifer Carling."

She said it so loud, it echoed at least three times around the gym.

Ed glanced at me and shrugged, an obvious "Who?" on his face. Unlike the other girls, whose hesitation read some fear, some loathing, or a bunch of both, Jen trotted directly to the space between us.

"Hi, Jon," she said, ignoring Ed, who was as busy ignoring her.

"Hi." I knew I said the word, but if Jen hadn't been watching me, she never would have noticed. I produced no sound, only swished out air.

Jen wore a tee shirt we both could fit in. Her shirt, shorts, socks, and shoes, all were sparkling and matching, bright white. In contrast, my gray shirt, jean shorts, once-white socks, and further-removed-from-white shoes, didn't match each other or her.

"Alyssa Cunningham."

Conspiracy!

Alyssa shuffled to the front center. "Hi, Stick Boy," she hissed at Ed. He stood as straight as a stick, trying to cover a smile, because we all knew to what she was referring.

"Lydia Mather."

Lydia was okay. She played the piano for the choir. We didn't talk much, but she was easy to get along with, a bit shy, but no worse than I was. She took the space on my other side.

"Hi, bass singer," she said.

"Hi, piano player," I replied.

We watched the teacher point and shoot girls onto the rest of the courts.

"Name your team." The next command echoed almost as long as Jen's name had. We converged in the middle.

"Sticks and Stones," Ed offered.

"You guys may think you're sticks, but we aren't stones," Alyssa snapped. "Beauties and Beasts."

Dan agreed. Ed followed suit. Lydia nodded. She was better looking than Alyssa, but not exactly a beauty like Jen. None of the guys was a beast, either, so it didn't matter. With a majority in agreement, without input from Jen or me, Alyssa proclaimed herself team captain and submitted the name.

Coming back, she announced, "I'm the libero."

"You are the what?" Ed asked.

"First contact. I dig the ball to the setter, like Jennifer, and she serves it to the outside hitter, Jon or Ed. Dan is the middle blocker. Come on guys, learn your positions."

"What about Lydia?" I asked.

"Lydia patrols the backline and covers the misses."

She faced Lydia, who shuffled her feet, and avoided eye contact with Alyssa and everyone else, acting like she wanted to disappear. "You gotta be able to hit it over the net from anywhere." She didn't bother to check for a response.

She made the guys practice rotating and staying behind some imaginary line when we were in the back row. Jen rotated into the middle, regardless of where she started. Lydia rotated to the corner opposite Alyssa. As Lydia didn't appear to want to play volleyball, this seemed fine with her.

"You ready to direct choir next period?" Jen asked as we resumed our original positions.

"Ready as I'll ever be," I replied, this time producing some noise to go with the air. Somebody threw us a ball, and the game began.

Jen was a natural as a setter, and floated the ball up for Ed and me,

To Face The World

mostly me. Although the rules forbid spike smashes, her perfect sets gave me the opportunity to look good at something. When complimented on a great set, she smiled, but didn't speak. In contrast, Alyssa wouldn't shut up, and she gave herself credit for everything. We didn't have to contribute.

I could see volleyball was not Jen's favorite sport. She was blurry quick, but too short to reach everything. After a botched set by Alyssa, which Jen managed to tip up in a dive and which I saved for point, she glanced up at me and sighed. It made two sighs, two years apart.

Taking my cue, I helped her up. This meant I touched her hand for the second time in my life. I remembered how warm her hand felt from two years previous when it lingered on mine for an extra second. A lavender mint had replaced her cocoa butter smell.

Letting go, I asked, "What sports do you like?" Nothing prepared me for her response.

"Running. I like to run. Distances, like 5K runs. Have you ever run in one?"

Stupid! Stupid! Stupid!

I had never considered competing in the 5K or 10K runs going on all over the place in the spring and summer, usually on Saturdays during my lawn mowing.

"I don't compete, but I do like to run." I had blurted it out, but at least it was a complete sentence. Flush with my success, I continued. "I have a forest to run through, all to myself, with fences and creeks to jump. On Saturdays, I run to my yard job on Cartier and to my job on De Soto." I snuck in the street names so Jen would know I worked on her street.

"I live on Cartier. Do you take care of Mr. Dunlap's yard at 1611? It's beautiful."

Of course I do.

"I think it's 1611. It's the one with the picket fence in front of a hedge, and rose bush--"

Just then, I discovered a volleyball in my face, which bounced off my nose and went straight up. Someone yelled, "Nice set." I was instantly blind, as my glasses went flying in the opposite direction.

Jen picked up my glasses, smiled when she handed them to me, and said "Sorry." I was too embarrassed to speak and played the rest of the game like a zombie. For the second time in my life, my heart moved into my stomach.

Fortunately, no one besides Jen noticed, and I survived the class. We won, three games to one, and took the entire class time. Other groups had finished sooner, and this resulted in an immediate guy-girl split, retreating to opposite sides of the gym.

Jen whispered, "See you in choir, Jon; good luck," before she left, and I waved in response.

John C. Pelkey

However, my joy and terror from PE quickly disbursed when I realized my next class held the moment of reckoning. I was the last one out of the shower and barely arrived in time for choir.

We took our places and warmed up. I thought we would sing something else first, but no go. I followed Mr. Dobson's waving up to the podium and took the baton. I fumbled with the music on the stand and swished the baton a couple of times, but couldn't think of any reason to stall further.

When I turned to Mr. Dobson, he jumped up and addressed the class. "Mr. Perone is now directing. As such, you will give him your undivided attention." He jumped back down and sat behind Lydia.

How do I begin?

A sudden idea jumped in, something Mr. Dobson did for sight-reading. "Lydia, could you play it through once?"

Like me, she had seen the music before. At the beginning, she played better than Mom did, but probably had practiced it more. What Mom had done and Lydia didn't was point out the most difficult place. Instead, she stumbled over it.

"Stop, stop, stop."

She stopped. I stepped down next to the piano. Pointing at the music, I said, "LA, LA, LA, LA," for each of the four introductory parts, as Mom had done to help me learn. "Now, Lydia, let's go over it. Sopranos first, altos second, tenors third, bass fourth. Play the first. Stop. Play the second. Stop. Play the third. Stop. Now, the last."

After some hesitation, Lydia played it through okay. The second time sounded better, and I had her play the entire piece front to back. When the class began to squirm, I jumped back and tapped the baton.

"Hopefully, we all paid attention to the song, and each of you listened to your part. This is a sight read, so let's go ahead and see what happens."

Remembering what Mr. Dobson did, I waited a few seconds, tapped the music stand, waited a few more seconds, raised my hands, waited a few more seconds, and started Lydia.

The choir came in when I wanted them to, but the singing left a bit to be desired. Nevertheless, we moved along, right up to the four-part entrance. The sopranos stumbled, the altos fell flat, and the guys broke into laughter. They stopped when I banged on the music stand.

I could see instant irritation on almost every face due to my attempt to correct them. They glanced over at Mr. Dobson, who stood.

"When Jon takes the baton, he's in control. I expect you to do *what* he tells you *when* he tells you. If I want to jump in, I'll let him know. Otherwise, you watch him, not me."

As he had done when introducing me, he laid his hand out flat, pointing at me. "Jon, you are doing fine. Keep going."

I had Lydia began with the sopranos. They didn't get it any better

32

this time than I did when Mom first played it. I gave up on the singing as a group and made them sing it one at a time, beginning with the lead soprano. She stumbled once, but got it well enough. Alyssa was next and made a big show of singing it perfectly.

"Good job, Alyssa, thanks."

"Yeah, whatever."

Mr. Dobson was instantly up. "Class, I'm only going to say this one last time. When Jon is directing, he is in charge. You will do what he asks. If any of you have an issue with this, see me after class and we will discuss your future in choir. Clear?"

"Clear," I mumbled, the only one who responded.

The girl between Alyssa and Jen did okay. I thought about going back to them as a group, but decided to hear Jen. Directing her individually felt so different from standing next to her in PE. I had to fight to keep my hand from shaking.

Jen had the beat down pat, but was flat on half the notes.

I thought about having Lydia play it for her, but decided another tactic. I stepped off the podium and stood next to her, as I had done with Lydia. She was inches away, staring up at me. I could feel her warmth and smell her lavender.

What am I doing? I'm directing; it's what I'm supposed to be doing.

Flush with the victory over myself, I told her, "Listen, and copy me."

I pointed at the music on her stand, brushing against her shoulder. I thought she would instantly move away, but she didn't. For a second, maybe two, we touched.

I went through the first six notes, holding each until she matched. After a stumble, she followed perfectly. From my position next to her, I had the entire section step through one note at a time.

As I returned to the podium, I ventured with, "Thanks, Jenni, for bearing with me. Thanks, sopranos. Now, altos."

Either they had paid attention, or they didn't want me to do any personal instruction, as the rest did fine and we continued. By the third time through, we began to sound like a choir. To my surprise, the bell rang.

Mr. Dobson took back his class. "Okay, choir, this time we sang the song. Next time we interpret the song. Well done."

While the rest filed out, I returned to my seat for my backpack. Mr. Dobson followed me, holding out his hand for the baton, which I had forgotten to give him.

"Sorry," I muttered, reminding myself of Jen.

"It's okay," he said. "You'd have had figured it out in a second or two."

As I stashed the music in my backpack, he sat in the next chair and swished the baton as I had done. I thought he wanted to talk, but he waited until I was ready to go. He did want to talk.

John C. Pelkey

"Jon," he said, standing, "I didn't know what to expect from you. I anticipated spending maybe five, ten minutes with you attempting to direct today and later providing some private instruction. In my wildest dreams... For starters, you kept an even tempo the entire time. How did you do it? Have you directed before?"

"My mom plays the piano, so I learned the parts. The rest is doing what you do. The tempo is just swishing the baton."

"Just swishing the baton." He shook his head as if in disbelief. "Well, keep swishing away. I'm impressed, and am so glad you paid attention. Thanks, Jon."

I edged toward the door; he followed behind, still swishing. "Jon, you direct only on Mondays. Don't spend tonight trying to figure out what I meant by attempting to interpret the song."

You are too late.

At the door, I stopped. It seemed he had something more to say.

"Jon, how well do you know Jenni Carling?" he asked.

The question floored me, almost literally. Not having a clue how to answer, I could only blurt out, "I don't know her at all. She was on my PE volleyball team last period."

"She didn't want you to direct for any particular reason?"

"No reason I'm aware of. She doesn't talk to me much."

"Now I'm even more impressed. Thanks, Jon."

I had no idea what I had said to impress him. I mulled over every word and came up empty.

Chapter Five

While washing the dishes, I practiced asking Mom how to interpret music. I wanted a head start on the next Monday. Finished, I got all way the way to, "Mom?" when the phone rang. She answered, ahead of Beth, who yelled, "I'll get it," from the upstairs bathroom.

"It's for Jon," she said into the receiver. "Beth, hang up."

As I took the phone from her, she whispered, "It's a girl."

A girl? Alyssa has called enough for Mom to know her voice, so scratch Alyssa. I don't know another girl willing call me.

"Hi, Jon. This is Jennifer Carling."

Instant shock. *After two years of zero conversations, we're having multiple conversations in one day?*

"Hi Jen... ni."

Almost blew it.

"Thanks for helping me and not getting angry because I sang flat."

Say something, Jon, anything.

I jacked up my courage. "You didn't hear how badly I sang the first five times I tried it. In comparison, you did fine."

"You practiced it? I could tell. You were incredible, so polished."

"My mom helped; she plays the piano."

"I play the piano, too. It's how I learn the sounds. Not so good when we sight read."

Sounds? Okay, you lost me. Why would you need to learn the sounds?

I thought of *My Fair Lady*, and Eliza needing to learn the pronunciations, how proper English sounded. Was Jen from another country? Considering her accent, it would make sense. Something to ask her someday.

To cover up my space-out, I asked, "I was thinking, if you play the piano, do you know how to interpret?"

"Do I know how to what?"

"Interpret the music."

"Just a sec."

I waited about a minute, wondering what she was doing or if I should hang up. My indecision paid off when she returned to the phone and said, "Sorry I took so long."

"You don't have to say you're sorry."

"Really? Not saying you're sorry is what love means."

What?

I gasped to myself, completely lost. I had no idea how she introduced love into the conversation.

John C. Pelkey

"The movie song, 'Love means you never have to say you're sorry.' My dad sang it to my mom once."

I remembered, *Love Story*, which was about twenty years old. I had watched it when Beth picked it out at the movie rental, and later read the book to see what the movie missed. I had no memory of the song, only the part about the girl dying.

"She died." Brilliant conversation maker, me.

"So I heard. I've never seen the movie; I have read the novel and heard the song."

You read. Something else we have in common. Maybe we could compare.

"I read *Love Story*. She was a Jennifer, too."

"Well, Oliver, I promise to do my best not to die on you."

For some unknown reason, her promise sent a huge rush of warmth throughout me.

Jen played the choir song. I could hear it clearly through the phone. Maybe she had a speaker or something. As I listened, I realized she played what I asked, interpreting the music.

My backpack was within reach, and I had the music out before she came to the entrance. She went right into it, each part louder as she introduced them. The whole song grew louder. I noticed the notation above the soprano entrance, *piano*.

The entire sheet of music jumped out at me, *ret., forte, moderato, glissando*. Jen played what the words meant. When she finished, I could only sit there, gasping.

"Jon, sorry, I have to go."

She broke my reflection as quickly as she had caused it. I managed a, quick, "Bye," before I heard the click. I never knew why she called.

I searched for Carling in the phone book in case I ever became brave enough to call her. The two Carlings listed were Elise Carling, Realtor, with no street address, and Ralph Carling, with a local phone number for a downtown Seattle business address. Without a local address, I didn't know if either had anything to do with Jen.

*****

Tuesday lunch brought the next set of changes. Instead of me by myself, or occasionally with Tom and Trish, who were far more popular and in demand, Lydia sat down across from me. Normally, she was a fringe in Alyssa's group, including when I sat with her.

"Can I talk to you?" she asked.

"Sure," I replied. Lydia talking to me was a major step up from no one.

"I thought you were a good selection for director up until you corrected me. But then, the way you helped Jenni, you were amazing and so professional. How did you know? I guess it was nice what you

To Face The World

did to help me, too. So now, I want you to know I was wrong."

"Thanks, Lydia."

"You are our best volleyball player, too. Jenni is second best. In volleyball, I'm the only player on the team worse than Alyssa. She is so impressed with herself. Her grades, her singing, her volleyball expertise."

"I don't think I've impressed anyone, with volleyball or directing. When Mr. Dobson appointed me director, Alyssa dumped me."

"Not for directing. Alyssa broke up with you because you like Jenni. Everyone knows it. I do anyway."

"How?"

"I see the whole choir where I'm sitting. When Mr. Dobson is doing something, you're watching Jenni. I thought maybe you were watching Alyssa, but I know who now."

Lydia said nothing more about Jen because Tom and Trish joined us, followed by Ed and Dan. A surprise, I had somehow become popular. The transformation from an occasional pity sit by Tom and Trish turned into a group gathering in a single day, but without Alyssa. No Jen, either. She didn't have my lunch period. Her friend Jamie did, and sat next to Lydia.

The conversation bounced between volleyball and my directing with no mention of Jen, to my relief. I smiled my gratitude and mouthed *thanks* to Lydia for keeping her mouth shut. She nodded and smiled back. In one conversation and non-conversation, Lydia moved from non-existent in my social life to a friend.

*****

In volleyball, Jen and I had our first significant collision when she nailed me while saving a tipped ball. To try not to hurt her, I took the hit like a charge in basketball, falling backward. She managed to hit the ball up about six feet, and on its way down, I clobbered it while lying flat on my back. It went all the way up to the rafters and slowly wandered down, almost an exact aim at the net. Both sides watched, frozen, as it caught the top of the net and dribbled down their side. Our point.

Jen's shoe had skidded across my knee. It turned red, and the scrape initiated the worst situation possible for any public team sport gathering -- blood -- about two drops. Immediate chaos.

"He's bleeding!" Alyssa yelled it loud enough to scare the blood back into my knee. The entire gym fell into silence.

"Don't move!" The girls' PE teacher's directive rang across the floor.

Easy for me to obey, as Jen was sitting on my feet. "You okay?" she asked.

"Other than bleeding, I guess so. Are you?"

"I think I'm going to have a bruise."

John C. Pelkey

I conducted a thorough search of her legs for any bruising, but everything appeared to be okay.

"It's a tiny bit higher up," she said, a shy smile forming as she watched me watch her. "But thanks for checking for me."

I could feel my face burning. She didn't move, but she did smile and give me lots of eye contact. As I had sort of found with Cindy, I found out more so with Jen. Unlike Alyssa, she had no space issues.

The girls' PE instructor brought a container of wipes and a box of Band-Aids. She tried to hand them to me, but Jen intercepted. In a move too fast for me to follow, she had taken both and had a wipe ready.

"I wasn't handing them to you," the teacher snapped. "You shouldn't touch him. He's contaminated."

"He's not diseased; he's only bleeding a little," she snapped back, a surprise to both the teacher and me. Jen cleaned off the blood with one wipe and held another against my knee.

"Are you sure you know what you're doing?" the teacher asked, having calmed down a bit.

"I do it all the time," Jen replied quietly, acting in complete control while sticking on a Band-Aid. "It's not like I'm going to kiss it."

With a, "Harrumph," coming from the teacher, and after some finger pointing, Jen trotted toward the girl's locker room with the spent wipes.

"Wash your hands!" the teacher commanded as she trailed along behind her.

When Jen returned, Alyssa demanded, "Now, can we play volleyball?"

My leg felt fine and the Band-Aid fit perfectly. I wondered what Jen meant by her, "I do it all the time," comment, but it became another question I didn't ask. Maybe someday I would.

*****

As with the other classes, volleyball and choir flew by for the rest of the week. Under Alyssa's command, we won all the volleyball matches, although the Friday game was due as much to a miracle as our skill.

We split the first four games, and in the fifth game, the score stood at fifteen to fifteen. We botched the set off the serve, and the ball floated over the net. Jim Stone, their leading hitter, couldn't wait and clipped the net, as he not so carefully slammed it down our throats.

While they fought about who should have done what, Jen slipped a serve over the net, dropping the ball in the middle of their argument.

"What are you doing?" Jim screamed at her.

"I'm trying to win the game for our side," she replied, devoid of emotion.

"We weren't ready."

"We noticed," Alyssa snapped. "That's why we served, and that's why we won."

Without giving them an opportunity to dispute it, Alyssa headed for the scoreboard and indicated a win for our team. Jim went after her, but only watched as he couldn't push a girl and at the same time act totally suave and in control.

"We'll play you again," he muttered when they returned for the after game cheer, "and you won't be so lucky next time."

"No," Alyssa said, with way too much swagger. "Next time we'll cream you."

With five wins, we were in first place. Jim's team sat in a tie for second with one loss, but had beaten the other team. We would play the other team Monday, right before the next time I directed. I hoped the weekend would take forever.

*****

Friday night, Jen called again. "I only have a minute," she said. "Tell me about your forest."

My forest. Sounded strange, as if Jen thought it was mine.

"You know Notch Hill?" I asked.

"Everyone does. I can see The Notch from my house. It's a cliff, hundreds of feet up and completely enclosed by a ten foot high fence with barbed wire at the top."

"Not completely. It's fenced because people tried to climb the cliff part. One of them fell and died, and his family sued the owner. However, our field only has our fence, and not the high one. It's so the animals can go in and out."

"Do they?"

"Don't think so. They have nowhere to go out, but I can go in."

"Do you?"

"All the time. It's not steep from our side. I've made trails to run. It has a neat creek to jump. I have to be careful if I jump over the fence, though. We have cows."

"I would like to see where you run, someday. Not much chance, though, as my parents would never let me and you already have a girlfriend."

It came out of nowhere and I froze, but managed to choke out, "Had a girlfriend."

"So it's true."

Silence, long silence. I had no idea what to say, so I waited.

"I think I figured it out playing volleyball. I know you don't want me to say I'm sorry, but I suppose I should be if Alyssa and you broke up. She and you are so smart together."

Like when we play volleyball.

"How's your bruise?" I asked, trying to change the subject.

John C. Pelkey

"I have one, but no one but you will ever know where."

She gasped into the phone. "I don't think I said it correctly, two giveaway conjunction references in the same sentence. Freudian slip, maybe? Ha!"

Her laugh was musical, like listening to someone singing, and it was contagious. For the first time, even if for only seconds, I felt comfortable talking to Jen.

"Where your bruise is, well it's half of what Alyssa called me, so you don't have to worry about her breaking up with me."

"What did she call you?"

"Butt slime. I'm not going to make up with someone who calls me butt slime."

"Something for me to remember," she said, still laughing, a tinkling bell sound I tried to memorize. "Got to go, bye."

Again, I had no idea why she called. Or why she could only talk for a minute or two. Or why she was so easy to talk to on the phone and so hard in person. Even so, I had no complaints. We weren't going together or anything, but we were talking to each other. If only I could work up enough courage to ask her for her number.

*****

Saturday broke our winter drizzle with the first sunshine of the month. I took advantage and cleared up the debris left in Mr. Dunlap's yard from a late February storm. Three weeks of rain had left it a mess. While raking under Mr. Dunlap's roses, a shadow appeared, Jen, dressed in an oversized jogging suit with a big "1301" pinned to her top. She bounced up and down and shook her outstretched hands.

"Hi. My dad wants to know if you could work in our yard. He thinks you do a wonderful job. It would have to be on Thursdays, as my parents aren't available on the weekends."

I'm petrified. What if your dad doesn't like my work and fires me? What if you come home with another guy while I'm working at your house? He would be your boyfriend and I would be your hired help. I would die!

I realized I wasn't ready to enter her life as a lawn mower.

"I'm turning out for track next month," I lied, "and my dad only lets me have two yard jobs during the school year. I could do it this summer after school is out."

I had instant guilt about lying, but Jen believed me.

"Oh, I'm turning out for track, too. I'll tell Dad. He's not happy with the job the real yard workers do. He should be ready to hire you by summer. See you."

Off she went to the 5K or 10K run, or wherever people who wore numbers went, while I stuck myself on the roses trying to turn around to watch her. My brilliant effort in making small talk during the volleyball match came back and landed at my feet with a thud.

What am I going to do?

I was afraid to turn out for sports. Too many kids had laughed at me for my lack of athletic ability too many times on too many playgrounds. Didn't matter, I had to try for Jen. If she found out I lied, it would make death an improvement.

I tried to think of how to convince my parents. They weren't thrilled with my running. Or with lying. After dinner, I prepared to broach the subject. It was win-or-lose time. If they said no... I went for broke, and for Dad.

"Do you think I could turn out for track this spring?"

Dad glanced up from his paper. "Why not? Dave does. You like to run so much, you may as well put it to good use. You could be the second Perone making all-league. No quitting, though, if the going gets tough."

My lie was now the truth.

*****

Mom and I spent Sunday afternoon practicing the song. I directed her playing, using my hands to designate tempo and volume. Although the music indicated the four-part entrance was to begin soft and build as each section entered, I thought it sounded better if each section began loud, and then softened to let the next one take over. Not like a round, but letting each section carry the melody. If they all worked it together, we would better showcase the choir.

The phone interrupted us. I hesitated, breaking my concentration. Mom waved me toward the phone. "Go see," she said, all the encouragement I needed.

"Hi, Jon."

Cindy, not Jen.

"Dave's not here."

"I know; he's with me. We're buying pizza for fend-for-yourself-night. What do you like?"

"You're asking me?" Dave never bought food for other family members, and he never asked me anything. Cindy followed a different drumbeat than Dave's previous girlfriends, making Dave different, and maybe a plus for me, and for the rest of our family.

"Well?" she asked.

"Pepperoni, olives, sausage, lots of cheese."

"Coming right up. See you."

True to her promise, they showed up with pizzas, including an individual one for me. While everyone gathered around the kitchen table, I fetched napkins and glasses for the pop they included. Cindy helped with the glasses, leaving us isolated for a second.

John C. Pelkey

"Thanks, Cindy," I said. "No one has bought me my own pizza before."

"Well, they should. Being nice never hurt anyone. Besides, you deserve something."

"For what?" I asked.

"For putting up with my boyfriend your entire life, for starters," she said, studying my face. "Besides, I like you and hope we can be friends."

"Come on, glasses and napkins people, sometime today already." Dave interrupted us and rescued me. For once, I didn't want any rescuing.

Chapter Six

Monday's volleyball became a train wreck. Alyssa couldn't dig anything, Lydia fell twice trying to save Alyssa's miffs, only to have Alyssa criticizing her for poor play. When Dan opened his mouth to object, Alyssa jumped all over him, although he hadn't done anything.

When they served during our argument, I yelled, "Cover the back," at Lydia. She dug it out fine, letting Jen float one to me for a perfect spike.

"What are you doing?" Alyssa screamed, at whom I didn't know.

"Trying to win," I snapped, despite myself.

"I'm covering the back." Alyssa waved Lydia away.

"Cover half; let Lydia cover the other half. You aren't playing well; give us a chance."

While Jen got ready to serve, Alyssa got ready to cry. "If any of you had periods," she blubbered, "you would know how hard this is and cut me some slack."

Periods, something Beth groused about on occasion, but without any details. I knew what they were from health class, but not what emotions or pain they created. PMS was a vague term for a crabby girl.

"Go easy on yourself, Alyssa. Let Lydia help; she's doing fine." To Lydia, I added, "You aren't having one, too, are you?"

Alyssa shot daggers at me, Lydia broke into a smile while shaking her head, and Dan and Ed gave me, *Are you out of your mind,* looks. Then they all gawked at Jen, who was holding her breath.

Instant crisis.

When Jen's knees buckled, I caught her. "Jenni, what's wrong?"

She sagged in my arms. I wrapped one arm around her stomach and bent her over, thinking she may be choking. After a few more scary seconds, she began breathing and laughing.

"Oh, Jon," she said between gasps. "You are so..." More laughter. Dan and Ed joined, along with Lydia, while Alyssa pouted along the back line.

"Serve it already," she snapped.

"You okay?" I asked, standing her up after her breathing returned to normal. Jen nodded, so I let go. It dawned on me I had been holding her for over a minute, but I was too concerned to notice. I tried to remember the feeling of touching her as we continued.

I felt certain I had committed some major crime asking Alyssa and Lydia such a personal question, but with no adult in sight, I considered myself safe, even if embarrassed.

43

John C. Pelkey

We rallied with Lydia covering most of the back line and Jen setting both of us like a pro. Alyssa continued to pout, but at the same time played better. Maybe the pressure to be perfect was off with her admittance. At two games each, the class ended with our first tie. If we won the next three matches, we would go in the final with the best record.

*****

I accepted Mr. Dobson's wave to the podium after our warm-ups. This wasn't becoming old hat, but at least I knew what to do. When he didn't give me any further direction, I let the choir through the song, picking up from the previous week. They stumbled at the four-part entrance again, but I let them muddle to the finish.

"Okay, we made it, more or less." Some scattered snickers, but this time they don't face Mr. Dobson.

"Now I want us to focus on intensity adjustments."

"Aren't we going to fix our mess?" one of the guys asked.

"Yes, when we get there."

My rather mundane answer got me a bunch of surprised stares.

Yeah, the kid choir director is going to do something new. Get over it.

"Okay, this is how I signal by sections." I used the baton to indicate the section and my hand to indicate the volume, and initiated a simple, "Ah." After a few stumbles, the choir understood, and I had them singing their single note louder and softer, together and apart.

At the four-part entrance, I brought the sopranos in loud, took them down in time for the altos, the altos down for the tenors, and last, the tenors down for the bass. They seemed intrigued with my attempt to modulate the volume and didn't stumble. Successfully, we sang it together, and each section had their moment.

My effort brought Mr. Dobson to his feet and up next to me.

"Jon, you are not singing it as the music is written."

"You said we need to interpret it. I'm not changing the words or the notes, only the dynamics. The music gives the introductory lead to the sopranos, and then each section competes at the same volume as they enter. The song gets louder when it doesn't have to in order to reach the audience, and so the message misses out. I want to bring out each section with the lead, which I think follows the intent of the music."

"What are you talking about?" he asked.

"We are singing about a triumph as four separate entities working together and supporting each other, giving each the opportunity to shine. If only the sopranos get to lead unopposed, and only because they come in first, we don't show it. We show the opposite of what we sing. The song is only words."

I probably said too much, but at the same time, I took a stand instead of simply going along. Maybe the little bit of directing taught me something. Maybe not.

Mr. Dobson scrutinized the music, and then he scrutinized me. He said, "We are done for today."

I handed him the baton and crawled back to my seat, thoroughly humiliated. So much for directing. Although we continued with other pieces for the spring concert, my heart felt like a rock and my singing like loose gravel.

Nobody spoke to me as I made my way to the bus and home, as if the entire school knew I had blown it as a director.

I didn't expect to hear from Jen. People didn't call losers, so I decided, except she called.

"Hi, Jon. I wanted to call to thank you for holding me up when I couldn't breathe."

"I didn't mind; you aren't heavy."

"I felt so stupid. I have this..." She stopped talking.

"You have this what?"

I didn't find out what she had, because what I had was the dial tone. I plunked the phone down.

"So Alyssa dumped you." Dave, leaning on the counter next to the phone, mimicked a violin. "I even heard about it."

Dave acted as if he was an eagle in the sky and I was a mole in the dirt, his dirt someday.

"Oh, you forgot to say goodbye just now when she hung up on you."

"It wasn't Alyssa." I pointed at the phone. "She didn't hang up on me; she had to go."

"Well, who was it, Lover Boy?" he asked, making curvy motions with his hands.

"What difference does it make?" I asked, making flat motions back.

"None to me. A skag is a skag is a skag." He copied my flat motion.

Jen wasn't a skag, but nothing I could say would matter to Dave. So I kept silent.

Cindy popped up next to him, touching his stomach, and for some reason, making me incredibly jealous. Of what, I didn't know.

"Heard you are directing choir," she said. "Congratulations." She held her hand up for a high five. Since I had nothing to gain by telling them I got the boot already, I tapped it lightly. Instead of letting go, Cindy squeezed it. She flashed her eyes at Dave and gave him a shove.

"Thanks, Cindy," I said, wondering what she meant by her action.

"Yeah, okay, good going, LB," Dave muttered, pulling on Cindy's hand.

They walked away, leaving me hot and anxious, and not knowing why.

John C. Pelkey

*****

The next day, I decided I could make up for being a lousy director by being a good volleyball player. This included my initiating an insurrection against Alyssa for dominance of the team, something I wouldn't have dreamed of doing a week ago.

I made my move before the first serve, after a curt greeting to everyone and a wave to Jen. "Ed, you rotate to the back and play Alyssa's position with Lydia. Dan you are the other outside hitter."

"Why are you switching Dan and Ed?" Alyssa demanded. "You didn't ask me and I don't agree."

"I'm not only switching Dan and Ed. I'm switching Dan, Ed, and you. It will give Ed a chance to dig, Dan a chance to hit, and you a chance to block. You want to be the center of attention. Now you are. About whether you agree or not, I don't care."

Comparing her complaining to my encouragement made an easy decision for everyone else. Ed did fine on the back line with Lydia, Dan made some hits and some saves, and after her mandatory pout, Alyssa scared everyone on the other side away from the middle. We won in straight sets, the other team failing to reach ten points in any of them.

As soon as we finished, Alyssa left to record our win, Ed and Dan left to find a wall to hold up, and Lydia waved as she went to the girls' side. With almost half the class time left, I searched for the team we would have to beat in the playoff and found them in the corner by the boys' locker room entrance. To my surprise, instead of following Lydia, Jen followed me.

Pretending to expecting this, I pointed them out. "It's the team we have to beat. I'm checking for weaknesses."

"Arrogance," Jen said. "They are like team Alyssa."

Despite my low feeling about choir, I had to smile, probably for the first time since Mr. Dobson booted me off the podium.

Maybe there is life after failure.

"Sorry about hanging up last night," she whispered.

"I figured you had to go, like the other times, so it was okay."

"You did a good job of directing," Jen said, switching subjects, "both the choir and our team. You took a risk for each."

"Less of a risk for the team. We could have beaten them in any formation. Not so good for the choir. I tried..."

No point in continuing the conversation, or watching the other team. If we win, we win. If we don't, we don't. By next week, it won't matter.

I decided Ed and Dan had the right idea and sagged against the bleachers.

"Don't give up, Jon," Jen said.

On what? Volleyball? Choir? My brother? You?

Jen's silence matched my silence. She sagged with me and our

To Face The World

elbows touched, another terrifying, magic moment. I froze in place, with three inches of her skin nestled against three inches of mine. I wondered if she noticed.

The team we were to play also swept their opponent, only taking a bit longer. Jim Stone dominated, but watched us more than he watched the other team, as if he wanted to be certain we saw every hit.

After the game ended, the girls moved toward their locker room. Jen joined them, but stopped long enough to wave. I waved back. Waving didn't hurt anything.

I dreaded going to choir, but held my head up and marched in and to my seat, one of the first to enter the classroom. No sneaking in for me. I was an up front and showing it failure. Nobody said anything and life, as usual, moved on.

*****

During volleyball, Jen and I visited casually as we played. I lacked the courage to ask her real questions, like for her phone number, or why she held her breath, or what country she emigrated from, or how she knew about Band-Aids, or, most important, if she liked me. I felt more disappointed in my lack of effort with Jen than I felt elated in my effort to lead the team. I found connecting with a group easier than connecting with one.

We won the next two matches and went into the championship against Jim's team, where Alyssa almost got us into a brawl. She had given into me leading the team with no further argument, although not speaking to me contributed. She took it out on the teams we played by intimidating them from the middle.

We were slightly ahead when Jim got the perfect set. We braced for what was coming. All except Alyssa. When she blocked his spike, it bounced off his head and out of bounds.

"You hit it out of bounds," he shouted.

"Yeah, off your head," she countered.

"It didn't hit my head."

"What about the big red spot on your forehead? Oh, that's right. It's not from a hit; it's where your brain leaks."

They were toe-to-toe, inches apart with only the net between them. I realized how tall Alyssa was when she could look Jim right in the eye.

"Did it bounce off his head?" I asked the girl standing next to him.

Her eyes darted at Jim and her teeth clenched. She was clearly scared, but still nodded.

"What are you doing?" he snapped. Then, for some reason, he softened. "Okay, it hit my head. I was just trying to win."

"You were just trying to cheat," Alyssa snapped.

They were almost toe-to-toe again, but Jen slipped between them.

47

John C. Pelkey

Although several inches shorter, she managed to back them both up. What she said next absolutely floored everyone within hearing.

"You two aren't mad at each other; it is only sexual tension."

It came at a lapse in the normal gym noise, and I could feel a collective, "*What?*" from everyone around. Alyssa gasped and Jim turned fire engine red. They both perfected my previous zombie imitation for the rest of the match. As Jim was their best player, we won easily.

The second the match was over, Alyssa fled to her locker room.

Jim yelled, "No way," pointing at Jen. He backed up and followed Alyssa's disappearing lead in the other direction.

The rest of both teams cracked up. I spun, surveying Jen to make certain she was breathing, but she smiled, waved, breathed in and out for me, and said, "I'm okay. Thanks for checking."

With Alyssa gone, I marked our win on the scoreboard. The other teams were still playing for third, fifth, seventh, and ninth.

Our PE teacher noticed me. "Nice job of leading the team, Jon."

"Alyssa was the captain."

"Maybe, but you were the leader. If you hadn't taken over, you wouldn't have won."

As I mumbled a thank you, he added, "We don't only score how the teams play each other; we also note how each of you work together. Alyssa is a tough cookie, but you handled her. Good job."

"Well, we had the best player on our team."

"Jon, you are excellent, no doubt about it, but--"

"Not me, Jennifer Carling."

He stared across the gym. When I followed his eyes, I saw Jen standing next to the girl's locker room door. She waved at me and disappeared.

"Maybe you're a bit biased. Still, you could be right. She is fast. Plus she did a good job of breaking up a tiff between your team and the other team. What exactly did she say?"

I froze in place, my mouth stuck in open. I could feel the air going in and out, but the words were hiding under my feet.

After a few seconds, he asked, "Is it best if I don't know?"

I nodded vigorously, and he waved me toward the locker room.

*****

After a weekend of no music, no phone calls, and no Jen sightings, I slogged into Monday. In PE, we moved on to dodge ball. I had hoped we could stay a team and take everyone on again, but they shuffled us, with Alyssa, Lydia, and Jen all placed on other teams. The gym could handle five volleyball courts, but only two dodge ball matches at a time. Playing on a team with fifteen provided less opportunity for conversation.

Jen's team played mine. As it was our first effort of the year, players

To Face The World

fell like dominos. Unlike volleyball, the players on both teams, once eliminated, watched as a group. We were getting to know each other.

I had a brilliant plan. After I took out Jen, someone could take me out and I could join her on the sidelines, at least long enough to ask one of my questions.

Without me communicating anything about my intent, Jen directed her next attack against me. I threw at her legs, my best play, but she was too quick and easily jumped my ball. To take one for our relationship, whatever it was, I let her clobber me, but acted good enough not to get razzed.

"Nice try, Jon," Dan said when I joined him on the sideline. "She has a wicked throw. Thanks for taking one for the team."

I almost have guilt about it.

Jen's excellent effort got her into immediate trouble, as the team sacrificed three more players to get her out. She trotted over to me, smiling.

"You let me hit you," she muttered quietly.

"As if. You're the team's best player. Maybe--"

"No maybe about it."

"I wanted to get your phone number."

There, I did it. Spilled the beans, took the step, made the big gesture.

Jen glanced at me and sighed, her third.

Not good.

"You wasted your effort. I don't give out my phone number."

Instant crush, as if she had slugged me. She noticed. "Jon, it's not you. I would love for you to call me. It's my parents. They don't allow calls to or from boys, not without a good reason, and I have to ask first."

"You call me."

"Only when they are busy or not home. If they're home and busy, I make the call because the phone doesn't ring. If they're not home, the second I hear the garage door open, I hang up."

"They monitor your phone calls?"

Her eyes flashed in instant anger. "They monitor my life, birth to now. Phone calls are minor compared to everything else. I have to be perfect." She softened, her anger drifting down to the floor. "Jon, I'm sorry. You didn't know."

I do now.

Taking Jen out provided my team a surge in confidence and our side won. It was short lived; as the second game proved she had allowed our team to eliminate her in the first match. She didn't give anyone opportunity to gang up on her and took out all of us. I managed to stay afloat the longest, but when it came down to us two left, she beat me again, deflecting my best throw with her ball and clobbering me.

"Perone, you have to stop letting your girlfriend beat you. Come on. What's more important, her, or our team?"

John C. Pelkey

Coming from Dan, who should have been on my side, this was a bit of a putdown.

"She's better than I am," I said, loud enough for everyone to hear.

Fresh off the duel defeat, due to my failure to play dodge ball and live life well enough, I trudged from PE to choir, the last class before it was time to retreat into my shell. Maybe I would stay there this time.

After Mr. Dobson ran us through warm-ups, he tapped the music stand. "We are switching music for the contest. Please pass it in."

So much for my director role, as passing the music in hammered the last nail into the coffin.

After he collected them, he passed out another set of music. This went quietly until one of the sopranos said, "This is the same as what we passed in."

"Not quite. I searched around a bit this week. Seattle has an excellent music school. They were willing to provide me another set of the music, which has a slightly different interpretation from the standard. I think Jon will notice it follows his suggestions. It isn't a perfect match to what Jon may want, but we can adjust to meet his expectations without losing our ability to compete."

The class gasped in unison, and all eyes swiveled in my direction.

My expectations?

I had been so certain he fired me for taking a risk; I never dreamed he would reward me. I didn't know what to say.

"Come on, Jon," he said, waving the baton in my direction. "Let's give it a test drive."

I took the baton and tried to study the music through blurry eyes. "Thank you, Mr. Dobson," I said, more of a stall technique than anything else.

Ignoring everyone, I scanned it without much comprehension, but came to a quick conclusion.

"Lydia, play the choir parts through slowly. Not your part, play what the choir sings. Follow the dynamics as much as you can. It is more important we hear the tone of the song than only the song itself. We already know the words and the notes."

Lydia played it slowly until she reached the entrance, where she slowed even more. The four parts came, each overshadowing the previous. I could sense the excitement. We had invented something.

We took it on. Unlike some practices, no one complained if we worked a section too long or if somebody didn't get it. Even the section leaders got involved. After all, it was their music, too. Flush with our success, we ran it through one more time, ignoring the bell signaling the end of school. I could feel the energy in the room. We were a choir.

After we finished, Mr. Dobson jumped to the podium, shook my hand, and gave the choir a personal ovation, joined by me. Almost as a cue, the choir applauded back.

To Face The World

I acknowledged the smiles as I waited for everyone to file out before retrieving my backpack sitting by my normal seat.

"Good job, Jon," Mr. Dobson said as I approached the door. "If they could have heard us today..."

Alyssa waited for me in the hall. "You are getting to be so good at things. Who would have thought?"

I scanned the hall for Jen.

The last thing I want is Jen to see me talking to Alyssa. Alas, I'm too obvious.

Alyssa noticed my one second search. "You don't have to worry; your girlfriend is not in sight. Here I was about to take you back. What was I thinking?"

"You can't take me back, Alyssa; you like Jim, and he likes you."

I thought she was about to pounce, but instead she spun on her heels. She snapped, "You don't know anything, Jon Perone," over her shoulder.

I almost yelled, "I know you think I'm butt slime," but kept it to myself.

As Alyssa stomped off, I could feel the relief flowing through me. Although I was not about to say it aloud, she was right. When it came to girls, I didn't know anything.

Girls were hard to understand, despite how well Dave thought he did with them. Girls like Alyssa, with their "my way or the highway" attitude, they were worse. She had been dominating all along, even telling me where to sit at lunch. I simply hadn't noticed. Better put, I had nothing to compare her with until now. Jen didn't appear to be like her at all.

I hoped for a call from Jen sometime during the week, but the phone kept to itself, unless it wanted Beth. Now I understood how girls felt when guys didn't call. Still, I was being unfair, since I had never called a girl

Jen said she would need a good reason to call me. If only I could think of one.

51

Chapter Seven

The final week of March brought the first middle school track practice. I survived the form requirements, doctor visits, and parental approvals. Wearing my official South Valley Middle School Track Team sweats and my first pair of real running shoes, I trotted onto the field, joining Tom, Dan, Ed, Jim Stone, and a bunch of other guys in the eighth grade group. They stood away from the seventh graders, acting like we lived in two different worlds. Maybe we did.

Jen waved, and Trish left the girls to join us. Tom held his hand up for a high five. Not much from Dan or Ed, but they didn't say much any other time.

"What do you do in track, Trish?" I asked, trying to break the ice, which had layered the group by my arrival.

"I carry what Tom throws," she said, beaming, "and I measure it when it lands." She waved a hundred foot tape.

"And a fine job she does," Tom added.

"Figured you'd be here," came from Jim, as he pointed over at Jen, who was talking to her friend Marianne.

"Where's Alyssa?" I asked him, to move the conversation to focus elsewhere.

"She's way too good for track," he muttered, shoving some dirt around with his foot.

"You asked her?"

"No, I didn't ask her," he retorted. "She was your girlfriend once, not mine."

"So what? She isn't anymore. You do like her, don't you?"

Probably not a good question to ask in front of a bunch of posturing kids. Everyone became silent, hanging on whatever he would say next.

Jim, aware of the sudden audience, hesitated before saying, "Na, she's way to bossy for me."

"So boss back."

"Yeah, like you ever did?"

No, I didn't, not while she was my girlfriend. If I had, she would have dumped me sooner.

The track coach broke up our conversation with, "Listen up. I'm Coach Harris. I teach economics at the community college and have a class at Aurora Valley High School. My track experience, I pole vaulted in high school. Went to state a couple of times. My assistant, Coach Davison, held the state record in the shot put a few years ago. While I conduct tryouts for the seventh graders, he'll take care of anyone falling

To Face The World

through the cracks."

Coach Davison waved at everyone and added. "I teach math and statistics in high school, so you might get me, too."

Coach Harris said, "We don't have a state meet at this level, but we do have North Valley to fight with for our final meet. We haven't won two years in a row, so I'm counting on you to reverse the trend. We have a goal this year; it's to beat them and win the league championship."

He failed to mention we would still have to be in contention by the last meet. I guessed everyone assumed it. I was about to ask, when he added, "Hands for anyone in eighth grade with no track experience and who hasn't tried out yet."

I was the only one who had to raise a hand. All the other eighth grade kids, including Jen, had participated before and already knew their specialties.

After Coach Harris's opening pep talk, the eighth graders went to their areas on the field. He took away the seventh graders, leaving me with Coach Davison. He inspected me, up and down.

"Jon Perone, Knowledge Bowl MVP. Are you going to be the track MVP?"

"I hope so. I want to at least contribute."

Mostly, I want to see Jen.

I thought about what would happen if I didn't make the team. Instant turmoil. I could still watch, but watchers had no status.

I have to do this.

"At Knowledge Bowl, you and the tall, slender girl?"

"Alyssa."

"Yeah, her. What you couldn't answer, she did. You made some people quite unhappy there, cleaning up on those snob schools."

"We won fair and square. We had to qualify first; some of them didn't."

"They are into winning; 'fair and square' comes only when it is convenient and doesn't conflict."

I liked knowledge bowl, but the idea of spending four more years with Alyssa contradicted any enjoyment. I must have made a face, as the coach showed an immediate concern.

"Don't let me scare you. With a good team, we can make a go of it. I hope Alyssa and you continue to participate. I'm the high school advisor. I generally don't select freshmen, but I would make an exception for you two. One of the reasons I can coach middle school track this year is the high school team quite miserably failed to qualify for the tournament rounds. Think about it. We began in January."

Wow, he wants to recruit me. It's a neat feeling, being wanted. I haven't thought about high school much, except classes, English, math, history, science except biology, French, music. Cross country and track with Jen. Otherwise...

"Okay, Jon, back to track."

53

John C. Pelkey

How quickly neat feelings change into queasy.

"You can participate in three individual running events plus a relay, or all three field events, or all four jumping events, or any combination of three. What can you do?"

"I can run."

"I figured as much. You would have surprised me if you said you were a field man. What do you run?"

I had no idea. I could run fast, but I had never perfected a quick start. I didn't know if starting blocks would help or hurt. When we raced measured distances for time in PE, my runs were above average, if not spectacular. However, once I got going, I could go. I had won the twice-around-the-school race by staying close to the leaders until the race was nearly over. Then I had beaten them with my closing kick. I searched for someone to ask besides the coach, but we were alone. I winged it.

"The mile, maybe a relay." No one used blocks for the mile. Although I had no idea what relays they ran, the relay runners had running starts, except the first guy.

"I can jump too," I said, and instantly regretted it. We had not done any significant jumping in PE. The only jumping I had ever done was over the creek for distance and over the fence into the cow pies.

"Warm up, and when you're ready, we'll time you for sixteen hundred meters. We don't run the mile."

I felt an alarm ring in my head. I had never raced for time beyond four hundred meters. I kicked myself for my still too narrow horizons. The other kids had been competing for years. I hadn't known what to practice.

Sixteen hundred meters was four times around the track. A button on my digital watch turned it into a stopwatch. Maybe, if I timed myself, I could figure out how fast to run.

"What's the record for running sixteen hundred meters? For eighth graders?" I sounded like an idiot, but I didn't know what else to ask. Coach Davison had a good chuckle from my question.

"If you can run four laps in five minutes, you make the team."

I warmed up for a couple minutes, pretending to skip rope, three fast and ten slow, and practiced my breathing.

"What are you doing?" he asked.

"Increasing my heart rate and oxygen flow." Something I had read about and practiced before sprints, but had never tried it in front of anyone. "Doesn't everyone?"

"No, most people trot around a little, line up, and start running when I say go." As I walked to the starting line, he added. "You might want to take your sweats off, unless you don't have anything on underneath."

A small crowd formed to watch, and laugh, with Jen right in the center of it. I threw off my sweats and tried to think. Five minutes was

To Face The World

seventy-five seconds a lap. I would aim for seventy seconds a lap, thirty-five seconds a half lap, and if I came close enough, maybe I could make the team.

I started fast, trying to count the seconds to the half lap marker. It quickly became apparent thirty-five seconds a half lap was a bit fast, and more apparent that I could not run and count. I managed to maintain the pace for the first two laps, but lost of the time in the third lap. I was unable to compute the time I needed to make it up in the fourth lap, so I ran as fast as I could, and hoped for the best.

The team was silent now. I realized they had been cheering for me on the last lap. Coach Davison stared at his timer and at me at the end of the race. "Where have you been?" he asked. "I was kidding about the five minutes. Five minutes was the field record for boys. You broke it, and you didn't even have anyone to race."

The sideline crowd dissolved and reformed around me. They slapped me on the back, gave me high and low fives, and pelted me with "Nice going" and "Good job." After Jen added her smile and hand to the others, I trotted over to pick up my sweats. I wanted to hold the feel of her hand on mine.

Coach Davison told the other kids to get back to work, and they scrambled away. I watched Jim and Dan head for the jumping area, and Jen and several girls left to run around the track.

I slipped on my sweats and practiced some light stretching, the touch the toes, touch the ceiling kind.

"Now what are you doing?" Coach Davison asked. He seemed to find something amusing by my effort.

"Light stretching." I said.

"You didn't stretch before you ran."

"Wasn't warm then."

Am I doing something wrong?

"You've never ran in track before today?"

"No. I've run lots for years, always by myself."

"Who taught you the exercises?"

"I did. From books. Reading."

"Very impressive. You appear quite advanced in your track regimen. Now let's see if you jump as well as you run."

How far is it from the top to the bottom, and how long does it take to get there?

In less than a sentence, I learned how short and how fast it was.

"Since you are running one event, you can't jump in all four events. Pick two."

Coach Davison accompanied me to the jumping area. I had an instant decision to make. Should I pretend to be able to long jump, high jump, triple jump, or pole vault?

We watched Jim warm up with a pole, bending it and bouncing it

John C. Pelkey

around, showing off more than practicing. He took a run at nine feet, five inches, and cleared it with ease. Hopping up, he offered it to me. "Come on, Perone, see what you can do."

I shook my head and eliminated the pole vault. I had never touched a pole and had no idea he made it work so easily. We moved to the high jump and watched Dan take out the bar at five feet, jumping about six inches short.

I had jumped the creek more than the fence. I passed the high jump and moved on to the long jump area, empty of competition, and checked it out, pretending I had experience.

I trotted along the runway, visualizing the run and the launch. Coach Davison watched without saying a word. This time I didn't ask what the record was. I pictured the creek where I jumped and pretended to be there. The runway was much longer than my runway at the creek. Therefore, I could go faster and, I hoped, jump farther. I launched at what I pictured was the creek bank, stretched as far into the air as I could, and landed on my feet, then pitched forward on my face. At least the sand tasted clean as I spit some out.

He measured the distance, and he measured me. "You jumped far enough, well over fifteen feet. You do need to work on your technique. It might help if you jumped with your eyes open."

He led me over to the high jump and placed the bar at four and one half feet. We watched Dan barely clear it. I came next. Our fences were at least as high and I could jump them. If Coach Davison thought my long jump technique was bad, he wouldn't like my high jump.

"I haven't high jumped over a bar before," I said, hoping to warm him up to the impending doom.

"I figured as much," he responded. "Let's see what you can do."

I cleared the bar on the first try, and landed, as usual, on my face. The pad felt better than sand until I thought about the butts previously landing where my face was.

Ignoring the other kids, he moved the bar to five feet. I came so close, nicking it on my way down, and still managed to land on my face.

Dan helped me up. "Nice jump," he whispered. "Maybe you can beat Jim."

Coach Davison beckoned me away from the pit and pointed at the warm up bench. I sat.

"You can clear five feet and more with proper technique and some practice, high enough to get us some points and give Jim a run for his money. You can do the 1600-meter run, the 1600-meter relay, the long jump, and the high jump. We have to work on your landings though, or you'll embarrass the team."

I glanced up to see him laughing.

We watched Dan try again at five feet. He still wasn't close. Jim cleared it, and didn't land on his face.

To Face The World

"I can teach you how to land," Coach Davison said. "You'll do fine. You should place in the events most of the time. Welcome to the team." He extended his hand to shake mine. "You can run, no doubt about it."

*****

I did fine. I ran. I jumped. I ran some more. I jumped some more. I didn't run much faster, or jump much longer or higher, but with his guidance, I did manage to stop landing on my face.

School seemed a complete turnaround. Guys who would barely speak to me a week before were now my buds. Teachers and students said "Hi" in the halls. Even Jen's friends talked to me, more than she did.

Jen hadn't changed, friendly yet reserved toward me and toward everyone else. I witnessed one incident when Jim Stone, who we all connected with Alyssa, tried to ask her to out right in front of me.

"Jenni, my babe," he said. "How about ice skating with me this Saturday?"

"Thanks for asking, Jim," Jen replied, shaking her head no.

"Come on girl, it's in the daytime. I'm not even talking romance. Besides, I'm the best you're ever going to see. I have some moves to freak you clear past supper time."

"Thanks, but no thanks. Stick with Alyssa; she's more your type."

Jim grabbed Jen's hand. In a move too quick for me to follow, she snapped his hand back and spun away, right into me.

"Uh, sorry, Jenni," I stammered.

"It's okay, Jon, my fault." She almost smiled at me, but walked on. I watched Jim go the other way, mumbling and rubbing his wrist.

Too bad.

In the locker room after track practice, I found out Jen had a reputation of being a cold one, and a little spacey. I chanced into a conversation about her.

"...she acted like she had slept through the whole thing. When the teacher asked Jenni about the movie, I thought she was going to cry. Since Jenni gets good grades, the teacher, she didn't do nothing."

Someone else spoke. "Once I watched Marianne walk up behind her and say, 'Hi Jennifer.' She pretended Marianne wasn't even there. A second later, she said, 'Hi, Marianne.' It was like she suddenly came back to earth."

"Earth to Jennifer. Earth to Jennifer. Anybody home?"

"She's cute," Dan said. "She could warm up somebody's life."

"I think ice could warm up her life." Jim was still a bit negative after his hand snap.

"I know you like her, Jon," said Tom, jumping into the group's discussion.

"So?" I retorted. "It hasn't done me any better than anyone else." I

57

John C. Pelkey

sounded as negative as Jim, and kicked myself inside. I tried and failed to give Tom a signal to shut up.

"Hey," Tom countered, ignoring my signal. "She talks to you. She doesn't talk to me, or any other guy I know of. What's your secret?"

"If it's a secret, it's a secret to me." No way was I going to tell anyone Jen had called me.

The conversation drifted off into, "Did you see what the new girl wore today? Lisa Martin, she is so hot..." leaving me alone with my thoughts.

I tried to think of why Tom wanted to connect Jen with me, but remained clueless. Fortunately, not all my thoughts were as lost. In my hours of noticing her over the years, other than the one time of Jim's botched effort, I had not seen her in lengthy small talk with any guy. Her comment about her parents managing her life came back.

How much does she risk talking to me?

*****

Three weeks and many practices later, Friday came, our first track meet. Posters and banners decorated the school. I even found my name on some, with a picture of me breaking the tape as I won the 1600-meter run. The meet was at our school, and everyone who cared about middle school track would be there. I wasn't even tense, not until school was over. When I was tense, it wasn't from thinking about running.

I saw Jen waiting in the hall on the way to the locker room. After checking to see no one around, I walked right up to her and held up my hand for a "five," fingers spread apart, so she could clasp it instead of hit it if she wanted to. She clasped, *wow*, and smiled. We walked the last two feet to the locker room doors together.

"We run the same race," she said. "Not together, of course."

"Let's sweep them," I said, challenging her. "You win your race and I'll win mine."

"Sure, you're on," she replied. As she entered the locker room, she stopped and turned back to me, still holding the door. She gave me the same shy smile from our first day, which turned into a smirk. "Betcha I beat you." She disappeared inside.

"Betcha you don't." My voice followed her into the girls' locker room.

Betcha she better not, jumped out at me from the back of my mind and followed me into my locker room.

I started with the long jump. We jumped in reverse seeding, so with no previous jumps, I jumped first. I remembered the creek jump, pictured it better than before, took off just short of the mark, and didn't land on my face. The scoreboard put me into first place. It held up past Dan, but not to the two top jumpers, Jim and one on the other team.

58

To Face The World

I improved on my second jump, passing their lead guy, but didn't come close to Jim. Nor did anyone else. Still, my first track competition earned me a second place ribbon. Thus, I officially became an actual contributing member of the team.

"Congratulations, Jon," came from Jen. Although only two words, it was two more words than any other girl said.

The relay came next. Ed seemed a bit ticked when Coach Davison said I was to anchor, but recovered when he got to be the lead runner.

"Good thing," Ed said, "since I have starting block experience. You don't."

Dan had a different perspective. "If Ed gets a lead and I still have it through the third lap, don't lose it. If I don't have it, go get it."

Like I have a clue?

Ed did get the lead and Dan did keep it, but I almost lost it on the handoff. We had practiced handoffs during the week, but not in a real time situation. Dan let go before I gripped it, and I had to bat it in the air and bring it in before I could continue.

My bobble put me behind, so I took off after their runner. Instant decision concern. I could catch and pass him on the backstretch, but I didn't know how badly it would wear me out. If I waited until the final stretch, I had half the distance, but I only had to take the lead, not try to take it and maintain it.

If I'm not faster, it doesn't matter.

I waited.

Coming off the turn, I slipped out from behind him and floored it. He met my challenge with his challenge. I thought it was over, but I kept digging and slowly eased past him and across. I had won by a heartbeat.

This time congratulations came easier, from my running mates, from Jen, and from others. Even a "Good job," from Jim Stone. "Nice catch, butter fingers," he added, negating anything positive.

Jen followed, anchoring their girls' 1600-meter relay. The other team held the lead for three laps, but it didn't matter. She took the handoff and caught their anchor before the first turn, essentially ending the race.

"Hey, we matched," she said, being ultra-nice in comparing her blowout win to my hair width.

I had barely gotten my breath back when they called for the high jump. This went different from the long jump. They set the bar at four feet, nine inches, and called for anyone who wanted to jump. I went first and cleared it, jumping up to dead silence.

"What?" I asked Dan

"Waste of time and effort," he said. "When you know you can clear higher levels, why bother?"

"Sissy jump," Jim said, adding to his "butterfingers" compliment.

Uncertain what they meant, I noticed I was now at the top for the board, same as with the long jump. Only two other participants on the

59

John C. Pelkey

other team attempted the first height, one failing after three tries, and they moved the bar to four feet, eleven inches. Five of us left.

This time Jim and Dan jumped, and cleared it, Dan barely. The two guys on the other team cleared it, too. I managed to join them on my last of three jumps. Surprised, I still sat tied at the top, despite taking more tries than anyone else did.

"Doesn't matter if it takes one, two, or three tries. Clearing it is what counts."

I appreciated Dan being willing to talk. Everyone else stood closed-lipped, more posturing than talking.

At five feet, one inch, Dan cleared it, but bounced the bar off. So did I. Only Jim cleared it on his first try. On the second try, their lead guy cleared it. Dan and I bounced it again, but it stayed. Four of us left.

At five feet, three inches, Jim and their lead guy cleared it, but Dan and I didn't. Surprising me, they awarded me third.

"I should have jumped at four nine," Dan muttered. "We could have had a jump off at five two for third."

By jumping the unnecessary "sissy" jump, which Dan skipped, I had placed. My first real track lesson. Don't bother with the posturing part. Instead, jump at the initial height.

Compared to the other events, the 1600-meter run was the least exciting. I eased into third, sat there for three laps, and passed the two lead runners on the final backstretch, finishing in five minutes, two seconds, just short of the school record.

Jim Stone won my two jumping events and the pole vault, which was okay. At least he didn't run. Dan didn't place in either jump, and I felt bad for him, but not bad enough to let him beat me.

"You scored enough points to letter in your first meet," Tom lauded, while we listened to the final 1600-meter results. "Five points for the win, one and a quarter for the relay, three for the second, and one for the third. You have ten and a quarter points, and you only need ten to letter." Tom and Jim each had fifteen points from their wins, so I wasn't exactly the team leader.

Still, Coach Davison congratulated me. "You did well, but you jumped better when you landed on your face." We shared a laugh. I belonged, a great feeling.

The feeling of unexpected success was weird, unnatural almost. Good grades and math competitions had never brought it. Winning them, I felt more like I had averted failure than anything else. The only time I could equate to winning the race came when I directed the choir.

The boys didn't need my 1600-meter win, but the girls would only win if Jen did. Her 1600-meter run was the last event. She had to scratch on the 800-meter run when they delayed it to the race before the 1600, not leaving her enough time to meet the mandatory rest between events.

She came up to me and gave me another five, holding it longer than

To Face The World

she had to. I was ready to run another 1600 meters.

"Why didn't you run the 800 instead?" I asked. "You'd be done."

"Better to run this one and beat you."

She became serious. "Coach Harris said we needed points from both races to win. Marianne and Sandi ran the 800 and got second and third. No one else on our team is going to place in the 1600, so I'm not taking points away from a teammate if I win."

What Jen said made sense. I had a moment of guilt for Dan, who placed fourth twice. If I had tried different events, he would have placed third twice. The problem quickly came to a conclusion. My goal was to beat Jim. Dan's goal was to beat me.

My time of reflection ended when Jen asked, "What time do I have to beat?"

"Break five minutes and you beat me," I teased, remembering my tryout.

"Piece of cake," she pronounced, rather smugly.

She stayed right behind the leaders for the first three laps and blew them away in the fourth. Still, her time was almost thirty seconds slower than mine was. We grouped around her to offer congrats.

"It's not fair; the girls are all too slow," she complained. "I want to run with the boys." Her comment produced a good laugh from everyone.

I wanted to compliment her without embarrassing her or me. I tried out, "Hey, you won, and you looked good."

Close enough.

"I could do better. You did. You ran one of your fastest races when you had no one to compete with."

She had reminded me of my tryout day. Since I couldn't tell her I had messed up, I threw out, "I kept track of the time in my head," and got a good laugh from everyone.

Despite my silly remark, a sudden flash creased across my brain.

Timing can work. I need to learn to keep better track of the time in my head. Then I can run faster than the day I tried out. Today I had only run fast enough to stay with the pack until the last three hundred meters. I can do this.

I practiced the concept for a week. I timed everything in my head, both in school and at practice. I got to the point where I could count a minute while running and be off by only a second, close enough. People wondered what I was doing. Jen even asked, in our now pre-meet ritual at the locker room doors.

"Watch my race and you'll see," was all I would say. I was going for the school record in the 1600-meter run. The field record I had set in the tryout didn't count because it wasn't in competition.

The jumps were first. I moved up to second in the high jump, but could not beat Jim, who again won both jumps. It was okay; we still scored most of the points. Jim shared a five with me when we got our ribbons, almost a breakthrough.

61

John C. Pelkey

I didn't have to run the 1600-meter relay. The second runner dropped the baton, disqualifying our team. He wanted to continue, but the coach said, "No." Better for my race.

Except at the beginning, I ran the 1600 meters as I had at the tryout. Off the line, I blew away everyone and ran all by myself for the rest of the race. Only this time I didn't get lost in the third lap. When I finished, I had the school record, an amazing 4:53. More important, I didn't even feel tired.

Coach Davison told me to take a victory lap, something Coach Harris rarely allowed. "Jon, you set a new South Valley record. Enjoy the moment." I did.

However, "enjoying the moment" left no time to talk to Jen before her 1600-meter run. She waved to me from the starting line. The guys noticed, especially Jim.

"You and Jenni are getting somewhere," he muttered. A little jealous, perhaps, another first for me.

Jen took off like a rocket. She ran the first four hundred meters in sixty-five seconds, faster than my first lap, and fast enough to win the event anywhere in girls' middle school land. She ran the first eight hundred meters faster than she had in winning the race an hour before. I hurt inside when I realized how this was going to end. She finished the third lap much slower.

In the fourth lap, half way around, it happened. She came to a stop and bent over, gasping for breath. She could run no farther. Maybe, if she hadn't run the 800 meters earlier, she could have finished. She stepped off the track and waited for the pack to pass before stumbling toward the locker room, still gasping and holding her chest. I was on the far side at the finish line and my best run got me to the door as it was closing behind her.

"Jen, wait!" I shouted through the still open crack in the doorway.

She heard me and came back out, tears streaming from her face, still trying to catch her breath. "I really botched it," she blurted out between gulps of air. "I lost the race. Everyone thinks I'm stupid."

I couldn't believe it. Those were my kind of words; they shouldn't be hers.

"You can do it," I countered. "You had my time beat for almost three laps. You had a terrific start. You ran the first 800 meters two seconds faster than your winning time. You still had me beat at the end of the third lap."

Or close enough.

"If you skipped the 800 meters, and you ran the second and third laps differently, you would have more left for the fourth lap. Jen, you can do it. You can beat my time."

To my surprise, she ignored my commentary and focused on one word. "You called me 'Jen.' You have never called me Jen before. No one

To Face The World

has ever called me Jen."

Before I could catch myself, I launched a burst of words. "I called you Jen because I think of you as Jen. Because no one else does. Because it makes your name special. Because you are special." Now I'd done it. All I had to do was add, "Because I love you," and my stupidity would be complete. I would have "becaused" her to death.

My feelings for her were lying on the ground. She could pick them up, or she could stomp on them. She picked them up and handed them back to me.

"Thanks for caring about me, Jon. You have helped me more than you know. I don't know if I am ever going to run again. If I do, I'll run your way. Right now, I want to be alone."

Poof, she was gone.

We won both meets, even without Jen's finish. My win had been the difference for the boys. I had a school record and a victory lap. I was the big hero I had only imagined. Somehow, it didn't seem to matter anymore. What mattered, I had spilled my guts to the girl in my dreams who had responded by wanting me to leave her alone.

One of Dave's favorite lines, "Nothing ventured, nothing lost," exactly fit how I felt.

I ventured. The result feels like Dad's dump truck sitting on my heart. Why does venturing have to be so hard?

In the locker room, no one complained about Jen's non-finish. When the guys weren't congratulating themselves and me on how good we all were, they commended her effort. "Hey, she won the 800 and the relay; what more does she have to do?"

When I left the school, I saw her talking to Coach Harris and the same silver-haired man I saw the day I found out where she lived. Coach Harris waved us all away. I wasn't going to find out what the score was, between her and track, or between her and me.

Later, I sat on my bed, wondering about life, girls, and Jen. I felt I was grasping for something, so desirable, and at the same time quite difficult to comprehend and even more difficult to obtain. It wasn't only Jen for herself; it had more to do with being with Jen, mixing her presence with my presence. Together. Like connecting one-half of a puzzle to another, without knowing how the pieces fit.

The feeling of Jen existing out there sent shivers of both joy and terror through my body.

What is this? I've had symptoms before, never the full measure cruising though me now. Love? What is love? Will I ever find out and understand? Friday, May third. How many years will pass before Monday?

Chapter Eight

Saturday morning blossomed in full spring color, as beautiful a day in May as the Pacific Northwest allowed. In contrast, my heart awoke cloudy as I recalled the events of the previous day.

I had spilled my feelings to you, Jen, the object of my dreams for over two years. I will not go back to being your shy observer from a distance. I took a huge risk. Worse, I left the ball in your court. What will you do with them? With me? Anything?

I both dreaded and hoped for answers when I arrived on Cartier Street. Instead, I found silence.

As I worked in Mr. Dunlap's yard, I wanted to run across the street and find out, good or bad, how Jen was doing, and more important, what she thought of me. Fear, my faithful best friend, kept me on my side of the street and I didn't see her. I took an extra hour to weed three feet of weed-free flowerbeds and gave up. Most likely, she wasn't even home. I ran to Dr. Canfield's house.

When I found the garage side door locked, I had to knock at the front door. Dr. Canfield met me with a smile and a one hundred dollar bill.

"Let me explain this," he said with a snicker, as my eyes must have been popping. "The little woman and I are jetting out this week and will be gone the next two weekends. So this is an advance. I know it's more than your usual. I want you to come by now and then to check up on the place beyond your Saturday maintenance. I know you'll do a good job keeping the place sharp."

I wasn't about to argue with one hundred dollars.

"Here's the key for the garage while we're gone. It's a spare so you can keep it. You will need to get on my deck."

He led me through the living and dining rooms to his deck. Although the garage shared a wall with the house, its back door opened onto the deck, which seemed a strange arrangement.

"I want you to water the plants here. Once a week should take care of them; they've grown used to mistreatment."

A hot tub, partially recessed and two steps up, took up the center of the deck, surrounded by miniature palm trees. It appeared as if from a scene from some desert movie, except for the tulips lining the deck in a planter. Maybe like a desert in Holland.

"If you have time, jump in the hot tub. I wish someone would use it since I'm paying to keep it going. Otherwise, all it does is warm up the atmosphere."

To Face The World

I couldn't tell if he was serious or not. Rather than test him, I asked, "Where are you going?"

"We own a condo on Maui. Mrs. Canfield has to play in the annual spring bridge tournament. Myself, I'd rather be pulling teeth."

"You're a dentist?" I didn't know at what he doctored.

"Na, I'm an OB... Wan Kenobi. Well, they're stupid initials. Sorry. I'm a baby doctor. I never pulled a tooth in my life, wouldn't know how. Sometimes I think it would be fun. 'All right, buddy. This is what you get for not brushing your teeth for the last twenty-seven years. Take that!' Be a change anyway."

"Don't let him snow you, Jon; he delivers babies," Mrs. Canfield said as she passed by with some clippers.

"I like delivering babies. I must have done twenty thousand of those little suckers. Took about four thousand to pay for this house, and another two thousand for the condo. I did nine in one day once. I used to count them, but I lost track about twenty years ago. I love 'em though, ever last one of them. Wouldn't trade my life for nothin'. Nor the little woman either."

We watched Mrs. Canfield bend over to snip the tulips for a bouquet. She was not a little woman; "ample" was a better word.

Dr. Canfield was on a roll. "You know, I married her for her boobs. Oh, I had other reasons, but she had some beauties. The rest of her weren't too bad neither, thirty-five years ago. She put me through med school with her bod; she was a dancer. Now we're older and those are bygone days. I don't mind now, she's a blast. I lucked out. She's as good inside as outside. Wouldn't trade her in for a younger model."

I had no idea where Dr. Canfield was going and didn't want to think about Mrs. Canfield. I tried to picture Jen with "beauties." She didn't wear tight things, even when running. I wasn't positive about the size of her figure or even if she had one. I knew she wasn't big, at least not yet, and probably not ever. It was okay.

I realized when I pictured Jen, the body parts I saw first were her legs. She had great legs. I mostly saw her face, her eyes, her smile, her funny shy look I had seen twice. Now her face with tears from the last time I saw her. My stomach knotted slightly.

"Pay attention here!" Dr. Canfield said.

I came back.

"You ready to get married, you find somebody who's good inside, understand? The outside doesn't count and doesn't last if it does count. I've seen twenty thousand women, and they were all about the same outside. Some of the best outsides were the worst insides. So you concentrate on the inside, and if the outside ain't sugar for life, it's okay. Their plumbing all goes bad in forty to fifty years anyway. And from having those babies. Ah, but I love birthing babies. Love making them, too."

65

John C. Pelkey

With a snicker over his own audacity, he walked over to his wife and gave her a whack on her ample behind. She laughed and went into a jiggling dance routine, including a bump knocking him about three feet. Watching her routine, I wondered what kind of dancing she had done to get him through medical school. I also wondered how he had learned about her "beauties." Dr. and Mrs. Canfield went into the house with their arms around each other. Jen or no Jen, I hoped for the same kind of relationship after thirty-five years.

Finished with the lawn, I was applying touchups by the front door when I heard someone running. I glanced up to see Jen, wearing a sweatshirt several sizes too big and bouncing a golf ball on the sidewalk. The ball hit a crack and caromed onto the lawn. She hesitated, but kept running. I picked up the ball and ran after her.

"Jen, stop. Please."

She rounded the corner to the back of Dr. Canfield's, and slowed to a stop, like a grounder rolling through a grassy outfield. She stood staring away from me out onto the golf course. When I caught up to her, she spun around to face me. Her eyes were red and her cheeks had wet marks trailing down from her eyes.

"I watched you all morning at Mr. Dunlap's. I wanted to see you, but couldn't get through the door. When you left, I followed you here and went home." She waved her hands back and forth. "I hoped you were here, but by the time I got this far, I was crying again. I wanted to run by you and just keep running. I didn't want you to see me like this. I'm sorry about yesterday. I really bungled things. With running, and with you."

She appeared so tiny and pitiful standing there in her oversized sweatshirt. She wasn't crying exactly, but I saw a tear ran down her cheek. Watching her, my heart came apart. Without thinking, I launched into a pep talk, placing a hand on each of her small shoulders.

"Jen, you didn't bungle anything. You carried the girls' team to the win before you entered the last race. You had a free run to experiment. It didn't work, but so what? You know more than you did before the race. You have limitations; everyone does. You are the fastest girl I have ever seen. With some minor adjustments, you can break five minutes and even my record."

Minor adjustments? I sound like my choir instructor.

This was the longest time I had touched Jen, even longer than when she had trouble breathing. She didn't seem to mind. We stood there, watching each other. I could see she was thinking about something, and waited. With a quiet sigh, she came to some decision. Catching myself, I let go. We stood there, eyes locked and inches apart.

"Remember my first day?" she asked. "In sixth grade two years ago? When you sacrificed your hand to open my locker?"

I must have grimaced at the memory because she hinted at a smile.

To Face The World

"You said if I needed something, I should ask and you would help me. I know it's rather late, but I need something and I'm asking. Will you help me now? Will you teach me how you run?"

My moment had arrived, fragile and fleeting.

You're only going to get one of these opportunities, ever, Jon. Make it count.

"Sure. I would be happy to."

How to teach you to run. You put one foot in front of the other faster than anyone else. No, I have to do better.

I stumbled backward over the rest of what she said. My thought process worked, but so slowly.

You have bungled things, with running, and with me. With me? What do you mean? What things with me did you bungle? How can I ask you to explain?

Since I couldn't think of how to ask, I decided not to. She wanted my help; she was going to get it.

She had watched me carefully while I went through what must have been a bunch of facial expressions. I ended with a smile, which I hoped would cover for the rest.

"Thinking," I said. "Remember, the horizon thing?" I swished my hand. "Like directing, this is a new horizon."

Not like I have a clue about what I'm trying to say. I need more time.

"Can we talk after I finish? I only have a few minutes of work left. You could wait on Dr. Canfield's deck, there by his hot tub."

I pointed up at the hot tub; only on the lower side, we couldn't see it. Too much deck. As we walked up around the house, I showed Jen the problems involved with power cords. I had to guide the electrical mower around trees and edge three hundred feet of sidewalk, both sides, while always watching for cords everywhere. She smiled for the first time.

"You do a great job. My dad can hardly wait to see you work your magic."

I could hardly wait, too. The fear from two months ago was gone. If what the guys said was true, I wouldn't have to worry about Jen coming home with someone else.

Jen wandered out onto the deck when I unlocked the door for her. I finished, cleaned the tools, and put them away. When I peeked out from the garage, she had pushed the corner of the hot tub cover back a little and was swishing her hand through the water. As I approached, the hot tub suddenly sprang to life, water boiling and frothing all over. As suddenly as it started, it stopped.

"Oops," Jen said, smiling ever so sweetly. "Sorry."

"Dr. Canfield said I could use it while he's on vacation, but I have never been in one." I wasn't the world's greatest conversationalist.

"You should try it. It's great for relaxing and for sore muscles. We have one." She dropped her voice to a whisper. "If you do try it, and no one is around, take off your bathing suit for a minute or two when the bubbles are running. It feels neat."

I must have turned a bit red, because she laughed. "Jon, you are so sweet. I didn't mean to embarrass you." She appeared to be enjoying it to me.

"Do you?"

"Only when no one is home. Our hot tub is inside, in an atrium. It's not like this." She paused, unsure of herself, before continuing. "I'm not as bold as I sound. The slightest squeak and everything is back on." Her turn to turn red, she was more like pink compared to how I felt.

Back to the subject at hand, I began. "Training. We need to train separately from the track practices, so maybe on weekends?" She nodded. "Will your parents object to us..." I had no idea how to finish.

Jen squirmed, but looked me in the eye. "I asked my dad before I came to find you. My mom would say no. She says no to everything. Dad said it was okay, as long we focus on running."

"Our target will be the last meet at our school in three weeks. We work tomorrow and the next two weekends to get you ready to set a new record."

"Your record" Jen added.

"Yeah, whatever, my record."

"Will you be okay with me if I break your record?" she asked, studying my face again. All I could do was nod.

Jen did tons of face contact when we talked. It made me nervous, excited, and created a whole herd of feelings I didn't recognize or understand. All I could do was nod.

I didn't want to leave, but couldn't think of any reason to stay. I felt in a sensory overload absorbing her presence. Nothing like with Alyssa, who was predictable... yeah, bossy and safe. Jen wasn't bossy or safe. My feelings went to a level never before known, like uncharted territory. I could hear Tom summing me up. "You, Jon Perone, have a massive, incurable case of the hots."

Yeah, I do.

If the Canfields saw us on their deck, they didn't complain. We put the cover back on and left. I glanced back before closing the door, memorizing the scene of our first minutes alone together.

I moved Jen out into the driveway, and ran back to close the garage door behind her. I had a second of uncertainty as I locked the side door. Maybe she would lose her nerve and take off. She didn't, and stood exactly where I left her, waiting for me.

"I'll walk you home, okay?" My first time ever asking a girl person to do something with me outside school, and it came with her first answer.

"No."

No?

Jen's reply almost crushed me. Before I could respond, she added,

To Face The World

"You can run me home." Off she went up the middle of the street, not even realizing what she had almost done.

I caught up with her and ran on her right. After a few feet, she switched to my right. For some reason it felt funny, so I switched back to her right. Jen accepted this with a shrug. I didn't know how to tell her it felt more comfortable with her on one side than on the other. I didn't even know how to tell me.

For our first lesson, I timed the distance between blocks. I quickly realized we would need exact distance as well as time. We slowed to a walk as I tried to figure out what to do. I didn't want to admit I didn't know what I was doing.

"We need a defined distance, more than running up and down the street. Something we can measure like our track."

"We could use the high school track," Jen volunteered. "It's open on weekends for jogging. The middle school is too far away."

We resumed running, and I kept an even pace for about a half mile. When Jen began to lag, I stopped us. "What's wrong?"

"Aren't you tired yet?" she asked, breathing hard.

"No," I replied, "are you?"

"No, but I need to catch my breath."

I went into instant concern mode.

Is something wrong inside you? Cancer? Heart attack? Or germs in general? The laughing incident when you couldn't breathe?

I had not heard Jen breathe while we were running, not in any rhythm. "Breathe for me," I directed.

"Do what?"

"Breathe, you know, in and out. Show me how you breathe when you run."

"I don't breathe," she said, still gasping. "I mean I don't think about it. I just run. I used to hold my breath, like swimming under water, but I don't anymore."

Instant shock. Everyone knows enough to breathe when they ran, don't they? No, they don't. I learned to breathe from reading about it and practicing every day for four years. I have three weeks to teach you.

"No wonder you..." I blurted it out, and stopped.

"No wonder if I what?" Jen snapped, before breaking out a smile. "No wonder I run so poorly? Well, fix me, okay?"

My second life-changing moment had arrived.

"Listen to my breathing." I practiced breathing in through my nose and out my mouth, following one of the books. When she appeared not to understand, I tried harder. "In, in, out, out. Keep a rhythm. In, in, out, out. Now, you try."

"I don't know what you did."

I thought I was obvious, but, maybe not. "Okay, stand up straight." Jen did, like at attention, as much as she could while still trying to catch

69

John C. Pelkey

her breath. "Don't watch the ground; face ahead to keep your chin up. Breathe in through your nose and mouth, two breaths. Breathe out through your mouth, two breaths. Or maybe two breaths in, then three breaths out. What you are doing is forcing air into your lungs and establishing a rhythm. The point is this; you control your breathing, not your breathing controlling you. Got it?"

She didn't. Worse, I noticed her stomach didn't match her breathing. It was going in the wrong direction, which meant she wasn't fully using her diaphragm to breathe. All her breaths were shallow. I took her hand.

"I want you to feel my stomach when I breathe in and out. It means I'm using my diaphragm." I put her hand on my stomach and forced myself not to notice. I breathed in, pushing my stomach out, a bit exaggerated, and sucked it in when I breathed out. "Now, you try it."

To my surprise, Jen took my hand and put it on her stomach. It was so tiny; I almost could wrap my hand around her. She tried breathing like I did with her stomach matching, failing at several attempts before she was in balance.

"Don't push your stomach out, let it happen naturally."

"If it happened naturally, wouldn't it happen?" Jen sounded slightly irritated, but wouldn't let go of my hand.

"It will become a natural habit, after you learn how and practice. I took weeks to perfect."

More like months, but who's counting? We don't have months.

Jen practiced, with my hand bobbing in and out, less after a while as she figured out what needed moving and what didn't.

"Okay," I said, wondering if I should take my hand back. I left it under her hand, still touching her stomach. "Now breathe in rhythm, in, in, out, out. Got it?"

She nodded, but didn't let go. Reluctantly, I pulled my hand away, with her hand lingering on mine after I was no longer touching her stomach. Another surprise, she touched my stomach again and waited for me to breathe, which I did. Then she touched hers and smiled. "Got it."

We resumed running. I breathed extra loud, but it didn't appear to help. Jen waved her hand at me to leave her alone while she practiced. Within a few hundred feet, she established something consistent that seemed to please her.

"Wow," she said. "Breathing in a rhythm really works. Thanks." She broke out a great smile.

I smiled, too. I had done something right, and Jen had let me touch her.

We continued at the same pace together until we reached her block. She stopped and checked her stomach again, and wanted me to check it. Touching her stomach made me tingle and shiver; full of happy messages, even more so the second time.

70

To Face The World

"See, I can do it now," she said, holding my hand against her, beaming up at me. Whatever irritation she had earlier appeared to be gone. Plus she liked holding my hand. Things were looking up.

"Catch me," she said, and off she shot. I caught her as we reached her driveway, but maybe she had slowed down. She was incredibly fast! Being she was so little; it didn't seemed possible.

"You'd better do better, or it will be my name on the track records wall, in the guys' section, too."

Inside I agreed. Outside I said, "Yeah, well we'll see." Jen's challenging smile kept my bravery going. "How does tomorrow at three sound?" I couldn't believe it; we were almost making it a date.

"Could we begin at four? I go to church at eleven, and we have Sunday dinner. I need to let things settle. It's okay I go to church, isn't it?" Jen appeared to be searching for help. It was our first awkward moment, at least in the last half-hour anyway.

I realized something about Jen my adoration toward her had missed. She was a real person. She didn't have the complete self-confidence I had bestowed on her in contrast to what I lacked.

"I go to church too, with my family. Trinity Lutheran Church, it's across town. I sing in the choir."

I could see the relief spreading over her face.

"I go to the Assembly of God, two blocks from here. My parents rarely attend church, and not at all after we moved here. I went to an Assembly of God Church in the last place we lived, so it was easy to continue. There is nowhere else to go I can walk to."

"I'm one of the middle school representatives on the City Youth Board. Your minister, Pastor Kamorkov, is the chair, so I know him a little. He's nice."

I realized she probably didn't hear me, as her thoughts appeared to have floated off somewhere.

She took my hand again, completely unexpected. "Church," she said. "Outside of school and running, going to church is the only thing they let me do by myself. Would you like to go with me?" She carefully searched my face.

I had my second opportunity, another one of those stunning snapshots of time where the entire world's future rests on how well I answer. This was even more important than running. I wanted to step aside and practice my own breathing, just to get my heart back into my chest. She had asked me. This would be our second scheduled together time, and it would happen before our first. It had nothing to do with school, or running. It had to do with us -- a her and me us.

I wanted to shout something, something stupid, probably. Part of me wanted to go hide, too, the self-centered, fearful beast part, which had always said I wasn't good enough. I decided to ignore it.

I can do this. I am good enough.

John C. Pelkey

I repeated it twice and felt better, but I didn't how could I say yes. My parents expected me to attend church services with them as a family, although I sat in the choir section.

I took too long. Jen's face reacted to my indecision. I winged it. "Logistics. I don't sing this Sunday, but my parents expect me to attend church with them. Still, I could ask and you could call me this evening."

Her smile, accompanied with an, "okay," proved I had saved us.

Maybe I'm getting the hang of this girl relationship thing, if possible, provided you can call me. Now if only this call can fit within your parents' requirements of either important or training for phone calls.

"I need to ask, too," she said, reading my mind. "This isn't about running, but it is important. I could call you. Or..."

Or what?

I waited.

"I could give you my number." Her smile alleviated my instant concern. "I asked if I could call you to talk about music. Mom didn't like the idea of me using her phone to call boys so Dad gave me my own phone line. He told me I was old enough to have one, and it would keep theirs free for business. I would have said something, but I didn't know how to tell you to call me without sounding..."

I repeated it slowly. "Without sounding?"

She squirmed again, but didn't back off, her eyes locked on mine. "Like Alyssa."

I took her hand, made a small space between our index fingers, and said, "Horizon with Alyssa." Still holding her hand, I stretched her other arm out straight and my other hand out opposite, and moved us apart to as wide as we both could reach. "Horizon with Jen."

She squinted at me with one eye closed, but said nothing.

It must be the expression for when you think I'm completely nuts. I'll have to expect more of them because I am completely nuts, over you.

She disappeared into the house and came back carrying her mother's real estate card with the number I had seen in the phone book. She had written "Jen" on the back with her personal number, the first time she had referred to herself as Jen.

"What group do you sing in?" she asked, keeping the conversation going.

"The church Senior Choir. We sing every Sunday except the first one of the month, when the Children's Choir sings." It sounded funny. Some of the Children's Choir "children" were my age.

"I would like to hear you sing."

You would? Another time together? Could be, but how?

This would be hard, as either her parents or my parents would have to take her. However, with enough time and some parental warm-ups, maybe I could work something out.

"I have a solo the last Sunday we sing before the choir goes on

72

summer break, the second to the last weekend in June. It's 'Amen'. If it's okay with my folks, maybe we could pick you up."

I had practiced the solo part with encouragement, but I wasn't sure I wanted to sing it in front of people. Maybe now, with a real purpose I did. Besides, if Jen wanted to go to church with me almost two months from now, it meant we would see each other after school was out and for something besides running.

"Okay. Guess I'll see you tomorrow, and you'll call me tonight. I hope you can go to church with me."

I wanted to touch her but didn't know what to do. I put my hand up for a five, like I did before track meets. Jen made like to hit it hard, but stopped short and tickled my palm instead. With a laugh, she turned and ran into the house, pausing at the front door to wave, her fingers spread apart like when we clasped hands the first time.

I floated home.

*****

Although the fearful beast part of me still tried to push me down, I was beginning to picture us together. The real picture kind, not the imaginary kind I had been doing. More than us walking to school together next year. This was hard. I had too many "downs" to picture myself in an "up" for long. Most of my downs were due to my own lack of confidence, or so people loved to tell me.

Jen was as human as I was, but the concept was hard to grasp. I had placed her on a throne in my mind, with me at her feet. I would need time to be completely comfortable with her. I wanted to gain the confidence to walk up to her anywhere, knowing she wouldn't put me down.

She had never snubbed me, nor given me the slightest indication she thought little of me. At the same time, she remained reserved, not only with me, but also with everyone. She appeared to be alone all the time, even with lots of people surrounding her. She wasn't cold at all, but she was terrifically shy. The confidence I needed couldn't come from her; it had to come from me.

Chapter Nine

"Do you think I could go to the Assembly of God Church tomorrow?" I directed the question to the air in front of me at the dinner table.

The air responded, "Why do you want to go there?" My precious brother used his older, bigger, wiser, and knew-it voice. He was counting down his days left in school. I was counting down his days left at home.

"Someone invited me," I responded in my best younger, smaller, and dumber voice.

"Who?" Mom jumped into the interrogation.

"A friend I have been running with. Her name is Jenni." Now I had blown it. I waited for Dave's inevitable put down barrage.

Mom stared Dave into submission. "Oh, how nice," she said. "When do we get to meet her?"

Dad wandered into the conversation. "Pass the potatoes, please. You run with a girl?"

"The Sunday I sing 'Amen,' you could meet her. I invited her to come with us. Is it okay if she does?" To Dad, I added, "She is a fast girl. I mean she can run fast."

"She has to, to get away from you," Dave snapped, as expected.

I ignored Dave. My parents had not objected yet, and I wasn't going to give them any unnecessary ammunition by whining. I thought of something to help my cause.

"If you want to meet her before I sing, come to the next track meet at home. You can meet her and see how fast we are."

I felt certain lead balloons floated better than my idea, and I was right. Together, my parents groaned at the thought of rearranging work schedules to watch, with each race taking up about five minutes.

Maybe to compromise. Please.

Mom said. "Since you are not singing this Sunday, I guess you can go to another church this once."

Yes! I won the battle. Winning the war would have to come later.

After dinner, I snuck into my parents' room to use the phone in private. Jen answered on the first ring. "Hi, Jon."

"How did you know it was me?" I asked, forgetting to say hello.

"Besides my parents, you are the only one who has my number so far."

I wasn't sure if she was serious or not. "What about Jamie or Marianne?" She had other friends, but they were the two most important.

To Face The World

"Not yet. My parents, my mom. I think she's testing me, and I don't want to ruin it. Can you come to church with me? I asked my dad, and he didn't say no."

"Yes, they'll let me, but only this one time so far. I asked if you could come with us to hear me sing in June. They were okay about including you." Like her dad, they didn't say no.

"Jon, where are you? You're not doing the dishes," echoed through the house and the phone. Mom had yelled this from the doorway, not realizing I was about two feet away. Jen heard it, too, and laughed.

"Okay, see you tomorrow about 10:30. Thanks, Jon. Bye."

For what are you thanking me?

"Why are you in our bedroom and not washing the dishes?" Mom demanded.

"I used the phone to call Jenni to tell her it is okay. I wanted to be alone."

I had talked to Alyssa in their bedroom during our three-month romance, so it wasn't something new. Beth had an extension in her bedroom, but I had to make my phone calls from the kitchen, where everyone could listen.

"Another girl. You aren't going to tie up the phone for hours like Beth does, are you?"

One phone call for fifteen seconds doesn't equate to tying up the phone for hours. However...

"It would be my life's pleasure to live on the phone with Jenni. Her laugh is like silver bells tinkling in the wind. Her thoughts are like brilliant rays of sunlight on my face. Her--"

"Enough hogwash. Do the dishes."

Mom must have felt guilty about yelling at me while I was on the phone. After I started the dishwasher and while still finishing up in the kitchen, she came in to see me.

"You like this new friend of yours?" she asked.

"I've known Jenni since sixth grade." I thought of the first day. "I don't know her well. I would like to, though."

There, as close to my bare soul as you are going to get.

"I suppose it is okay if you use our phone. I want you to ask first. Then I won't be yelling for you."

Ah ha! You're afraid Jen would tell her mom about you being a yeller. It's okay to dump on the kid as long as another adult isn't involved.

Instantly, I felt bad for thinking it. Mom was making a major concession, and I was the one dumping on her, in my mind anyway.

"Your brother never talks for long. It would be nice to have only one person dominating the phone." Finished with her discussion, Mom wandered back to the family room.

Dave's phone conversations went like, "Hello... Yeah, uh, I donno... Okay... Yeah bye." By then, he had exhausted his telephone vocabulary.

John C. Pelkey

The complete opposite, Beth's exercised an inexhaustible telephone vocabulary. If she spent five minutes on the phone with one of her many guys, she could spend hours discussing it with ten different girls, who would discuss what their guys said. She had to go out on Fridays. It took all Saturday to finish talking about it to everyone.

As she had her own phone, I wondered if Jen called up any of her friends to discuss our fifteen-second conversation. I hoped she didn't. I didn't intend to tell anybody about talking to her.

I had a calendar hanging next to my bed, featuring pictures of scientists. I could put notes in code for each day, depending on what happened. I wrote, "start," and drew my impression of a hot tub and Jen's phone number backward in the box containing the four. May fourth. I could almost see Einstein smile.

*****

I presented myself at Jen's house at precisely 10:30. When I knocked, the same man I had seen with her on Friday opened the door. He appeared to be about fifty, which would make him ten years older than my father, and he had perfectly combed silver and black hair. He wore a designer polo shirt and matching slacks. My sport coat and tie looked frumpy in comparison.

"What a nice young man. You must be Jon. Come in. I'm Ralph Carling." He sounded like a politician ready to kiss a baby. "Jenni will be with you in a minute."

I now knew why she would jump at a squeak when naked in the hot tub. Standing in the entry, I could see the living room and through four huge floor-to-vaulted-ceiling windows into the atrium, and into the hot tub. I saw the curtain she could pull from the inside. It was lovely, but without the curtain pulled, quite exposed.

"Jenni says you are almost as fast a runner as she is." He smiled at his supposed wit.

"I have the school record in the 1600-meter run. Jenni wants to break it."

Jen came into the living room and saved me from further conversation, and at the same time almost blew our relationship.

She wore a pale green dress with the skirt part short and with pleats, a dark green blazer, and white-lace stockings. The stockings made her already terrific legs look, well, even better. The top of her dress was tight enough to show she had a small figure, the outline visible even under the blazer. Her hair, instead of being straight or in the fluffy ponytail she wore while running, was in sweeping curls with her ears showing, and a single curl in front of each ear. She appeared as perfect as I could imagine.

Fortunately, her father was staring at her, too, or he might have

To Face The World

sailed me out the door. Fathers would not like their middle school daughters gawked at the way I gawked at Jen. I recovered in time.

"Isn't she a knockout?" her father asked, still watching her.

"You look great, Jen... ni." I almost forgot the last part. I hoped it was an acceptable compliment.

She took her cue, giving her dad a teeth smile. "I'll be back right after church. Jon and I are going to run later in the afternoon at the high school."

"Practicing for your record? Okay." He turned to me, "Take good care of my little girl."

For the rest of my life if she'll let me.

"Yes, sir. Goodbye." We escaped out the door.

Jen's smile left as soon as the door shut. She flashed the same expression as the day I volunteered to direct choir, intense hostility.

"If my dad saw the way you drooled at me," she scolded as we walked to the end of her block. "I'm not a piece of bacon."

"I'm sorry. I hadn't seen you quite like... I mean in a dress before. I did remember to call you Jenni instead of Jen. I didn't know if your dad would object."

She almost smiled, but appeared to force the grim expression back to her face. Something bothered her. "I don't think my parents care if you call me Jennifer, Jenni, Jen, or hey, you." She glowered, thinking about it.

When we came to the corner of her block, she turned left toward the church, already in sight. I turned right to cross the street.

"You're going the wrong way." She pointed sarcastically, not believing I was unable to see the church. I turned back to face her, but didn't move in her direction.

"Jen, I think we need to walk some more before we get to the church. Something is wrong, something more important than the way I looked at you."

I went out on a limb. If she went the other way, our relationship could be going the other way along with her, a repeat of me giving in to everything as I had done with Alyssa.

Jen hesitated a bit before making up her mind. She trotted a few steps to catch me. We walked in silence for about three blocks.

In a moment of daring beyond my belief, I took her hand, casually, pretending I did it all the time. She didn't pull away, but held my hand loosely, gradually moving on to tighter, and finally applying enough pressure to about break it. She had an incredible grip. She stopped, let go of my hand, and stood, facing me. I rubbed my hand, which now had gone through its second sacrifice for her.

"It's my mom." She rolled her eyes and faced away, blowing air out in apparent frustration. "You haven't met her. She's quite attractive. My mom wants to compete with me. It's like in 'Snow White,' where the wicked queen goes 'Mirror, mirror on the wall?' Only Mom goes, 'Who's

John C. Pelkey

the fairest in this house?' Today, she decided I was the fairest. I think she is going shopping for a poisoned apple. I hope she eats it."

"Jen, what do you mean?"

You aren't making any sense.

"Last night Jamie Collins came over. You know her. She has red hair and is about my height."

I know her.

She was one of Jen's friends who used to gawk at me. Lately, she had been eating lunch with Lydia at our table. Jen had company when I called.

"Jamie wants to do hair for a living. So she gave me a perm. Mom said it came out well last night."

It came out well this morning, too.

"It's like this dress." She held her pleats out. "Mom helped me pick out this dress and stockings."

We examined at her lace-covered legs together. I was more like trying to see through them. She hadn't gotten any uglier since we left the house.

"Pay attention!"

I am paying attention, quite good attention.

I went back to her face. She formed a smile. "You made me lose my thought."

"Your mom helped you pick out the dress." I was myself again.

"Yes, she did. This morning when I came out wearing it... Well, she was studying herself in the hall mirror fixing her... uh, straps." Jen paused, glancing at me to see if I knew about what she was talking. For once, I did.

"Mom is kind of... Well, she's built differently than I am, or will ever be. You'll find out when you meet her."

Jen struggled, and I didn't help much. However, I did give her my full attention, and not to the part in the discussion. I waited for her to continue.

"Well, something bugged her about me today. I don't know exactly what it was. When she saw me in this dress, and checked my hair, she got all upset, and said I looked like a call girl. She said I had too much makeup on. Jon, I don't have any makeup on. I went around her and walked in on Dad and you. Do you think I look like one?"

Not knowing exactly how a call girl should look from anything but movies, I was at something of a disadvantage. I did know if being a call girl made them as cute as Jen, then the world needed a bunch more. I decided not to share my conclusion.

"Jen, you're different dressed up than when you have your hair in a ponytail and wear a sweatshirt."

Usually ten sizes too big.

"You surprised me this morning. I didn't expect you to change so

78

much. I was wrong."

"I noticed your 'surprise,' Jon. Guys have leered at me before, so I know what it means."

"Jen, I didn't mean to leer, honest. I couldn't help it. You're so incredibly..."

"Incredibly what?" she demanded, still flashing anger and backing away.

I took a deep breath, stepped right up to her, caught her shoulders, gazed into her eyes, and said it. "You're so incredibly beautiful."

I'd heard of a phrase melting someone before, but had never seen it happen in real life. Jen's anger melted like an ice cream cone on a hot sidewalk. The smile I'd been missing flowed down her face, nothing like the fake one she had given her father.

She dropped her eyes. "Thanks," she said, scraping her shoe. "I think I knew what you wanted to say." She shook herself and faced me again. "Still, it was nice to hear it, Jon."

"Jen?"

She waved me into silence and blurted out, "You wear your thoughts. It's okay you do. I like it, although I'm not used to, well... you. You see, you're my first guy... uh, boyfriend. No. Well, whatever you are, you're the first. It doesn't mean there is a second or anything." She stomped her foot and grabbed my hand. "Let's go."

We walked in silence to the church, Jen alone with her thoughts, me about two feet above the ground.

I'm her first guy, which means if, no, not if, when. When we kiss, I will be her first kiss. Sure, she'll be mine, too, but so what and not important. If I'm hers, my lips could be the first lips her lips touch in the first base way. Bigger than any so what and very important.

We reached the church, still holding hands. I was for sitting in the back, but she went straight to the second row, towing me behind her.

"This is where I sit, so I pay attention instead of watching the people," she explained. Jen was all seriousness.

Unlike some members, Jen didn't belt out the opening hymn, but I could distinctly hear her words. I toned down, but the people next to us gawked at me. They probably wondered how the skinny kid could make so much noise. "You sing so low," Jen said, using her deepest voice.

Pastor Kamorkov came forward to greet the congregation. He was Russian, a great big bear of a man, always excited about everything and everybody. This was a considerable contrast to our minister, Pastor Anderson, who was a small, quiet man.

The Assembly of God Church and the Lutheran Church were the largest, most influential churches in the city. The Assembly of God sat on the hillside in the well-to-do section where most of the Lutherans lived. The Lutheran Church nestled in the valley, where most of the Assembly of God members lived. So the people passed each other going to and

John C. Pelkey

coming from church. This created an unending source of conversation and friendly rivalry.

Pastor Kamorkov studied the congregation and spotted me. "Ah ha, we have a visitor from the competition. It's young Mr. Perone, from Trinity Lutheran."

"Boo!"

"And our City Youth Board."

"Ah!"

"Jon's brainstorm was the New Year's extravaganza, which gave our city's youth an alternative to liquor and other debauchery." The congregation cheered.

Debauchery? No one says that word in my Lutheran Church. No booing or cheering allowed either.

"Stand up and say hi to everybody," he commanded.

I stood up, turned and waved, and sat down quickly.

"Whoa, wait! Introduce the little girl you brought with you."

The voice yelled from somewhere in the rear of the church, where I wanted to be. Jen froze, a pained expression enveloping her face. The people in her own church didn't know her.

Pastor Kamorkov couldn't help but notice. "You, back there, have been sleeping through more than my sermons. Jenni Carling has been with us for some years, sitting in the same place every Sunday. You need to get out of your pew ghettos."

He made everyone stand, move around, and sit in a different place. However, after first moving somewhere else, Jen pulled me back to the now empty second row. She wasn't willing to give it up, even for Pastor Kamorkov.

The man who made the blunder came up and apologized. "I'm sorry; I didn't recognize you, Jenni."

"It's okay," she said, sniffing. When everyone finished moving, the congregation remained standing.

What next? Do I want to know?

I didn't.

"Now it's hug time," the pastor boomed, and bounded into the crowd, throwing hugs left and right. Completely focused elsewhere, Jen moved past me out into the aisle.

I quickly found out why. The pastor came to her and gave her a soft hug, not the bear type he gave everyone else. He whispered, "Sorry," to her, loud enough for me to hear.

He recovered and gave me an airmail bear hug, landing me several feet away. When he put me down, he whispered, "She is fragile; you be gentle with her," soft enough for Jen not to hear. Off he went again, throwing hugs left and right.

Thinking of her parents, her mom anyway, I wondered if Jen's front pew selection was more for the hug than for the concentration. I

To Face The World

understood the concept of what Pastor Kamorkov said, but it came with pieces missing.

I walked back to Jen, who faced me, her eyes glistening. She met me, almost a collision, and held me tight, far longer than she had to. Our first hug came in the presence of four hundred people. The feeling of her against me sent happy messages to all corners of my body. I wanted never to let go.

"Hug time is over," the pastor announced. "Too late if you missed somebody. You'll have to wait until the service is over."

Back in our pew, Jen sat closer now, touching me from her shoulder to her knee.

"What extravaganza?" she whispered, facing me.

"All night skating and pizza party. Not exactly an extravaganza, but Dave and Beth said they liked it."

"You thought of it and didn't go?"

"High school only."

"Maybe next year, we can go," she said.

Together.

When the sermon began, she leaned against me and put her hand over my elbow. I covered it with mine, about as close together we could get in a church. The sermon was about caring, and caring about Jen is what I wanted to do the most.

After the service, we walked to her house, hand in hand, not saying much. When we came to her block, she slowed down, squeezed my hand, and let go. I thought I understood why. She didn't want her parents to see.

At her front door, she turned on the first step, and held up both hands for fives. When I leaned forward to clasp them, we bumped heads, more of a nudge, fingers entwined. I hoped no one, especially no parent, saw us. Jen mumbled something about acting like football players, and stepped back to the door, opened it and turned around.

"See you at four," I said.

"Okay, bye," she replied, but without moving. She stood at the door watching me and I stood on the walk watching her. It was as if we were trying to will time to stand still. She waved and went in.

Chapter Ten

I arrived home to our after-church dinner in progress. "Everyone missed you this morning," Mom said as I sat down. "How was the service?"

"The minister gave out lots of hugs and preached on caring. It was a good sermon. They are much nosier than we are."

I didn't say anything about the booing and cheering, or about Jen. I did get to hear about Pastor Anderson's sermon on responsibility, at least what they could remember.

After dinner, everyone went their own way, leaving me alone in the house. While washing the dishes, I watched Dad mow the lawn and Mom gather some flowers. No one had even mentioned Jen. I felt relieved and, at the same time, let down.

I finished my homework, and announced to Mom at 3:30, "I'll be running at the high school, some extra practice. Okay?"

"Be back by dark," Mom said. Dark was about 8:30.

I took my time getting to Jen's house, wondering how she and her mom were doing. When I turned onto her block, I could see her sitting on her front steps. She wore her normal oversized sweatshirt and her hair in a ponytail, smashing the curls. She bounced a golf ball between her feet. When I approached, she kept bouncing the ball and didn't look up.

"Hi. You ready?" I asked, staying out on the sidewalk, uncertain if she still wanted to practice or even see me.

She hid the golf ball under the steps, ran down them, past me, and up the sidewalk. I followed for a block, and when she slowed, I caught up. She moved over to let me be on her right.

"The ponytail is ruining your curls," I ventured, testing the waters.

Jen didn't offer a response, so I dropped talking and focused on our warm up jog. When her breath came in sporadic pants, I stopped.

"What?" she snapped.

"You aren't breathing."

"I am, too." Another snap.

"You aren't controlling your breathing. You are letting it control you. Breathing right isn't something you can perfect in five minutes. It takes practice."

"Fine. We'll practice when we practice." Off she went.

I followed her onto the stadium, with the track surrounding the combination football and soccer field used for league play. We were the only ones in sight. I stopped at the edge of the track, wondering what to do. When Jen ignored me, I showed her my frustration by walking away from her. She shot by, spun, and faced me, putting her hand on my chest to get me to stop.

"Jon, I'm sorry. You are nice to me every day. You don't complain; you don't criticize. You listen; you always try to help. You've been a great guy."

Been?

My heart thumped faster than when running. As she was touching my chest, I knew she could feel it. I wanted my words to match my heartbeat, but could only come up with a lame, "Jen, what's wrong?"

She let go of my chest. Instead, she took my hand, and studied my fingers and my palm. I tried to focus on her problem instead of what she was doing to my insides. She was thinking, and I let her think, not even allowing my breathing to disturb her. Finally, a second before I was ready to burst, she spoke.

"I don't know what's wrong. Not for sure. I think my dad and mom don't like each other anymore. They're keeping it from me. When they include me, they use me to play against each other."

"Can you talk to them?"

"Sure. I can say 'good morning' and 'good night' without getting into trouble. If I say anything more, they filter all my words, searching for insubordination."

Since I barely understood what she said, I had no answer for her. "We better start before we get cooled off. We can talk when we're done." I was stalling. I thought ten years would about do, and a psychology degree.

I wondered about her use of "been."

Maybe it's how she phrases sentences. If I ask, she may answer in a way I don't want to know.

Despite how well the last two days had gone, the fearful nasty beast part of me still waited for the bubble to burst.

Jen took off her sweats to reveal her running suit, with a tee shirt and longer shorts underneath, the same as what she wore in the meets. Although she had done this as part of race preparation, watching her take off her sweats suddenly became a lot more exciting than ever before. As I took off my sweats, I realized I forgot to wear a tee shirt.

She smiled for the first time. "Wow," she said. "You have chest hair. I think I can see at least ten."

"Well, don't count them," I muttered.

So of course she did. "One, two, three..." She quit at ten, and added, "I could go without a top, too, and no one would even notice."

I thought I would get red again, but instead I felt irritation, perhaps for the first time in reference to Jen. "You had a top this morning," I said, trying to sound neutral. She had more curves in her dress than in her running clothes. I didn't speculate why.

John C. Pelkey

"You noticed more than my legs?"

"What I noticed is you are not controlling your breathing."

I went over the routine, but this time without touching her.

"I think you need to show me," she said.

I had an idea on a new approach. I led her to the stadium seating, about thirty rows. Standing at the bottom, I said, "Run to the top."

Jen frowned at me, and then took off, with me following. I had begun to doubt my brilliant plan, but about twenty-five rows up, she faltered. At the top, she gasped for breath. Although it wasn't easy, because I had prepared, I didn't.

"You're going to stand there and breathe normal?" she asked, still trying to find enough air.

She walked along the top and back, and sounded better. "I realized something," she said, watching me. "You breathe normal after your races, too. Everyone else is dying, and you are barely winded."

"Now you get my point," I said, smiling.

"Yeah, it means you could be running a lot faster than you are."

"And with proper breathing, so could you."

No way do you get to move the focus to me.

Jen's breathing had returned to normal by the time we walked back down to the first row.

"Now, try it again. In, in, out, out. Watch your stomach."

She took my hand and put it on her stomach again. I noticed how tense she felt. "You need to clear your mind and relax. Let it happen. Think about something you like."

She must have listened, as I could feel her relax. When she breathed properly in and out three times in a row, I let go.

"We jog to the other end, breathing properly, and run back to the top. Ready?"

She waved, more focused on my instruction than on me. After nodding to indicate ready, she shot across the bottom walkway. At the other end, she turned and flew up the stairs twice as fast as before. At the top, she was breathing hard, but not gasping.

"Notice the difference?" I asked.

"You are breathing much harder this time."

"No, your difference."

She ran back down, much faster than it was safe, and left me behind. She waited for me on the track.

"Okay, I'm not the best student," she muttered when I caught up, "but I got your point."

Do you know how stupid it is to sprint down cement steps?

I thought it, but I didn't say it.

We practiced half laps for time, running faster each time. We walk-rested a half lap and ran a half lap. Jen ran three straight half laps at less than forty seconds each without me telling her the time. We tried a series

84

To Face The World

of whole laps, again faster after each rest-walk. She had more trouble with the time on the full laps, missing by several seconds. We stopped for a break, pouring water over ourselves from the drinking fountain.

"It would help if somebody could read the half lap times," she observed.

"I guess I could, with Coach Davison's permission." I wasn't about to ask Coach Harris. I didn't think he liked me.

"Let's run four laps for time, try for five minutes," she offered. "You tell me the time at the half laps. Come on; we can do this."

"Jen, we have been running for hours." At least it seemed like hours.

Still, I quickly agreed. After the opening mess, we had become more comfortable while running together and I didn't want to reverse it. I watched her trot to the 400-meter starting line and followed.

I set my watch, and we took off, seventy-five seconds a lap. Jen kept the pace smooth, while I yelled the time every half lap. We were a second ahead on the first lap, a second behind on the second lap, right on time. The third lap was agony, but she picked up the pace. We were three seconds ahead. Halfway through the fourth lap, I wanted to die, but she ran faster, her breathing only a little labored. We were both hurting close to the finish line, so we had no closing kick.

I stopped short and hit the button as she crossed. The time read 4:51. With one day of practice and some simple breathing lessons, even after hours of running, Jen had broken the boys' school record I had set only two days ago. It seemed like two years ago.

We were too tired to cheer, but I could see her smile reflecting in mine. We picked up our sweats and tried to walk out our muscles. I made us finish with some light stretching. With a smirk, she waved goodbye to my chest hairs. I pushed my watch back to the regular time. It was almost eight o'clock.

"We're late," I muttered. Too tired, we walked to her house in silence.

Jen stopped on her front steps. "I did it; I broke five minutes for 1600 meters." She seemed pleased with herself. "I wouldn't have made it if you hadn't kept running; thanks, Jon."

More like you kept me running.

"Plus teaching me to breathe right, now it makes everything easier. You are so smart."

In her race two days ago, she had to stop. If she had known how to breathe correctly, she may have been able to begin with a sixty-five second lap and finish ten seconds faster than what we had run today. A shudder went through me. My three-week goal of getting Jen under five minutes for time had come and gone in a single day. I was at my best and she in warm up. I would have to try harder, much harder. Much, much harder.

"You okay?" she asked, probably wondering where my mind had

John C. Pelkey

gone.

"Jen, you're fast."

She cocked her head and shrugged. "You're fast, too." She made parallel whooshes with her hands, indicating the same speed.

"No, Jen. You are *fast*, fast. In the history of our school, no one has run 1600 meters faster than you did. No boy or girl, ever."

"Which means?" Her face turned into a huge question mark.

You don't get it. You have no idea you could be the fastest human female ever in existence. I'm exaggerating. Or am I?

Her father appeared at the door. "You're late," he growled.

"Dad, I broke five minutes for 1600 meters," Jen said, stepping past him.

I heard her mom speak from somewhere in the house. "What have you been doing?"

"We've been running, all day." Jen peeked back out from behind her dad. "Bye, Jon. Thanks."

As I backed away, her dad called to me. "Jon, Jenni says you have been a big help. Thanks." He closed the door, ending any further conversation and my almost glimpse of her mom.

Alone in my bedroom, I drew a hand on my calendar, Jen's hand, next to the numbers: 4:51. I added some dashes; only I would know they stood for chest hairs. May fifth. Two days ago I had wondered how long before Monday and seeing Jen. Now, a pile of wonders had replaced my single one. My life had become more complicated than from any previous experience. To make sense of it, I tried to merge my fragile view of the present with specific events and feelings from the past. Regardless, it all pointed toward an uncertain future.

Tomorrow, we have school and the first day of our future together in public. Or do we? Are we together? I don't know.

*****

I awoke, shaking with anticipation and uncertainty.

What will today be like? Will she be there? Will she pretend to be indifferent to our relationship? Do we have a relationship?

I was all questions, waiting for Jen to supply answers. I still felt like the little boy, afraid of his own self, hoping for a miracle created by someone else.

No, today I stand on my own two feet.

My answer came when I stepped off the bus. Jen, waiting in front of the school steps, gave me instant turmoil inside. I ignored it and focused.

Her curls had survived the previous day's trials. In a sweatshirt, though, Jen's curls didn't change her appearance as when in a dress. Jen wore a different sweatshirt every day, and they were all too big for me, much less her.

To Face The World

When I opened my mouth, she put her finger to her lips. "Shhh. We don't tell anybody about anything. I want it to be a surprise."

"Fine with me." Telling anyone about our extra running could get us in trouble. I decided to look at the school rules I had stuffed in my locker. I didn't want to ask in case somebody had a rule against it.

As she walked away with her friends, I decided Jen wanted to keep more than running a secret. So much for me standing on my own two feet. I realized how little I knew about relationships, having been in two, and so far both controlled by the girl.

Disappointed in myself, and with a sunny day, I decided to go golf ball hunting after track practice. Although Mr. Hernandez worked weekends for the most part, the golf course still accepted my donations in trade for course time. Maybe I could practice putting.

My golf ball patch missed me. I gathered four dozen in less than a half hour. I didn't expect Mr. Hernandez to work Monday evening, but saw him on the putting green giving tips to some ladies and sinking thirty-foot putts like free throws.

I dumped my golf balls in the machine that cleaned and striped them for range balls, getting a "Thank you" from the head pro.

Mr. Hernandez waved a putter for me to join him. We played putting horse. He gave me half the distance and still nailed the E on me before I could get him an R. "I miss you since you began track," he said, as we walked back to the pro shop.

"I practice running every day, weekends now, too."

"Maybe you could come by Sunday after you run," he said, with a sly expression. "I might have a surprise."

I latched on to the idea. "Can I bring my friend, Jenni? We practice running together. We could run here."

"It work out like I said, remember? You are a friend first?"

"I hope I am. I'm trying to be one. I'm not certain I'm succeeding, though."

"A girl is something precious. Liking a girl is no easy game, not like sinking a putt. You need to read the position carefully and take charge. When you swing, you do not think, 'Maybe I can,' you think, 'Yes, I will.' When you miss, you keep trying; you do not give up."

Keep trying. I haven't even attempted a try; instead, I go along with whatever.

"We'll be here," I said. "We should run some first."

"Good. I see you both. Come before the light goes away."

I wondered what Mr. Hernandez had in mind. I wanted to show Jen I had other interests we could share, which would only happen if we stayed together.

Wait. We have to get together first, stay together second.

*****

John C. Pelkey

Tuesday morning, I didn't expect to see Jen waiting for me and she wasn't. Instead of going along with *whatever,* I searched her out and found her in the hall in front of her first class, visiting with her friends. The second she saw me, she waved and left them.

"Hi," she said, flashing a smile. I realized how much I missed her from one day.

Taking a deep breath first, I blurted it out. "I don't want it to be a secret."

"Me going for the record?" she asked, clearly confused.

"No, not the record. Us. I don't want us to be a secret."

"Okay." She lapsed into silence, leaving me to swim or sink.

"When my bus comes..." I faltered, my courage sinking.

"I get here before you do," Jen said, jumping in and throwing me a line. "Maybe I can meet you outside the door if it's nice or inside if it's raining."

"Okay, great."

The bell rang, ending our conversation and saving me from acting any more foolish than I already felt. I reached out, and she met me halfway, touching hands for a second. On the way to class, I felt as if I had aced a five-syllable French spelling test.

*****

After practice, while walking up Notch Hill Road from the bus stop, I spotted Pastor Kamorkov at the intersection behind me. I waved, wondering if I should walk back.

His, "Wait, Jon. I'll walk with you," took care of my decision.

"Do you live around here?" I asked.

He pointed to the street down the hill on the other side of the intersection. "We recently moved. I wanted to be closer to work."

On a rare occasion, I ran down the street by his house and looped around back past Dr. Canfield's house.

"I can walk to church from here. It's much less than a mile." He stopped and smiled. "You walk there, too."

He continued with me, talking about the City Youth board, how he enjoyed working with my pastor, and, as an afterthought, with me. I waited for him to mention Jen; he did.

"Nice to see Jenni with someone. In two years, you are the first person outside our congregation she has ever sat with in church, so you must be special to her."

"I hope so," I said, wondering if he was fishing for something.

"You're fourteen?" he asked. I nodded. "This isn't easy for you to understand. I hope you see Jenni as a friend more than anything else."

Where have I heard that before? You know Mr. Hernandez?

To Face The World

I opened up, a major risk. "It's hard to see Jenni as only a friend. You saw her Sunday. She is so beautiful; it hurts just looking at her."

He laughed his hardy bear laugh. "Young girls look pretty good to young boys. I'm fifty. Under twenty, and you all appear as children. Jenni does, even if she's been a teenager for almost a year."

"Jenni is thirteen?"

"Yes, her birthday is June first, less than a month from now."

It seemed like a good hint. I wondered if he had planted himself at the corner on purpose.

We arrived at my driveway. "You live up here. It feels like we are in a different part of the state, and back maybe about fifty years. You are lucky, Jon." He waved down the street. "I like to take walks and this is nice. Maybe I'll see you when you run by."

I kept the quip of, "Not if I see you first," to myself.

Chapter Eleven

Friday brought the first of our two away meets. We sat at our typical spots on the bus and talked with our typical friends. We ran our typical races, and placed in our typical places, first. Although Jen's winning time at 5:19 came in twenty seconds behind my winning time, she still set a new school record for girls in the 1600-meter run.

"Ha, little do they know about who's going to break what record," she whispered as we picked up our winning ribbons.

We agreed to meet at Jen's house, Saturday at four. As expected, her mom met her at our school and whisked her away, while I waited for the home-delivery bus.

*****

I finished Dr. Canfield's yard ninety minutes before the time to meet Jen. I even cleaned the bathroom in the back of his garage, and silently thanked him. It had become the only bathroom in my life from the beginning of the yard jobs to my return home after running.

Before leaving, I spent a few minutes on his deck, swishing my hand through the water in the hot tub. Only one week ago, Jen and I had spent our first time together and alone here. She had told me I was sweet and embarrassed me. I would never see a hot tub without thinking of her.

She appeared as I finished edging the sidewalk in front of Mr. Dunlap's yard, sitting on her steps and bouncing the golf ball. When I crossed the street, she put the golf ball away and trotted out to meet me. She was in much better spirits, complete with a smile.

"Hi," she said, swishing her hands back and forth inches from mine. "Come on."

"Someone's hand," I muttered, watching it pull a curtain back a few inches in the front window. I waved at it, but it didn't respond.

Already on her way, Jen missed my remark and the cozy little, private non-conversation I had with the curtain.

When I caught her at the corner, she stopped and peeked back at her house.

"Dad and Mom are up to something. They won't tell me what it is. They did say I could stay out longer because running is so important to me. They are acting weird, especially Mom. Mom hates running. Mom even hates sweat. So there she is, encouraging me to run hard and give it my all today."

To Face The World

We watched the Mercedes back out of the garage. It appeared to be enough for Jen and she darted out of sight. "Aha," she said, almost with a snicker, when it turned toward the freeway. "They're going somewhere, but had to ditch their daughter first. Come on."

We ran to the school in silence, but a togetherness silence. This time I remembered my running shirt. Jen cried out in feigned agony. "Oh, I miss your chest hairs. I spent all week naming them: Frederick, Jeffery, Marvin, Theodore, William."

"Okay, okay. So I'll take it off." Which I did.

Before we began our workout, Jen counted my hairs as if to make sure I hadn't lost any. We ran similar to the previous week, with better results. She was accurate to the second for a half lap. Her breathing appeared to work just fine. She accentuated it a couple of times, to show she knew I wondered.

"Breathing is so simple once I learned your way. I practiced it all week in PE. We ran track there, too. I won all the races." She acted proud of herself, even patting her own back.

"What do you mean?" I asked, knowing the results, but wanting her to tell me.

"I won four races, 100 meters, 200 meters, 400 meters, and 800 meters. I didn't try hurdles. I won the long jump, too. Maybe I'll add it next year. I'm only running two races and the relay."

She didn't ask how I did and I didn't volunteer. Of the same events, I had won the 800-meter race and finished in the top five of the rest, not close to measuring up to her. With no secrets in our school, she probably already knew my results, the same as I had known hers.

We practiced getting Jen out of traps, in case other runners boxed her in. Her solution, slow down and go around, could work in long races. To be certain, I made her try to slip past me at a dead run given an inch of space. She grasped it faster than the breathing.

Jen had no acceleration issue. In a thirty-meter race, she would blow me away. I considered shorter races as she didn't have to run my race. My best times were for longer distances. Her best times were at any distance. Since she wanted my record, I kept silent.

I noticed she nodded to count when she ran. It was almost imperceptible, and I didn't tell her, afraid she would become self-conscious and disrupt herself. The full laps weren't perfect, so we continued the idea I would call out times for the half laps.

About 6:30, I called it quits. We had accomplished what we needed to for the week.

Jen said, "Stopping is good. I hurt for two days after last Sunday."

I still hurt from last Sunday.

We had to go through the new ritual of her saying goodbye to my chest hairs, calling them by name. Not to be outdone, I in turn, waved goodbye to her legs.

John C. Pelkey

"You do like my legs," she said, analyzing me. "Thought so. It's okay. I like your legs, too, and your chest hair. You could like my chest, too if I had--"

"If you had what?" It was more of a retort than a question.

She stared at the ground and bit her lip. "I was going to slam myself again."

Before I could stop me, I caught her hands and pulled her against me in a hug, not a good one, but better than doing nothing. She didn't fight or complain; instead, she hugged me back and didn't want to let go even when I did.

"You wanted to hug me, why?" she gasped after I gently pried her loose. "Don't I smell?"

"The hug is for not slamming yourself," I said, trying to feel as confident as I sounded. "Besides, we both smell."

"So," she said, smiling up at me from inches away, still holding both of my hands. "Every time I don't slam myself, you promise to hug me?"

"Maybe, depends on the circumstance." I touched her face, a first, running one finger across her lips, and said, "You can hug me whenever you want to. You don't have to ask."

Jen shuddered and took off, leaving my finger caressing the breeze. She slowed down when I caught her, and bumped me, to make up for her desertion. We ran an even pace back to her house, slowing to a warm-down walk when we entered her block.

I reached for her hand, and caught myself.

"What?" she said. "You can hold hands whenever you want to. You don't have to ask." She flashed me a smirky smile.

"On your block?" The smile disappeared faster than it came.

She nudged me back around the corner and stepped in front, facing me, touching my cheek, and running one finger across my lips, as I had done hers. I froze in place. Her finger felt like electricity.

"You don't even flinch," she said.

"If I did, you'd stop."

She dropped her hand, but smiled. "Next time, I'll hold still better."

At her front steps, I remembered Mr. Hernandez. "Tomorrow, instead of running at the track, could we run to the golf course? Someone I would like you to meet."

Jen gave me a funny glance, more sly than shy. "You play golf?"

"Yes, on Sunday nights. Not so often now I'm in track."

"Oh," she said, trying to hide a snicker, and failing.

What do you know and aren't telling me?

We did our fives, bumped heads for a second, and she ran up the steps. She waved goodbye, and I turned to leave. When she tried to turn her door handle, it didn't move.

"Jon, wait. They're gone. They said they'd be here."

My imagination pictured dead people or hostages, but we had seen

To Face The World

them drive away.

"Maybe they will be here in a minute or two. We didn't practice as long as last time."

"Or maybe not," Jen mumbled, smiling. "Come on." She led me toward the hedge. To my surprise, it had an angled opening no one would notice without seeing it from the house side. Even directly in front, it was invisible.

Now I know how she did her disappearing act two years ago.

"This is clever," I ventured, jumping from one side to the other.

"It gets less clever when you point it out to everyone."

Oops.

Her back yard fit in with upscale neighborhoods, fenced on three sides, with flowering trees along the fence and lawn in the middle. Behind the house, a huge deck started about a foot above the lawn and held a covered barbeque.

A recessed stone fire pit surrounded by low, circular, cement wall for seating sat at the far end of the yard. I could see formal events flowing out onto their deck and informal ones held around the fire.

Jen stepped onto the deck and continued to the far corner of the garage. "We keep a spare key here." She showed me the key hidden inside a fake rock partly buried in a pot.

You trust me, another step in our relationship.

After unlocking French doors, she motioned for me to come in. I froze in indecision. Our relationship was moving faster than I was. Jen helped decide by stepping behind me and pushing me through the door. We walked quietly into an informal eating area off the kitchen.

"Why are we being so quiet?" I whispered.

"I don't trust them," she replied. "They're up to something."

Maybe they are up to seeing if you bring guys in the house when they aren't home.

I turned to leave.

"Wait, here's a note." She took it off the refrigerator and read it.

> *Jenni, we have gone to the city for some fun, Mother's Day, you know. We will be spending the night there. Hold things down for us. Go to bed on time. No talking with your friends half the night. See you after church tomorrow. -- Mom*

"Well, we solved one great mystery," she said, more of a grumble. "They could have told me. I guess we would have known they were gone before you said goodnight, and maybe I would have snuck you in the house." She smiled for a second. "I suppose you should go."

I suppose I should.

"Wait!" she cried, grabbing my hand. "Let me show you my house. It will only take a minute."

93

John C. Pelkey

She led me around the house, waving at everything with one hand. Kitchen, dining room, living room, and down a hall with closet door mirrors lining one side, the location where her mother wasn't so nice. The other side had a closed door and a bath. We entered a bedroom turned into her mom's office, full of real estate stuff.

Her dad's office came next. It had a computer sitting on a huge desk and two walls of bookshelves, including a section with recent releases in fiction. Someone had arranged them in alphabetical order by author. Auel, Brooks, Christie, Crichton...

We took the back way into the atrium, which included another bath and a locked door.

"Dad doesn't let anyone inside this door. I think it has the furnace and water heater, but I don't know what else."

When I examined the hot tub and the curtain, she giggled. "Pretty much out in the open, unless the curtain is pulled. Dad and Mom pull it and tell me to stay in my room for a while, just not lately." Jen first appeared depressed, then hopeful. "Maybe, after today, they will again."

You are so sweet. How can anybody treat you mean?

I wanted to hug her again, but, being there, I was already out of bounds.

Jen wandered back into the hall. We paused at the end in front of a set of double doors. She watched me, a sneer masking her face, daring me to say or do something. I didn't know what to do and waited, feeling stupid standing in front of the doors.

What if your parents are on the other side?

I silenced my thoughts.

Finally, she pushed one door open. We stepped into a bedroom, the biggest I had ever seen. It came with a stone fireplace and sitting area, a large screen television, a VCR, and a bunch of movies whose titles I didn't recognize. She continued into a large bath. On the way, we passed two walk-in closets. The bath had two sinks, an oversized bathtub with holes in the sides, a glass-surrounded double shower in the middle, and a door, which she opened. Inside stood a toilet and a drinking fountain, set too low.

"What's that thing?" I asked, wrinkling my nose and pointing. "Why would anyone want a drinking fountain next to the toilet?"

Jen, to my surprise, said nothing, but stood there holding her breath, like during the volleyball game. I reached for her, but I wasn't fast enough. She went down to the floor, a rather thick white carpet, and burst out laughing. I felt helpless and even more stupid, staring at her, then at the thing. She propped herself up on one elbow, tears streaming down her cheeks. I studied my face in one of millions of mirrors. It was bright red, and I didn't even know why.

"Jon, you are so incredible!" she exclaimed, trying to sit. "I'm sorry. No, I'm not." Back down to the rug she went, laughing hysterically. I

To Face The World

turned to leave.

"Wait!" She jumped up and grabbed the sleeve of my sweatshirt. She used it to wipe her eyes and nose.

"Thanks." I said, more of a pout, pulling away. She continued to laugh, but managed to control herself, barely.

"Jon, if I tell you, I'm going to be so embarrassed. It could help if you were embarrassed, too."

I'm already as embarrassed as I can get, and I don't even know why.

"Jon, I like you much more than anyone else in my life. I don't ever want to hurt you, believe me. I'm sorry I laughed at you."

She forced herself to freeze her laughter and grabbed my arm, stretching my sweatshirt. She pulled me over to the thing, bent over it, and turned it on, without letting go of me. It shot up a stream about eight inches, and still looked like a drinking fountain. She put my hand into the stream. It was warm, like bath water.

"It's a *bidet*." She pronounced it *bid day*, but it sounded French. "It's used by a woman to clean a certain part of herself after she has been with a man. When I first saw it, I thought it was a drinking fountain, too. Mom explained it to me. I've never used it, duh. Haven't needed to." Her explanation ended with a smirk, but her face had turned as red as red as I felt.

She pulled me back into the bedroom, spun me around, and let go. She danced around the room, highlighting each item, like a game show hostess. "This is the best master suite money can rent."

Jen plopped on the bed and gazed up at me, sniffing. She wasn't laughing anymore. I lent her my other sweatshirt sleeve. She blew her nose on it and said, "Thanks."

Since you ruined one side, you may as well ruin the other side.

She smoothed out the bed and checked the room to make certain they were as they had been. Once she had me in the hall, she scooted her foot across the floor to erase the footprints, followed me out, and closed the door behind her. She had become subdued now, drained of energy.

"One more room to show you, I saved the best for last, my room." She led me to the closed door, opened it, and motioned for me to go in first.

Larger than mine, it had two windows, one facing across the street into Mr. Dunlap's front yard. The walls were white, where I could see them. Posters of exotic foreign places filled up every available space. Two more doors broke up the endless posters, one to a walk-in closet and the other to the bathroom.

Jen kept her room spotless and wrinkle free, except for a bag on her dresser. She didn't strike me as the throw-stuff-on-the-floor type. Her telephone was antique, sitting on a matching nightstand. The bed headboard and dresser matched, too. Everything matched. Nothing matched in my room.

95

John C. Pelkey

I studied a black box attached to the phone. It wasn't an antique. "What's this do?"

"It picks up the sound and filters the buzzes. It makes things clearer. Sure made your mother clearer." Jen giggled nervously. "We have one on all our phones."

They did, and they didn't. I saw it on the phone in the kitchen and on the phone by the piano in the living room, but not on the phone in her parents' bedroom. Maybe they could only afford three.

I saw a corner of a photo peeking out from the bag. As I moved toward it, she paused in front of me and stepped aside. "I didn't want you to see it yet, but I guess it's okay." As I picked up the bag, she stood next to me, even more subdued now.

I slipped out the photo, set in a plain, black frame. I studied Jen, who bit her knuckle, but said nothing.

In the photo, she stood, leaning forward with her legs apart, her hands on her knees, her head cocked slightly sideways, with a curl partly covering one eye. She had written, "To Jon," in the top left corner, and in the opposite bottom, "Love, Jen." Somehow, her dress seemed shorter in the photo than I remembered, falling about half way to her knees.

"I took the photo last Sunday, after you left. You liked me in the dress. Well, you liked my legs at least, so I took their picture." I watched a smile dance across her face. "I noticed you liked my legs today, too. The skirt part came out shorter than I thought, so I wasn't sure if I should give it to you. Since my shorts are shorter and you've seen enough of my legs, it's yours if you want."

"I want. I don't have anything from you."

She scrunched her nose, deep in thought, before popping her smile back.

"You want something? I'll trade you, your sweatshirt for one of mine."

"It's all smelly." I glanced at the mess on my sleeves.

"I can wash it, silly."

Jen showed me her closet full of sweatshirts, some imprinted with foreign countries, all large and colorful. I picked out one she had worn recently, showing a wolf running through the snow, with the word, "Whistler," printed below it.

"My Whistler Wolfie. One of my favorites. I'll like seeing it on you."

"What is Whistler?"

"It's a ski resort in Canada."

"Do you ski?"

"No, I've never been there."

She glazed over, as she did the first time I asked her about where some place was.

Why does Jen have shirts from places she had never been to and might not even exist?

"You sure you want mine?" My sweatshirt was plain, white, with a tiny red logo, "Trinity Lutheran," and nothing else on it. Plus it was dirty, full of sweat and covered with other stuff on the sleeves.

"Yours is great because it's yours, except for my snot," she said, giggling. "It will come out. Your mom won't get mad, thinking you blow your nose on it."

I let her pull it off, catching my glasses at the last second. There she was, undressing me in her bedroom. I let her put her sweatshirt on me, too; she seemed as happy dressing me. It fit okay, a bit large.

"Your parents won't mind?" she asked.

"No," I replied, truly uncertain, but not willing to say so aloud. I checked myself in the mirror over her dresser. "I'm wearing the better of the trade."

Jen fingered my sweatshirt logo. "Your shirt means more to me than mine does."

I checked my watch, eight o'clock. I had been in her house more than an hour.

"I guess I should go. Except..." I turned to face her. "Why did you say, 'This the best bedroom suite money can rent?'"

She returned my stare. "My parents don't own anything. The house, cars, the big TV, even my furniture, all rented. This was the best rental house Mom could find available in this town. We couldn't rent over by your Dr. Canfield. It's why I knew where he lived; we tried there first. We rent everything so we can move on a moment's notice to wherever Dad wants to live. Mom can find a new job selling houses. Simple isn't it? No extra baggage except me."

Jen broke eye contact, her signal for me to be quiet. I silently waited for her to reconnect. She pointed at the walls. "See these pictures, these sweatshirts. All bought in places where Dad and Mom went. I have never been to any place, except new houses to live in. I used to stay with my grandparents when my parents went places; now I stay with me."

She sat on the bed and stared at her feet.

Now I understand a little of what Pastor Kamorkov said.

With thoughts flashing in my head, I knelt in front of her and took her hands in mine. I waited until she found my eyes.

"Jen, please listen to me." She nodded. "I think you are the most beautiful and wonderful girl ever. Sometimes it hurts, looking at you. When you said I was your first guy, I couldn't believe I could be so lucky. I have been crazy about you since the first second I saw you in the hall, two years ago. I want to be more than your first guy; I want to be someone you can always count on, so you will never feel alone and without someone, at least to talk to, no matter where you are. I want to know you a long, long time, even if you end up with someone else. I want to be your friend, and I want you to be my friend."

Jen smiled at me through a tear. "What you said, it is the most

John C. Pelkey

unbelievable neatest thing anybody has ever said to anybody. Now, you better go before we do something we'll both regret." She stood, catching me with both hands, wanting a hug.

The moment faded when she stepped back and gasped, same as she had after the first hug. "I can't hold my breath any longer."

"You hold your breath when you hug me?" I asked.'

"Have to. Don't dare breathe. We should hug first, run second."

"I don't mind your smell. Not as bad as mine."

"It's not you, Jon, it's me. You've been running forever and have learned to live with your smell. I'm not used to living with mine."

For the first time I noticed a bit of her mom in Jen.

How much more of your mom will I find, and how well will I do with it?

Walking through the living room, I noticed it was missing a TV. The house had one TV, in her parents' bedroom. "Where's your TV?" I asked.

She glanced at me, shaking her head. "I don't watch TV, so I don't need one. I would rather read."

"Those books?"

"Book club. I get five a month. More if I want. My parents don't read, but my dad lets me store them in his office. Sometimes, I reread one if I'm caught up."

I would rather read than watch TV, but we still had one, and I still watched it, especially movies.

The sun had dipped behind The Notch when Jen walked me to her back deck. I stepped down on the grass, which made us the same height. We did our fives, clasping hands and bumping heads. More like leaned our heads together until I remembered her "smell" comment.

"Wait!" Jen slipped into the house, returning a minute later with her photo back in the bag.

"Tomorrow at four?" I asked.

"Tomorrow at four. Goodnight Jon, my friend." She disappeared into the house.

I walked through the hedge and onto the street. When I looked back, Jen stood at her bedroom window, waving. I waved back, and she blew me a kiss, our first one. I made a big deal about running out into the street and making a leaping catch, touching it to my lips.

I wanted to go back for the real thing, but it would come another day.

Chapter Twelve

The last rays of sunlight torched the cirrus clouds pink as Rex met me at the end of the driveway. We raced toward the house, Rex barking in the hope I would throw her ball. My third toss had her flying past the barn when I heard, "Jon! You're late." I found Mom and her grill routine waiting at the kitchen door. The sweatshirt caught her attention, and I watched the word, "Whistler?" soundlessly cross her mouth.

Before she could speak, I said, "Please let me shower first; then I'll explain everything," and reached for the photo I had left on the porch.

"What's in the bag?" Mom wanted to learn something.

"It's a picture of Jenni, taken last Sunday." I pulled out the photo and handed it to her.

"This is your little running friend?" Mom stared at the picture. As I ran up the stairs, she exclaimed, "Gas, you need to see this."

Great nickname for my dad, Gaston Perone.

When I came down in a clean tee and jeans, Dad, Mom, Dave, Cindy, and Beth still gawked at the picture. Beth had even given up the phone. Time for the family interrogation.

"The photo is of my friend, Jennifer Carling. Today, we ran at the high school, and we visited a bit. We traded sweatshirts, not the one she wore." Dave had opened his mouth. "She surprised me with the photo, which is why I'm late." Everyone accepted my story.

"She's cute," Cindy said, almost sounding jealous.

"Yeah," Beth added, squinting at me to see if it would make an improvement.

Dave handed me Jen's picture. "She's a sharp looking girl for being only fourteen. Great legs," he added, whistling. "You didn't just go buy a frame for its photo?"

Cindy gave him a slug on the shoulder.

"Hey, I was trying to compliment my LB on his taste, okay?"

"Jenni will be fourteen on June first," I said. "She's six months younger than I am."

Why did I tell them?

Then I realized why.

Mom co-owned a knit, sew, and notions shop. She liked to run a business and still be home to make Dad his dinner. Conveniently, it sat close to the library, across the street from the high school, and shared the building with a corner market. Mom sewed letters and designs on the school uniforms and jackets. She also made stuffed animals to order, of superb quality, so I thought. She had spent a month in training for it

John C. Pelkey

somewhere when I was younger. As far as I knew, it was the longest time Dad and she had ever been apart.

Jen had no stuffed animals or any personal things in sight in her room. I decided she needed something to put on her bed. I needed to figure out how to explain this to Mom without admitting I had been in her room. Without enough time to think, I winged it.

"Mom, will you a make a stuffed polar bear for me to give to Jen on her birthday? The biggest one you can, and a little polar bear, too, matching. Dr. Canfield paid me a hundred dollars last week. You can have it to buy materials. I'll pay the rest when it's done."

I knew custom-made stuffed animals were not cheap. I hoped my mom would help.

Mom seemed surprised at my request. Lately, she seemed surprised at everything I'd done. "The biggest stuffed polar bear we can make and a small one to match? Okay. It's going to cost you." She smiled and gave me a hug.

Other than playing the piano for me, I don't think I ever had asked Mom to do anything extra-special before in my life. I realized what was a little thing to one person was a big thing to another.

Beth went to her room and the phone, hopefully not to blab about me. I went to my room to hang Jen's picture on the wall next to my bed. I drew her house on my calendar.

Before going to bed, I did something I hadn't done in years. I got on my knees and prayed to God to take care of Jen. I asked Him to let me help if I could. Most of all I prayed He would take care of her, with or without me.

*****

Later in the night, I found myself caught up in a nightmare. Jen appeared in a prison cell and called to me through the bars. I tried to reach her for what seemed like hours, but could not. Every time I stretched out toward her a little farther, she reached out toward me from further away. "Jen, no! Come back!" As the dream faded, I awoke in an empty room.

"LB, what are you doing?"

My yelling brought Dave to my door. I cracked it enough to see him. "Nightmare. Jenni was slipping away and I couldn't reach her."

He pushed it open. "Look, kid. I saw her picture. Sooner or later, a girl as cute as she is will slip away. So don't get all worked up about thinking she is going to happen to you. You're too young anyway."

"You had your first girl when you were my age." *So you say.*

"Kid, there is a bit of difference between you and me."

"What difference?"

"I was a man at fourteen."

To Face The World

Your body was a man, but your brain was a pea. Still is.

"Face it, kid. She's gonna dump you."

"She is not. Jenni needs me, and not only for running."

"Well, someday she isn't going to need you."

I tried to think of a good, "oh yeah." Something popped up and came out before I could stop myself. "Well, someday Cindy is going to figure you out, and she's going to realize how stupid she is."

Brick brain.

"What are you talking about?" Dave snapped, shoving me backwards onto my bed.

I couldn't hide my surprise, not at him shoving me, but for me defending myself and saying something back. I basked in my accomplishment glow for about a half second.

"What are you talking about?" he repeated quietly, standing over me, chest out, shoulders back.

"What do you think I'm talking about, brrr... other?" I asked, barely above a whisper. I had almost said *Brick Brain* this time, but managed to keep it inside.

Still, I thought Dave was going to clobber me. Instead, he sagged against the wall. I stopped cringing and stood up, now at eye level with him. "Dave, what did I say? I'm sorry."

"You're sorry? Why should you be sorry? I'm the schmuck. Go to bed."

As I shut the door, I watched him trudge away, head down, as if I had beaten him. In bed, I tried to understand what had happened.

I've never said anything negative about you to you, and I'm not as mean to you as you are to me. Are you the type who can dish it but not take it?

As I had never tried to dish it before, I didn't know.

*****

I woke early Sunday as usual and crept down the stairs to go on my morning run. A muffled noise coming from the living room stopped me and I peeked around the corner. Someone lay on the couch under Mom's afghan. Cindy must not have not gone home. When she sat up, I fled into the kitchen.

Cindy stayed last night. Had she heard us? No. The distance is too far, and we had been whispering.

Cindy followed me. Alone with Dave's girl dressed in his tattered, old bathrobe wasn't my idea of how to start my day.

"Morning, Jon. Wait a sec. I want to make breakfast. Help your mom for Mother's Day. What do you eat on Sundays?"

"Um, eggs, bacon, toast, pancakes, hash browns," I said while tying my shoes. "The good stuff." My family hadn't joined the health club yet, but I knew it was on the horizon.

John C. Pelkey

"When does everyone get up?"

"When they smell your cooking, they'll get up. Promise." I shot out the door.

When I returned, my family had gathered in the kitchen, eating a tasty breakfast with compliments to the cook. Mom beamed from her spot at the table, an unusual place on Sunday morning. Cindy was more than a ditzy cheerleader; she was good cook.

The Lutheran Church service provided a quiet contrast to the Assembly of God Church the previous Sunday. I pictured Jen sitting alone there. I missed hug time. I missed her. I watched my family sitting in their "pew ghetto" as Pastor Kamorkov had called it, Dad, Mom, Beth, Dave, and Cindy. Cindy spent more and more time with us as a family. If her home life wasn't so great, I wondered how it compared to Jen's.

My parents had married too young, so everyone told them, Dad at twenty, Mom, nineteen. Dave came two years later, then Beth, then me. They took care of us and still had a life together. They went places alone, even overnight, and, although they didn't get mushy, I knew they still liked each other. My family was a family. We weren't perfect, and I often felt alone, but I never felt left behind like Jen felt.

Her family was two people living in the same house, stuck with a kid. Cindy's family was a demanding father, an exhausted mother, and seven little sisters and brothers. To Cindy, Dave, my less-than-stellar big brother, was like paradise. I wondered what Jen thought I was like.

When the choir stood up to sing, Dad and Mom smiled at me. For a change, I smiled back. Smiling made the day go better, as did the song. It wasn't so hard to smile at them. They were wonderful to me. I could try to be wonderful back.

Never, never, never smile at parents while standing in the choir.

They took it as a weak moment in my life, and they pounced on both the moment and me. They must have caught Beth smiling, too.

After the service, Mom stopped us as we walked to the car. "I have an announcement to make. Cindy is moving in with us."

Beth and I gawked at Mom, then at each other, then at Mom again. We started to speak, stopped, and looked at Cindy, who tried to find somewhere to hide. We stood there, silently staring at each other.

"Into the car," Dad said.

We continued our silence as Dad maneuvered through the greetings onto the street. Dad, Mom, and Beth sat in the front; Dave, Cindy, and I sat in the back. We had enough room between Cindy and me to put about six people.

"I'll explain," Mom said.

"No, let me," Dave interjected. "They can know the truth. It's our problem; we can share it." Beth turned around. We both watched Dave, who cleared his throat as if to make a speech. Cindy counted the specks of dust on the floor.

"Cindy and her dad aren't getting along. He was drunk on Friday and tried to get her."

The car became quiet, like on my morning runs. Dave's reference to "get" reminded me of something I once overheard him say, bragging to his friends about "getting" four girls in four years, one of them being Cindy. From the way Dave talked, I had already thought he did more bragging than "getting." Now I felt certain.

After a long, drawn out silence, tension as thick as butter, Mom turned around and softly said, "Dave, you're providing way too much detail."

Dad drove in silence, a bit faster than he usually did. He kept silent until Dave said, "Better to hear it from me than listen to all the crap at school."

"Dave!" rocked the car.

Dead silence, now. We in the back gathered our thoughts; carefully picking them up one at a time, afraid even of the sound of a thought dropping would further infuriate Dad. Only the engine made noise for the next mile.

"Sorry, Dad." Dave cleared his throat again. It sounded much dryer than the last time. "Look, Beth, Jon. This is how it is. Cindy's dad has a tough job. He is under a lot of stress. Her mom doesn't work, but has her own mom to take care of in Everett. She leaves all the kids with Cindy's dad. He drinks a little too much at night. He did the night before last. Sometimes when he's drunk, he takes it out on Cindy."

"Dave, get to the point." Dad appeared upset about something, although I wasn't certain what. I wanted to hear more. Dave hardly ever said anything interesting.

"Okay, Dad. The point is this. Cindy's mom told her she better move out. So we're moving her things to our house today."

How does this foul up Beth and me?

Mom read my mind, Beth's mind, too. "Cindy moves in with Beth until she and Dave marry, which will be on June thirtieth."

I checked out Cindy's finger, but didn't see a ring on her left hand. I checked my own hands to ensure I had perused her correct hand. "You guys are getting married?" I asked.

In light of you two getting happily married, Dave, I don't understand your reaction to my first ever come back last night. Something's not right.

I caught Cindy in the middle of a sentence. "...Dave asked me yesterday. I said yes. You were gone, and after we saw your friend's photo, we forgot to tell you." Cindy tried to smile, not quite successful.

"Congratulations. It makes you almost my sister."

I felt the tension fade in the car, and we went back to being a family again. It lasted for almost a minute, until Mom continued.

"After they marry, Dave and Cindy will move into Beth's bedroom, Beth will move into Jon's bedroom, and Jon will move into Dave's

John C. Pelkey

bedroom. Only for a few months, until Dave and Cindy find a place and can afford to move into it."

What? The tension did an about face and marched right back.

"Mom, you are kidding?" came from Beth. "Jon's bedroom sucks."

"Why involve me?" I asked, trying not to whine.

"Beth's bedroom is on the opposite side upstairs, and will give Dave and Cindy more privacy. Your room has the closet; Dave's has a bar. Beth has more things and needs a closet."

Silence again, except an occasional sniff from Cindy. I could see tears still flowing, silently. I could not even imagine what she could be going through. My whine seemed insignificant in comparison.

"What do you think? Beth?" Mom asked.

"Okay." Beth said it through gritted teeth. "I'd rather have Jon's bedroom than Dave's."

"Thanks, loads," Dave muttered.

"Jon?" Mom asked. "What about you?"

"Okay. Dave and Cindy are entitled to some happiness." I used a line from my favorite movie.

Cindy stopped crying and cracked a tiny smile. She whispered, "Thanks."

Dave nodded. "Ditto, LB."

"Oh," Mom said. "One more thing. We don't have much free storage space. We have to store Cindy's stuff somewhere. Jon, since you will have the larger of the two rooms, we're going to line the inner wall with her boxes."

So I go from a closet to a bar and a room full of boxes. Somebody else's boxes.

Cindy tried to change the conversation. "Jon, when are we going to meet your friend?"

Jen. Do her parents treat her like Cindy's dad treats Cindy?

Bad pictures tumbled out of my mind. I tackled my imagination before it broke away. "Maybe today. We're running to the golf course to see Mr. Hernandez at four."

"We might still be moving," Dave said. "You could bring her by on your way back."

Dave sounded like he meant it. A complete shock, in the same day he had said something worth listening to, and he had been nice about it.

Chapter Thirteen

After church, Dad treated Mom and us to a Mother's Day dinner in a nice restaurant. With the uncertainty of what would happen, we had a tough time eating and skipped dessert. After we came home, Dave and Cindy left in Dad's huge, crew-cab pickup truck. They took Dad along for reinforcements.

Mom, Beth, and I moved Dave's bed into Beth's room. Dave said he would sleep in his hunting bag. It was large, soft, and lived in the storage room for fifty-one weeks a year.

Beth eyed my bed. "If we move you now, you won't have to move later," she said.

"I don't want to move now or later," I muttered.

Beth held out a coin and Mom flipped it. I declared heads and lost. We swapped Dave and me. It didn't take long to move, the only casualty being the mesh lining to my box springs, which tore when Beth's hand slipped and I tried to keep it from crashing.

"Oops," said Beth, not exactly sounding contrite.

"I ripped it," I moaned, now more ticked at her for making me move.

Mom fixed it with a safety pin. "There," she said, "no one will notice." Since no one ever went under my bed, including me, no one would have noticed anyway. Somehow, her fixing it made me feel better anyway. Mom was good about that.

Soon we finished without any other accidents. My bed, desk, chair, dresser, photo, calendar, and what I stored in my closet, which I arranged on the floor in a corner of my new bedroom.

"You are so neat and tidy," Beth muttered, as she moved a pile of Dave's stuff between rooms. I helped Mom organize Dave's room while Beth rummaged for Dave's sleeping bag in the storage room. By the time our effort satisfied Mom and Beth, we had Dave's room tidy for the first and only time, and his clothes hanging in my closet.

"Perfect," Beth said, and disappeared into her room.

"Thanks for not putting up a fight," Mom added, as she walked down the stairs.

I headed for my room, caught myself, and trudged into my new home. "Get over it," I muttered as I sat at my desk, staring at Jen's photo and trying to focus on assignments instead of my new slum. It was hard, as I had lived in the other room almost as long as I could remember living.

I finished my homework and announced my departure. I planned

John C. Pelkey

to run to Jen's house and continue with her around Notch Hill to the golf course public entrance on the other side, about three miles. We could run back through the members' gate by Dr. Canfield. This way, we would get in a good run and see Mr. Hernandez first before I brought Jen home and introduced her to my family.

"We'll have supper tonight when we're finished moving Cindy. We all want to meet your friend. Just show up, don't worry about the time."

Mom's extra special invitation to supper at our house surprised me, as did her plan for an actual supper on Sunday night. After Mom prepared a huge and tasty dinner after church, supper became fend-for-yourself. I wondered how Jen would feel about supper, along with finding out about everything else going on with my family. I needed to warm her up to the idea. Maybe we could talk first and run second.

When I stepped out the door, I found the girl of my dreams in conflict with the dog of my reality. Jen and Rex faced off in the front yard, Jen trying to get her golf ball away from Rex. Her lack of success became obvious. She appeared to be afraid of Rex, who had figured this out and growled her best, *Try it; I dare you*, growl.

"Point at the ground; say, 'Rex, drop,' and she will."

With doubt written all over her face, Jen pointed to a spot well away from her and said, "Rex, drop," in almost a whisper. At once, Rex went to the spot where she pointed, dropped the ball, and backed up, jumping from side to side.

"She wants you to throw it." I waited to see what would happen next.

"She?" Jen picked up the golf ball, held it with two fingers, as if three fingers would trigger contamination, and threw it about five feet.

"Rex, stay!" Rex sat down and whined. "Like this." I retrieved the golf ball, took several running steps, and threw it into the scrub woods by the road. Rex tore after it, barking.

"You threw it away!" Jen cried.

"No I didn't. Even if I did, it's okay. Rex won't come back until she finds it."

I closed in on Jen. She wore my Trinity Lutheran sweatshirt. I reached for her hands and she met me halfway. We touched hands. Hands can send messages to all parts of the body and hers sent bunches. One signal finally reached my mouth.

"Hi, how did you find here?" I asked, my mouth not producing anything resembling what I wanted to say. Worse, I lost my signaling device when she let go. She moved in the direction Rex went, but only took a step, then spun and faced me. She pointed behind her, toward Notch Hill Road.

"I knew you lived in the last house on the road. This is the last house. I ran past to make sure. I worried you'd be gone before I came back. Rex came out of nowhere and took my ball. I couldn't get it back.

106

To Face The World

She is so big. It's my special golf ball, the one I bounce when I run and on my steps. Why is she called Rex?"

A bit chatty for Jen, I could feel her nervousness. I tried to think of what could calm her.

Rex came bounding out of the scrub to my rescue, with a strange bark to prove she had the ball in her mouth. Jen waved for me to get it.

"Go ahead," I said, trying to encourage her. "She won't hurt you."

Jen pointed at the ground by her feet. "Rex, drop." She spoke a little louder this time. Rex dropped it and backed up again.

I grabbed Rex's ball off the grass where she had left it yesterday and bounced it to get her attention. "Here, go find your own ball." I threw it over the house. Off Rex went, barking away. Without line of sight, she wouldn't so easily find it. She would spend a long time searching for it. Only food held more importance than dog ball.

I picked up the golf ball, cleaned it with my sweats, and tried to hand it to her.

"You keep it for now," she muttered. "It's still icky."

"You haven't been around dogs much. I used to sleep with Rex in the barn."

Jen wrinkled her nose. "I haven't been around much of anything, but I wouldn't sleep with a dog."

"You said you stay with your grandparents. You know, Grandpa chopping wood. Grandma making a pie. Living in an old farmhouse with a barn and fence in the country." I smiled at my brilliant scenario.

"My grandparents' high-rise condo in Florida overlooks a golf course and marina."

Thud. My imagined grandparents' farmhouse pictures are old-fashioned.

"They do have a boat, so I've been fishing." Jen wrinkled her nose again, showing her opinion of fishing. "Why is she named Rex?"

"Dad bought Rex for me six years ago. At eight years old, I couldn't tell the difference between a boy dog and a girl dog. Nobody would explain it to me. When I called her Rex, nobody argued. So she's Rex. Now she's an it."

Happy?

"Oh. Well, show me your place." Jen faced away, but I could feel her smirk.

I gave her a tour, pointing out the attractions as we walked. "The house is to your left. Dave's big car. Mom's little car. Dad's wagon. The building where Dad stores his digging equipment and dump truck is to your right."

She studied the dump truck and backhoe, sitting on a trailer. "Your Dad digs?"

"Yes. He digs ditches for water mains and connections. He contracts with Aurora Valley, some developers, and, occasionally the county or other cities. My dad's a ditch digger."

John C. Pelkey

"Oh." Jen absorbed this for a minute.

I wondered if his job made a difference. My dad didn't wear a white collar, or even a blue one. Usually, regardless of the original color, his collar became brown from the dirt.

"My dad hates dirt. My mom, too." She touched my arm. "It's their problem, not mine."

Relief. For a second, and not the first time, I wondered if we could be together. I kicked myself for my own doubt. Jen didn't show doubt.

She laughed at something going on inside her. "I guess our parents won't be entertaining each other any time soon," she said, more of a mumble.

I continued our tour to the barn. A cat came out with her tail up and ran to Jen, meowing for attention. She bent down, petted it, and said, "Nice kitty." Three more came out for some petting.

"Oh." She appeared nervous, but held her ground and petted them all. It got old for the cats and they wandered back toward the barn.

"Jen, have you ever petted a cat before?"

"Jamie's."

"How about a dog?"

"Little dogs."

"Have you ever had a pet?"

"You can't have pets when you live your life in rented houses. The agreements prohibit pets. If they don't, Mom makes sure they say they do."

I had launched into my own grill time, more like giving her a hard time. I could see her agreeability meter registering zero. "You ask me something."

Good catch and excellent recovery, Jon.

Jen glanced around, pointing at the flowers edging the garden on the house side. "What are those?" she asked. "The ones not ready to bloom, with their leaves looking like rushes."

"Day lilies, they bloom in July. Each flower has brilliant oranges, but only lasts a single day. They put everything they have into their one day, though. You'll see."

Meaning, in two months you'll still be seeing me to see them.

"At church, we have a painting of Moses in his basket in some rushes by the Nile. The rushes have the same leaf. They have orange blooms, too. Maybe they are the same." She glanced coyly at me. "I guess I'll find out. Be sure to tell me when the day lilies bloom so I can see them."

For some reason, this made me hot and shivery at the same time. Jen noticed and threw out a new question. "Who does your lawn? It's huge."

Our "lawn" combined volunteer grass, never-say-die weeds, and hopeful trees. We never watered it, and currently it stood about two feet

To Face The World

high and going yellow, except where Dad had mowed trails. There it was short and green.

"Dad mows it with a riding mower. He likes to make mazes."

"I like mazes."

I led her along the maze entrance, which split into separate trails. "Sometimes we play tag, usually right after Dad mows so we don't know the routes yet."

"Your parents play, too?"

"Well, yeah. Mom likes to run sometimes. She does okay."

"Your mom runs. Wow. My mom never runs. It would ruin her heels." She closed her eyes. "Nope, Mom running, can't picture it. Race you."

She went right, and I went left. My trail wove around more, so she ran ahead, until her trail came to a dead end on the other side of the house, almost to the driveway.

"Now I have to go all the way back," she muttered.

"Or you can walk through the tall grass," I offered.

"And ruin it? Never." After racing me back and winning, she asked. "What' next?"

We continued past the barn and walked up a slight rise to a knoll. Rex charged out of the woods with the ball and danced back and forth, waiting for me to tell her to drop it. "Last throw," I said, and rolled it down the driveway. Instead of running and barking, Rex slowly ambled after it. "Last throw" were words of death to dog ball.

Jen stood on the tip of the knoll, the exact highest spot and surveyed in all directions. "What's yours?" she asked.

"We have the pastures," I indicated the two fenced areas, one about four acres with the horses and cows, and a separate two acre section. "Dad planted the garden next to our house so Mom's view out the kitchen window wouldn't be at some farm animal staring in."

Jen flashed an, *I agree with her*, smile.

"We own the alders, by the road and on the north side." I pointed out where they had snuck under the east pasture fence. "Even those."

"Shouldn't you fix them? They are invading your pasture and closing in on that funny-looking, roofless, cement building... thing." She walked over to the fence to study it.

"It's for manure storage. We have to keep it separate from the animals and to keep from contaminating the water supply. When Beth and I clean the field and the barn, we dump it in there."

"Oh," she said, glancing at me, with one eye closed. "You actually go in there?"

"See the trail?" I pointed at the gap in the high grass where the trail clearly stood out, directly from the gate to the storage.

"If you put your horse and cow stuff there, how come it doesn't have anything in it?"

109

John C. Pelkey

"We sell it."

"You sell... Wait, somebody wants it?" She stepped away from the fence. "You're joking."

"No, I'm not. It grows flowers and vegetables. Our garden, the corn, beans, raspberries, and potatoes, among other things, and the marigolds and dahlias along with the day lilies. They all happily grow in our special mixture of dirt, peat, and 'horse and cow stuff.'"

"What's special about it?" she asked.

"I mix it myself, by hand."

Jen shuddered at the thought. "You put your hands in it?"

"I wear gloves and wash my hands afterwards."

Jen lapsed into silence, trying to come to grips with me, Jon Perone, farm boy, so different from her, Jennifer Carling, city girl.

"When potatoes are in the ground, they grow in the stuff?" she asked.

"So do carrots and radishes, anything growing under the ground, and what's on top, like the lettuce, sits on it."

"Do you step on the stuff when you walk between the rows?"

"Well, sort of. I don't walk barefoot, although I used to. I weed it twice a week. I shower after, okay?"

I decided not to say when I was ten, I used to collect cow pies, line them up on the side of the knoll, wet them, get a good run, and slide on them standing up in my bare feet.

Our different cultures had created a wall, Jen drifting away in her mind. I needed a quick fix. "Have you ever petted a horse?"

We had three gates where the pastures intersected with the rest of the property so we could get in and between them. I walked to the south pasture fence by its gate. Beth's horses trotted over and leaned on the top board. Jen slowly followed me, quite deliberate, but stood next to them. I demonstrated by petting Elizabeth, the rough horse, and she carefully touched Janet, the gentle one. Janet shook her head and blew through her nose.

"Oh!" Jen jumped away, but didn't stay back.

"Want to sit on her?"

She considered my proposal, glaring at me to show she thought I had slipped out of my mind absolutely. She softened her glare when she remembered something. "I almost rode a horse once, in Florida. My grandpa offered to take me, but my parents came back a day early."

I didn't ask for details. Petting the horse meant she had touched it, and I didn't want to wreck things.

"Come on." I opened the gate. For a second I hesitated, as she appeared about ready to bolt. Somehow, she broke out her courage and came in, staying behind me.

"This is how you do it." I grabbed Janet's mane and threw myself up and over, hoping I wouldn't blow it and fall off the other side. Janet

110

To Face The World

didn't object and stood quietly.

"I don't think so," Jen said, shaking her head and backing up.

"It's easy; come on." I jumped off and waited. She sighed and came over. "Give me your foot." I cupped my hands. She carefully put her foot in my palms and I boosted her up.

"Oh, wow, I'm doing it! She's hard." I put my hand under Janet's chin and pulled gently. She slowly followed me.

"Hang on!"

"To what?"

"Her mane."

"She won't mind?"

"No, and press with your feet."

I moved to a trot and Janet responded, causing Jen to bounce.

"Oh, oh, oh, oh." She spoke in rhythm to the trot.

I went down the field, past the barn and shed, and then back, making a huge oval. Along the way, I checked the house to see if anyone watched. I could see a face in the dining room window, but not who. Somebody watched us.

At the gate, I asked, "Ready to get off?"

"More than ready, but this was fun, and different." She smiled, her eyes sparkling.

"Bring your leg over." She did, and I held out my arms. Jen slid into them. I held her as long as I dared, about one extra second, and let go.

Jen stepped in front of Janet and petted her. "Thanks, horse."

"Janet."

"Thanks, Janet? Janet is a horse name? What did you name the other horse?"

"Elizabeth. Naming animals is not a Perone specialty."

Jen nodded in agreement. "Jan and Liz. Named after your sister?"

"Beth? No, Beth's name isn't Elizabeth."

"What is it?"

Instant crisis. I can trust you, I hope.

"This is important; you can't tell anyone, ever, okay?"

She nodded, but her face contradicted her words.

"No one."

"Okay, I got it. Tell no one, ever. Promise. What?"

"My brother Dave is David from the Bible. They named my sister after his most famous wife, Bathsheba. She could have been Abigail, Ahinoam, Abishag, all worse, or Michal. I thought Michal would have been better. I could have called her Mike."

"That's goofy."

"Well, she refused to let us call her Bath or Sheba, so we call her Beth. If I tell anyone her real name, I'm toast."

"Good to know." When I frowned, she added, "I won't tell anyone, promise," and raised her right hand.

111

John C. Pelkey

One of the cows came over and Jen turned to leave.

"Ever pet a--"

"No!" With her courage still turned on, she stepped around me and walked right up to it.

"This is my first cow; what do I do?" She and the cow stared at each other.

"Nothing, it's what the cow does best. You'll make it feel right at home." My low opinion of cows came out.

Jen petted it anyway. "Hi, cow, what's your name?"

"Hamburger. Over there are Sirloin and Pot Roast." I pointed at the other cows. "They're steers. We grow them to eat."

"What a horrible life, stuck with a crummy name, never petted, and then eaten. Cows need love, too, you know."

"Fine. Cow love."

I stood next to Hamburger, flexed my fingers, and scratched down the top of his spine from his head almost to his tail, and back. When I stopped and backed away Hamburger came forward, one step. "There, you try it."

Jen wiggled her fingers and gingerly tickled his back. When she hit a spot in front of his tail, he mooed. "He must like getting tickled," she said.

"Maybe he likes you. He doesn't moo for me."

"That's because you're going to eat him." Jen scratched his nose again. "If I ever eat any of you, I promise not to make a pig of myself and have seconds. Don't suppose it makes anything better, does it?"

Hamburger had no comment, having used up his moo for the day.

"We better get going. Mom wants you to have supper with us if you can."

The horses followed us to the gate. Hamburger, unimpressed with the confrontation, went back to doing nothing.

"Why do the horses follow us and not the cows?" she asked.

"Horses like people and each other. If Beth rides one and leaves one, they both have issues. Separate the cows and they think, 'More for me.'"

"If I eat with you, does it mean less for everyone?" she asked.

"We aren't like cows; we're like horses. Everyone wants to meet you."

For some reason, I could feel a thud from my response. Jen turned away, and I knew the wall had come back. I didn't understand at first, and then realized she could be comparing my family to hers. I had still not met her mom, but so far, my picture of her wasn't positive.

"Jen?"

She turned back, facing me. "My family doesn't allow guests, not without prior approval."

"My family is a little less formal. Trust me; they will like you, especially Beth and Cindy."

To Face The World

"You sure?"

"I'm sure. Before we run, do you want to ask your folks first?"

"My 'folks' called me early this afternoon. They're staying in Seattle to see a dinner play. They won't be back until late, which is why I could come over. No one home to say no. They did tell me not to let you in the house while they're gone. Since they don't want you in the house when they're not gone, it doesn't leave much."

Jen sounded angry about something. The talk we didn't have last week haunted me. I wished a second time for the ten years and the degree.

"Jen, what's wrong?"

Most likely, nothing you'll ever tell me.

"I don't know. Well, maybe I do."

She paused for a moment to think. "They knew I had other plans today, but they didn't know two months ago when they bought the tickets. First yesterday, then today. They knew they weren't coming back as they had planned to go a day early. They don't tell me anything. They don't share anything; to them, I barely exist. When they do get along, they live in their world without me. When they don't get along, they use me to hurt each other. And Mom..."

And Mom what? What, Jen? Talk to me.

"Jon!" Beth, standing with Mom on the porch, saved her. We walked back in silence.

Mom spoke first. "Hi, I'm Emily Perone; this is Jon's sister, Beth."

"Mom, Beth, this is Jennifer Carling." I swirled my hand down like a French aristocrat.

Jen waved me off and slipped into a formal hostess, *so happy to see you,* manner. "Hello, Mrs. Perone. Hi, Beth. Jon said you invited me to supper. Thank you. I would be happy to attend."

Her demeanor didn't surprise me. It reminded me of her earlier comments about being perfect.

Mom would have none of it. "I refuse to believe I am old enough for anyone to call me Mrs. I'm Emily. Please remember this; you are always welcome here."

Mom pulled Jen into a hug, which surprised me, followed by another surprise when she returned it. Beth stared at me suspiciously.

"Dave called," Mom said. "They are still negotiating with Cindy's father. It's a good thing Dad went. Cindy is eighteen, so her father can't stop her from leaving. That aside, he doesn't appreciate anyone, especially his daughter, questioning his authority. Dave said they will finish eventually."

Mom didn't usually share with a stranger. Mom didn't usually hug people she didn't know. For today, usually had gone out the window.

Beth gave me a, *we're going to talk soon, little brother,* stare.

Mom gave me a, *we're going to talk soon, son,* stare.

113

John C. Pelkey

I gave them both a, *you can't dig deep enough to get anything out of me,* stare back.

Mom and Beth watched us warm up with some light exercises. We set off at a good pace, waving goodbye. The second Mom and Beth disappeared into the house, Jen stopped and asked, "Who is Cindy? Why did you say she will like me?"

"She's my future sister-in-law, and she will like you."

Jen gave the impression of being serious, no smile, and not a time for joking. When I shared the conversation we had in the car, she quietly let it sink in.

"Your family is so nice. You all are sacrificing to help Cindy, and you do it together." She stopped, but her tight expression told me she had more to say.

I felt helpless. I didn't know what would make things better.

Jen must have noticed, as she dropped the subject. She glanced through the trees toward the golf course and pointed. "You can reach the golf course through there? Is it where you find your golf balls?"

"Yes, but let's go to the gate by Dr. Canfield." We had wasted enough of our running time.

"Don't you want to share your golf ball patch?" she asked, suddenly chipper.

How do you know about me gathering golf balls, or my "golf ball patch?" I don't remember mentioning it. I don't remember mentioning where I live either.

She acted so perky and hopeful, as if hunting for golf balls would be like unwrapping Christmas presents.

I faced a choice; we could run or we could hunt golf balls. We couldn't do both.

We had not worked our way through a difference of opinion situation like this before, and I did not know how to solve it. Jen did. When she faced the street, I touched her shoulder and turned her toward the trees.

"Follow me close and be careful. Lots of branches, sticker bushes, and mud."

She smiled a sweet *thank you*. I decided I could give in to her, as long as I didn't make it a habit. One time didn't constitute a habit -- yet.

Chapter Fourteen

I led Jen into the forest of maple trees and underbrush on the other side of Notch Hill Road, weaving along a faint trail around a swamp to my grassy golf ball patch by the lake. She caught herself once in some stickers, and I had to undo her.

I'm so glad you wore sweats over your shorts. Better to unsnag sweats than skin.

"You could make a real trail," she said. "It would make this much nicer."

Right. I should have made a real trail for someone who didn't know this place existed.

I hadn't picked golf balls there since visiting Mr. Hernandez. Jen found her first ball, and another. "This is like Easter egg hunting," she said, smiling.

Okay, maybe this isn't such a bad idea.

We divided the space in half, and gave ourselves ten minutes to gather golf balls. I let her choose the side she wanted to search. There were no golfers in sight on this part of the course.

We dropped our golf balls in piles next to each other. I ended up with nineteen; Jen found fifteen.

"You're better at this than I am," she said, pretending a sniff.

"You gave me the good side where the most of the golf balls land."

Jen snooped through my side and found five more in about a minute. "You didn't even have to try," she said.

I searched five times as long on her side and found one, keeping my mouth shut. Truthfully, she was much better at it than I was. We now had forty, and each found half.

I took Jen's ball from my sweatpants pocket and dropped it in the pile. "Adding this makes forty-one."

"No! It's my favorite." Jen tried to follow her ball's bouncing around as it joined the others.

"It's easy to spot; Rex put a ding in it." I picked it up and showed the scar Rex had made. "You can have another one to bounce on your steps."

"I don't want another one."

"Here, you can have it back. It still works." I cleaned it thoroughly again. This time she took it as if it were too precious for me to hold for her. I thought about the lack of things in her bedroom.

"How are you going to carry them?" Jen studied the golf balls, and the sweatshirt I wore. "We can't jump the lake and walk to the pro shop with them bundled in the bottom of our sweatshirts."

John C. Pelkey

How do you know about the lake? You shouldn't know about the lake, or the golf balls, or the trail, or my house.

Jen completely misread my thoughts. "If you aren't going to volunteer your sweatshirt, I'll take mine off," she said. She raised it far enough to reveal her navel, a cute little indent. She caught my ogle and giggled. "Since we aren't sprinting today, I'm not wearing my racing clothes. If you want me walking into the pro shop showing what's underneath?" She pulled it up further.

"Here's mine!" I whipped my shirt off, losing my glasses.

Jen took my shirt. She counted my chest hairs again, making a big deal of waving her finger in front of each one. "Hi, Fred. Hi, Jeff. Hi, Marv. Hi, Ted. Hi, Bill." I wondered if she would still be counting them when I turned fifty. If we were still together at fifty, it would be okay. I might even have more.

Jen fished my glasses out of the sleeve, cleaned them off, and carefully put them back on my face. "Did you ever think of wearing contacts?"

"No, why?"

"Cause I like you in glasses, not all the time though."

When wouldn't you like me in glasses?

I wanted to ask. Without asking, I wouldn't get an answer. I added it to the list of unanswered questions, now piling up.

Instead, I asked, "Would you have pulled your sweatshirt off?"

"Embarrassing you would be fun and would serve you right for taking so long to decide," she said, shaking her head. "No, though. I would be more embarrassed."

I packed the golf balls in my sweatshirt and moved on to our next problem. The lake narrowed to about twelve feet across, but we had no room to get a running start from this side. One day when I didn't mind getting wet, I moved a large rock into the center. It rested an inch beneath the surface. I could jump across, touching the rock and not get wet. Although the water couldn't be more than a foot or two deep, when I had missed a couple of times, I had been thoroughly soaked.

I explained the jump, and showed her. Jump, jump, and I landed across. I put the shirt down, planning to jump back, but she went for it. She bounced off the rock and stumbled on her landing, almost falling backward into the lake. I grabbed one arm and reeled her in.

"We did it!" She put her hands up. I clasped them and we bumped heads.

"*Fore!*" Something shattered our moment, a lone golfer calling from the fifth tee.

The fifth fairway teed off on top of a rise, followed the lake at the bottom, and doglegged sharply to the left. The lake doglegged with it. A line of trees bordered the side opposite the lake, ending with the largest one at the inner point of the dogleg. The space to make the turn past the

116

tree, but not crossing the lake, had to be about fifteen yards wide. Many golfers misjudged the distance partially due to the slope and hit their ball into my golf ball patch. They took a drop and went on. If they hit it short, they hit their second shot to my patch and took a drop.

I grabbed the shirt, and we ran behind the last tree. The golfer bounced his ball over the lake into my patch. As he picked up his club, I had an inspiration. "Use your seven, no eight. Use your eight!"

He stopped, thought about it, pulled out a club, and teed up another ball. He hit the ball high; it landed five feet past the tree and stopped. Although he couldn't see it from the tee, he had a clear shot to the green.

"Sorry about being in your way," I said to him as he approached.

"It's okay. Watching you two is more fun than playing this hole. I always hit an old one in or over the water, take my drop, and hope for a five. It's better than hitting it short."

He stopped talking when he saw how well he had placed his ball. "Well I'll be damned." He studied at his ball, and then studied us. "You teach this game, kid?"

"No, but I collect lots of golf balls across the lake. This hole is deceptive. Most people hit the ball too hard. A seven or an eight iron will get you past the trees and short of the water."

"What should I use now?"

"This side is longer. Use your hybrid; I would use my fairway wood."

He took out his hybrid, readied himself, and hit the ball to less than five feet from the pin. "Well I'll be damned," he repeated. "Thanks, kid. I've never hit par on this hole. This is the closest I've come. Here's something to add to your collection. You won't get another one from me." He threw me a new ball, probably expensive.

He gave Jen a closer look. "Hello, Ms. Carling."

"Hello Mr. Shoeman."

He left us, me staring at Jen.

"Who's he?"

"He works for my dad." She wrinkled her nose.

"Do you think he will tell your dad about us?"

"Dad already knows about us."

Your dad already knows what about us?

Her nose wrinkled further. "Well I'll be..." she mimicked, glaring at his retreating figure. "You know what I left out?"

I know.

"Pastor K talked about language today. Some people think in swear words and obscenities, and say whatever comes out. Some people substitute for swearing and obscene language with words nicer to hear, but mean the same thing."

She unwrinkled her nose and smiled. "Something I like about you,

John C. Pelkey

Jon. You don't either use bad words or substitute words. Most guys do; most girls do, too, except maybe in front of guys, and they mess up when they aren't careful. Thanks for not being like everyone else."

I digested her revelation.

People think in terms of swear words. Even if they don't say them, the words are always on their minds, waiting for the chance.

I didn't usually swear or say obscenities, but used some pseudo swear and obscene words on occasion in normal conversation. My favorite was "crappity-do-da" when irritated.

The question: Do I think using them? I conjured up a couple, and felt uneasy doing it. No, I don't. The result came as a surprise, a pleasant one. I couldn't help but smile.

Jen noticed and scrunched her face into a question.

"Do you use swear words?" I asked.

"What? Jon, have you ever heard--?"

"Not when you speak, but in your mind. Do you think them?"

Instant silence. As we walked to the pro shop, I could almost see the smoke coming off the wheels spinning inside her head. We kept silent, both lost in our thoughts. I tried to picture Jen swearing, but doing so made me uncomfortable.

Before going inside, I dumped the balls into the range ball machine, saving Mr. Shoeman's; one of the few times I kept a golf ball. As it was a gift, not somebody's lost ball belonging to the golf course, I thought it counted differently, like Jen's ball did.

As I put my sweatshirt back on, Jen made a pretend pout and I read the sign by the door. "No shirt, no shoes, no service."

She grabbed my arm as we stepped in. "No, I don't," she said. We traded smiles.

We found Mr. Hernandez visiting customers, so we checked out the golf clothes and clubs.

I would like to own clubs.

I once had thought about buying some clubs, one at a time. Mr. Hernandez told me to wait until I was older and finished growing, a better idea.

"The clubs I give you to play are better than what you can afford. When you buy clubs, you buy the best. Otherwise, you waste money."

I had been eying a good putter so I could practice at home. Too late now, someone else had purchased it.

Oh well.

The people left and Mr. Hernandez joined us. "Hi, Jon."

He smiled at Jen, who smiled back. She appeared to have a giggle ready to burst out.

"Mr. Hernandez, this is my friend, Jennifer Carling. Jenni, meet Mr. Hernandez."

"Pleased to meet you, Miss Carling."

To Face The World

"Hi, Melvin." She waved, trying harder but failing to suppress her giggle.

Hi Melvin? How do you know his name?

She gave Mr. Hernandez a hug, and they both glanced at me and laughed. They were the same height. Jen let go of him, took hold of my hand, and gazed up into my face. Her eyes sparkled and her mouth dazzled. For the first time, I had an incredible urge to kiss her, but didn't. Mr. Hernandez watched us for a second, and went into the back.

"We joined the country club when we moved here. My parents like the social calendar as much as the golf. Mel has been giving me golf lessons on Saturday mornings each summer since sixth grade. Some good advice too, on occasions." Jen ended with a smirk.

Like where I live, my golf ball patch, and a bunch of other secrets, not so secret.

"That's how you knew where I lived?"

She still held my hand, something we hadn't done in front of anyone since our walk from the church our first Sunday together. She gazed up at me, her soft eyes showing uncertainty. "May I show you something?" I shrugged.

She pulled me into Mr. Hernandez's tiny office. An aerial map of the golf course and surrounding area took up one entire wall. We studied it together. I found Dr. Canfield's house and traced the route to my road. The map ended half way through the pasture behind my house.

"Your house," she said, pointing. "Harder to tell from the street." She continued pointing. "Bushes, golf ball patch, lake, narrow spot." She handed me her golf ball. "Doesn't it look familiar?"

I studied it. The brand was unusual, Clover, like the first four golf balls I found, almost two years ago. I had not paid attention before. Jen had bounced the same ball into Dr. Canfield's yard. "You hit them?"

"From here." She tapped the spot where Mr. Shoeman's ball landed on his second tee shot. "Maybe a hundred yards? I used a seven to clear the trees."

"Why?" I couldn't hold back my irritation. "You could have hit a car or something. Why do all the secret stuff? Why didn't you say something?"

Her eyes dropped to the floor, and back to me. "I know it was a dumb idea. We listened for cars and didn't hear any. I didn't know what else to do. I wanted to talk to you a thousand times. Do you know how hard it is?"

My anger disbursed, and I nodded. I knew.

You hit golf balls at me. I got a lawn care job across the street from you. Are we so much different?

"I could have said something, too."

"Every time I like someone, anyone, we move, and I lose them

John C. Pelkey

forever. It happens over and over. This time I don't want to go through losing someone, not with you."

Not with me?

"Have you ever moved?" she asked.

"I slept in the family room until Dad partitioned Dave's room. I moved upstairs a few months before I turned three. I still remember, although it's hazy. It was quite the shock, being in a small room alone. I know it's not what you meant. No, I have never moved."

"Moving upstairs," she said, shaking her head. "I've moved a dozen times, not across the house, across the country. Every time we move, I lose every friend I have. I make fewer friends and it gets so much harder. Most of the kids you know, you've known since you've known people. When I moved here, I didn't know anyone. You were the first kid person to speak to me. You were so... You cared. I felt this huge... thing, inside." She tapped her chest, probably meaning her heart. "It made me crazy. I couldn't talk to you about anything without..." She stopped.

I continued. "Without feeling like everything is going to come apart forever if you get the tiniest hint of rejection?"

Her mouth popped open. "How did you know?" she asked.

"I didn't know. It's how I feel."

"You? You're the smartest kid in school. Even Alyssa thinks so. You intimidate everyone."

"Why?"

"Because around you, we think we sound stupid."

My turn to shake my head. "Jen, you have it backward. You're popular; I'm not. You were -- you are -- way too good looking for me. My brother says I am a skinny kid. Alyssa is skinny, too, so she fits. Did fit." I almost said, "Skag," but managed to force my mouth shut.

She pulled me back to the clothing section. A full-length mirror hung on the wall. She posed with me. "You aren't skinny. Maybe thinner when compared to Tom, but so is everyone else. How big is Dave?"

"Dave is bigger than Tom, and my dad is bigger than Dave. Or as big, anyway. I'm the runt."

"You weren't a runt when we played volleyball. You could jump higher than anyone else, even Jim." She stopped and smiled. "They asked the girls for preferences and concerns, mostly so they wouldn't accidently place a girl on a team with a guy who hits on her. I asked them to place me next to you. Alyssa and Lydia did, too, but none of us knew about the others. They didn't tell us before they announced the teams."

"They didn't ask us. I thought they picked at random."

"So they want you to think. Otherwise, guys would be asking to be with girls they could hit on. Girls generally don't hit on guys. None of us did. We wanted to play on your team. Jamie said, in her class, Trish asked to play on the team with your friend Tom. They almost refused for

120

To Face The World

obvious reasons."

Trish and Tom, the one other real couple our age. Because of Tom, Trish was the only girl who regularly said hi to me before I met Jen.

"You know Trish?" I asked.

"A little. She spends most of her waking hours either with Tom or thinking about him."

Kind of like what I do with you.

"How tall or how strong you are doesn't matter. Who you are in here does matter." She touched my chest. "Like in volleyball, you always helped; you never laughed at me. When you took over the team, you didn't do it to help yourself look better; you did it to help us, even Alyssa. It worked, too. Now you help me by being my friend, even when I whack golf balls at you."

Her conversation roamed all over, but at least she talked long enough for everything to sink in, except... "Jen, were you going to turn out for track?"

Or am I the only liar?

"Not until you said you were. I knew I could run. I ran the fastest in my last school, boy, or girl, for at least the short distances. Not so good at longer distances, until now. Dad insisted Coach Harris test me privately, so I didn't have to go through what you did."

Like make a fool of myself asking about the record? Which, if I had not done, maybe we wouldn't be here together.

"This is the most important. Yesterday, Dad said we could stay here until I graduate from high school, but not to tell Mom."

Now everything makes sense. Jen acts reserved because she doesn't want to make friends just to lose them. What's my excuse?

Jen faced away and bit her knuckle, something I noticed she did when she felt nervous. She continued. "Mom doesn't like us being together. Dad knows I like you. He may have kept Mom away this weekend so I could spend it with you. I wish Dad would talk to me more. I wish Mom would go away." She shook her head. "There's more I need to tell you, but not yet, so maybe later."

When she headed for the restroom, I wandered back into Mr. Hernandez's office. No Mr. Hernandez. Instead, I found a set of clubs in a golf bag leaning against his desk. The clubs were used, but in good condition, except for one, my once-dreamed-about new putter.

"Surprise!" They appeared behind me.

"What do you think of them?" Jen asked.

I didn't know what to think, until a little message found its way to my brain and said the golf clubs were now mine. "Wow!" Good or bad, it would have to do; nothing else came out.

I tried out the clubs, one by one, ending with the putter.

"They're great. How did you know?" I made some practice swings. "How can I take them? They're too expensive."

121

John C. Pelkey

"Expensive, no," Mr. Hernandez said. "Our rented clubs are all the same brand. We replace them when sets get old and have broken clubs. We bought a new series for rentals and sold the old ones cheap. Since you have kept us in range balls for two years, I can give you a set. These are the best ones. I put on new grips and bought covers for the woods. Mr. Marek, the owner, threw in the bag for free."

"What about the putter?"

"Jenni bought the putter. I told her which one."

Facing me, Jen became reserved and quiet, much different from the chatty girl of a moment ago.

"I don't know what to say. Thanks."

"You are welcome, sir." Jen spoke a bit formal, but she smiled for me.

"We kept good secret from you. For years. Now it is over." Mr. Hernandez tried to appear glum, but couldn't. "Hey, it is okay. Maybe now us three play sometime?"

He had obviously enjoyed listening to me talk about Jen for the last two years, knowing who she was. It meant he listened to her talk about me, too, and told her what I said.

He read my mind. "What you say about Jenni, what Jenni says about you, I keep here." He pointed at his heart. "Only tell my Juanita. Remember; keep no secrets from your woman. Or lies. Except when she is old, you say she's still young. Not a real lie, she is still young inside."

He pulled a set of keys from his pocket. "Time to lock up. I have to go home now. My granddaughter's boy is five today. Big party tonight. I drive you to the gate." When I objected, he said, "No, come on," and beckoned with his hands.

I picked up my new clubs and followed Mr. Hernandez. Jen ran over to a display and came back. She found a putter cover to match my wood covers. "Can I buy this? I'll pay you next time."

"Tell you what. I'll trade it for your old golf ball."

Jen studied the ball and Mr. Hernandez. I could see she didn't like the idea at all.

"Why would you want my ball?" she asked, holding it against her heart with both hands.

"I want to return it to my collection." He turned to me. "It will remind me of you two. The Clovers are a rare brand. I retrieved the others from your first take, Jon, except number four."

I had only found four of the five balls.

"Okay, I guess you can have it. It is your ball." She gave it up with a shrug.

"Here, you can have Mr. Shoeman's." I tossed it to her.

"Yay?" I could tell she wasn't impressed. "It's a nice one, though."

I put my clubs behind the single cart still left out. The cart only had two seats.

Mr. Hernandez hatched a plan. "Jon, you drive the cart; Jenni can sit on my lap."

"Good idea." said Jen, suddenly agreeable. I didn't feel agreeable.

"Nah, you are too good looking. You sit on me, too hard on my ticker. You sit on Jon's lap."

"Well, alright." Jen played it up. Mr. Hernandez helped.

Three can play this.

"If you would rather, Jenni, you can drive and I'll sit on Mr. Hernandez's lap."

"Okay," they chorused. Jen jumped in the driver's side. Mr. Hernandez sat on the other side and slapped his lap. They played better than I did.

"I'll walk," I said, pouting.

"You'll beat us," Jen said. "I've never driven a cart."

Seizing the opportunity, Mr. Hernandez showed her how the cart worked, and directed her around the parking lot while I watched. When she managed to drive to the end and back without hitting anything, I gave her a standing ovation. She jumped out and came up to me, putting her hands up for fives. I clasped them and we bumped heads.

"Thanks," Jen said. "You're a good sport."

I won't be if you sit on Mr. Hernandez's lap instead of mine.

Mr. Hernandez moved over to the driver's seat. I sat down and Jen slipped onto my lap, facing in and putting an arm around me. Much better than hugging, now she touched me all over. I put one arm around her waist to hold her and laid one arm across her legs, taking her hand. She didn't object. Holding her was easy; she felt lighter than I thought she would be.

Instead of heading directly toward the gate, Mr. Hernandez drove along the first fairway. "What is bumping heads?" he asked. "You kids bump heads instead of kissing?"

Jen caught my eyes for a second, but faced away, slightly blushing, and squeezed my hand while I considered his question.

I know the answer, Jen. We high-five and bump heads to say hello and goodbye, and to share a second together. I've never kissed you. Or even come close. Not yet anyway. Other kids our age are kissing and doing worse stuff. Better stuff? Other stuff, which doesn't always match what either one wants. I want us to match feelings. I know we came close to kissing and maybe even other stuff the night in your room. When it happens, it happens, probably years from now.

When I didn't respond, Jen swished her eyes, indicating she wanted me to answer.

"Bumping heads instead of kissing," I said, watching Jen. "I guess so. We invented it by accident."

"It's much safer when parents are watching," Jen added, "and it means the same thing."

John C. Pelkey

It does?

"It means we're happy to say hello, and sad to say goodbye, 'Congratulations' on the track, and 'I like you' at other times." She bumped my cheek with her nose, another brand new feeling.

"I like kissing," Mr. Hernandez said, "and so will you. So young now, both of you, you have plenty of time for many things to happen in your life."

We listened to his first sermon preached to us together, this one about taking our time. As if we had some choice in the matter.

When we came to the gate, Mr. Hernandez tapped in the combination and it opened. Instead of letting us out, he continued. "Okay to drive golf carts all the way to your street. You can sit together some more and pretend you do not like it."

The cart rode much smoother on the street, but we still held on to each other. All my nerve endings reacted happily where we touched, even with our sweats on. The feeling of Jen nestled against me, like a journey into wow. Mr. Hernandez helped by spinning the cart in semi-circles, forcing us to hang on tightly. I thanked Mr. Hernandez in my heart and determined I would continue to search for his number four Clover golf ball.

He let us off on my corner with our thanks. "We golf, soon," he said. "Maybe with your Dad, Jenni?"

Jen gave Mr. Hernandez a peck on the cheek goodbye and we watched him spin back and forth as he drove away. I now understood the sign, *Be aware of golf carts*, posted across the street for traffic driving toward Dr. Canfield and the gate. More like *beware*.

We walked up Notch Hill Road in silence, me carrying my bag, Jen bouncing her new ball. I wondered when she would ever sit on my lap again. I couldn't recall anyone sitting on someone's lap without a necessary reason. I knew I lacked the courage to ask her. I added courage-improvement courses to the psych degree on my future list of things to learn.

"We didn't run much today," I ventured. Today's running covered maybe two hundred feet.

"We have another weekend before the final meet. We'll work twice as hard." She bounced her ball off my bag. It didn't rebound right, and she had to chase it. "I'm hungry," she announced, catching up.

We hadn't discussed food or eaten together. This would be another new thing.

"Do you think they'll like me?" she asked.

"My family will like you lots, and wonder what you see in me. Does your family like me?"

"My family doesn't like me, so you don't have a chance. My grandparents would like you. They're nice."

"You miss them?" I asked. She nodded. "Maybe you can visit them

To Face The World

this summer."

She kept walking, but stopped talking. I could feel another wall growing between us. Anything about her family resurfaced it.

I wanted to kick myself the rest of the way home. With Jen, the highs were like mountaintops -- with sheer cliffs on all sides.

Chapter Fifteen

We finally reached my house after playing a game of bounce the ball to each other, something Jen was willing to do. We didn't talk much, including me not pointing out where her wayward golf shots had landed. Not talking had a good side. I needed time to digest the many surprises she had shared. My watch said 6:30. The last three hours took forever, and at the same time, went by in a second.

Beth sat on the front steps, hands on her chin. She didn't move when we came up. "Hi. How are things going?" I asked.

"Mike called me. He said he's seeing Nancy Palmer now because he wants to go places on Sunday evenings and I can't."

Who is Mike? What happened to Derrick, Scotty, and the rest?

"I think I'll be a nun."

"You can't be a nun, Beth, you're not even Catholic."

I tried without success to picture Beth in a nun's suit.

Beth's issue struck home.

Does Dad's dating rule for Beth apply to me? No. They don't allow me to go out at all. Or do they?

I changed the subject with, "Has Cindy moved in?"

"They've finished moving and called me to supper a minute ago, so you're right on time." Beth didn't move.

I set the clubs on the porch by the door. Jen put her ball in one of the pouches. As we passed Beth, she asked, "Where did you get them?"

"Mr. Hernandez gave me the clubs. Jen gave me the putter."

"Oh, how nice." Beth still hadn't moved.

In the kitchen, Mom and Cindy worked on creating a tray of leftovers to munch on. Dad and Dave, sitting across from each other, had a knife and fork in hand and rapped them on the table, singing "Rub a dub, dub; let's have some grub." They stopped when they saw Jen.

"It's not like it looks," Cindy said. "You would have to be here from the beginning to understand." She set out a selection of sandwich meats and bread, raising the bar for our fend-for-yourself night.

She flashed a smile at Jen and said, "Hi." They traded lengthy appraisals, hopefully with positive conclusions. Jen had barely given Beth a second glance.

I remembered my manners and introduced everyone. I did okay until I got to Dave's fiancée, Cindy. I didn't remember Cindy's last name.

"Carson." Dave reminded me. I didn't know if I had heard it or not. He turned to Jen. "Hi, Jennifer. Uh, we pretended to be barbaric Huns, returning from victory against the Romans. We demanded homage and

To Face The World

supper after we finished carrying our pillage, well, Cindy's hope chest, upstairs."

Cindy has a hope chest? What hopes need to go into a chest?

"You do know what a hope chest is, Jon?" Cindy also read minds, my mind anyway.

"Yeah, sure. Uh, no." Not much reading material in my mind.

"Dishes, towels, linens, things to begin a home with. A mother and daughter work together to fill it. It is an old tradition and uncommon now." Jen helped me out.

"My mom wanted to do something for me to make up for..." Cindy stopped. "Do you have one?" she asked Jen, trying to smile away whatever it was she couldn't mention.

"No, you have to have hope first," Jen snapped.

Her terse response caught me by surprise, everyone else, too. "Beth has no hope either." I said, breaking the silence. It didn't stop them all from staring at me.

"I'm fine, thank you." Beth shuffled in. "You're right about hope, Jennifer. When it comes to guys, it's better to be a nun." Beth sounded like a stuck record.

Cindy went behind Dave's chair and gave him a hug. "I have hope, thanks to all of you." Dave gently pulled her head down and kissed her, right in front of us. Still, it wasn't much of a kiss, more like a peck. I wondered how Jen kissed, and if I would ever find out.

With Dave's kiss for openers, we settled in to eat. "Jon, it's your turn for grace," Dad said.

Nothing like putting me on the spot.

I thanked God for the food, and for having Cindy and Jen with us. I also asked him to give us all hope. My family chorused, "Amen."

Finished, I watched Jen study the pattern on her plate, obviously embarrassed.

Why did you lapse when you usually are quiet and guarded? How am I going to explain you to my family? What do I say the next time we are alone? Lots of questions. No results.

The initial table conversation faltered a bit, with single sentence questions and single word answers. Cindy took up the task to repair the situation and asked me some real questions. I had to explain the golf clubs on the porch and Jen's attempt at the school record.

"You mean the girls' record," Cindy inserted.

"No, Jenni already has the girls' record. I mean the school record. My record."

Dave couldn't help himself and jumped in. "You're going to let her take your record?"

"When I said Jenni was faster than anyone I knew, I included me."

"I don't think I am faster than you." Jen finally said something.

"Well, you're not slower. You should race Dave. It would help him

John C. Pelkey

get the picture." Cindy could beat Dave. Jen would blow him away.

"Not after eating supper." Mom's admonition refocused us from my dumb remark.

Cindy and Dave talked about their wedding. Dad kibitzed. Beth mourned. Mom made sure everyone had more food than they could eat. Jen memorized her plate. I watched.

Cindy fished around for a subject to involve Jen, and finally found something to include her, her favorite class at school.

"English, my favorite class. I like to read and I belong to a book club."

"You should see her library," I chimed in.

"I would like to," Cindy added. "Especially the poetry."

"Hiawatha?" Jen asked.

Cindy opened with, "By the shores of Gitche Gumee..."

Jen jumped in. "...By the shining Big-Sea-Water..."

Together, they continued. "...Stood the wigwam of Nokomis, Daughter of the Moon, Nokomis..."

They followed the required rhythm and sounded poetic until Cindy forgot a line.

Beth, who loved all things Shakespeare, took on Macbeth, speaking the part of the woman. "Lo you! Here she comes. This is her very guise; and, upon my life, fast asleep. Observe her; stand close..." She motioned to Cindy, almost a challenge.

Cindy took the part of the doctor, and she and Beth traded lines.

When Beth got to, "...It is an accustomed action with her, to seem thus washing her hands. I have known her to continue in this a quarter of an hour..." they motioned to Jen to take Lady Macbeth.

Jen hesitated, scrunched her nose at me, and added, "Yet here's a spot..."

Cindy yelled, "Hark! She speaks..."

Jen cracked a tiny smile at the literary pun.

Cindy continued with a sly smile. "...I will set down what comes from her, to satisfy my remembrance the more strongly..."

They again cued Jen, who yelled, "Out, damned spot!" I could read the disbelief on her face as she covered her mouth and turned deep red.

I remembered her talk earlier on swearing and tried to reassure her. However, she cracked up the rest of my family. Their laughter echoed through the house; even Beth forgot her misery. Soon Jen broke out a smile, and I breathed a sigh of relief.

I realized how much tension she had much of the time, so afraid to make a mistake. Making a mistake didn't faze my family, as evidenced by Dad and Dave's supper song. Making a mistake appeared to be a problem in Jen's home, at least for her.

With the poetic spell broken, we finished supper. I volunteered Jen and me to wash the dishes, my ploy to keep her longer.

128

To Face The World

Mom objected. "Jon, we don't put guests to work."

Jen countered with, "I would like to contribute," the first words after her blunder.

Mom smiled defeat, and she and the rest of the family moved into the living room.

"I'm sorry about my dumb remark about not having hope, and about my swearing." Jen scrubbed the dishes, trying to make up for things she thought she had done wrong. I had planned to put them in the dishwasher, which I did when she handed them to me.

"Jen, in my house you can say dumb things. It's okay; I do it all the time. So does everybody else."

It was always okay, but more so lately. Everyone in my family, even Dave now, made a special effort to be nice to everyone else. An outside crisis, Cindy's family troubles, had unified us and reminded me of how good things were in my family. I resolved to continue smiling at my parents from the choir loft.

"Aren't you guys finished yet?" Cindy gave us only a few minutes to ourselves. "We're going to play Pictionary and we want you to play, too. Even Beth is going to play."

Cindy and Dave helped us finish cleaning up. Dave had never helped me before. This truly was an unusual day.

For Pictionary, we knew Dad, Dave, and I could not draw. Mom and Beth could. Cindy and Jen were unknowns. Dad decided to be the judge. Dave and Cindy formed one team. Jen and I formed another. Mom joined them and Beth joined us. Old against young. An artist, a non-artist, and an unknown on each team.

Without realizing it, we had selected even teams. Mom and Beth made easy to understand drawings; Dave and me fouled up. Cindy took right off but Jen paused. She drew a clown juggling, but missing one. "Dropped," I said. We were ahead. Jen could draw, and so could Cindy.

The game came down to us sharing the last square before someone winning, with Dave and me stuck with drawing. The word was "Chocolate Mousse." I first tried to draw a pie, no luck, and then a moose. It looked like a duck with antlers. Dave tried to draw a candy bar. When Cindy said, "Chocolate bar," Jen said, "Chocolate Mousse," and we won.

As Beth, Jen, and I locked arms and danced around the table, I noticed the growing darkness outside. My watch said nine-something.

"We better go," I said. Jen nodded. My heart went into my stomach. What if her parents were already home? Her stricken face echoed my thoughts.

Mom noticed our concern. "I'll drive you," she volunteered.

"No, Cindy and I can."

Dave wants to drive me somewhere? What is the world coming to?

We accepted.

John C. Pelkey

Dave's car had seen better days and grumbled at the thought of going anywhere. It had a huge back seat though, the site of Dave's *Missions Accomplished*. I now believed a better title would be *Fantasyland*. Jen and I took up one corner, sharing the seat belt, and she slipped her hand into mine, resting her arm on my leg. This was as good as the golf cart ride.

Dave, to tease, moved his mirror where he could see us. Cindy moved it to where he couldn't see anything. We were almost to the road when Jen cried, "Stop! My golf ball."

"Your what?" Dave asked.

"I'll get it." I ran to my bag, still on the porch. When I returned, I heard the tail end of Jen's story of hitting Mr. Hernandez's Clovers.

"Wow, just like *Romeo and Juliet*." With one reference, Dave exhausted the extent of his knowledge of romantic literature.

"We'll end up like Romeo and Juliet if we don't get Jen home."

I hoped Dave would get us lost, though. Maybe forever. He didn't, not with her help, and too soon, we were there. Seeing the dark house, I breathed sighs of relief.

"Don't they know where you are?" Dave acted like he couldn't believe Jen would be sneaking around.

"They've been gone since yesterday, so I didn't ask. I don't think they would approve." Jen was serious, but Dave wasn't.

"They were gone all last night? You blew it kid-- *Oof*!" Cindy had whapped him.

Thank you, Cindy.

"We're going to drive to the store," Dave announced. "Be back in about five minutes."

"What are we going to get at the store?" Cindy asked, glancing out at us.

"Nothing, we're going to drive to the store and be back in about five minutes." Dave drove away with a gleam and a snicker.

We felt our way through the gap and around to the back of the house, still holding hands. I found the key and gave it to Jen. She unlocked the back door and went in, saying, "I'll be back in a sec."

She turned lights on around the house and in front, but left them off in back. When she returned, she handed me the key. "Put it back." I did. It would have helped if she had turned the outside light on, but I could feel Jen's tension. She matched my sigh of relief after I returned to the steps.

"We did it," she chirped. "Again." We clasped hands and bumped heads, leaning against each other.

"Don't tell Mr. Hernandez," Jen whispered. "We're kissing, a long one,"

No, we're not, but we're close.

I let go and wondered what to do next. A car's lights flashed from

130

the driveway, reflecting in the trees. The car was much too quiet to be Dave's.

"It's your folks," I deduced. "You better go."

I'd better go, but I don't know where. I can't go through her house.

Except for the gap in the hedge, I had not seen any other way in or out, only a back door to the garage.

"Wait behind the house until the garage door closes. Go through the hedge and follow it to the neighbor's driveway. Don't run. They'll never know."

I wondered if Jen had someone sneak out before me. Not the time to ask.

"Goodnight, Jen. This is my new favorite day. Thanks for the putter, and for everything else."

"Bye, Jon. Thanks for being okay with me... being... me."

She stepped up on the deck, stopped, grabbed my face, and she kissed me hard, right on my mouth. Before I could respond, she disappeared, and the door closed, leaving me reeling in her back yard.

I hid on the deck below the kitchen window and listened to her greeting her parents. No, we hadn't gone running; she had been reading a book. How was the play? They moved out of hearing.

You lied for us. You shouldn't have to, but what choice is there? Either you lie, or I can't see you anymore. I hurt for you inside. You are so nice, so caring, and never want to hurt anyone. You live with people who aren't nice, aren't caring, and don't mind hurting you. It isn't fair. What can I do about it? Nothing.

I crept around the side of the house, past her parents' bedroom and through the hedge. I followed it to the neighbor's driveway and then on to the street. Dave's car came noisily around the corner. When he saw the lights on, he didn't stop. I met him at the end of the block. He motioned me to sit up front.

"Everything okay?" he asked. I described the escape, but left out the kiss.

"You forgot to kiss her, but I'm proud of you anyway, LB." Dave was accepting me as a fellow conqueror of women, or at least an eluder of their fathers. Only in this case it was eluder of Jen's mother. I didn't think her father objected to me.

Cindy came out point-blank. "Why is Jenni so uptight? Why do you have to sneak around? What's going on? You can practice on me because you won't get past your folks."

"Jenni's mother torments her. Jenni feels she has to be perfect."

I can do point-blank, too.

"I'm sorry." Cindy sounded defeated.

"I'm sorry, too," Dave added. "She's a neat kid. Good on the eyes. You do all right by her. You have to fight to keep her, like I fight for Cindy. Don't you go stepping out on her either."

John C. Pelkey

Dave gives me advice he never takes. Or does he?

Dad, Mom, and even Beth waited, all ready for the interrogation. They marched me into the living room. Mom and Dad waved to send away the rest, but I said, "No. Cindy and Dave shared; Beth shared; I can share."

And share I did. I started with what Jen said about moving and not owning anything. I moved on to how her parents left her by herself, what her mom said about her green dress, and why she wore sweatshirts. I ended with how bare her room was.

"You were in her room?" Mom groused. "You shouldn't be in there when her parents aren't home. You shouldn't be in her house."

"Mom, I know; I'm sorry. Other than showing me around, she didn't do anything. I didn't do anything, either. I wouldn't have known she needs something for her room if I hadn't been in there."

I pour out my heart, and you get all excited over mere details.

I glazed out for a minute.

To be honest, I do think of me in her room. I think of how I felt the night when she said I'd better go or we would do something we would regret. Maybe she's right. Although I don't know why, I do know she excites me when I look at her and more so when I touch her. When she kissed me, yeah. I guess I'm old enough to know what it means.

I realized they were all staring.

With, "I want thirty seconds," Dad shooed everyone away, even Mom, and I faced him alone.

"Jon," he said, "you just might be a bit too young to attempt to build a relationship with a girl, much less a girl with a difficult family situation."

You're telling me?

"I'm not going to tell you not to see her. It's obvious you and Jennifer like each other. I don't want you in her house when her parents aren't home. I am glad you felt it was important enough to tell us, knowing it was wrong. You are growing up, Jon, like Dave and Beth did. Soon you will find out, when you are alone with a girl you like, you will know a lot more than you now think you do."

Dad, you are a minute behind me, and way beyond anything I thought we would ever discuss alone. On the good side, we are talking, and talking makes up for it, I think.

"Thanks for sharing, Jon."

"Thanks, Dad."

We talked and I'm still alive. This is good.

Dad called the rest back, including Beth. "Jon willingly shared; what he said stays in this room. Understood?" We all watched Beth.

"Understood." Beth knew she was a newspaper to her friends.

I escaped to my new room; this time I remembered to go past the old room door. I spent a long time sitting at my desk, gazing at Jen's

132

To Face The World

picture. Sunday, May twelfth, Mother's Day. It began with finding Cindy in the living room, and ended with Jen kissing me. I felt like I had lived half of my life in a single day.

This must be what it's like to be a June bug, ricocheting through life, scratched out one minute at a time.

I sketched Jen's lips on my calendar, too poorly drawn for anyone else to decipher.

She, Jennifer Carling, has kissed me, Jon Perone. So fast, but I will never forget it. My first, first kiss. Hopefully, Jen's, too.

Less than two months to the first day lily. Will each day be as exhausting as this one? If Jen can be in each one, it will make it okay.

Will she?

John C. Pelkey

Chapter Sixteen

Monday morning. I had always been the first one up in my family. However, heading to the bathroom, dressed only in my towel, I met Cindy, coming out of Beth's room, also in a towel, a short one.

"Hi, Jon. I thought if I got up early enough, I would stay out of everyone's way. I should have remembered yesterday morning. You go ahead." She turned around. "Oh, nice legs," she said with a smile, before disappearing.

Yeah, you have nice legs, too, and nice thighs, and I should try not to notice them.

Since I had noticed them, I thought of Jen and felt guilty.

I had seen Cindy's legs before; she bounced around in a skimpy little cheerleader outfit all the time. However, the comparison didn't work for a towel, knowing she wore nothing underneath. I had seen Beth in a towel, big deal. At six and four, we used to bathe together. Cindy made me nervous.

Yesterday a bathrobe, today a towel, what will tomorrow bring?

I wanted to see Jen to chase the vision of Cindy out of my mind. When I stepped off the bus, I found her waiting. It worked. Jen in an oversized sweatshirt and jeans nailed the top of my happy list.

"Hi, Jen. I'm so glad to see you."

She wrinkled her nose and cocked her head, closing one eye. "Okay, you're so glad to see me. Why?"

You'll never know.

"I miss you, and seeing you reminds me of how great you look."

I'm not lying; you look great. Your blond hair curls, just right. Your eyes sparkle, just right. Your sweatshirt comes halfway to your knees and completely disguises the rest of you, just right. I'm glad you dress modestly. If you wore the micro-skirt and see-through top like Lisa Martin, the girl who's now wiggling by, I would be unable to concentrate.

Although, after a long and detailed second opinion of the subject matter, I wasn't certain losing the ability to concentrate would be entirely detrimental. More knowledge didn't necessarily equate to more wisdom.

Jen completely misread my purely objective comparison. We had been walking close together. Now I noticed a growing space between us.

Time to confess and do it without getting the other foot in my mouth.

"Yeah, I saw Lisa. I'm glad you don't dress like she does."

"You are? Why?" Jen glared her doubts, but she did stop to listen.

"Jen, you're so beautiful, regardless of what you wear. If you dressed like Lisa, I could never get past your appearance. I would never

134

To Face The World

get to know you inside. Then we wouldn't be good friends, which is far more important to me than spending a few seconds ogling somebody's bod, and never knowing who they are. I'll never know who Lisa Martin is."

Thanks, Dr. Canfield.

"Besides, if you wore skimpy stuff, every guy in the school would want to follow you around. We would never get a minute alone together. Anyway, they don't need any more opportunities to leer at you. Okay?" I sounded like what the cows left in the pasture.

To my surprise, she bought it, especially the last part. "You would be jealous of other guys?" Her smile returned.

Jealous of other guys, maybe. Terrified of other guys, definitely. Up close, I know how incredibly cute you are. Going from Alyssa to you is a huge climb, accompanied with the fear of what goes up can also come down. I need to answer your question.

"Of course, I would. It's nothing you will ever have to worry about with me."

I don't have a history of girls left drooling in my wake.

"Jon, I think you look fine. Really. You have great legs. Other girls have noticed."

Two legs compliments in one day. I'm on a roll. However, I can't think of any girl you know who will say something about me, especially who will say something about me to me. So I have no idea of who the "other girls" are.

"If other girls have noticed me, they've managed to keep their excitement to themselves."

Jen laughed at my poor attempt at humor. I had survived the crisis and used it in my favor.

*****

Jen and I connected when we could during the day, which wasn't often due to having only PE and choir together and to not sharing lunch. Still, the guys at the lunch table noticed.

"You and Jenni are getting to be tight." Tom waved both hands with fingers crossed.

"Not like you and Trish yet."

"Trish is getting old," he said, pretending to whisper with a hand covering his mouth. "I'm going after Lisa Martin." This garnered a laugh from everyone and a slug from Trish.

A recent transfer, most guys considered Lisa the most attractive and desirable girl in the school, best built anyway. She wore the clothes to prove it. Even high school guys were after her.

Lisa sat across the lunchroom, sharing a table with the future hookers of America group, as Trish called them, all about attitudes and clothes, with little left to the imagination. Lisa hadn't gotten into trouble

135

John C. Pelkey

for her clothes, or lack of clothes, mostly because the others wore even less.

I thought she looked a bit like Jen, but when I mentioned it once, the response from the guys was mostly static. One made huge curves for Lisa and two parallel lines for Jen. Since I didn't like guys commenting on her figure, or comparing her to Lisa, I didn't mention it again. I was goofy anyway.

Who would compare slender Jen with curvy Lisa?

It was doubtful I would ever know anything about Lisa, who had no idea I even existed.

So who waited for me in the hall between Math and PE? Lisa. She brought a chorus of "oohs" from the guys on their way to the locker room.

"Hi Jon. Can I talk to y'all a minute?" Lisa had a southern accent, probably faked, but I couldn't tell for sure. I wondered how she even knew my name. Lisa wiggled down the hall next to me, the same wiggle I almost got into trouble for watching.

"I want to write an article on Jennifer Carling and y'all for the school paper. You know, running and stuff."

You want to write an article about me. You, the same reporter who headlined Jim Stone, whom you referred to as Mr. Golden Boy, when he lost his comb in the girl's locker room on the same day my new school record got one line on the back page.

"Y'all both have the school records for the same race, I don't remember which, and y'all run together on weekends; everybody knows it."

Some reporter, no facts messing up your life. Who is everybody, how does everybody know we run together, and how do you know they know?

"Can you wait until after next Friday?"

Then you will have something to write.

"Way too late. After next Friday, the season is over and nobody will care."

I'm glad you think so.

"Jenni has already agreed. We're meeting tomorrow after track practice."

She has? I'll believe it when I hear it.

"See y'all then, okay?"

Lisa walked away, leaving me a little on the dazed side. I had spoken to her for the first time, volumes in my mind, but in reality, one whole sentence.

"You and Lisa. Does she want your body?" Jim had to throw it out in front of everyone.

I tried not to show my irritation. "Lisa wants to interview me after practice tomorrow for an article about Jenni Carling and me, and our school records for some race, but she doesn't know which one."

To Face The World

"I would be happy to take six months to explain which one to her on a deserted island," offered Ed the Stick.

"Feel free. Why don't you two leave today?"

"What? You want me to miss the interview?" he asked, gasping in pretended shock.

I want me to miss the interview.

After last period choir, Jen and I walked together to the locker room for track practice. "Did Lisa talk to you?" she asked.

Now I believe it.

I made a face, which she noticed.

"She asked you then. Did you agree?"

"I didn't have to agree, Lisa agreed for me."

"You don't want to do the interview?"

Jen appeared confused, and a little hurt. I needed to correct the situation. "I don't want to do an interview with Lisa. She doesn't even know which race we run, and she doesn't care either."

"I thought all the guys wanted Lisa." Jen's smile told me she thought differently.

"They may say they want her, for show. Most guys would rather be with someone they can count on and be themselves. Like you."

I'm hot with the compliments today.

Dan interrupted us. "Jon, did you hear? Rafer Washington from North Valley won the 1600-meter run six seconds faster than you won last week. We run against them next week."

We were South Valley, located at the south end of Aurora Valley. North Valley, sitting at the north end, was one of the other middle schools in town and our archrival. Although I hadn't killed myself winning the race last week, six seconds came close to my record. I didn't want to lose a race the day Jen broke my record. Losing the record would be bad enough.

"I haven't raced anyone close yet."

Except Jen.

"I guess it's time I found out what I can do." I planned to keep her secret to the end.

*****

The next morning, I rose five minutes earlier. It worked; I saw no one. Cindy was the next one up. When she appeared in the kitchen, I asked, "Can I make you something for breakfast?" I was either succumbing to a fit of stupidity, or attempting to reward her for showing up in more than a towel. I didn't know which.

"Why thank you," she said. "Eggs are fine. Scrambled. Okay?"

I managed to land them in the pan, but I lost momentum.

Cindy rescued me and together we made enough eggs, bacon, and

137

John C. Pelkey

toast for everyone. To my surprise, we worked well together, flipping the eggs and dodging the bacon spit. Cindy seemed a lot less dangerous with all her clothes on. She came across brighter than her cheerleader image, maybe brighter than Dave. For the first time, I talked to her like a friend. I even told Cindy about Lisa interviewing us, something I would never mention to anyone in my family.

*****

Lisa came to practice and watched us, sitting in the stands in her usual clothing, advertising the goods. A woman photographer took pictures of us running, jumping, and throwing. The guys ran, jumped, and threw extra hard for some reason. The coach noticed. As the practice ended, he told us we had better work as hard tomorrow.

Someone whispered, "If we don't work hard tomorrow, do you think the coach would punish us by having Lisa sit there every practice?"

A quick reply came. "He better not. You would be too tired to run in the meets."

Lisa and the photographer joined us. The coach dismissed the guys with some difficulty. They all planned to watch, or at least make a big deal out of it. The coach stayed.

I wondered about the woman. She took some pictures of us separately, together, with Lisa, and with the coach. After the photo session, she and the coach walked away, leaving Lisa with Jen and me.

Lisa sat on the bottom row of the stands. She crossed her legs and didn't even attempt to pull down her skirt. I sat on the same level facing her and managed to maneuver Jen into sitting between us. I memorized the number of steps in the stands behind us, half as many as at the high school.

Lisa's first question to Jen caught me by surprise. "Why do y'all wear extra clothing under your uniform? Nobody else does. I wouldn't."

"It's comfortable. No other reason." Jen seemed ready for her.

"Do y'all like running with a girl, or does she slow y'all down?"

How am I supposed to answer you?

"I seem to be doing all right," I said. "I haven't been beaten yet."

Maybe I'm ready for you, too.

Lisa mumbled something into a tiny tape player. I hadn't noticed it before. For a second, I thought she sounded like a real reporter and knew what to ask. Only for a second.

"Are y'all concerned about Ralph somebody beating you?"

Ralph Somebody? A girl with a broken southern accent and dementia is interviewing us.

"Rafer Washington. If he's faster than I am, he'll beat me. Otherwise, he won't. I'm looking forward to the challenge."

I realized this mental mycoplasma would not give us any questions we would struggle to answer. What she printed, though, could be another matter.

Lisa turned back to Jen. "I'm told you're really fast. Why do you run the longer races when you could win the shorter ones and run less?"

Now she spoke with a foreign accent.

Make up your mind. Well, get a mind, first.

Then it hit, as if revelation had struck me.

Lisa, you sound exactly like Jen when she first arrived two years ago, as if you are copying her.

I missed half of Jen's answer.

"...I run the long races because I like to run. I wish we had a 3200-meter race like the high school."

Before Lisa could ask her next question, I blurted out, "What state did you move here from?"

She appeared surprised by my request, and fumbled for a minute. She said, "Connecticut, and before that, Florida." She flashed a smile, almost a blush. "You noticed my accents. Duh. I like my Florida one better, but the Connecticut one wins out when I don't pay attention."

For the first time, I had an inkling Lisa wasn't as dumb as she projected. When she spoke with the Connecticut accent, her questions became sharper, even if non-threatening.

The interview continued smoothly until Mr. Carling's arrival interrupted us. I sensed the tension rising in Jen. If her father made her tense, what did her mother do to her?

He had on his best, baby-kissing smile on right up until he saw Lisa. A look of terror flashed across his face, from which he quickly covered.

What is that all about? Does Lisa trigger something?

As hard as he tried, Mr. Carling could not get his smile back to baby-kissing.

After introductions, conducted by Jen, Lisa turned her legs and her reporting brilliance toward Mr. Carling, who nervously pulled on his collar.

"How do you like having a daughter who runs?" she asked. He appeared more prepared to answer, "How do you like my legs?"

"I'm proud of her, and I'll be even prouder when she breaks Jon's record."

No! Don't say that!

"Which record?" Lisa asked.

Fortunately, Lisa faced away. Jen drew a line across her throat.

"It was a joke, and not a good one, I guess," he said, rolling his eyes.

Lisa accepted Mr. Carling's answer. "I guess I'm done," she added.

After one last long gawk at Lisa's legs and mumbling something indecipherable, Mr. Carling spun around and left in a hurry, Jen trotting behind. She waved and said, "Bye," over her shoulder.

Mr. Carling said, "Thanks," over his shoulder.

John C. Pelkey

Thanks for what?

They left me with Lisa and her legs. I got up to fetch my sweats.

"Wait, Jon." Lisa stood. Her skirt seemed shorter when she stood than when she sat. "You and Jenni are boyfriend and girlfriend?" she asked, the tape still running.

"Are you going to print that?"

"No," she replied, snapping off the tape, "I promise I won't. I could tell, though. You knew where she was and she knew where you were all the time, without having to look."

Lisa, your mind could be suspect, but your vision isn't.

"What are you trying to say?" I had forgotten my status level. Lisa had, too.

"Of all the guys I know, none of them are like you; none of them are aware of another person, someone else... me, like you are aware of Jenni. Do you know what I mean?"

I know what the guys think. You aren't like Jen either.

"Maybe it's your clothes. Wear something like a baggy sweatshirt and old loose jeans every day for a week. Maybe you will find someone who is."

Lisa gave me a scrunched-nose questioning look, smiled, said, "My clothes, huh? Jon, thanks." She wiggled off into the sunset. Her questioning look appeared to be exactly the same as Jen's.

I survived my first interview. However, my thoughts haunted me.

Lisa, who are you? Why are you suddenly in my life?

Chapter Seventeen

I hurried through a shower and dressed as I dashed to the bus, but talking to Lisa took too long and I missed it. Instead, I ran into her again, in front of the school.

"You missed your bus," she observed, as we watched it disappear around a corner. "You wouldn't have if I hadn't asked you to wait. I'm sorry. I thought about what you said. Do my clothes give guys the wrong impression?"

She spun around to give me a close appraisal from all sides. I wasn't certain about the "wrong" part, but they certainly gave guys an impression. "Well, do they?" she repeated.

How can I describe my impression of a girl wearing a short and tight black skirt, an even tighter thin, white see-through blouse with the top two buttons unbuttoned and the rest struggling, and underneath, a long, black, low-cut, lacy thing with thin straps?

"I think you look like you're, uh, well, kind of available."

"I am available." She sounded as available as she looked.

Help!

Help arrived, disguised as Lisa's mom, in a large, beat-up station wagon with a bench front seat, reminding me of Dave's car. I opened the door for her, said, "Bye," and casually walked up to the school front door. I found they had locked it, like twenty seconds after I went through.

Lisa, sitting with the door opened, asked, "Would you like a ride?" She had me trapped like a rat.

"Uh, yeah, I guess so." Either I rode with Lisa or I walked for two hours.

Lisa scooted over, about three inches, and invited me in next to her. Her legs, covered with about an inch of skirt, stared at me harder than I did at them. I hated riding in a back seat by myself, but I would have gladly made an exception this time. However, Lisa surprised me.

"Mom, this is Jon. He's a track star. I interviewed him today with his friend, Jenni. You should see them together; they make such a cute couple."

How do I respond?

Since I badmouthed her in my mind, I apologized, also in my mind.

Lisa's mom looked like what Lisa would look like in twenty years if she stopped eating, sleeping, and taking care of herself. She could be quite attractive, like Lisa, if she put out even a little effort. I wasn't too concerned, as I didn't anticipate a future of seeing her beyond the few

John C. Pelkey

minutes she would need to get me somewhere closer to my house.

I didn't want her to drive me home and have someone see me with Lisa. I thought of Dr. Canfield, who had asked me to check out his place occasionally. I hadn't been by during the week, although I carried his key every day.

"What's Jenni's last name," Lisa's mom asked. She sounded a bit tense.

Lisa glanced slyly at me and giggled. "Perone," she said, winking. Her mom didn't notice.

"Where do you live?" she asked, now sounding more tired than anything else.

"Notch Hill Road, but you can drop me off by the golf course."

Lisa asked me about school things and track, nothing I needed any thoughts to answer, and nothing embarrassing me. She was genuinely nice, not self-absorbed as I had imagined her to be. I realized I liked talking to her. Although she was sitting against me, she didn't attempt to make me more uncomfortable than I already was. I certainly didn't attempt to do anything toward her.

Lisa's mom dropped me off at the street corner about five houses from Dr. Canfield's. I thanked them and said goodbye, trying not to give Lisa's legs the same long gawk Mr. Carling had, but not with any more success.

"Can I talk to you in school tomorrow?" Lisa asked.

Not knowing what else to say without being an ingrate, I replied, "Sure."

I walked to Dr. Canfield's house and snooped around. Everything seemed okay. Since I had the key in my pocket and some shorts in my backpack, I decided to change and run home. After changing into the shorts, I checked out his deck and hot tub, and remembered Jen's comment.

Dare I sit naked in a hot tub, outside for God to see me, even if no one else? I could wear my shorts and maybe slip them off for a second. Or I could try it out first and then decide.

I dropped my clothes on the deck, pushed back the cover, and swished my hand in the water. As the place where we were first alone, the hot tub felt special. While trying to decide if I was brave enough to get in it, I noticed something quite wrong with the kitchen window. I heard noises in Dr. Canfield's house and felt the hair on my neck rise. Someone had broken in.

I snuck quietly through the garage and sprinted to the house next door, ringing the doorbell like sending out Morse code. A man about Dr. Canfield's age answered it.

"Someone is in Dr. Canfield's house!" I screamed in a whisper at him.

"Who are you and how do you know?"

142

To Face The World

"I take care of Dr. Canfield's yard. He asked me to check on his house while he was on vacation. There's someone in his house right now!"

He looked me up and down. "You check his house dressed only in a pair of shorts?"

"He said I could try his hot tub."

Do I ever sound lame.

The neighbor called the police and stayed on the phone. They told us to remain in the house until they arrived. It seemed like we waited hours, but it wasn't even two minutes. Police cars appeared, one in the front, and when we peered out over his deck, we saw one in the back. Three police officers took up positions. One, a lady, had a loudspeaker.

"We have the place surrounded! Come out with your hands over your head and lie face down on the front lawn!"

After a minute, a small man in a dirty tee shirt and greasy jeans opened the door, came out, and lay face down on the lawn. The police in the front ignored him and continued to watch the house until another officer drove up.

Two police officers cautiously went through the front door, like on the TV shows. After another eternity, they came out. They cuffed the guy, talked to him, and put him in a car.

The lady police officer knocked on the neighbor's door. She talked to the neighbor first, with him pointing at me. Then she motioned me outside. "I want your name, age, and address. Do you have a key to Dr. Canfield's house? Do you know how to reach Dr. Canfield?"

"I have a key to his garage for mowing his lawn. His office should know how to reach him." Another officer wrote down my response, as if it was important or something. I thought we were done, but she had not finished, or come close.

"You seemed dressed a bit casual to be mowing his lawn. Show me what you did."

I showed her everything; I even swished the water in the hot tub like before, and covered it. I managed to pick up my school clothes lying on the deck. Good thing the burglar didn't notice.

"You were sneaking into his hot tub in his absence?" she asked, while examining my clothes.

"He told me I could when I came over to check his place out for him."

It's not even a lie, but it sure sounds like one.

"Well, how about putting your clothes back on? You might appear less suspicious."

I quickly changed in Dr. Canfield's garage bath, silently thanking him one more time.

The lady officer and two other officers examined the window, which the burglar had broken around the frame. A bent limb on trailing

143

John C. Pelkey

plant below showed where the burglar had climbed up the trellis to the deck. One officer photographed everything, including me, and then they secured the window with some heavy black tape. After a thorough examination, she let me lock the garage.

Two officers left with the burglar, leaving me with the lady and the neighbor.

"You been taking care of Dr. C's yard now for a while, haven't you?" he asked. "His yard makes my yard look like crap! I pay so-called professionals one hundred fifty dollars a month; what do you charge?"

"Dr. Canfield pays me twenty-five dollars a week."

I regretted telling him the price. It sounded like I expected him to pay the same. I thought of a way out. "I can't do any more yards while I am still in school. Thanks, though, I'm glad you like his yard."

Mr. Dunlap paid me ten dollars a week for his yard, but I wasn't going to give up my spot across from Jen's house.

I wanted to leave, but the lady officer, with a nametag saying "Thompson," didn't agree. "Please allow me to drive you home."

I didn't think the request had room for a "no" in it. At least I didn't have to ride behind the screen, but sat in the front seat next to a monster shot gun.

My parents were extremely not pleased to see me arrive home late and in a police cruiser. After introductions, Officer Thompson insisted on talking to them. The grilling wasn't over. "Did Dr. Canfield assign your son to watch his house during an extended absence?"

Mom remembered the one hundred dollar bill. "The doctor paid Jon extra to care for his yard for three weekends and to watch the house while he is on vacation. Jon has maintained his yard for almost two years now."

Good going, Mom.

"Thank you, Ms. Perone," Officer Thompson replied. "You have a great son here."

She and I traded smiles, mine with more teeth. I could have run home in my school clothes and been sweating less.

"Jon has facilitated in the apprehension of what appears to be an intruder inside Dr. Canfield's house. The Aurora Valley Police Department appreciates his alertness and assistance. I expect you will be hearing more from us on this incident, Jon. Thank you and good evening."

She grabbed my shoulder and walked me to her car.

"A word of advice," she said, facing me with her car door open. "I won't mention what you wore in my report. It is not relative to the investigation. Yes, you probably did get Dr. Canfield's approval to use the hot tub. However, think about this. Sometimes appearances are more important than reality. Had someone reported you sitting in Dr. Canfield's hot tub, this would not have gone as well, even if you were innocent. Remember that."

She drove away in her monster car with its monster gun, both glaring at anyone daring to peek in the windows. I breathed a long sigh.

I survived, I don't have to explain how I arrived at Dr. Canfield's, and nobody knows the only reason I went there was to get away from Lisa Martin, the most desired girl in school. Nobody except me.

Dad and Mom grilled me with looks, but, because they were so pleased I wasn't in trouble, they didn't ask me much of anything. I certainly wasn't going to share any more than I had to. Mom felt more upset about Officer Thompson calling her Ms. instead of Mrs. than about anything else.

"Gas, couldn't she see my wedding ring? It cost us enough; she could have at least checked."

Dad smiled. "Now Emily, the police have to call you Ms. It's the law. You could have been a libber in disguise."

"Horsepucky!" It was as close as Mom got to saying anything colorful.

"Jon, you did well," Dad announced, putting his arm around my shoulders. "I didn't think you were taking the time to watch Dr. Canfield's house. I know how conscientious you are, so I should have known better. I'm proud of you, son."

Dad, don't rub it in!

I felt my silence was as bad as a lie. However, it was much too complicated to explain. Mom joined Dad in putting her arm around me, and together we walked into the house.

Dave, Cindy, and Beth wanted to know what was going on. "Dad, can you explain?" I asked. "Mom, can I use the phone?" They agreed; I had caught them in a weak moment and escaped. To ease my conscience, I needed to tell somebody the truth.

"Say hello to Jenni for us," they recited in unison.

Jen answered with, "Hi, Jon. I'm glad you called. Dad was in a hurry to get home because he and Mom were going out, without me of course. Since they're gone, now we can talk forever, or until they come home. Did you see the way Dad ogled Lisa's legs? Disgusting. I'm so glad you didn't. What happened after I left?"

You sound so excited; I wish I could see you. Your eyes must be sparkling. You have pretty eyes when you smile. You have pretty eyes all the time, and I've never told you.

"I talked to Lisa for a while. She wanted to know if we were boyfriend and girlfriend."

"What did you tell her?"

Careful, Jon.

"She told me. She said she could tell because I knew where you were and you knew where I was all the time, without looking."

"She could see our auras intertwining."

John C. Pelkey

Right.

"She asked me why guys didn't see her the way I saw you. I told her to wear a large sweatshirt and jeans for a week, and maybe somebody would."

"You told Lisa Martin to wear casual clothes to attract a guy?"

"Well, yeah, to attract a different kind of guy."

"Like you?"

"Yeah, someone like me, but not me. I'm already attracted to somebody else."

"Who?"

"You, whom do you think?"

"Just wanted to hear it. Then what happened?"

"Promise you won't get mad if I tell you?"

Silence, so much I thought the phone went dead. Then Jen spoke. "Jon, if you're afraid I'll get mad, then don't tell me."

I blew it. I've made you mad even before I said anything.

"I'll tell you, and you can get mad if you want to. I don't blame you if you do." I paused, but she outlasted me. Time to confess. "I missed the bus, so Lisa's mother gave me a ride. I didn't want her to take me home, so she dropped me off by Dr. Canfield's."

"You were afraid to tell me about riding with Lisa? I trust you. Besides, her mom was there. I thought you could miss the bus. I wanted Dad to wait, but he was in too big a hurry, as if someone was stalking him. I didn't even get to shower."

"There's more." I paused to think of how to explain the rest. Jen's bravado disintegrated.

"Jon, can I say something? Remember when you told me you wanted to be friends more than anything else? I feel the same way. If you like somebody, I want you to tell me. Jon, I care for you too much to let anyone ever spoil our friendship, even if we aren't together."

I had hurt her by pausing too long, as if I was going to break up or something. I hurt, too.

"Jen, there isn't anybody else. You are it. My eggs are all in your basket. Don't you believe me?" Now we were both hurt and mad.

She sounded subdued. "Most guys say nice things to girls without meaning anything; it makes for conversation."

"I'm not most guys, I'm your guy. What I'm going to try to explain is something wrong with me." When Jen tried to talk, I interrupted. "Let me say it first, and then you can yell at me."

"Oh." Jen sniffed. She still hurt. So did I.

"Lisa and her mom left." Big sigh. "I was swishing my hand through the hot tub water, trying to decide if I should jump in, when I noticed someone had broken the window to Dr. Canfield's kitchen. I could hear him inside. I told the neighbor to call the police, and they arrested him. Everybody thinks I did a good job."

To Face The World

"I think you did great. Jon, you're a hero. I'm sure Dr. Canfield thinks so, too, or will. What's wrong?"

"Jen, I had Lisa's mom drop me by Dr. Canfield because I didn't want anyone to see me with her. If I had caught the bus, I never would have gone there."

"Not true. You could have told Lisa's mom to drop you anywhere. You could have walked home when she did. Instead, you checked out Dr. Canfield's house like he expected you to, and by doing what you agreed to do, you caught a burglar."

"I only went on the deck because I wanted to see where we were on our first day."

"I remember. You helped me. Now maybe I can help you. Sometimes good things happen because people are in the right place at the right time to do the right thing. You were, and you did. It's what happened. Don't worry about what didn't happen. It's what I do. I worried so much you wouldn't like me because I ran the race badly, remember? You still liked me, and you told me at the locker room door. Then, when I blew it again by running away, again, you still liked me."

I still like you, Jen, more than ever. Although I'm not exactly certain I understand what you're saying.

"Now, more important subject. What is Lisa's mom like?"

"Jen, I love you, I really do."

"I love you, too, bunches. Now what is she like?"

Nothing like being persistent. Why do you care about Lisa's mom?

"She acts like she doesn't care. She could be eye-catching like Lisa, if she wanted to be. Dr. Canfield told me the outside is only good for a little while. We should love people for their inside because it lasts. Well, Lisa's mom, her outside hasn't gone bad yet, but it will if she doesn't try. So I hope she has a good inside. She did give me a ride, but I think it was because Lisa wanted her to. Lisa is much nicer than people give her credit. She told her mom about us. I also don't think she is as dumb as she pretends to be. Last thing, she doesn't have a southern accent, either."

It is more of an accent like yours.

"Lisa said she lived in Connecticut. I lived in Connecticut before I moved here."

"Did you ever see her?" I asked.

"No," Jen said. "I think if I did, I would have remembered. I lived in Florida, too, but I never got a southern accent. I don't think our coming from the same place was a coincidence."

"Why?"

Jen was silent for a moment, and I wondered if I had pried too much. However, she came back.

"'Why' needs to be my question, but not to you. Dad asks about Lisa, like how well she does in school and how well do I know her. Lisa's first day here was the same day you volunteered to be choir director. I remember, because it's the day my parents started fighting. I don't know Lisa. Today was the second time I've spoken to her. On the way home, Dad asked me to try to make friends with her. Between his request and the way he leered at her, it's creepy."

I think so, too.

Something interrupted her. "Dad and Mom are back. Means they are fighting again. Guess I had better go make myself scarce. Thanks for calling me and sharing. If I want call you some time, I mean with your folks and all, do they allow you to get calls from girls? I remember the one time your mom yelled at you. I wanted to call tonight, but didn't know if I should."

"She yelled at me because she wanted me to be doing something. You can call. They haven't minded you calling me so far."

"I mean when I haven't anything important to say."

"Jen, everything you say is important."

I could feel her smile though the phone.

I hid in my room to think about our conversation. Jen had to hide from her parents. It wasn't her fault they didn't like each other. I tried to think of the better parts.

I had told Jen I loved her, and she had told me she loved me, bunches, although mine seemed more sincere. Still, she had said the words, our first shared *I love you*. Wednesday, May fifteenth. I marked it my calendar with a heart. Better than marking it with people fighting.

Someone knocked on my door. Dave. "Hey, little brother, it was a real swell thing you did. You know I always thought you were a big pain, taking half my room and all. But you turned out okay. You're nice to Cindy. You got a cute girl. You sing good. You run good, even from Jenni's folks. I want you to know you're all right by me."

A week ago, I would have choked. Now we seemed able to have brotherly conversations. I didn't feel different, so Dave had changed.

"Thanks, Dave," I said. "You're all right, too. I'm glad things are okay with Cindy and you."

As long as I never see Cindy with less on than she wore yesterday morning, we'll be fine.

It seemed a year ago.

Chapter Eighteen

Jen met me at the bus and took my hand for the first time at school, watching my reaction to make certain I thought it was okay. I tried to act like it happened all the time, but couldn't stop smiling. After standing in the rain, her hand felt like ice, so I rubbed it and her other hand, too. A bunch of kids saw us holding hands, even though I let go when we reached the entrance.

I asked her to be quiet about the burglary and she nodded in agreement.

What am I worried about? Jen never says anything to anyone. Nobody knows yet. Smooth day.

It was. Then came lunch.

I was the first to sit at the table shared with our ever-growing group. When someone approached, I didn't look up until she sat across from me. Lisa. She wore a sweater a bit too tight. I couldn't see what else she had on and didn't want to.

"Can I eat with you this once? Can we talk?" she asked.

I remembered her request, forced a smile, and said, "Sure, we have room."

I noticed Tom and waved him over. No way, he and Trish sat at another table. Everyone joined them, leaving me alone with Lisa.

Lisa's table reacted, too, the girls giving me dirty looks and one even yelling, "What's with you?" at her.

Lisa ignored them, and focused on me instead. "Jon, I don't want to be a pain. People will think I'm trying to hit on you. I'm not. I need your help."

I can't believe this girl, who'd never even acknowledged I existed before two days ago, wants... What?

Thinking of Dave's, *nothing ventured, nothing lost,* I jumped in. "What can I do, Lisa?"

I had used the word for her name in a sentence, something my English teacher told us to do when we had a difficult time with certain words.

Lisa. I certainly do have a difficult time with you. I don't know the exact scientific term for it, but you put my fear emotions on overload. Lisa anxiety syndrome, maybe.

After waiting patiently for me to come back from my blip out, Lisa said, "It's my mom."

I blipped again. I had heard the phrase before, the exact words spoken with the exact voice. I couldn't stop the shiver descending my

John C. Pelkey

back.

What next?

"Sorry," I muttered.

"It's my mom," she repeated, pausing in case I blipped again. "We don't see things the same way, mostly about me. She is so messed. She has lots of money, but we own a shabby car and we live in a tiny apartment. She spends wads of money on clothes to make me look... Well, you said it. Available. Available and cheap."

"What about your dad?"

Good question.

I patted myself on the back.

"My dad? What dad? I never knew my dad. Mom said she couldn't marry him because he married someone else. It has always been us two." She stopped talking and studied her food, but didn't touch any of it.

"What else?"

I can't believe I asked. I should slap my hands over my mouth. She stopped. Why do I want her to continue?

"She spends a lot of time on the phone talking to some man. He never calls her; she calls him. She makes me leave the room, but I can still hear. They argue, sometimes about me. She tells him he is getting what he deserves, but I don't know what it means."

"What about you do they argue? Do you know?"

She nodded, but stayed silent, glancing around. "I can't talk about it here. Can we go outside?"

Now? While we're trying to eat lunch?

"Maybe after school, I can call you, talk on the phone?"

Much safer.

She shook her head. "After school will be too late."

"Too late for what?" So far, she had talked a lot, but without saying anything.

"Too late for me. Mom sets me up to date older guys, men. She dresses me to appear older... and available."

Your mom sets you up, like on a date? Adults don't date children, even if they look available, not for date, dates.

"I thought it was all a game, guys pretending I was somebody hot and desirable. Big joke, me. When I saw you and Jenni, I knew I was fooling myself. You two have something real. I want something real. I want to stop pretending I'm older. I want to stop pretending, period."

"What do you do on these dates?" I asked.

Probably not a good question, as I don't think I want to know.

"Can we go outside?"

Outside we went. Lisa hugged the wall next to the cafeteria doors, while I checked around to ensure we were alone. With the rain ready to return any second, no one else came outside.

"Okay," she said, after taking a deep breath and turning around.

150

To Face The World

"You can't tell anyone or Mom could get into trouble, deep trouble."

"Tell anyone what?"

Lisa hesitated. "I shouldn't tell you."

For the first time, if such a thing was possible, Lisa irritated me. I forgot about how much of a knockout she was, and how she petrified me.

"Lisa, if you don't want to talk about it, let's finish our lunch."

When I started back inside, Lisa grabbed my arm. "Wait, please, Jon. I can do this. Give me a second."

I waited. I noticed Lisa didn't let go, but I ignored it. I wanted to focus on getting her through this, not focus on her touching me. I felt jumbled enough.

She took another deep breath, let go, and waved one hand in front of her face. "Okay, here it is. Mom sells stuff, mostly to men."

"Stuff?"

"Drugs. She wants me to go with them to help..." She stopped and grabbed me again.

"Help?" I sounded like a repeating machine. When I saw the tears, I tried to control the shivers already sprinting up and down my back.

Some help I am.

I went for a revelation point, pulled her hand away from my arm, and forced her to look me in the face. "Lisa, what do you do with the men?"

"Make them happy?"

I got an image of Lisa making men happy. It didn't have anything to do with drugs. It had to do with girl parts.

"The last guy I saw; well, he wasn't happy with how little I was willing to do. He wanted me to... Never mind."

She paused, her eyes willing me to understand something I would rather not know.

"Jon, I don't want to live like this anymore. I want to be like Jenni, with someone like you to watch over me, to care about me. I want to care about them, too, and watch over them back. I want what you and Jenni have. I want out of my life. How can I get to be like you?"

Wow! Never before has anyone wanted to be like me. What can I do?

I needed to get my mind away from what Lisa could do to make men happy. I had no idea where out was, or how Lisa could get there. Lisa's girl parts, starting with her face and working in any direction, simply outmaneuvered everything else.

Focus, Jon, focus. Focus on what? When in doubt, change the subject.

Changing the subject, I said, "Your mother sells drugs," nodding my head to get Lisa to agree.

The tears streamed down her face now. No way we could walk back inside and pretend nothing happened. I wanted to get everything out for sure. Lisa had already said this once; she could say it again. "Say it," I

John C. Pelkey

snapped.

"Yes, my mother sells drugs," she snapped back, glaring up at me, but softening, "when she's not too smashed to stand up. I know; I've seen enough of them."

"Do you use drugs?"

Lisa had faced me eye to eye. Now she shrunk back and refused to look at me. I knew the answer. I could see she was on the verge of falling apart. No more questions.

Now what?

I thought of Cindy and Jen.

Is my family the only family, family? The together kind? Normal dysfunctional instead of dysfunctional, dysfunctional?

I didn't know what to do. Lisa had too huge a problem for me to solve alone. I took too long.

Lisa couldn't stand my silence. "Jon, I'm sorry. Please, talk to me. What can I do? If I tell anybody, they will put Mom away. She already has a record from what she did where we used to live. I don't know what they will do with me, but it could be worse than it is now."

Lisa, what could be worse than your mother forcing you to take drugs and have sex?

"Jon, I don't want to use drugs. I wouldn't do it last time, but I helped the guy do his. Then he wanted to... I lied to him about being, um, about it being the wrong time of the month?"

Her sentence ended in a question. I nodded.

I know what you're trying to say.

"I offered to do something else for him, but he didn't want it that way."

Now I don't know what you're trying to say. I do know what you need goes beyond me. Regardless, I won't pretend I can save you.

"Lisa, I don't know how I can help."

"You are helping. You're listening."

Right. Now your problems are my problems.

Without knowing what to say, I tried anyway. "Lisa, you have to find someone who honestly can help. Now. You have to get out, physically. Away from your mother if she sells drugs and sets you up. You can't worry about what happens to her more than what happens to you. Getting out doesn't mean leaving your mom to go somewhere else to do the same things. Next time you could end up doing both."

"Next time is tonight."

"Then don't go home."

"I have to; they've already paid Mom."

They? The word caused the shivers to attack again. How can your mom sell you to a "they" to share for drugs and sex? Adults don't sell their children. Mom could never sell Beth. What kind of person...

Before I could stop myself, I grabbed Lisa's hand and towed her

152

To Face The World

inside. Instead of going back to the food, I aimed at the foyer and the principal's office.

Lisa struggled at first, screaming, "Jon, what are you doing?"

Everyone watched our fight as we continued toward the doors to the foyer. I pulled one way; she pulled back. She was stronger than she looked, but I was more determined.

When she realized I wasn't going to stop, she blurted out, "Jon, you can't tell them. My mother. They will..."

I let go, but had to grab her, as she was pulling so hard, she slid backwards. Instead of her falling, we collided. From inches away, I asked her, "Lisa, do you want to die?" Dumb question, but I couldn't think of anything else.

"What?" My close proximately and unexpected question clearly confused her. She backed up and swiped at me with her free hand.

"What she is doing to you, your mom is trying to kill you. We go there; you live." I pointed toward the office. "We stay here; you die." I pointed toward our food. "You decide."

The lunch monitor, stunned at first, had recovered enough to charge toward us, yelling something. Lisa saw him and stumbled in the wrong direction. I forced her to stop.

"You have about two seconds!" I shouted in her face.

"I want to live!" she shouted back, loud enough for everyone in the cafeteria to hear.

Her response stopped the monitor for a second, enough to allow me to pull Lisa through the doors ahead of him. We shot across the foyer and burst into the reception area, toward the principal's office and past his secretary.

"You can't go in there!" she screamed.

Wanna bet?

The principal, Mr. Koffman, had three visitors, a woman, a police officer with bars on his collar, and someone I couldn't see. "What is the meaning of this?" he demanded, jumping up from behind his desk. "You can't disturb this meeting!"

Before anybody could do anything else, I blurted out, "Lisa has been sold by her mother to some men to take drugs and have sex with tonight!" I may not have gotten it right, but I did get it loud. "Will you help her? She can't go home!"

Silence. I watched Mr. Koffman's face go pale. I let go of Lisa's hand and she slumped into the only vacant chair. I noticed her skirt. It was short, but not like yesterday, and it wasn't tight. Lisa had tried. I turned back to stare at Mr. Koffman, both hands gripping his desk.

"Well, Mr. Perone, you certainly don't do things half way, do you." Pastor Kamorkov revealed himself as the third visitor.

The woman, the photographer from yesterday, caught Lisa, who was about to fall out of the chair. She completely lost it, sobbing out of control, and blubbered, "They'll take my mother."

"You said you wanted to live." I chucked it back at her before she could make any more decisions, like change her mind and accuse me of something.

"I do. I want to live!" She screamed it at everyone.

Things got blurry. I tried to let go of the desk, but found myself stuck. The desk was the only thing holding me up.

Pastor Kamorkov steered me from the desk into his chair. I managed not to fall out of it. "You were the subject of this meeting, Jon. But you're going too fast. We can't keep up."

"Can you help?" I asked anybody.

Mr. Koffman's secretary popped in. "Shut the door!" he snapped. She popped out, quietly latching the door closed.

"I can help." The police officer picked up the phone on Mr. Koffman's desk, gave the cord a jerk, and moved into a corner.

Mr. Koffman came around his desk and knelt in front of me. "I take back what I said about being disturbed. If we can't help, we shouldn't be here."

Pastor Kamorkov stood between us, one hand on me, and one hand on Lisa. I realized he was praying, right there in front of everyone.

The police officer hung up and announced, "I have some people on their way, coming here and going to Renee Martin's. We know where she lives."

Sitting there, I realized the police officer knew who Lisa was, and what was going on.

Why didn't anyone do anything about it before now? Why are they meeting to talk about me? Nothing makes sense.

My mind swirled around, oblivious to everyone.

When I snapped back, Pastor Kamorkov had let go of me and was introducing himself to Lisa. He ended with, "I've known Jon for a while. You picked the right person to trust and confide in. I am greatly impressed with your courage, Lisa."

The photographer introduced herself. "Jon, I'm Mrs. Koffman, his wife." She pointed at Mr. Koffman, who smiled sheepishly. "I work for the Aurora Valley News."

The police officer mumbled something, but spoke up when Pastor Kamorkov motioned encouragingly at him. "Captain Phillips, I'm the head of criminal investigations for Aurora Valley." He didn't seem greatly interested in talking to me, which made us a match.

Mr. Koffman fumbled around in front of me, looking lost. "I guess you can go back to class, Jon, with our thanks."

Go back to class?

With my arms and legs complete rubber, I couldn't even stand.

As I was about to try, Lisa screamed, "You can't go, Jon! No! You have to stay! You are the only one who cares!" She faced Mr. Koffman.

To Face The World

"Please, let him stay. Please!"

"Okay." Mr. Koffman put his hands out, palms up, defending himself. "He stays for now."

Minutes passed, like with everyone holding their breath. Lisa calmed down, and the life returned to my arms and legs, a tingling sensation from the blood flowing again.

Pastor Kamorkov touched our shoulders in encouragement and left. Captain Phillips followed, but didn't trouble us with a goodbye. Mrs. Koffman stayed with her husband.

When in doubt, do something. I did. I've made Lisa's problems my problems. I'm not going to let go, now.

"Mr. Koffman, to get Lisa to come in here, I promised her I would stick with her as long as possible. With the situation and her mom, she doesn't have anyone else."

I sort of lied, but didn't think Lisa would object. Her attempt to smile confirmed it. If the concept of my words were true, Lisa didn't have anyone else. The feeling of helplessness buried me.

Mr. Koffman helped unbury me. "I think you have a great idea, Jon. Thanks."

I plopped back in the chair and vegged, letting the world continue without me. Mr. Koffman's secretary brought us some water and our untouched lunches. I picked at mine to be polite, but ate it all, as did Lisa. Tension made some people hungry, made us hungry.

We stayed in the principal's office with Mrs. Koffman. After an hour, two state social workers entered. They introduced themselves as Anabelle and Smitty, no last names, and gave Lisa and me thorough look-sees.

When they said I needed to leave, Mr. Koffman shook his head. "Unless you have some specific reason or the legal authority to remove him, Jon gets to stay."

"He's a bit young to be her lawyer," Smitty said.

"The State of Washington allows all respondents of interviews conducted by state employees to have a support person present," Lisa said, indicating this was not her first, but one of many interviews.

"Yes, but for minors, the support person generally is a parent or guardian," Anabelle added, making them like a tag team.

"My 'parent' is about to be arrested. I don't have a guardian, so I choose Jon."

Anabelle and Smitty gave me another visual examination, shrugged, and asked the Koffmans to leave. Mrs. Koffman gave us a tight smile and a finger-wiggle wave. Mr. Koffman pointed out the door at his secretary and said, "If you need something, step out and ask." Then he left.

Anabelle produced a paper listing the interview questions. After some hesitation, she gave me a copy. The first questions requested

John C. Pelkey

technical and standard personal information, like name, address, and phone number. Then, some of the questions got down and dirty.

Have you ever consumed in any manner an illegal substance or a legal prescription written for someone else? If yes, list by substance and method consumed.

Have you ever engaged in intimate or sexual activity with a person or persons of either sex over the age of eighteen, gratuitously or for compensation? If yes, identify the activity and participants by name if possible.

"Does Lisa have to answer all the questions?" I asked.

"To be accurate in our assessment, Lisa needs to provide the information requested and..." Anabelle paused, her icy stare clearly revealing her irritation, "...the most truthful answers."

"However, to answer your question, Jon, no, she does not," Smitty said, almost a contradiction. "Why do you ask?"

"The questions about drugs and sex seem misleading," I said, trying not to show irritation back. "What if she was forced? I don't see that question."

"You mean like if she was raped or molested?" Anabelle asked. "She doesn't need a separate question. At thirteen, it makes no difference, forced or consensual. In other words, it doesn't matter." She turned her glare toward Smitty, daring him to contradict her.

"What matters to Lisa is what matters," I muttered. I sounded like a three-year-old, but I wasn't going to back down. In their data collection, they left out Lisa's feelings.

Smitty broke out his smile. "She does have her lawyer with her. Think of it this way. Lisa can elaborate her responses to show the circumstances. We record the conversation, as we don't want to miss anything. Does that work for you?"

It did. They asked Lisa the questions. Somehow, her saying yes to the drugs and sex questions, regardless of the circumstance, defined the interview. Her mother collecting money and handing her over to strangers, both gave me a solid punch in the gut.

Whose mother allows, much less forces, her own child to go with strangers, and why? If what Lisa says about their finances is correct, they don't even need the money. If people know about it, like the police, why don't they make her stop? Nothing makes sense.

They finished, and left without taking Lisa. We shared surprised looks, but said nothing. When the bell rang, I stood and walked around, watching the regular school buses load. I wasn't about to leave Lisa, not even for track practice. She followed me with her eyes.

"You did the right thing," I said, "deciding to let me turn you in."

To Face The World

"I decided?" she asked, almost smiling.

"Yeah, if you had said no, I wouldn't have done it."

"I'd rather everyone think you decided. It takes me off the hook."

"Okay, fine. I decided," I muttered. "Think of it this way. Had you said no, I probably would have ratted on you."

"Thank you." This time she smiled.

"I wonder what they're doing now."

Lisa, why they haven't taken you somewhere?

Lisa read my mind. "First, they have to arrest Mom. Next, they need to arrange for an emergency placement. I've been through this before. It's why it took so long last time."

It's why what took so long?

"When the man she talks to moves, we move, too. Last time he moved when Mom was in prison, so we had to wait for her to finish her community service before we could move here."

"Have you met this man?"

"I think so, but it was a long time ago. I was like six. Mom meets with him, but I don't."

"Is he your dad?" I asked.

"Maybe. I don't know."

After a while, Mr. Koffman knocked, and opened the door. "I didn't want to startle you," he said, trying to explain the knock on his own office door. Smitty followed.

"They have your mother," Smitty announced. "Also, the two men she had set you up with. Kudos to you, Jon, for your concern to bring this to light. Kudos to you, too, Lisa, for allowing him."

"See?" Lisa said, not trying to hide an, *I told you so,* expression. "This is all your fault." We did a stare down, but Lisa lost when she attempted a smile, a tiny one for sure, but better than crying.

"Well, okay. I guess it's a good thing," Mr. Koffman said, trying out his own smile.

"Where are you taking her?" I asked Smitty.

"We have an emergency family for Lisa to stay with. A nice, older couple who have volunteered. They belong to Pastor Kamorkov's church, and he connected us." He turned to Lisa. "They live a short distance from here. You can easily walk to school."

It certainly sounded better than hauling her away to some place I had pictured like in *Annie*. I wondered what roles they had played. All of them, Mr. and Mrs. Koffman, Pastor Kamorkov, and Captain Phillips, had done things and pulled strings we never would know about.

He continued. "This is a temporary placement, like an emergency fix for now. We will continue the process after you have some time."

Lisa nodded, but didn't seem to be as upset about her mother's capture as I thought she would be. She came up to me. "Thanks, Jon." She stopped and faced Mr. Koffman. "Can I hug him?" she asked.

157

John C. Pelkey

"We'll give you a minute," he replied. They both stepped out. Seemed odd they would leave us alone, but they had left us alone for more than an hour, twice.

Lisa took my hands, swinging them together and apart. "You saved me, Jon. I knew you would. I'll never forget what you did for me. I hope someday my mom understands. Maybe I can explain..."

She crashed into me. It wasn't as much a hug as a hold-on-for-dear-life crush. I held her tight, trying not to think about hugging a girl I had been terrified of three hours ago. Now, she seemed more like an old friend.

She let go, smiling. "I hope we can stay friends," she said. "Maybe I can call you. Tell you where I'm at and how I'm doing. Ask about Jenni and you, how you're doing?"

Mr. Koffman had a sticky pad on his desk. I wrote my name and phone number. For some unknown reason, I wrote Jen's name and phone number below mine.

"Here," I said. "You can call both of us."

"Jenni will talk to me? She seems nice, but she doesn't say much."

"She never says much to anyone. This is different. I think when I fill her in, she will talk to you."

"Thanks, Jon," she said, hugging me again, this time comfy, like friends. I felt a kiss on my cheek, along with the lingering scent of roses from her lip gloss.

When she let go, I touched her nose. "Are you going to be okay?"

"Yep. New Lisa, beginning right now, drug-free." She held out her hand, and we shook, right in time for Mr. Koffman to come in and see.

"Ready?" he said. He didn't seem to know what to do, but accepted Lisa's hand when she offered it.

"Thank you, Mr. Koffman. Your wife, too, and the officer and minister." She turned to me. "See you tomorrow?" she asked.

"You'll be back tomorrow?" I hadn't thought about seeing and talking to Lisa in person at school so soon.

"The new Lisa has to debut sometime. May as well be now." With a blown kiss and a wave, she disappeared with Smitty.

Mr. Koffman watched her go, and turned to me. "Thanks, Jon. You did well, today. You are too late for track practice, but I've excused you, so you still can participate in the next meet. I've excused you from your math, PE, and choir classes, too." He handed me a paper. "Your math assignment. You didn't have to turn anything in today."

He paused, pre-wording his next discussion item. "I called your mom and briefed her on the situation. I didn't say what you did for Lisa due to confidential restraints, but I said you contributed to a smooth transition and told her much we appreciated your efforts. From the situation and the strain it put on you, I asked her to pick you up. She instructed me to have you call her as soon as you are ready."

158

To Face The World

Mom answered on the first ring. "What is going on?" she asked.

"What did Mr. Koffman tell you?" I asked back.

"Well, basically... nothing. Are you in some kind of trouble?"

"It wasn't about me. I helped someone else. Things got a bit complicated and emotional, but everything is all right now."

"Well, I'm leaving to pick you up. I have a bank appointment, so you will have to come along with me."

Great, instead of track practice and seeing Jen, I get to sit in a bank. No good deed goes unpunished.

I got my books and backpack, and reached the front of the school at the same time as the first kids from track practice arrived.

Ed spotted me and ran over, with Dan and Jim trailing.

"What happened?" he asked. "What did you do to Lisa? Did you get in trouble?"

"You missed practice," Jim added.

"I didn't get in trouble and I'm excused from my classes and practice. However, I can't talk about it, legal stuff."

"Bet you can talk to her," Jim countered, pointing behind me.

I spun and found Jen, watching us and probably listening, too.

I left the guys and caught her, steering her away from everyone. We walked toward the street, as close as we could get to each other without touching. Her hair was still wet from showering, and I could smell a mixture of aloe and lavender.

"You smell good," I said to her cocked head and eye squint.

"What's going on?" she asked. "Everyone says you drug Lisa Martin into the principal's office during lunch and stayed there."

You covered the public version well enough. The private version?

"We need to talk, lots."

Jen smiled a response, which instantly broke into a frown. I followed her eyes to the green Mercedes coming down the street.

"Mom," she said. "Quick, what happened to Lisa? Mom will want to know. She asks about her enough."

"Your mom knows Lisa?"

"Dad and Mom both do, but they try to keep it a secret." Her mom stopped and honked. "Two second version, hurry."

"It's too complicated. Can I call you?" I asked.

"Calling me is complicated. If I call you, my phone doesn't ring."

As usual, Mrs. Carling had stopped on the street. Jen waved, but didn't get a response.

As we approached, the shock of my life smashed into me as I gaped in the window. The woman driving had cleaned up, but not enough to change her appearance, even with wearing better clothes, combing her hair, adding makeup, and sitting up straight. I tried to move, but found myself glued in place, as if shot with a stun gun.

No!

159

John C. Pelkey

"What are you doing?" the woman demanded through the open side window.

The voice clinches it. Zero doubt now.

Jen hesitated before opening the door, long enough for me to unfreeze, run up, reach out, and catch the end of her sweatshirt, pulling her away from the car.

"Jen, don't get in," I whispered. "That's Lisa's mom."

She froze, probably thinking I had completely lost it. "Jon, what are you talking about?" she asked, crinkling her nose. "That's *my* mom."

Chapter Nineteen

"Your mom?" I flailed my fingers in her mom's direction, trying to point without pointing.

"Yeah," Jen said. "My mom. You haven't seen her before, have you?" Her eyes caught mine. She wasn't lying. "Why do you think she's Lisa's mom?"

I took the opportunity check out her mom, quickly trying to find differences between her and Lisa's mom, without success. Maybe she weighed less. I was certain, given the right clothes, makeup, a diet, and some sleep... "They look exactly alike."

Mrs. Carling wasn't the most patient person. She waved at us and yelled, "Jennifer, what are you doing? Why is he pawing you? Leave him and get in the car right now."

Jen left me and peeked in the window. "Mom, meet my friend Jon."

"I know who he is." From the tone in her voice, I was a criminal with my face plastered on the TV.

"Mom, he wants to meet you."

I do?

"Jennifer, please already, what does he want?"

"Mom, Jon says you look exactly like Lisa's mom. Do you?"

Without registering anything perceptible, Mrs. Carling ignored Jen and pointed at me. "You, get over here."

I approached the car as if it was on fire, even putting my hands out to ward off the heat. When I got close enough, she asked, "What do you know about Renee Martin? Tell me, right now."

I tried to think of something brilliant and vague, but blurted out, "They arrested her," before I could stop myself. I clamped my mouth shut with both hands, but it was too late.

"Arrested her for what?" she demanded.

"Selling drugs and Lisa--"

"That fool women. Can she not be so obvious?" Mrs. Carling snapped out of whatever blip she went in. "Jennifer, you go back in the school and call your dad to pick you up. Understand? Right now!"

Jen didn't hesitate, but turned around and silently walked toward the school, her eyes betraying her despair as she passed me.

Mrs. Carling pointed at me, said, "You... You stay away from my daughter," and drove away.

Yea, though I walk through the valley of the shadow of death, I will fear no evil.

I caught Jen, as she wasn't setting a land speed record to get back into the school. When I touched her shoulder, she spun and spit out, "What do you mean Lisa's mom looks exactly like my mom?"

"Jen, they look alike. Not like close alike, like exactly alike. As if they are the same person. They don't have the same accent as Lisa and you do, but just as you two sound the same, they sound the same, exactly. They even use the same words."

"Lisa and I sound the same?" Jen asked.

"When Lisa isn't trying to sound like she's from the south, she sounds exactly like you."

I watched her absorb my revelation. "Now I understand some things, but I don't understand why Mom refuses to tell me. She asks about Lisa. Dad asks about Lisa. They want information, but they won't share something as basic as Mom has an identical twin sister and Lisa could be my cousin? Do they not think I would like to know?"

She flexed her fingers into fists, ready to hit something, but sighed instead. "Why would I think Mom would be any different with this than she is with everything else?"

She had shouted the last part. Although the late busses had arrived, the kids stopped climbing aboard and stood, staring at us. A honk behind me caused us both to jump. Mom had arrived.

"Come on, Jen. We're leaving."

"I can't; I'm supposed to call my dad."

"After what you yelled? You'll have every adult in the school clamoring to find out what's wrong."

She didn't need any more encouragement, and followed me. As we weren't interesting anymore, the kids resumed loading, and I didn't see any adults in attack mode.

Mom's car was tiny, bucket seats in the front separated by a floor shift, back seats too small for Jen to sit comfortably, much less me, and it didn't even pretend to have a middle seatbelt. Mom had stuff piled on the front seat, so we would have to squeeze in the back. At least her trunk was empty when I opened it for our backpacks. She did move the passenger seat forward to give me a couple more inches. I felt like a sardine.

"Do I want to know why you have Jenni?" she asked, once we settled in. "Does it have to do with what happened to you today? The principal told me the girl's name was Lisa."

"I want to tell Jenni what happened. Her mom had to go, so I thought we could talk while you're in the bank."

"When do you plan to explain it to me?" Mom demanded.

"Can we wait for Dad?"

"Jon, the school called me to come pick you up."

"Mom, it's not about me, it's about what I observed."

Yeah, and what are my observations for today? Lisa was about to become a prostitute and drug user, maybe not for the first time. My ratting got Mrs.

Martin arrested. Lisa's mom looks exactly like Jen's mom. Lisa's in some kind of placement. Mrs. Carling's in some kind of crazy. Jen's about ready to come apart. Another normal day. If I mark my calendar with an atomic explosion tonight, I'll nail it.

"I helped somebody through a tough situation. It got a little emotional, as I had to do some convincing."

"Who, exactly, were you convincing?"

"The principal, Mr. Koffman. He said I did well and excused me from class and practice."

"That's why you spent the afternoon in the principal's office?"

"Yeah, more or less. There are details."

Mom laughed. "There always are." She thought for a second or two, and came to a conclusion. "I guess I can wait to hear it with Dad, but I'm going to be a while. This is an important meeting, and I don't have time to drive Jenni home first. Jenni, maybe you can call your dad from there."

Jen nodded. "Okay, Mom, she agrees," I said. If it got Mom going, I would agree to anything.

At the first traffic light, Mom's next question was, "Should you be telling this to Jenni?"

"I think so. It concerns her in a roundabout way." To get Mom refocused, I asked, "What are you doing at the bank. Is it exciting?"

She laughed. "Exciting, no. Necessary, maybe. It's a refinance. We want to help Dave and Cindy, so we are freeing up some money."

"Helping them so they can move out?"

"Yes, eventually. It won't happen right away, but maybe by fall."

It worked. Mom continued to talk about Dave and Cindy, and I only needed to chip in with a word or two now and then. She may have forgotten about Jen, who sat completely silent, except for her hand lightly touching the seam of my jeans at my knee.

Mom's bank was in the civic center, next to a tiny, triangle-shaped park, including grass, a couple of benches under trees, and a fountain, where the crisscrossing streets had left a space too small for much else.

Mom parked in the bank lot, across the main street from the city hall. I pointed out the park. "May we talk for a minute first, right over there? Then Jenni can call."

"Okay, for a minute. I'm going to be in an office, so I'm depending on you to be responsible."

"Maybe I should call now," Jen said, her first verbal contribution.

We followed Mom into the bank. When Mom asked Jen if she had change for a pay phone, she replied with, "I have an account number."

While Jen dialed a series of numbers she had memorized, Mom met two bank employees, a man and a woman, and disappeared with them behind a door, waving at the last second.

Jen got through, but only said, "Ralph Carling, please," and, "I'm Jennifer Carling, his daughter." After a long pause, she ended by saying,

John C. Pelkey

"Thank you."

"He's gone," she said when she hung up.

"Did your mom call him?" I asked.

"No, he's been gone most of the afternoon. If I had stayed at the school, I wouldn't have reached him."

She touched my arm. "I think I'm ready to hear about what happened," she whispered, her eyes glistening. "They said he left due to a family emergency, way before Mom knew."

We walked to the park, and I sat on the bench where I could see Mom coming out from the bank. Jen sat facing me, slipping one leg under the other. When I reached for her hand, she met me half way. Now I had my opportunity, but I wasn't certain this was a good idea.

"Are you sure you want to know all this?" I asked.

"My mom looks exactly like someone else and you think I might not want to know?"

I got a now familiar glare, with her eyes flashing fire. Jen could change moods instantly. She could change them back, too, as she switched off the anger. "Okay, Jon, tell me exactly what happened today. Don't leave out a detail. I want to know everything."

I started with a comparison of Lisa's mom and Jen's mom and explained the best I could remember, except I left out the social worker questions about sex and drugs I didn't want to think about. She didn't interrupt once, but I did see tears.

"Did you want to know?" I asked when I finished.

She nodded, deep in thought. "Write it down or something," she instructed.

"Why?"

"You will have to explain it to more people than me. Hearings and trials and stuff."

Great. Exactly what I want to dredge back up.

Jen shifted from facing me to one knee up, resting her chin on it. "I may have an aunt and a cousin I didn't know about, who live in the same town, and maybe have lived near us all my life. My aunt subjects her daughter, my cousin, to prostitution when she's in eighth grade at thirteen or fourteen. Jon, she's our age. She could be me, and me her. Why?"

When I saw tears, I skipped the handholding and scooted over to her. She leaned her head against my shoulder and touched my chest with her hand.

"I don't have anyone in my life I can trust," she whispered.

"Yes, you do," I countered. "You have me."

As I held Jen, behind her I watched a car approach on the street adjacent to the park and the bank. A green car, a Mercedes. It stopped in a no parking zone right across the street from us, under the sign labeled *City Hall and Police.*

164

To Face The World

I tried not to cringe when I watched Jen's mom get out, but failed. Jen felt my reaction and glanced up, but didn't move. Not noticing us across the street, Mrs. Carling entered the building.

Seconds later, a silver Nissan 300ZX cruised up our side of the street. The driver couldn't miss the Mercedes and spun a U-turn, parking behind it. Before he got out, I already knew whom he was.

As I tensed again, Jen sat up, wondering what I focused on. She followed the direction I faced. "Dad," she mumbled, although with the traffic going by, screaming it wouldn't have made a difference. "Mom's car, too." She slipped around behind me, using my body as a shield.

Without even glancing in our direction, Mr. Carling stood in front of the building, watching the street.

"Guess I could go over there," she said, but not moving.

Mr. Carling didn't have to wait long. A new Cadillac parked behind the Z, and a chunky man with slicked-back hair and a briefcase got out and trotted over to him. They shook hands, Mr. Carling gave him a small package, and together, they went inside.

"Lawyer?" I asked. He looked like a lawyer. As Dad would say, I could see grease marks on the sidewalk.

I wanted Mom to hurry, but at the same time, I didn't. We couldn't leave now, right in the middle of everything. Sitting behind me, Jen rested her chin on my shoulder and I held up a hand for her to hold. Nothing happened for five minutes, although she about broke my hand. I finally forced her to let go. After whispering, "Sorry," she massaged it with both hands, but neither of us spoke or watched what she did.

After five more minutes, give or take, Mom coming out of the bank coincided with Mr. and Mrs. Carling coming out of the police station, along with the lawyer and a woman in an orange jumpsuit.

I almost gasped, but Jen beat me. There she was, Mrs. Carling in duplicate, the slightly dull-looking version in the jumpsuit, and the more polished version facing her. Mrs. Carling had to be over thirty, but she didn't have any trouble slowing traffic in the tight top and short skirt she wore, something I hadn't noticed during my earlier zombie observation.

Lisa's mom in the jumpsuit didn't quite match the curves, didn't have makeup on, and didn't have the same hairstyle, hers being the messy version, but still, even from across the street, no way was she not a match.

"They could look exactly alike if they wanted to," Jen whispered, her mouth next to my ear. "All this time, Mom never said a word."

"Your mom is quite striking," I whispered back in her ear.

"You noticed?" Jen exclaimed, not whispering. "She tries to ooze sex, but worries about me if I show a hint of anything."

I thought about the circumstances required to bring the four of them together. Mrs. Carling was the closest relative to accept the release of Lisa's mom. Mr. Carling brought the money. The lawyer sprinkled his

165

John C. Pelkey

expertise to streamline it. They took about ten minutes to get her released, and the plastic bag Mr. Carling carried meant she didn't bother to change. Like with Lisa's placement, more strings pulled, more shortcuts taken.

The four stood in a face off. I wondered who had the hockey puck. We could hear noise, but the traffic kept it from being clear enough to understand. Then people using the crosswalk light stopped all the cars, and the noise.

"She's your sister," Mr. Carling yelled, pointing at the Mercedes.

The argument is over cars?

Mrs. Carling yelled back, "Maybe she is my sister..." She pointed at the Z.

The traffic started, but not fast enough to cut off, "...but she's your whore."

Gut-punched. Right where it stops everything and takes away all the air. I felt like I was about to throw up. Mom waved and yelled, "Come on, Jon." I ignored her.

We watched the lawyer set a new world record for the fifty-foot-run to his car, not even looking as he started it and pulled out in a single motion. Mrs. Carling followed suit, also failing to kill anyone in her departure, and leaving Mr. Carling with Lisa's mom.

The fight wasn't over cars, but with whom Lisa's mom should ride.

Mr. Carling took off his coat and used it to cover half of the jumpsuit. Still, the jumpsuit alone should have been enough for someone to run out and holler, "Escape!" No one did. He handed her the bag, they walked to the Z, he opened her door, and she got in.

Although I sat frozen to the bench, Jen stood and walked toward them, putting her in plain sight. I jumped up and caught her, in case she attempted to cross the street without paying attention to the traffic. Mr. Carling steered into a second U-turn to go in the opposite direction, right in front of us. By doing so, he couldn't help but see Jen. I could read the surprise on his face, but he didn't stop. As suddenly as they all had appeared, they all had disappeared.

Mom came toward us, saying, "Who were they? Why are you standing--?"

As she stopped speaking when she noticed Jen, I turned, dreading what I would find. She hadn't moved, but her eyes had become Niagara Falls. She moaned a single word, "Jon," and buried her face in my chest. I waited for the sobs to come, and she didn't disappoint.

"Jon, what is going on?"

"Please, Mom. Home. Our house, now. Please don't stop anywhere. I will explain everything, I promise. Please!"

Mom took a breath, but didn't speak. Instead, she led us to the car. Inside, Jen scrunched against me as much as her seatbelt would allow. I held her as best I could, but felt completely lost and defeated. How could

To Face The World

anything make up for what she had seen and heard? Mom drove slowly, took over twenty minutes to get home, and Jen cried every foot of the way.

When the car stopped, I forced her to sit up.

Mom's only words were, "Jon, shouldn't we call--?"

"No, Mom. We shouldn't call. Calling is the top line on the things we shouldn't do list."

I ran around the car to get the door opened for Jen, but she beat me, standing outside the car before I reached her. "Your house," she said, looking around. "Better than my house."

I fetched our backpacks, carrying both to the house behind Mom and Jen. Dad and Cindy were cooking in the kitchen, but more like making a mess.

"We wanted burritos, but I think we've moved on," Dad said.

Mom gave everything a thorough inspection. "Moved on to what?" she asked.

"Well, when we get there, we'll know," he replied.

"What's this," Mom asked, pointing at something bubbling on the stove.

"Our mix," Cindy replied proudly.

"I see. What's this?" Mom pointed at the floor.

"Our accident," Dad said, and sounded every bit as proud.

Mom began to clean it, completely forgetting about Jen.

"Em, we can clean it up," Dad offered.

"If you were going to clean it up, you would have already cleaned it."

I led Jen on a retreat to the living room. I caught almost a smile as she followed me.

"That was so cool," she said. "Like a family."

"I don't think Mom thought so."

"They didn't even notice me."

They did. Before I could put Jen's backpack down, they flowed in behind us.

"I'll be right back," I muttered, and slipped by them with my backpack in front, so they couldn't see my wet shirt. In my room, I dropped them both on the floor and came back wearing Jen's exchanged wolf sweatshirt.

Mom had seated everyone except Cindy, who stood at the entrance. "Um, I should go?" she mumbled.

"Sit," I directed. She sat on the couch opposite Jen. I sat between them. Dad and Mom shared the loveseat, facing us. Jen scooted over until her shoulder and leg touched mine. She checked out my shirt and said, "Hi, Wolfie," to the wolf. I took her hand and rested it on my leg. Since Mom had already seen us holding hands, it didn't matter now.

"Dave and Beth?" I asked, trying to think of a diversion.

167

John C. Pelkey

"Shopping. They're catching something to eat before they return."

Dave and Beth are shopping and eating dinner together? This is different.

I could see Dave and Cindy shopping, and Cindy and Beth, but not Dave and Beth.

My inside smile only lasted a second.

"Let's hear it," Mom said, opening the inquisition. "Take your time; we shut off the stove."

I wanted to say, "Where's the bare bulb and the brass knuckles?" to lighten things, but I didn't think they would buy it. I checked with Jen; she nodded.

Now to explain enough to satisfy Dad and Mom without saying anything. Right.

Ignoring the admonition to myself, I covered everything I could remember about Lisa, from her first wiggle two days ago, to the sports interview with Jen, to the lunchroom, and on to the principal's office. They didn't interrupt once. Not even when I described my discussion with the social workers. They did notice, when I waved my hands, Jen didn't move hers from my leg. I ended with, "I'm not going to discuss Lisa's answers to the questions."

Dad agreed. "No, you're not. We don't need to know. However, you had better make notes. You could be a witness in court."

Double great. Dad and Jen are on the same page. I don't want to be in the same book.

"You did a good job with what you knew," Dad said, "making decisions and going to the right people. Lisa chose well, confiding in you."

"You're like a hero," Cindy added, trading smiles with Jen.

Mom thoroughly dampened the scene with, "What happened in the park? Who were you watching?"

I sucked in my breath when I saw silent tears. Cindy brought Jen tissues from the kitchen. I wanted to stop, but she pushed against me, so I continued.

If I didn't have their undivided attention before, I got it when I described the argument across the street. I left out the words, but told them Jen's dad drove away with Lisa's mom and saw us.

"Why didn't he didn't stop for Jenni?" Mom asked.

"Mom, his car has two seats."

She digested this and the entire conversation while we waited and watched; even Dad watched.

"We don't need to call because Mr. Carling knows Jenni is with us, which I understand. I don't understand why the Carlings would bail out Lisa's mother. Do you know why?"

I could feel Jen crushing my fingers. "Dad, Mom, Cindy, we need a time out."

"Answer the question first," Dad directed, "then you can have your time out."

It was almost imperceptible, but Jen shook her head. Everyone caught it. Cindy took the hint and left. Dad and Mom locked into mental combat with each other. I had no idea if either was on my side.

"Dad, I need to know Jenni is okay with what I say before I continue."

He broke off his contest with Mom and turned to me. "Jon, we are your parents. We get to know."

"Anything about me, yes, but this isn't about me. Please, give us a few minutes."

Dad faced Jen, who met him eye to eye. She didn't say a word, but no way could he misread her face.

"All right," he said. "We take a break. We'll be in the kitchen fixing dinner. When you are ready, come get us." Since he already had Mom's hand, he pulled on it to get her moving and slipped his arm around her. Mom reciprocated.

Jen leaned against me and whispered, "Thank you," about a dozen times in my ear, letting me slip my arms around her. "You holding up?" I asked.

"I guess I am," she replied, "but I'd like to think about something else for a second."

Without parental supervision, or more accurately, parental observation, I decided to give her something else to think about, like a kiss, only this time, I initiated it, nudging her upright, and facing her.

At first, she may have thought I wanted to let go. When I touched my lips to hers, she got a better assessment of the situation. Her eyes went wide, and she moved back. "You kissed me," she said, almost in anger.

"Something else to think about?" I asked, getting a solid glare for my effort, a little one sided.

"I wasn't ready," she said, snarling at me.

"Well, I wasn't ready when you kissed me."

Typical guy lame answer.

She softened, a smile replacing the frown. "Okay, let's try it again when we are both ready."

She moved closer, but waved her hands in front of her face and took two deep breaths.

"What are you doing?" I asked.

"Trying to get ready." She took three more breaths, shook herself, leaned forward, closed her eyes, and said, "Okay, I'm ready."

"Are you sure?" I asked.

"Sure," she replied. "Hurry, before I'm not sure."

All the encouragement I needed. Lips touched, like last time, except this time she stayed. I controlled the touch, softer and longer. I had a fleeting concern about the smack, but it came on its own.

John C. Pelkey

This is kissing, like in the movies or in books, except this time I'm participating, and get to share my lips with the most wonderful set of lips ever to exist. Everything is wow.

Jen looked flush, but not nearly as much as I felt.

"Have you kissed anyone before?" she asked, somewhat breathless, leaning back and watching me.

"No," I answered.

"Me neither."

I tried to act cool and grown up, while trying to figure out where the oxygen went. Finally, I had to gasp, realizing I'd been holding my breath.

"Ah ha. You hold your breath at the wrong times, too," Jen said. "We can work on that."

I'm ready and willing.

Parental concerns prevailed and brought me back to the subject of our moment together. "Okay, we thought about something else," I said, getting a soft smile without eye contact for a reward. "What do I tell them?" The eye contact came back, but the answer wasn't exactly on task.

"You tell them I love you," she replied, her eyes glistening.

That should go over well. However, it will get their minds off the current concerns, or maybe add to them.

"Okay, I'll tell them I love you and you tell them you love me."

"Do you?" she asked.

"I do," I replied, before I realized what ceremony it fit. "Oops."

Jen burst out laughing, her first laugh since longer than I could remember. She refocused, her hands fanning her face, with the slight hint of a pout accompanying her smile. It reminded me of Lisa, who did the same thing. I guessed it meant I was back to the subject.

"I tell them we think your mom is related to Lisa's mom. Since no one has verified it, we honestly don't know. We don't mention the words they said."

"I don't want to remember the words they said. It sounded like Mom accused Dad of sleeping with her sister."

"Maybe it happened a long time ago," I said, trying to soften the blow.

"Oh, like maybe nine months longer than however old Lisa is. That long ago?" Jen asked, sarcasm biting through each word. She shook her head and her shoulders. "I don't want to sound like Mom. You talk. Continue, please?" She squeezed my hands, pleading with her fingers and her eyes.

Dad interrupted, stepping in from the foyer. I wondered how much he had heard. "Let's eat first," he said. "Jenni, you are invited to join us since your alternatives to us feeding you are ambiguous."

I pulled Jen up. "Alternatives are ambiguous?" I asked as we walked by.

170

To Face The World

"It's how you'd say it," he replied, swishing my hair.

After grace and some food intake, I shared the revelation of how Jen's mom and Lisa's mom looked like sisters, which was why they were together in front of the police station.

"What was so upsetting?" Mom asked.

I had no idea how to respond. Jen leaned forward. She faced Dad and Mom, cleared her throat, and said, "I didn't know my mom had a sister. Lisa and I could be cousins. Everyone knows and no one would tell me. I don't trust..." She stopped, clearly trying to save what was left of her composure. "Sorry," she whispered, sniffing. The room went silent.

Mom broke the silence with, "I think I understand why you wanted the time out, Jenni. You have enough on your plate, learning you have an aunt and a cousin. You don't need anything added by us. We should contact your parents, right after we finish eating."

Good job, Mom.

I only thought it because if I had said it I would have undone it.

Dessert was peach pie Cindy had made with canned peaches, topped with ice cream. Jen shook her head when asked if she wanted some, but I cut an extra-large piece with two scoops and we shared it, feeding Jen and me alternating bites with my fork. This was fun until I realized everyone had stopped eating to watch.

The front doorbell proclaimed, like all good things, this had come to an end. Dad stared us all back into our seats and went by himself to answer the door. I could feel Jen tense when she heard her father's voice. Instead of Dad coming to fetch her, the front door closed, and the voices diminished. We watched them walk past the barn, Mr. Carling waving his hands and Dad listening. Although taller than I was, from behind, Mr. Carling could be a boy walking with a man when next to Dad.

Jen thanked Mom and Cindy, and added to me, "If I don't get to, please thank your dad." She picked up her backpack and stepped outside the front door. I followed, dreading what had to come next.

She leaned against me on the porch, holding her backpack in front. "Jon," she whispered. "I know I can't, but if I could."

"What?" I asked.

"Live here."

"Not as fancy," I offered.

"Don't care." I heard a sigh. "The kiss, you made the good better than the bad. I will always remember."

No way am I ever going to forget.

Too soon, they were back. "Ready, Jenni?" Mr. Carling asked. She shook her head.

Dad caught it. He walked past me, touching my shoulder. Since he didn't tell me to come in with him, I stayed. There we were, Mr. Carling next to his car, Jen on the porch next to me. Almost a standoff.

After Dad went into the house, Mr. Carling continued. "Jenni, I'm

John C. Pelkey

sorry you had to see the incident downtown. Emotions were running high and words spoken in anger. Yes, we've been keeping something from you. It's all in the past now. We will get through this."

Suddenly, he realized I existed. "Jon, I appreciate how you stayed with Jenni. I know Elise told you not to, but I'm glad you ignored her. Sometimes, we adults don't see things clearly and our decisions need further consideration."

He sounded like what a candidate would say in a speech, not what the parent says to the boyfriend, or even a sort of boyfriend like me.

He faced Jen. "For now, it's the two of us. Your mom and her sister left for NY to visit with their father. No, I'll be straight with you; he summoned them. Yes, you have a grandfather. I know; it's complicated. I promise to explain everything to you when we get home."

"I have a grandfather," Jen repeated, as if saying the word helped reinforce the knowledge. "Do I have a grandmother?" she asked.

"He's married, but she's younger than your mom."

"Oh, so I have a grandfather, married to someone who could be my big sister, along with an aunt and a cousin, and no mom, all in one day."

Despite her words, I couldn't help but notice the feeling of relief, the tension easing from her clenched shoulders, perhaps due to her mother's absence. She reached back and caught my hand, squeezing it three times, and handed me her backpack to carry for her, a clever way for her to give us thirty more seconds together.

I walked her to the Z, setting her backpack in the trunk when Mr. Carling opened it from his seat, and held Jen's door for her.

"Meet you at school tomorrow morning?" I asked.

"No," she said, catching me by surprise. "Meet you on the bus. If I walk three blocks over, I can catch your bus. Lots less than you walk."

"You can ride the bus?" I asked.

"I can. The person who tells me I can't isn't here to tell me."

I watched her ride away, her fingers spread across the window, and mine spread in response. I tried to keep back the eroding feeling this was the last time we would see each other, and wondered if it was going to rear up every time we said goodbye. Despite everything, all thoughts landed on Jen. I wanted to memorize every moment we spent together, every detail, every emotion. About her, I felt euphoric and terrified at the same time.

So this is what love feels like.

If I didn't know before, I knew now.

Chapter Twenty

As I turned back toward the house, I spotted Rex, and learned why she had not uttered so much as a single woof at either Jen or her dad. She ran around the corner of the house with her ball, wagging her tail. Instead of coming toward me, she slipped out of sight on the other side of Dad's car. I saw a hand motion and Rex went flying after the ball toward the barn. Cindy stepped out.

"I kept her occupied, so she didn't bark," Cindy said, wiping one hand on her pants. "Rex slobbers."

"She also ran to you instead of me," I said, trying to absorb the situation. "You've been playing catch with my dog?"

"Maybe. I get home before you do and Dave goes to work. Beth rides with your mom, so it leaves Rex and me to hold down the fort."

Rex scrambled back with the ball and dropped it. This time, they allowed me to throw it.

"Are you ready for your parents?" Cindy asked, as we watched Rex run down the ball.

"What do you mean?" I didn't like the forbearing in her question. After the grilling, the meal had gone smoothly, except for Mr. Carling interrupting us at the end.

"They have to be inside freaking out, Jon. Didn't you notice?"

"I noticed they were nice to Jenni. I think she noticed, too."

"We noticed a lot of things, mainly how much Jenni likes you."

Cindy made the next toss, this time toward the street. Rex had started in the wrong direction, reversed course, and actually growled as she slowly trotted by.

"Well, I'm glad you think Jenni likes me. I like her, too."

I do; I even said so, and used the other "L" word.

"I don't mean the holding hands and walking in the park like. More toward naming children and growing old together, a lot more than like."

"Why do you make it sound so ominous?"

"Jon, she wears you."

Cindy quit talking, and I wasn't about to get her going again. I wondered about her "wear" comment.

Jen wears me? Is it because she sits against me when next to me? Or because she leaves her hand on my leg when I stop holding it? Or because she's willing to share my fork? Or is it something else?

Rex walked back, but didn't want to give up the ball this time. We engaged in a nice discussion about dog ball, ending with the ball on the ground and with me trading a dog hug for a face lick. By the time we

John C. Pelkey

finished, Cindy had long since disappeared.

A sudden thought nailed me.

Was Cindy listening?

I didn't know where it came from, but I did know it wasn't about to go away. I also didn't know what to do about it.

"Women," I grumbled. It must have been a barkable offense, as Rex lit into a tirade, which I didn't understand until I turned around and noticed Dave's car, along with Dave and Beth.

"Some watchdog you are," I muttered at Rex.

Woof, she muttered back.

I followed them in the house, and Dad, Mom, and Cindy joined us in the entry. Dave and Beth handed each of us a brown package, tied with string, and with our names written in black marker.

"Bathrobes for everyone!" he proclaimed, after Cindy beat us all in opening hers. "Jon, Cindy told me about your meeting in the hall on Monday morning. Said you turned red when she teased you about your legs. Now you'll be covered."

More important, Cindy will be, too.

Dad seemed a bit skeptical about his plaid robe, but he did try it on. Moose size, it fit. Mine was green, the same color as Jen's eyes. I wondered if they knew.

"Anything exciting happen while we were gone?" Beth asked.

Dad and Mom traded silent admonitions of some sort. They engaged in a bunch of unspoken communication. I wondered if they had always done so and now, finally, I noticed.

When no one else spoke, Cindy did. "We had Jenni as a guest for supper."

"Again?" Beth asked. "Like she is becoming part of the family."

"Two times?" I snapped.

"Two times more than I have had anyone here, lately," Beth countered.

"Well, bring someone," I countered back.

"You have to have someone to bring someone," Beth retorted.

This is going well.

I took her remark as my cue to exit, and trotted up the stairs.

My shirt, still wet with Jen's tears, surprisingly, also came with her smell, aloe and lavender. Before today, I hadn't thought a great deal about her having one. I wadded the shirt, the tears, and the smell, and sailed all three into my laundry basket. I hadn't been a habitual girl-sniffer yet, and I wasn't about to become one.

Still, the wet shirt reminded me of what had happened. Jen cried more than anyone I had encountered, and for good reason. The worst situations my family worked through probably didn't compare to the average situations she dealt with.

I hung up my robe and dug out my notebook, turning to ten pages from the back. Despite my unhappiness in dredging up everything, I wrote what happened, similar to what I told Dad and Mom. It took well over an hour and used up eight of the ten pages.

I was about to congratulate myself for escaping Cindy's false parental alarm when I heard a Dad-knock on my door.

"Hi, Dad," I said, as a way of response. However, he wasn't alone, as Mom popped in behind him. "We need to talk," he said. I could feel Cindy's, *told ya*, floating in behind them.

They glanced at my bed, the only other place to sit in my room.

"How about I come downstairs," I offered. "Give me a minute to use the bathroom."

I mentally patted myself on the back for the excellent stall, and the time it gave me to rehearse. For what, I didn't know.

So what if Jen likes me. Young people have feelings. I have feelings, too.

I thought of an excellent defense, and, flush with anticipated success, I joined them in the living room. I could hear the TV going, so Dave and Cindy had squatters' rights in the family room. The phone rang once, but Beth, as usual, caught it upstairs. Since she didn't holler to anyone, it must have been for her.

Mom and Dad shared the love seat, so I took the couch. I sat where Jen and I had our first both-ready kiss. I tried to stifle a smile, but couldn't help myself.

With an encouraging nudge from Mom, Dad cleared his throat. I realized something almost too much for anyone else to understand; talking to me was harder for them than talking to them was for me.

"Go ahead, Dad," I said, trying to sound encouraging.

"Do you know what this is about?" he asked.

"Cindy--"

No, I'm not bringing up what Cindy said about Jen.

I clamped my mouth shut.

However, saying "Cindy" had thrown them a curve, and they had to reorganize, giving each other questioning looks and no answering looks back. Finally, Dad said, "No, this isn't about Cindy."

I had expected more, but silence again. I realized how difficult I had become to talk to; they thought they had to walk on eggshells around me. I remembered Jen's remark about kids feeling stupid around me, but Dad and Mom were adults. Since they stayed silent, I tried again.

"Dad, please tell me, because I'm not good at guessing."

Dad had decided something. "Jon, we are concerned about your interest in..." He stopped, not a stop like slamming on the brakes, but a stop like running out of gas.

You can't stop. Like telling a joke without the punch line. My interest in... What?

Dad tried again. "I've said this before. You are awfully young to maintain a relationship with a girl, now two girls, both with issues well

John C. Pelkey

beyond your ability to understand, manage, or cope with."

"One girl, Dad," I corrected. "Lisa isn't Jenni, and isn't ever going to be. When I see Lisa, I see a new friend. When I see Jenni, I see how you saw Mom when you were fourteen."

Gotcha. Two can play this, Cindy.

My well-rehearsed comeback fit right in after only four sentences. I mentally high-fived myself, and at the same time worried about overkill, but only for a second.

Dad and Mom didn't even disguise the looks they gave each other. They had been together since he was a freshman in high school. Mom had been the same age as Jen.

After forever, they slowly switched from a stroll down memory lane to parent mode. "Jon, you can't compare your mom and me to Jenni and you," Dad announced. "We're parents now. We have to do for you what we feel is right."

Silence. Maybe they expected me to argue, but since they hadn't shared what they felt was right, they had not given me anything over which I could argue.

"Are you going to tell me?" I asked, breaking the silence.

"Tell you what?" Mom asked.

"What you feel right is."

With, "Excuse me," as a lead, Beth entered the living room. "Um, Jon has a phone call, a girl."

"Who?" I tried to be first, but Dad and Mom, in unison, beat me by a half a breath.

Beth scrunched up her face and flashed her teeth, clearly tense and not willing to answer. Sighing, she mumbled, "Lisa Martin."

Mom opened her mouth, looked at Beth, and closed it. Dad and Mom conferred silently, now becoming a habit.

How am I supposed to know what they want if they never speak to me, or to each other?

Dad waved his hand and said, "Talk and come right back."

Needing no more encouragement, I took off after Beth.

She stopped me in front of the stairs. "You know Lisa Martin well enough for her to call?" she asked, more of an accusation. "Isn't she kind of, well, like beyond you?"

"Lisa's in my class, so yes, I know her. How do you know her?"

"Everyone knows her; she's the hottest girl in high school, and she's not even in high school."

"Wait, the phone rang ten minutes ago."

My turn for accusations.

"I told her you were busy for a moment, so we talked. She named the guys in my class who have hit on her often enough for her to know their names, so I could scratch them off my future considerations list, should I ever be in a position to consider any of them."

176

To Face The World

"For ten minutes?" I asked.

"She's been hit on a lot."

"What did you talk about?" This time I made more of a demand.

"Okay, she mentioned a couple of guys, already, and she mostly talked about you. Like you have become a rock star or something, but she didn't tell me why."

I shot up the stairs, and crashed to a halt in front of Beth's door.

What can I say to Lisa?

I had anticipated some parental limitations on our conversation, but Dad and Mom had been quiet. From the sequence of today's events, Lisa couldn't know she and Jen were cousins, unless she already knew and didn't say anything. I decided on the best thing to do, nothing.

After hellos, Lisa began. "You said I could call. I wanted to hear a friendly voice." She paused, and added, "Your sister is nice."

"You know my sister?" I asked.

"No, but we found we have something in common; we both don't like the same boys."

"Which boys?"

"All the boys we both know."

"Thanks."

"We don't count you as a boy."

I didn't know if not counting me as a boy was good or bad, but with Dad and Mom waiting, the small talk had to go. "Has anyone official talked to you?"

"Someone called Fred. My mom is out on bail, but has a no contact order. If I try to compromise it, she goes back to jail. They said she had someone place everything from our apartment in storage and I don't have access. So this is like day one. For starters, Martha had to take me clothes shopping."

"Fred and Martha? Where are you?" I asked.

"I'm one block from the middle school. I'm staying with Fred and Martha Van Buren; he is related to a former president."

Yeah, a one hundred fifty years ago president.

"They go to the same church as Jenni Carling. They said they met you. Do you go there?"

"Jenni attends the Assembly of God church; I visited there with her once."

"Well, I get to go to church for the first time ever next Sunday. Hard to imagine being involved with drugs and sex one week and going to church the next. Who knew? I guess I'll see Jenni there sometime, maybe."

If Lisa could sit with Jen in church, Jen wouldn't have to sit alone. I need to get them together. Time to make my pitch.

"Lisa, you need to call Jenni."

"Jon, I don't know Jenni."

John C. Pelkey

"You will. She will be another friendly voice, really."

"What if I get her creepy dad?"

Nice description of Uncle Ralph, although him leering at you doesn't make him someone you want to be alone with. In his defense, you advertise, and I've given you my share of looks, too, probably bordering on leering. However, Jen has her own phone.

"Lisa, you shouldn't get her dad; the number I gave you goes to the phone in her bedroom. If you do get him, tell him whom you are and ask if you can talk to Jenni. If he hangs up, call me back. Okay?"

"Okay. Call Jenni. If I can't talk to her, call you. If I can talk to her, will you let me talk to you about things tomorrow?" she asked.

"You really are coming to school tomorrow?"

"Jon, I've done this before, more than once. Mom's been arrested twice before for drugs. Last time, my placement was for almost two years. Moving into a new home is like, 'What did you do today? Nothing much.' Sure, I could stay home and pretend to need to get over it, but, I'm not going to. I don't want to go back to same old, same old. I want to start my new life as soon as possible, so to answer your question, yes I am."

Wow. What I could barely imagine happening to Lisa, to her it was like cleaning her fingernails. Done and time to move to something else.

"Jon, I talk a good game, but it doesn't mean I won't cry myself to sleep. I need you to help me keep my game face going. Someone who won't criticize..." She stopped.

"Nothing to criticize, Lisa. You took the best step you could. You got out. Now, the next best step you can take in your new life is to call Jenni; call her, now."

"Call her now. Thanks, Jon, for everything. You won't regret what you did for me."

Regrets. I already have regrets. I'm not so sure sending you to Jen is a good idea from your point of view. Jen's family isn't top notch, or anything close to it. Otherwise, you and Jen would already know each other, would have all your lives, and you would be living there instead of in a placement, as you call it, with who knows what for a future.

I regret sending you to Jen from Jen's side, too. I don't like the idea of Jen getting the call cold. However, if someone is to tell you, it's better Jen shares and you begin to be cousins than for me to be stumbling around and making all the dust bunnies reproduce.

I passed Beth going up on the way down, giving her a *thank you* smile and getting a *welcome* one back.

Ha, Dad and Mom, you aren't the only ones who can communicate without talking.

I peeked into the family room. Dave and Cindy shared the couch, Dave asleep. Cindy waved. Strange for a couple their age to be doing nothing. They didn't even touch.

To Face The World

Back in the living room, Dad and Mom hadn't moved. Dad asked, "What did you tell Lisa?" to begin the conversation.

"I told her to call Jenni. If Lisa gets to know, better if she hears it from Jenni than from me."

They smiled, visibly relieved. "A fine thing you did, Jon," Dad said, "letting Jenni decide what to tell Lisa instead of tooting your own horn."

I sat back on the couch and waited. When they waited longer, I opened the next round with, "What's right? Remember? You were about to tell me before the phone call."

Dad cleared his throat, again and said, "Jon, you are too young to have a girlfriend, but it is obvious both you and Jenni think she is your girlfriend."

Time for another counter attack.

"Did you mind Alyssa being my girlfriend?"

"Think about it, Jon. However long she was your 'girlfriend,' we never met Alyssa. She and you limited your time together to school hours, lunchtime mostly, if I remember correctly. Unlike Alyssa, we've seen quite a bit of Jenni. Since you mentioned, more than once, how bossy Alyssa was, we knew you weren't going anywhere with her, so it didn't worry us. We have noticed you have a completely different view of Jenni."

Warning, counter attack failed.

I made plane-crashing sounds in my head.

Time for the next counter attack.

"You want me to dump Jenni right in the middle of teaching her how to run?" I mentally congratulated myself for my brilliance and quick response.

They appeared baffled for a few seconds, but got over it way too fast. "Jon, are you supposed to be training Jenni?" Dad asked. "Even if you do knock a few seconds off her time, it doesn't matter much."

Doesn't matter? I was playing nice, but now the gloves come off. Which means what? I have no idea. Doesn't mean I can't try.

"Dad, I have the school record in the 1600-meter run. It means I have the fastest time ever in the history of the school."

"Jon, there isn't much history for a school that hasn't been open for twenty years."

"Dad, there are no track records older than twenty years. If the school had been open for a thousand years, I'd still have the record."

"And?"

It wasn't much, but at least I had their attention.

"In nine days, Jenni is going to break my record, and probably the state's middle school record at the same time. She's going to be the fastest girl ever for 1600 meters."

"All because of your coaching?"

"Yes, all because of my coaching. I'm not only teaching her how to

John C. Pelkey

run faster, I'm teaching her to believe in herself, and how her running can make a difference. While I'm teaching her, I'm also teaching me how to believe I can make a difference."

"How to believe?" Mom asked.

Inspiration slapped me in the face.

Could it be?

I had never been a deeply thoughtful person, in terms of higher purpose. Miraculously, I felt like I had one.

Did God put me on this planet to teach Jen how to run? Maybe.

My far away thoughts tumbled back into the living room. Dad and Mom, the two most patient people on the planet, sat quietly waiting for my return.

"Yes, Mom, how to believe in something, like teaching Jenni how to run, maybe it's my purpose, my opportunity to make a difference."

They both smiled, caring smiles, more at each other than at me. Dad picked up his feet and made a broom sweeping motion.

Okay, so, maybe I've come on a tiny bit thick.

"Are you trying to negotiate something here, son?" Dad asked. "I feel I need to ask for the sticker price."

Dad thinks I sound like a used car salesman, one of the occupations at the bottom of his trust level, so he says.

He smiled to soften it, but it still stung.

"No, Dad, we're not negotiating. Negotiations are between peers."

This time, Dad stopped for over a minute and, ignoring me, focused on Mom. When he faced me, his fatherly composure had turned into an angry bear snarl.

"Peers? Where did you get that, son? Negotiating with you is like climbing the Empire State Building, from the outside." He shook his head. "No, we are not negotiating because you don't make the decisions. What is it you want me to consider?"

Like I can win the battles and still lose the war. No, I don't want a war. I want them to understand how important this is.

I carefully phrased my response, slow and precise. "I want eight more days to prove a decision to let us continue running is a good one. Please come to the track meet a week from Friday, and then decide."

Dad and Mom conferred, facing each other and holding hands. I got up to leave, but Mom waved me back. She whispered a bit more, Dad nodding and shaking his head. They turned to face me. When Mom caught me smiling, she said, "Jon, we haven't told you our decision yet."

"I know, Mom; it's not why I'm smiling."

"Okay," Dad said, "I'll bite. Why are you smiling?"

"Because you guys have been married almost twenty years, and you still like each other."

It wasn't an attempt to sway them, but telling parents how cool they were couldn't hurt.

180

"Thank you, son," Dad said. When he paused, Mom bumped him. "Like you, we know Dave had a girlfriend at fourteen, although we didn't meet her. You know we told Dave and Beth they couldn't go out alone with someone until they turned sixteen. They objected, but we held firm, especially for Beth."

Poor Beth. All this did was keep her out of the pool of available girls until everyone else had experience and an increase to their level of confidence.

Having gone awry with Alyssa as my first attempt, I know how much experience means, even with what little I have. It helps knowing Jen isn't the pushy type. Any decent comparison would have derailed Alyssa eventually, even without any external event.

While I blipped, Dad had been rattling along about how tough Beth had it, something I already knew. I tried to refocus before I missed something important. Hopefully, I succeeded.

"...assess the situation, as now with you. Well, it is a little different. We recognize the distinction between wanting to date and having a goal. So we will defer until after the track meet."

Yes! I wanted to jump up and pump my fist, but remained obedient, quiet, and attentive.

"...need you to recognize how tough it would be to allow you to regularly see a girl at fourteen when your sister isn't seeing anyone at sixteen."

I knew you don't mean it like it came out, but you indicate if Beth has a boyfriend, she won't make waves about me having a girlfriend, and to you, keeping the peace is as important as is anything else. It isn't much, but it is a glimmer, even if I don't have any hope of Beth finding someone.

What to tell Jen? Nothing, easy answer. This isn't her problem; this is my problem. I need to work harder.

I slowly made my way upstairs, finding my dateless nemesis waiting at the top.

"You know Lisa Martin? Ten guys in my class would become your best friend if I told them."

"Lisa has enough trouble with males; she doesn't need my help."

When I turned to walk away, she added, "Not why I wanted to talk. I wondered if I got you in trouble. My comment about Jenni living here."

Were you listening, too?

I wanted to make a snappy comeback, but shrugged instead. "They are coming to my track meet a week from Friday to see if I've been any help to reducing Jenni's running times. Then they'll decide something."

"Want me to come?" she asked, now contrite.

"Sure, it would be great."

"Maybe I will. Not like I need to be home to get ready for a date or anything."

Beth disappeared back into her room. It dawned on me why I saw more of Cindy than Beth. Moody Beth lived in her room, so Cindy

John C. Pelkey

stayed out during waking hours.

Speaking of which, there she was, Cindy, following me through my door. "Got a minute?" she asked. Without waiting for an answer, she plopped on my bed. I sat in my desk chair.

"I met Jenni once, last year in the mall. I was spying on Dave and she caught me. I was about to tell her to butt out or something worse, when she said, 'If you like him, go say hi.' I asked her not to tell anyone, and she promised she wouldn't."

"She didn't."

"I thought as much. I'm good at keeping secrets. Jenni is way better."

"Maybe she doesn't remember."

"She remembers. We both remembered the first second we saw each other the day I moved here."

So now I know what their first meeting, lengthy, mutual appraisal was all about.

"What did you do?" I asked.

"I went up and said hi to him, just like she suggested. The rest, as they say... Well, here I am."

Cindy got up, but stopped at the door. "Jenni is so sweet. You both are good for each other. I'm glad for you, even with the issues."

"Thanks, Cindy," I said. She blew me a kiss and disappeared.

Sitting on my bed, I could feel exhaustion trying to overwhelm me. So much had happened between when Lisa wiggled past us only a few days ago and now, including Cindy's new revelation. My life was spiraling, up or down, I didn't know. I needed to regain control, if such a thing were possible.

Tomorrow is going to be a calm day. I am going to stay out of any and all situations.

I had made up my mind.

I drew the explosion on my calendar. Since I was into warfare, in a preemptive strike, I drew a straight line through the next day.

Nothing is going to happen tomorrow.

Chapter Twenty-One

Anticipation accompanied me step for step to the bus stop at the bottom of Notch Hill Road. The concept of riding to school with Jen had never been even a dream before. Today, it would become a reality. Thinking about Dad, Mom, and their concerns, I changed reality to maybe. I didn't want to count on anything until it happened.

Will I get to sit with her?

Seemed a silly question, but it was foremost on my mind. At my stop on the beginning of the route, the bus wasn't crowded, and with only me to pick up, it didn't change much. However, lots of kids lived between my house and Jen's house, plus her street was on a different route. I wasn't certain they would even let her on the bus from a stop not matching where she lived.

All thoughts scrambled as I approached the intersection, maple tree, and bus stop. Jen stood on the corner, watching me watch her. Instead of her normal sweatshirt, jeans, and running shoes, she wore a red, brown, and green plaid vest over a light green blouse, a short, pleated dark-green skirt, knee socks matching her blouse, and fancy, soft, brown jester boots. Now with her clothes fitting tighter, she had more curves than I remembered, on top anyway.

I need a camera; you are as pretty as a picture.

When I stopped, she spun around, giving me a three hundred sixty degree view and even more leg when she swished her skirt. She alluded cute from every angle. "Whatcha think? Dad said I could wear girl clothes today. He took me shopping last night."

"You look great," I said, taking her hands. "What are you doing here?"

"If I'm going to catch the bus, I may as well catch it here. Here is no further from my house than it is from your house."

"How did you know where I caught it?" I asked.

"I didn't. However, there's no other way in or out." She pointed up the street. "The bus had to come by here sooner or later."

She let go and waved at the tree. "Will you do something for me?" she asked. When I nodded okay, she added, "Leave your backpack."

I set it down next to hers and followed her to the tree. She ran her fingers along the side and slipped around to the back. I found her leaning against it, one knee up and bent so her foot could rest on the bark. The pose made her short skirt shorter and the rest of her cuter.

"Okay, now the best part," she said, "only if you want to."

"Best part?" I asked.

John C. Pelkey

"If it is okay and you want to, well, like I want to, share our first ever good morning kiss. Maybe? Of course, it means we have to do it, kiss, that is, each other... here... now."

Although I felt trapped, along with the guy feeling of wanting to initiate all the innuendos, I decided not to object.

Not to object? I need to slap myself upside the head. What other guy, breathing, conscious, and in his right mind, would object to a girl as lovely as you asking for a kiss?

I put my hands on the tree on each side, leaned in turtle-slow to enjoy the anticipation, and...

Honk!

Oh no. I've forgotten about Dave.

Before I could think, I popped out from behind the tree. Dave, Cindy, and Beth sat at the intersection in Dave's car. "What are you doing behind there?" he asked. "Taking a leak?"

Cindy slugged him in the shoulder and he waved and drove off. Cindy waved, too, but Beth focused on the backpacks, the green one next to my brown one, and not on me.

"Wow," Jen said, giggling, as she peeked around the other side of the tree after they disappeared. "Close call. Good job of covering, I hope."

"Except Beth noticed two backpacks."

"We didn't do anything," she said, more of a pout. "We didn't get the chance."

I thought of Officer Thompson's admonition. *Perception.*

"Well," she said, staring at the ground, then up at me. "If we are going to be accused..."

The distant bus sound interrupted us. As Jen didn't appear to notice, I said, "Bus is coming." Maybe she didn't know what a distant bus sounded like. With reluctance, I led her to our backpacks.

She leaned against me as we waited, her hair fluffed and in my nose. I remembered the scent from yesterday, the aloe and lavender.

Here I am, sniffing her again, after I promised myself I wouldn't.

We watched the bus climb the hill to the intersection, like a big, yellow turtle. I let Jen go first, a good thing. The bus driver stuck his hand out to stop her and she slipped backward off the top step. I was there and fast enough to catch her.

"Oh dear," he said. "I am so sorry. Thank you, Jon." He pulled out a clipboard, and while reading it, said, "It's just... I don't know who you are and don't have you on my list, whoever you are. Are you new?"

Jen kept silent, maybe a bit stunned, so I jumped in.

"She's Jennifer Carling. You don't have her listed because this is the first time she's ridden the bus."

He wrote her name down. "Do you have to cross a street to walk here?" he asked, facing her.

Oh, oh. Jen has to cross half a dozen streets to walk here.

184

"My dad drops me on his way to work. It is the most convenient location. I don't walk across any streets."

He bought it and let her go. I felt relief and a bit slimy at the same time, realizing we had shared in some conspiracy.

She sat in the first row, where she saw me when we met the bus at school. "This is where you sit," she said, running her fingers along the top as if it were a shrine.

I would have preferred further back, but like with Pastor Kamorkov's congregation, each year, everyone had informally assigned themselves a seat on the first day of school. For all of middle school, this had been mine.

As I kept my backpack in my lap, Jen leaned hers against mine and caught the seam of my jeans right above the knee with her free hand. I held her backpack, and she held me.

"Didn't you say the distance from your house was the same as from my house?" I whispered.

"I did, and it is. I didn't say I walked. Dad doesn't want to leave me in the house when he goes to work. He doesn't want me standing at a bus stop alone or with kids I don't know. His choices were to drive me to school or leave me here. So here works. I'm not alone and I know you. Problem solved."

"Your parents left you for two days."

"Yeah, and they got in big trouble, too."

"From who?"

"From whom, not from who." She laughed at the face I made. "I learned a little about my grandfather from Dad last night. His name is E. H. Martin; my 'grandmother' is Sarah. She's still in her twenties. He's not someone to mess with. He is furious with Lisa's mom. Dad thinks he will send her to stay with relatives back in Italy."

"Italy?" I said it too loud. "You're Italian?"

"Shhh." Jen let go and put her finger to my mouth. "We shouldn't talk about Mom here."

I stopped talking and started thinking.

Italy? Lisa and Jen are blonde. Tiny noses. Not Italian. However, their moms have dark hair and big honk... No, they have some nice noses, even if a little bigger. No, a lot bigger. Still a resemblance, though, the eyes and especially the cheeks. They make the moms and Jen appear younger than their age. They would make Lisa appear younger, too, except some of her other assets negate the younger girl look with an older girl look.

A countering thought interrupted my other thoughts, something to consider later.

Yes, they resemble their moms, but do they resemble Jen's dad?

The next thought dismissed the other thoughts.

Italian. Her grandfather, someone not to mess with and Italian?

These thoughts swirled throughout my head. Of all the thoughts

John C. Pelkey

swirling around, the ones in response to, *shouldn't talk about it here,* swirled the most.

If Dad seems concerned about my relationship with Jen without knowing this, what's he going to think now? Into what do I have myself?

Jen noticed my composure decomposing. She whispered, "I'm sorry."

"No, you're right. We need to think this through carefully before we draw any conclusions. Babbling about it in public isn't careful thinking."

What I said relieved both of us and readied Jen for my next question. "Did Lisa call you?"

"Yes, we talked for a minute or two. Dad said to wait until we know more to tell Lisa. I didn't say anything, except we would meet her at school."

I felt creepy checking to see if anyone listened, but I did it anyway. No one cared. Jen caught me and had to work to stifle a laugh. "Way too obvious," she whispered.

Obvious. Something about the word. What? I don't remember.

Jen flashed me hand signals in sequence and I realized she knew sign language. We had referenced it as a separate American language it in Honors English and I had a book, but all I knew was the alphabet, and barely enough to follow her, even if she went slow.

After she repeated it several times, I figured it out. "Obvious."

She smiled. Not her normal smile, but one I had not seen before, an expression of gratitude, no teeth, and her lips pursed.

You're grateful because I can barely read sign language. If we practice, me especially, we can communicate without words, something I already know you do quite well. I need to catch up.

As we left the bus, Jen grabbed my hand and turned us away from the school entrance. "Come on. Lisa asked if we could walk her to school to help her get through this. We have enough time before school starts."

When we reached the sidewalk, we could see Lisa standing in front of a house a block away. We walked; she walked, and we met her halfway. She wore a pair of long, baggy shorts with a bibbed top and a white blouse, not the see through type.

"Whatcha think?" She spun around in front of us. "I tried a baggy sweatshirt. It's you, Jenni, but it's not me. This is okay, isn't it?" She stopped talking and gave Jen a thorough evaluation. "Excuse me for being blunt, Jenni, but you are so cute today."

"Okay, so are you," Jen said, rolling her eyes.

"I know where I'm good, boobs and legs, but you are way more than looking cute. You're like Caesar; you came, you saw, and you conquered cute. No wonder Jon likes you so much."

Any thoughts of accidently revealing the cousin situation or worrying about her transition went south as Lisa dominated the conversation, a complete contrast to Jen. Even more interesting, none of

186

To Face The World

Lisa's conversation was about Lisa. Chatty and controlling, yes; self-centered, no. She talked like a news reporter in everyday conversation.

Did she always like a reporter?

I realized I didn't know because before a few days ago, I had never had a conversation with Lisa or even listened to her talk to someone else.

All Jen had to do was nod or supply a short answer, something she was already good at. Me, walking on the outside and even holding hands with her, pretty much forgotten.

While walking next to Jen and trying not to blatantly check her out, I noticed a reason for her massive amount of cute. Although well applied, for the first time I could remember, Jen wore makeup, including a light eyeliner and something on her cheeks.

The next school hurdle was the front steps, with Jim, Ed, and Dan acting like the three amigos, lurking in front of the doors. The closer we got, the more their faces lit. I thought of letting go of Jen's hand, but it had become a vice, something she did when tense.

Before they could do or say anything, Lisa took control. She trotted up the stairs ahead of us and walked directly over to them. They were unprepared for her and had no opportunity to escape.

"Hi, guys," she said. "I'm Lisa. You're some of Jon's friends. I saw you hanging around with him at track practice."

She held out her hand and forced each of them to shake it and tell her their name. She repeated it back to them, twice.

While this event occupied their time, I managed to pry loose Jen's hand. Lisa grabbed it and towed her toward the office, saying over her shoulder, "Jenni has this plan to help me move into the empty locker next to her. See you at lunch?" Lisa's bravado diminished the closer she came to the office, and she skidded to a stop. "Jenni?" she mumbled.

"Come on, Lisa" Jen waved at me with her free hand, and in a reverse of how they started, she pulled Lisa through the door, leaving me with my three "friends," all in various stages of Lisa encounter recovery.

"All this time," Ed said, "we try to meet Lisa, and all we had to do was hang out with you."

"Now she thinks we're your wing men or something," Dan added. He and Ed walked away, shaking their heads. I wandered toward my locker, but found Jim matching my stride.

"Everyone thinks Lisa's hot," he said. "But Jenni, what happened? She was a cute ten-year-old yesterday. Today's she's smokin'."

He shook his head, giving me the opportunity to jump into the conversation, but I didn't bite. At the intersection, he caught my shoulder and mumbled, "Sorry," stopping me. I still didn't bite, as keeping my mouth shut also kept my foot out.

"Look, Jon," he said, letting go and slipping his hands in his pockets. "Don't get me wrong, okay? Two months ago, you were the mayor of

187

John C. Pelkey

Dorksville. Now you're Joe Stud. I didn't see that coming. You appear to be the same to me."

"Appearances can be deceiving," I said quietly, watching him strain to hear me. "As Lisa would say, read the book before you write the book report."

I had no idea what Lisa would say, but it was fun to leave him standing with his mouth open as I walked away.

At lunch, Lisa waited for the group to assemble at our table before asking to join us. Ed and Dan made a huge space between them for her to sit, but Tom negated it by gently nudging them both over and leaving her room on the end next to Trish and across from me. He moved to my side next to Lydia.

After the morning's exchanges, I wondered what Lisa would do, be quiet like Jen, or be something else. Lisa opted for something else as she talked to everyone at our table. I could see how nervous she made the guys, except Tom. With Trish with him, he wasn't about to go fishing.

Lisa's first contribution to me was, "Today, I finish my article on Jenni and you. Mrs. Koffman supplied a photo. I heard you caught a crook, Jon. You've been busy. Everyone wants to know about it."

Lisa was correct. The school had been circulating two stories, starring me. They heard the burglar one correctly. They knew Lisa had moved in down the street, and I had something to do with it. They didn't know any more details, but they pumped me as much as possible between classes, I told everyone I couldn't discuss either story. So far, they had all bought it.

No way is it going to work with Lisa moving to our lunch table. The more people see her talking to me, the more they'll want to know why.

Lisa's second contribution came after I finished eating. "Can we talk a sec?" she asked, pointing outside with her eyes. It felt like everyone watched as we disposed of our trays and dishes, and stepped outside instead of going into the hallway.

I led Lisa to the school sign by the street and leaned against it. I wanted everyone to see we were on the up and up. Lisa leaned on the other side, giving us about six feet of space.

"You know what happened to my mom."

It wasn't a question. I felt cornered. How could I tell Lisa and how could I not.

"I think you should know something." She stopped talking and moved closer, ending less than two feet away. "I know."

You know what?

She studied me for a second, complete with eye contact. "It was Jenni's idea to move away from my used-to-be friends, who now aren't so friendly. Her idea for me to ask to join your group for lunch. Everyone else I know is caught up on my old life."

She dropped her eyes. "Drugs," she whispered, "among other

188

things. If I don't want to do drugs, I have to change friends. No more flaunting, too. I don't fit in with them anymore. I want to fit in with you, except at your table, I scare everyone. When I talk to Ed, he shakes. Dan isn't much better. Jamie and Lydia don't give me any eye contact and mumble when I ask them questions."

"Tom and Trish aren't scared."

Lisa laughed. "Tom is the only boy in this whole school who doesn't know I exist. He is like married to Trish, and she is to him. Even more than Jenni and you."

"Talk to Trish. You won't intimidate her. Everyone talks to Trish. Since Tom's the biggest guy in the school, neither of them care about who talks to whom. The boys have no chance and the girls aren't jealous."

"Okay," Lisa said, "I'll talk to Trish. I guess I've already started with you, thank you, and Jenni came after you. Now, Trish. We have the next class together. If I hurry..."

Lisa paused, but smiled a goodbye and split when I mouthed, "Go ahead."

As I watched her wave before going in the door, I realized another huge difference between Lisa and Jen.

Jen always looks directly at me when we talk, virtually never breaking eye contact. Lisa's eye contact never lasts more than two seconds, and she mostly looks away, although not at other people. Jen looks, but doesn't talk, and Lisa talks, but doesn't look. Interesting contrast.

I met Jen going from PE to choir. Even with her hair damp and the extra color on her face gone, she still looked great. I helped carry her backpack, swinging it between us. It wasn't holding hands, but still fun.

Someday, we could be doing this with a kid, our kid.

I caught myself; or rather, a shiver caught me.

What are you thinking? You're fourteen already.

Track practice was agony. I didn't think missing one day would matter. I guessed my body revolted against the strain I had put it through the previous day. I picked a good time for it to happen. The coach considered the Friday meet a coast, as we played the weakest school. North Valley was another matter; like us, they were undefeated.

I noticed Jen struggling, too. Even back in her oversized sweatshirt, she appeared to be uncomfortable. "You okay?" I asked when we took a break at the same time.

"Not exactly," she muttered. "I have on the wrong clothes for running." She caught me checking her out and added, "Underneath."

"You look different today, really nice."

"You think so? I wear an inch of padding and show some leg, and everyone thinks I'm single and free on Friday."

She laughed at my frown and rubbed the space between my eyebrows until I relaxed.

John C. Pelkey

"It's a phrase my mom uses, the 'everyone thinks I'm single and free on Friday' part. Not the other part. Don't frown; I turned them all down. Now I know what Lisa goes through every day. Tomorrow I'm going back to sweatshirts and jeans."

She stopped and watched the sky, almost glazing over, before facing me. "Last time I wore a skirt to school was the day I met you. Remember, at the locker? When I told Mom I met a boy, she made me wear jeans to school from then on. Now she's gone for a day, and I'm back in a skirt. Didn't even think about it until now. Means I can stop wearing a ton of clothes when I race. No Mom to tell me not to."

"You said you were comfortable."

"I lied."

I tried to conjure up something intelligent to say, and, failing, considered saying something stupid. Instead, one of Dave's, *I know way more about girls than you do,* speeches filtered out the rest.

When you're with a girl, LB, sometimes it's best just to keep your mouth shut.

Jen, watching my face as always, added, "You'll have to suffer seeing me girl-dressed one last time today. I'm riding the bus home."

We went back to our separate running groups. Despite my best effort not to stare, I couldn't help but notice the difference after Jen pointed it out. Not only was she bigger, but she bounced, a tiny bit.

"Quit looking," she signed the next time she caught me watching her, exaggerating each letter until I nodded. I must have been too obvious, even from a distance. Despite her admonition, squinty eye, wrinkled nose, and flashing fingers, I caught her smile, again of gratitude.

Maybe she likes me looking. Maybe I'm clueless.

We met at the bus, Jen back in her cute clothes, me trying to keep my smile from breaking my face. The bus drivers rotated driving the late bus, so of course we got the one from my route. Unlike the regular bus, the late bus had no rules about crossing streets, as it only went on one route and everyone had to walk from whatever stop was closest, even if it meant crossing a dozen streets.

"Guess I'm getting off at your stop," Jen said, "or he'll be suspicious. Doesn't matter. I'll still beat Dad home."

"Want to wait for him at my house? You could call."

"Really? Sure." Now Jen's smile matched my smile.

Life had taken a turn for the incredible. We got off the bus together and walked up Notch Hill Road, hand in hand.

I watched her smile drift off after a few hundred feet. "Jon, I need to pick up where we left off."

We walked some more, but, without my encouragement, it became apparent she wasn't going to pick up where we left off or anywhere else. Finally, I said, "Jen, you can tell me. I'm not going anywhere. Doesn't matter."

"Thanks," she said, swinging my hand. After a bit longer, she said, "E. H. Martin -- don't know what the initials stand for -- is a powerful man, and not often a nice one. Supposedly for my sake or for some whatever reason, Dad and Mom asked him to keep his life separate from ours."

She let me digest everything. It explained why she didn't know she had a grandfather, but not why she didn't know about an aunt and a cousin.

Jen waited until I nodded, ready for the next revelation. "About Mom's sister, maybe Dad has been involved with her, like what Mom accused him of, but we didn't talk about it. He said they had agreed to keep everything a secret. Keeping Lisa separate from me was to protect us. Protect us from what, I don't know. Guess the secret part is over, anyway. There must be a lot I don't know, but now you know what he told me."

I tried to make sense of what Jen said.

Why do they need separation and protection? Do their moms fight when they're together, as we watched in front of the jail? If they fly to New York together, they have to get a long a little.

She looked glum, so I thought of a distraction.

"Was your grandmother Italian? Your mom's mother?"

"Good question," she said, stopping. "Give me a second. I want to write it down, plus any other questions we can think of."

By the time we reached my house, Jen had seventeen questions, the last being, "Are you Lisa's dad?"

"I can try one a day like vitamins. Maybe he won't mind. Not sure about the last one."

"If he would answer it?" I asked.

"If he would tell me the truth. Remember, they kept this from me for my first thirteen years and eleven months."

Rex and her ball greeted us at the end of the driveway. I managed to sail it well out into the field. Maybe it would take her more than a minute to find it. However, when we stopped watching Rex, and I looked up the driveway, I ran into a snag.

Usually, someone else was already home when I arrived. Mom held the role until middle school, when they gave Beth a key, which she lost about ten times. I hadn't needed a key with everyone else home first. Recently, Beth joined Mom in her shop after her school events, and Dave dropped off Cindy on his way from track practice to work at a hardware store, where he spent two hours a night restacking lumber. However, today, Dad's pickup and car were gone, meaning Cindy had his car.

"What's wrong?" Jen asked, searching my face.

"No one is home."

"Should I leave?" she asked.

John C. Pelkey

"No, but getting in the house could be interesting if the door's locked."

With no one home, I usually found the kitchen door unlocked. When twice they forgot, I used the ladder Dad stored under the porch and climbed through my bedroom window. I kept my window opened a crack for air, but now we had swapped rooms. I had two windows partway up the roof in a dormer, but only half the size. Dave kept his window locked, as I found out when I tried it.

"What now?" Jen asked, as I climbed back down.

I walked around to the side and pointed. "I can try my window, but it will be a tight fit."

I set the ladder, climbed up and across the roof, removed the screen, and opened the window. I tried fitting through, but it was no go, as the window wasn't wide enough for my shoulders. However, in my effort, I found myself stuck, one arm in, and one arm out. I couldn't move forward, and had nothing to grip to push me back.

I felt hands on my flailing legs and Jen asked, "How can I help?"

"Pull?" I asked. She felt around for something to hold, and settled for the top of my pants, grabbing it and my belt. I wiggled, she tugged, and we managed to get me back on the roof.

"My turn," she said.

"Jen, you are wearing a skirt."

"So? I can still fit, even in a skirt. You have to help; hold my legs and push me through. You can't peek; though if you did, it would serve me right for not wearing jeans today."

She leaned into the window and her shoulders fit through. I held her legs from underneath as she carefully slid forward. As desperately as I wanted not to, I kept my eyes closed tight.

This worked until she said, "Okay, you can look now; I'm stuck," almost too muffled for me to understand.

When I opened my eyes, Jen was half inside, her cute little rear end barely stuck. "I have nothing to pull myself with and if I wiggle, I could tear my skirt on the roofing. You have to see to push me. You probably peeked anyway, so it doesn't matter."

"I didn't peek," I said, defending myself.

"Well, stop being such a gentleman," she snapped. "I could squish my top through, but not my bottom. If you push down on it a little, you could help me fit. It means you get to touch it, like a two for."

"What's a two for?"

"You get a look and a touch."

Following her directions, I pushed down on her rear end and she inched forward. I only glimpsed a flash or two of pink, but enough to reveal a completely new way of thinking about Molly Ringwald's movie.

She slipped through, stood up, and checked out everything. "Nothing on your floor." She patted the bed. "You make your bed in the morning." She opened a dresser drawer. "You pair your socks." Another drawer, underwear. "Whitey tidies? Do you fold them or does your mom?" She pulled out a pair and waved them at me. "Since you've seen mine, now I've seen yours. Every one of them white. You could be more adventurous, you think?"

"Not in front of the guys in the locker room."

She folded and returned them to the drawer, then disappeared.

By the time I got the screen back on and the ladder put away, she was back outside. "Dad's coming here; but he won't be leaving for an hour." She spun around and asked, "Are we inside or outside?"

I thought of the conversation with Dad and Mom. "Outside, and I should call my mom."

I hoped for Mom and not Beth, who could launch into twenty questions, and, for once, things went in my favor.

Mom asked, "Did you get in okay? When Cindy asked to use Dad's car, I forgot to tell her to leave the kitchen door unlocked."

"Climbed through a window." I didn't say who did. "Um, Jenni is here, as no one is home at her house. Nice outside. If it is okay, we're going to do homework on the porch."

After a long silence, Mom said, "I guess so."

Still, it is better than if you found Jen here and I didn't ask.

"I can stay?" Jen searched my face for an answer. "I should have walked home."

"If you had, I would be still stuck outside."

"Good point," she said, snickering. "Okay, what do you do when you come home?"

"Check the horses and cows."

The chin up bar got Jen's attention. "Can I try?" she asked.

"Remember your skirt," I countered.

"I'm not going to stand on it."

I gave her a sack of rocks for each hand to twirl. "To warm you up," I said.

When she was ready, I put both hands around her waist and hosted her up, a reverse of helping her on Janet.

She readied herself, and managed one. "Ouch, it hurts." She tried another. "Yup, still hurts." After a struggle, she completed five, and waited for me to catch her before she let go.

"Okay, beat five," she said, rubbing her arms.

"Count them."

I could do twenty on my own, but decided to add flair. I did five easy, and struggled from six though nine, gasping as I tried and barely succeeded with ten.

"Ten," she said. "Twice as many as me. Is ten a lot?"

After resting for a few seconds, I did ten more as effortlessly as possible.

John C. Pelkey

"Twenty. Now you're showing off." She still smiled.

I had never done thirty, but always a first time. Twenty-five and everything hurt. Twenty-seven and dire pain. Twenty-eight, barely. Twenty-nine, complete torture.

"You acted better the first time," Jen said.

"I was acting before. Now, I'm not."

As hard as I tried, thirty wasn't going to happen. I was ready to give up and let go, when Jen pushed on my seat, it made me lurch up, far enough to hang over the bar.

"Thirty," she said.

I let go. "Th-thanks," I stuttered. "You surprised me."

"Welcome," Jen said, beaming. "I got to look and touch, too, although your look and touch was better than mine." She cocked her head, squinting at me. "You're firm, solid like a rock. As I'm sure you found out, I'm squishy."

Walking from the barn, I thought about Jen's training. Five chin-ups were more than I managed to begin with, but still not a positive conditioning measure. "Jen, we need to add strength training to our routine."

She studied herself and noticed me following her gaze. "I appreciate your thoughtfulness, but I don't think strength training will make it permanent."

It took a little while for what she said to sink in.

"No," I sputtered. "For running. To improve your endurance."

I had no idea strength training could increase your... size.

I had a warm face to prove it.

Jen gave me a gentle nudge with her shoulder, all the time wearing a snicker. "Since Mom said exercise would keep me smaller, it seems like she would want me to run."

I invoked Dave's rule again and smiled, the toothy kind.

An hour later, Mom and Beth found us sitting on the front porch bench, doing our homework; our first time studying together, Jen became serious, even when leaning against me. The only interruption come with an occasional throw for Rex, who after a while decided she would rather sleep with her ball than chase it.

Mom smiled and said hi, but Beth appeared to be suspicious. "Been inside," she asked, eyeing our almost empty lemonade glasses and cookie crumbs.

I tried indifference. "Jen called her dad; I called Mom."

"Mom said you had to climb through a window. We keep all the windows locked."

"Upstairs window." I continued with indifference.

"Which one?"

I gave up, unable to hide my irritation. "Doesn't matter, Beth. It wasn't yours."

194

Mom helped by moving Beth. "Dinner in a half hour or so."

She paused, after pushing Beth around the corner of the porch. "Jenni, are you staying?"

"No, but thanks," Jen replied. "Dad's picking me up and I have to make our dinner."

Jen finished whatever she was doing, slid her books in her backpack, and returned to leaning against me, putting her feet up, and resting her chin on her knees. "Keep reading," she said, when I lowered my book. "Nice to sit here with you." She leaned and I read, with now and then a quick sideways peek at her legs with a tiny bit of skirt covering them.

We could hear the Z, and were up and around the corner of the porch before it came in sight. Jen had picked up her backpack, but she handed it to me carry to the car.

"Track meet tomorrow," she said. "See you at the corner."

I wanted to do something and, lacking the courage to kiss her, we fived and bumped.

"Today was so much better than yesterday," Jen said, smiling up at me. She added, "Had to be for you, too," as she swished her skirt to remind me.

Was better; I couldn't keep from laughing as she rode away.

I expected some backlash for violating the girlfriend alone rule, but at supper, all Mom said was, "Thoughtful of you to call. I'm sorry you had to break in. Cindy had an interview today, so she'll be using Dad's car this summer if she gets the job." She stopped and glazed for a second. "Jenni looked nice today. I hope you told her. Girls like that."

Mom, if you only knew.

Dad added, "You should carry a key, Jon. Everyone else does."

I wanted to tell them about Jen's key in a rock, but I didn't think I could work it into the conversation without the girlfriend alone thing, so I kept silent.

Beth solved it, to everyone's surprise. "Since I'm riding home with Mom now, I can leave my key here. I can hang it on the bridle nail. You have to remember to put it back."

Not as nifty as in a rock, but better than squeezing through a window, although I would never forget Jen's one time.

Bedtime, I drew a gold star next to my straight line. It wasn't exactly an accurate assessment, but I wasn't about to draw panties. The phone ringing interrupted my thoughts, and "Jon, it's for you," scrambled them.

Jen's hi sounded despondent.

"What's wrong?" I asked, skipping everything else.

"It's Mom," she muttered, adding a distinct groan. "She's coming back, tomorrow."

Chapter Twenty-Two

A subdued Jen met me at the bus stop. She had returned to straight hair, no makeup, and jeans and a sweatshirt, an indication her one-day vacation from following her mom's strict rules was over. The attitude change came with no attempt for a morning kiss, no leaning, and no conversation.

We survived Dave's drive-by, complete with a honk and with a wave from everyone inside, even Beth. Once on the bus, after a few minutes of silence, Jen shook herself and leaned close.

"Last night," she said, "I made chicken Alfredo, home-made dinner rolls, and asparagus, served on plates like in a restaurant. We stayed dressed up, lit candles, and toasted with wine glasses. Well, I drank sparkling cider; Dad drank champagne. Dad brought home strawberries, and we had shortcake topped with whipped cream."

She relaxed a little, and touched my seam. "We talked, too. Dad told me about his day, meeting with his favorite candidate for next year's election, closing a deal for some downtown construction. I told him about my day, riding the bus with you, walking Lisa to school, track practice agony, and you pushing me through the window."

"You told him?" I almost added a gasp, but managed to stifle it.

Jen tried out her first smile of the day. "Yeah, I told him. He laughed and said he hoped you enjoyed the show."

Ewww. Reminded me of him ogling Lisa, and now made me a co-conspirator of checking out girl parts. Although I certainly did with every reasonable opportunity that came along, it was not a distinction I wanted to share with the girl-part owner's father.

Jen seemed completely oblivious to my reaction, not even glancing my way. When she bumped against me and tugged at my arm, I took her hand. We had enough contact to satisfy her, and she turned to face me, mouthed a *thank you*, and continued.

"Jon, last night was like every night at your house. No arguing, no accusations, no eggshells to walk on. Dad felt the same way. He said we would not go back to the way it was, ever. He said, if and when I want to tell Lisa we are cousins, to go ahead. No more secrets. He even made a tee time for us to play golf, tomorrow at seven a.m., Dad, you, and me. I've wanted to play golf with you since forever."

My internal irritation softened.

Okay, her father isn't a complete slime.

Jen's composure faded. "Someone called. Dad answered, and went to his den; told me to hang up the phone when he got there." She stopped and turned away, gazing out the window.

"Did you hang up the phone?" I asked.

She came back, clearly uncertain of herself. "What?" she asked.

"Did you hang up the phone?" I repeated.

"Oh, I thought you said something else. No, I didn't; I said hello. An old-sounding voice, like gravel, asked, 'Who are you?' I barely understood him, even with the noise filter. When I answered with Jennifer, he said, 'So, you're the runner. Make me proud.' Dad came on and I hung up."

She laid her head on my shoulder, caught herself, and continued. "After about an hour, Dad came out, stiff and quiet like he had been told the world is ending tomorrow. He said, 'Mom is coming back.' He wanted to say more, but I think he was afraid. I asked if he had talked to her and he said, 'No, she wasn't on the menu.' When he said goodnight and went to his room, I called you."

She let go, moved away, and squeezed herself. "I'm sorry I was a big grump last night," she whispered.

I took her hand back and pulled her next to me, catching her eyes. "Jen, if you are unhappy about something, I want you to call me. I'm your boyfriend. It means you can count on me."

At least for now.

She nodded, giving me a warm smile. "Thanks," she whispered.

"You had to know she would come back." Her smile left again, and I felt like a heel for kicking it to the curb. "Sorry, Jen. Smile," I mumbled. "I'll miss you."

My silly remark bounced her smile back off the curb and onto her face. "Don't be sorry; you're right. I knew it would happen. I hoped it would be the year after I graduated... from college." She flashed her teeth to show she was kidding, too, and then sobered.

"It was so great to talk to Dad, and not worry about every word I said, wondering if it was acceptable or not."

Jen talked more on the bus than I remembered her talking in a whole day. I reminded myself, exactly as I said.

This is what boyfriends are for, someone to talk to about anything, and not be afraid, not walk on eggshells.

Jen relaxed, and she seemed calm when we got to school.

We set out to meet Lisa, who had already walked half way. A bit of a shocker, she wore a sweatshirt and jeans; almost a match, except Jen's sweatshirt was larger.

"Guess what?" Lisa said. "I get to attend your track meet today. This is my blend wear."

Lisa in blend wear means she wants to blend, quite the contrast from a few days ago. Although Jen goes from hot to nearly invisible by wearing a sweatshirt, Lisa in a sweatshirt still looks like Lisa. Is the difference is in her makeup or the fit?

197

John C. Pelkey

After further review, I determined it was both the makeup and the fit and drifted back into the conversation.

"...Since I wrote an article on you guys, I get to follow up at the meets this week and next week. Remember, Jon? You wanted me to write about next week, so now I will. You and Jenni will have to do something. Otherwise, I won't have anything to write."

I was impressed. "You remembered?"

"Of course, I remembered. It was our first conversation. Now I'm following up."

"Where's the article?" I asked.

"At the printer. You'll get to read it when it comes out Monday, along with everyone else."

So much for advanced warning. I hoped it left out us as a couple, well, half of me did. The other half wanted to flaunt it. Not good. The last thing Jen needed was a *Property of Jon Perone* sign on her.

*****

We had a long ride to East Valley, the worst team in the league and without a single meet win by the boys or by the girls. When Lisa boarded the bus, she had guys clamoring over who would get to sit with her. The coach solved their problem by placing her in the front with him and talking to her the entire way, breaking a half dozen hearts.

I sat with Jen behind Tom and Trish, another new branch on my horizon. Jen seemed more focused toward her mom coming home than on the meet, showing a cloud of concern in her eyes and tight smile. She wanted to continue our conversation, but this time, those on the bus would be all ears since they knew us. When she tried to speak, I shook my head and spelled out, "Later," to her. She nodded.

We did quite well without talking, so I thought, until I found Tom and Trish staring over the seat at us, laughing. "No wonder you two are so quiet," Trish said. "I'm calling a conversational foul. You guys are sharing secrets in sign language."

Yeah, so what if we are? It's a great idea, and for me a new horizon.

In front of the East Valley coach, Coach Harris told us, since this meet didn't matter, we could enter whatever events we wanted. We didn't even have to win the match ups. If we won next week, we were the champs. If we didn't, we weren't.

He caught Jen and me after everyone had had scattered. "Just between us. You guys enter your events. I want the team to have fun, but I also want to win." So we did.

The coach had Jen enter the first event, the 100-meter race. She won it easily. "It's no fun," she said. "Before you start, you're done."

It all changed when we heard the time. Jen had set a new South Valley Middle School girls' record and a new field record for their

198

school.

"You could set records in all the races." I envisioned the record board with a row of Jennifer Carlings on the girls' side.

"I only want one record, and right now you have it." Jen gave me a determined expression. However, to beat their best runner, she set a new record in the 800, too, nipping several seconds off the old time. Now she had three records.

Jim Stone decided to throw things: shot, javelin, and discus. Without him to beat, I won both the high jump and the long jump with personal records. Not school records, or even close, but at least I had something to compare with Jen's new school records for Lisa's article.

I realized how much I didn't miss Jim's, "Perone, you're an inch short... again." Our rivalry was friendly, mainly because Jim always won. Even without him competing, my good feeling and Jen's congrats lasted less than five minutes.

"Bask away," Jim said after I collected my ribbons. "It might be the only time you win."

Looking over Lisa's shoulder at what she wrote, he asked, "Are you gonna write about my PRs, too? I got three today, you know."

Lisa stepped away, turned, and faced Jim. "Let's see. Jon's jumping PRs today were better than your wining jumps last week. Plus he won. Your PRs were twenty to thirty meters short of Tom's school records. Plus you didn't win. What would you like me to say?"

Jim muttered, "Never mind."

Lisa threw him a carrot. "Set new jump records next week and I'll list you first."

Jim's pout turned into a smile. "You're on," he said, laughing.

It didn't seem like much, but I noticed how easily Lisa maneuvered a tight situation into a win for everyone.

Tom wanted to run the 1600-meter relay with me. "Come on; it will be great. I got third in the long jump, so I can do a crossover. This has to be easier than running hurdles. I'll go third, and you can make up whatever I lose."

When the coach agreed, I cringed, and tried to find someone to replace me for the fourth leg. Seeing Lisa in the area, Ed and Dan, our first two legs, proclaimed their support. "Ed blows them away in the beginning," Dan said. Ed nodded; thumbs up. "I increase the lead. Tom gives them false hope, and you crush them."

"Works for me," Ed added.

"I'm not writing that," Lisa said, ruining their two seconds of fame.

However, it played out exactly how Ed envisioned it. He got a lead, Dan built on it, and Tom threw it away. I was at least ten yards behind when he handed me the baton. Without thinking, I blasted off and caught their runner before the first turn. Doing so, I used up too much energy, and he passed me on the backstretch. I had to wait until the final

John C. Pelkey

turn to try to pass him back.

My legs felt like lead, and I flickered with the thought of letting him win. However, coming off the turn, I kicked it in and caught him. We went head to head to the finish, when my last inch lunge put me a hair ahead and we won.

Ed, Dan, and Tom high-fived each other, but I didn't join them. I still had a race to run, and less than a half hour to recover from wanting to throw up. I had put everything into winning the race.

"You got your third PR, Jon," Lisa said, after conferring with the coach. "Almost as good as Jenni's two school records. To think you are doing this just to give me something to write about, Jenni, too. You guys are great."

It wasn't exactly why we were winning. More of trying to meet our track coach's expectations.

I won my final race, the 1600, in an unspectacular time. Jen won hers about the same way, still trying to recover from the 800. Overall, our team won, though not by much. After the East Valley coach thanked Coach Harris for giving his kids a chance to win some events, he followed up with a glare at me. My last win put us over again. I was happy; I had won four events for the first and probably the last time.

On the bus ride back, Tom and Trish talked about their big weekend. Trish's parents were taking them camping. They were leaving right from the school. "We even get to sleep together, well, next to each other, as long as we don't try any hanky panky. Not much we can do with Trish's parents two feet away."

When they turned around, I signed, "I wish we could go off to some place and spend all day together doing nothing, or whatever Tom and Trish are going to do." I took forever and had spastic fingers half way through, but when I finished and Jen nodded in understanding, I had my own smile of gratitude.

She flashed back, "Me, too," along with a warm, friendly, inviting smile, the kind she could bring along wherever we went.

As we entered the school parking lot, we saw the green Mercedes with Jen's parents sitting inside, waiting.

Jen, who had held up for most of the day, began to deflate. "Could be worse; Mom could be waiting by herself," she said, trying to keep calm. Suddenly, she shoved past me into the aisle, before the bus stopped. "Lisa is in the front," she muttered.

Tom asked, "What's with Jenni?"

I shook my head. He could interpret it as I didn't know or I couldn't say, didn't matter which. Nothing I could do except watch.

The bus stopped before Jen reached Lisa. The coach stepped into the aisle to let her out first, blocking Jen. Lisa stepped off the bus, heading for the school; everyone else followed. I got off in time to watch Lisa and Jen walk through the school doors together. Lisa must have walked

200

directly in front of the Carling's car.

"Jon!"

Mr. Carling, standing next to his car, called out to me. Fighting an urge to run, instead I trotted over to see what he wanted.

"If you like, Elise and I can give you a ride home."

"Okay, thanks, Mr. Carling," I said, using my politeness as an escape clause.

After my shower, I stopped at my locker for homework, and eased by her locker, with no Jen in sight. I found them sitting on the floor against the wall by the front door. They were engaged in a private discussion, ignoring everyone, except me.

"She already knows," Jen said as I approached.

Not knowing what else to do, I leaned against the wall behind her. "Your parents offered me a ride," I stated, hoping I didn't ruin the conversation.

Taking my cue, they stood. "Lisa's going to wait until after they leave to walk out," Jen said. "We aren't telling them we know."

"We includes me." I didn't say it as a question, but their mirrored expressions of instant concern gave me the answer.

"If we know, they may decide to move me," Lisa said. "As long as we pretend we don't know, maybe they will leave me alone."

"You could move in with Jen," I said, not the wisest suggestion.

"Or they could move me to New York to live with Grandpa Martin," Lisa snapped.

I had envisioned their first shared understanding of being cousins as more of an event, at least more of a joyful one. Neither appeared particularly overjoyed about sharing the revelation of something both individually knew.

Jen hatched a plan. "When Dad and Mom are busy tonight, we'll talk in a three way conversation. They play music, so they won't hear."

Another reference to parental activity. I stifled all other thoughts and said, "Okay," echoed by Lisa. She motioned us toward the door and waved. Before we got there, Jen turned and set her backpack down. Lisa didn't hesitate. They hugged, laughing and crying at the same time, and both grabbed me to make it a threesome, my first ever group hug. As the activity busses had arrived, most everyone had gone, and we hugged in an empty foyer.

"Okay," Lisa said, "call at eight," and let us go.

I saw her tears, Jen's too, but we slipped through the doors, making certain we had pasted on our normal faces on before anyone outside noticed.

"How do we do this?" I asked as we walked toward Jen's parents.

"We stay silent," she said, wiping her eyes. "We don't tell anyone. Easier for me than for you."

"I can do this," I muttered, holding the door for her and trying to get

John C. Pelkey

an assessment of the climate in her parents' car.

Jen's mom smiled and said, "Hi, Honey," to her. It felt creepy, but I wasn't going to spoil it.

As it turned out, we didn't even have to try. Her mom described her trip, the private jet they flew in, what it was like seeing their father, and included Renee, pretending everyone already knew they were sisters. We were like actors in a well-rehearsed play, except the kids in the back didn't have a program.

When she paused, and we were almost to my house, Jen had an opportunity to begin the deception. "What about Lisa?" she asked. Not the direction I would have gone, but my deception skills were far less developed.

"Lisa doesn't get to know," her mom replied. "Unless you tell her."

"I haven't told her anything," Jen said, speaking both the truth and a lie at the same time. She sounded a little defiant, a surprise, facing her mom.

I waited for an attack, but instead, her mom turned to face us, a smile plastered to her face. "Better you don't for now. Lisa gets to stay where she is as long as she wants to. You can be friends, but let's not go any further. It's quite complicated, and we haven't worked out the details."

When her mom turned back, Jen wiggled her fingers to her ear, signaling phone. I nodded, silently squeezed her hand goodnight, thanked her parents for the ride, and beat a hasty retreat.

Things were quiet at home for the second night in a row. Dave worked late and Cindy camped out in the living room, reading. Beth moped in her room, her sophomore year now going badly in the Friday night dating realm. In the family room, Dad and Mom watched *Gone with the Wind* for the four hundredth time. I caught it for a minute. The "birthin' babies" line reminded me of Dr. Canfield. With everyone else occupied, the kitchen was empty.

The microwave clock bouncing to the eight coincided with the phone ringing. For once, I beat Beth. "Don't talk all night," she muttered after I told her to hang up.

Jen said, "I can't believe I almost gave it away. Thanks for not saying anything."

"I thought you pulled it off quite well."

"Mom was too busy reviewing her marching orders to notice. Otherwise, I think she would have figured it out. I need to try harder."

"What about Lisa?" I asked.

"Right, Lisa. Hold on; don't hang up." The phone went dead for about twenty seconds. "I'm back, and Lisa, too."

"Hi, Jon." Lisa said.

"So," I said. I tried to expand, but I needed to be the one listening, not talking.

202

To Face The World

Lisa started with, "Jon, remember when Mom drove you home and got all freaky over the word, Jennifer?"

"I remember. You told her she was Jennifer Perone."

"After you got out, I admitted she was Jennifer Carling and Mom got nervous and upset. Later, when she calmed down, she told me the truth. She said I was never to repeat it under any circumstances. I wanted to tell you so many times, and I almost did once."

"Outside at lunch?" I asked.

"Yes."

Lisa lapsed into silence. Jen hadn't said anything.

"Jen?" I asked.

"Lisa has more," she said. "Don't you?"

"Okay, Jenni," Lisa replied. "I saw your mom in the car. She does look like my mom. We didn't make eye contact, so I don't think she caught me. Your dad turned around, pretending to be grabbing something off the back seat. Your mom was facing him, so I got a sideways glance, mostly. If I didn't already know, I wouldn't have thought anything of it."

"How did you guys..." I had no idea what to call it.

"Connect? Jenni stopped me right after we walked through the door."

"I told Lisa we needed to talk."

Lisa added, "I made it easy for her by saying, 'Hi, Cuz.' She about fainted."

"Well, I didn't expect it," Jen said, "Still, now we know we know, so it's okay, thanks to you, Jon."

"Thank you from both of us," Lisa added.

"I just wish..." Jen paused.

"...that knowing we're cousins had been, like, one of our earliest memories, maybe?" Lisa asked.

"Yeah," Jen replied.

"You guys can finish each other's thoughts."

"We're working on it," they answered in unison.

They don't need me mucking with things.

"Jen, Lisa, I'm going to let you guys talk."

"You call her Jen? You're both so sweet. Jen and Jon. Can I call you Jen, Jen?"

"You guys talk," I said, and eased out of the conversation.

Upstairs, I found the storage room door opened, boxes rearranged, and Beth snooping in an old chest. She pulled out a funny hat and added it to the ancient dress she wore over her tee shirt and jeans, like someone out of an old movie.

"What are you doing?" I asked, wondering if I surprised her.

Beth didn't even jump; instead, she slowly turned to face me. "Did you know Mom was in theater in high school? This is from one of the

John C. Pelkey

plays she acted in, Jane Bennet in *Pride and Prejudice*. She was the trophy wife to one of Mr. Darcy's friends, whose name I forgot."

"Mr. Bingley."

"Oh, yeah. Figures you would know." She fingered the top of the dress, which formed an oval. "Kind of low cut," she added.

It was. I saw lots of Beth's tee shirt showing under the dress.

"Mom was a hottie in high school. She could wear this. I can't."

Beth took off the hat. I noticed she had pulled up her hair into a bun. "Women used to wear bonnets. They thought they were undressed without them. I wonder what it was like."

The dress came off next, and Beth carefully folded it and placed it back where it was, closing the lid.

"Did you know Mom gave up acting and almost everything else she did in high school?" she asked.

I shrugged, not exactly certain where Beth was going with this.

"She should have gone to college and become a lawyer or a doctor or something. Instead, she married Dad."

"Is it a bad thing?" I asked.

"Maybe. I guess it depends on what makes people happy."

"Mom's happy with Dad."

"I work with Mom in her shop. She is so smart, probably where you get it. She could run a corporation. Instead, she sews letters on jackets. Her fingers fly on her computer. Dad doesn't even have a computer."

Neither do the rest of us. So what?

"Do you want to go to college and become a lawyer or a doctor?" I asked.

"Go to college? Me? Hardly. I'd rather be a trophy wife like Jane, and find my own Mr. Bingley."

"Isn't a trophy wife where some old, rich guy marries a hot chick?"

"Yeah, I guess. You left out one important step. He dumps the old, former hot chick for a new, younger hot chick, but she cleans up in the divorce. I want to be different. I want to be the young hot chick who marries a young, rich, hunky guy, who isn't going to need a divorce in twenty years. Trouble is, I'm not the hot chick, not yet anyway, and I don't have the guy."

"Mom was the hot chick marrying Dad, the hunky guy?"

"Bingo." She shot me with her finger. "Except the rich part."

"Cindy and Dave?"

"Maybe."

Maybe?

I wondered what Beth meant. Maybe she didn't think Cindy was hot. I did. "You're okay, Beth," I said, changing the subject.

For a sister, I added to myself.

Beth took her hair down, shaking it out. She studied herself in an old mirror hung on the back of the storage room door. "Yeah, I'm okay,

To Face The World

just not a hottie like Mom was, or like your friend, Lisa. When she marries, it won't matter what she does. Everyone will think she is a trophy wife."

She opened the door, but shut it again. "Speaking of trophies, what happened to Jenni? Yesterday, she was like wow, right up there competing with Lisa. Today, she looked like your little sister again."

My little sister?

I had never wondered how we appeared to other people. Even if I had, it wasn't what I would have thought.

"Jenni got hit on a lot yesterday. Today, she didn't."

Or if she did, she didn't tell me.

"I saw the green backpack at the bus stop yesterday. Jenni went behind the tree with you. Can't imagine what you two were doing. Rumor has it you do one-on-one time with Lisa outside during lunch. Three days in a row, and after the first day, she moves. What's going on?"

The phone rang. Beth shot through the door toward her room and I wandered toward mine. I didn't even reach it before Beth hollered, "Jon, it's for you. You can take it in my room," and returned to the storage room.

"You didn't have to go," Jen said when I answered. "We did have a good visit without you. We want to figure out what being cousins means, even if we have to pretend. Lisa agreed to only you calling me Jen. She has a temper. She's mostly mad at her mom and grandfather for putting us in this situation. At one point, she yelled so loud, Fred and Martha came to see what was wrong. I thought they would make her hang up, but they didn't. I think they already knew. There's more."

After some silence, I asked, "You want to wait until tomorrow?"

"No, I want to get it out so I can go to bed knowing you know."

"Okay," I said, "Carry on."

"Lisa yelled first, and then she cried some. In the end, she said how happy she is to be my cousin. We're going to sit together this Sunday, and every Sunday if we can. Lisa wants me to help her understand what belonging to a church is about. Like I'm the expert or something? You should be the one sitting with her."

Me? Why would you think I'm an expert?

"Mom said Grandpa put Lisa's mom in a hotel in Seattle until the hearing next week. She gushed over how she wants us to continue running so you can help me improve, which can't possibly be her choice. It's like she wears some device transmitting instructions into her ear. Dad says, 'Don't ask questions; let it play out.' I do know this. Mom was difficult before, but at least she was Mom. Now, I don't know who she is."

"How's your dad?"

"He's taking charge, making the decisions, telling us what to do. I

John C. Pelkey

didn't realize how few decisions he used to make. Mom now says, 'Yes, dear,' and smiles. They hold hands, like they're dating or something."

"Sounds good to me."

"Maybe, but it's like a bubble. Sooner or later, pop." She sighed over the phone. I pictured it like her sigh on the first day.

"Let's talk about something else," she said. "Like this weekend. You can play golf tomorrow, can't you? Dad wants to know, too. Come a little early?"

I heard Beth tromping up the stairs, so I said goodbye, with a promise to be early and ready.

Early is easy, as seven isn't early. Ready? I don't know if I'll ever be ready.

"Cindy wants to talk to you before Dave comes home," Beth said.

Great, Beth probably blabbed and now she wants Cindy to drag out of me what she couldn't.

The movie over, my parents had moved into their bedroom and I found Cindy alone in the family room, slouched in a chair and watching TV.

She unslouched. "The conquering hero," she said with some noticeable sarcasm. "You are becoming famous, even in high school. You caught a thief; you saved the best-looking girl in middle school from who knows what. You hang out with her at lunch and with the second cutest girl before and after school. You direct the choir and you're going to help Jenni to set some kind of world record in track next week."

"Who told you everything?" I asked. Cindy knew a lot more than Beth did, almost unheard of.

"I hear things. For example, it seems someone has a little sister named Lydia. Anyone you know?"

I didn't hide my irritation, giving her my best icy stare. "You said you kept secrets, almost as good as Jenni. Why tell me?"

Why rat off Lydia?

"My secrets are on a need to know basis, and you need to know."

"I need to know what?" I snapped. I had no idea what I had done to tick off Cindy, but I was quickly joining her. For once, she didn't intimidate me, which came as a surprise at a time when she clearly was trying to. She didn't back down, and neither did I. We locked into a faceoff.

"Guys think you are hogging the market, and trying to be way cooler than you are. Guys who think a knuckle sandwich will help you reassess your over-reaching social status."

"I'm in eighth grade. I don't have a social status to over-reach."

"Pre-emptive strike before next year, when Lisa and Jenni are in high school and fair game. But you don't worry about it yet."

"What do you mean?"

"Dave has made it known if anyone so much as ruffles your collar,

206

To Face The World

they'll be sipping their steaks through a straw. I think it's how he put it."

"Dave sticks up for me?"

"Big time. Kids used to pick on you in grade school. Do they pick on you now?"

I tried to remember the last time someone bullied me, besides Dave. Maybe in seventh grade. I didn't strike fear in anyone, but the same kids who once bullied me, now they didn't. Some, like Jim, even said, "Sorry," when they accidently bumped me. I hadn't given it any thought, except to be glad I was able to stop hiding.

"Dave bullies me."

"As your big brother, he thinks he's supposed to. Haven't you noticed? Even he doesn't do it anymore."

"He teased me about taking a leak yesterday."

"He didn't tease you about making nice with Jenni behind the tree."

"I wasn't making nice with Jenni," I retorted, a bit too loud.

"Wait. Hold it." Cindy waved her arms in a peace gesture. "I'm not the enemy. I only want you to be safe. Pay a little more attention to what's going down around you. Not everyone is willing to play as fair as Dave does, even when he picks on you."

She forced a smile. I didn't. "Jenni is a sweet girl in a tough situation. Rumor has it Lisa is a nice girl, too, in a tougher situation. I know what Lisa was about to do when you pulled her into the principal's office. You are a good friend to both of them, and a better role model. So be watchful, okay? I care about you. You're going to be my brother-in-law come next month."

"You have a funny way of showing it," I muttered, cleverly ending the conversation.

Cindy got up and headed toward the kitchen, leaving me to watch a commercial to help make old people grow older slower.

Pay attention! Pay attention to what?

As I followed Cindy out of the family room, I noticed both of the doors were open so I glanced into the master bedroom. Dad sat at his desk, calculating something by hand, probably his bills. Mom sat by the window, mending Dad's overalls. It reminded me of the Norman Rockwell covers my grandparents used to show us at Christmas. I wondered if my parents had heard our conversation, but the TV was loud enough, so no chance.

"Thought I would say goodnight," I mumbled as an excuse to be staring at them.

They both stopped what they were doing, maybe to see if to see if I had something else to say.

"If we moved the TV to the other side of the family room, and pointed it away instead of toward your bedroom, it wouldn't be so loud," I offered.

"We don't even notice," Mom said. "Still, it was nice of you to think

John C. Pelkey

of us."

As I walked past the kitchen, I saw Cindy at the back door and heard Dave's car parking in front of the house. I disappeared upstairs before I caught them doing whatever couples did when they greeted each other.

There, Cindy, I paid attention.

Chapter Twenty-Three

Saturday morning, I stepped onto the putting green at 6:30. With the grass still wet, my putts left trails as they moseyed past the cups. Dark clouds lurked on the horizon. Our two weeks of nice weather was about to end.

Please be nice on Friday for the meet, or at least dry.

Today would be a long day. I had left my sweats and lunch in Dr. Canfield's garage so I could walk there after the golf and then on to Mr. Dunlap's. After yards, Jen and I could run at the high school. It sounded good in theory. It also sounded exhausting.

From the putting green, I watched Jen and her dad arrive in his Nissan 300ZX. Mr. Carling owned an amazing car, low slung and swoopy, with fat tires -- way cool. With two seats, I would have no chance ever to ride in it. I made a swishing motion for the Z when she got out. She saw me and swished back. For once, she wasn't wearing an oversized sweatshirt, instead, a sleeveless sweater with a white blouse underneath and slacks instead of jeans. Her clothes gave the impression of being expensive and made me feel poor in my sweater and jeans. Her dad looked even more expensive, along with tailored.

Oh, well.

After they fished out their clubs from the back, Jen headed toward me on the putting green while her dad waved and entered the pro shop. Too early, Mr. Hernandez wasn't there yet. I hoped we could see him after we finished.

Having practiced it for an hour the night before, I signed, "Missed you," as she approached.

Jen signed back, "Wow," and caught my hands. We moved closer and ended in a soft head bump, touching noses. Jen glanced sideways at the pro shop, spun back, and snuck in a kiss, with my help.

Wow, right back at you.

"Is everything okay?" I asked.

"If you are asking about Mom, she's at work, showing an open house today. It's the first time, well, in a long time."

She lined up a put, sunk it from about thirty feet, and waved her putter in triumph.

"Your dad?" I asked, trying to stay on the subject.

"Dad, okay. Dad is in macho heaven, thinking he is in charge. He barks out directions, Mom hustles to obey. She's like a Stepford Wife, on autopilot."

Jen made like an airplane with her arms for wings, and slowly flew

John C. Pelkey

in a straight line across the putting green and almost into a tree. "Crash," she said, tapping the tree. "That's what will happen."

"You saw the movie?" I asked.

"The movie? No. I read the book. It was a book first."

Jen tapped in one from about ten feet. "You're not putting," she said, trying to give me a push start.

I sunk a putt from five feet, my first. Jen put two balls down, pointed at a cup about fifty feet away, lined up her shot, and hit it, stopping about three feet short.

"Don't hit it short," she whispered as I lined up my putt.

I didn't hit it short, more like twenty feet past and down a slope. I felt a long golf day coming. I tried a comeback putt, carefully allowing for the slope up. *Go in; please, go in*, I silently pleaded as it slipped across the grass. It didn't look good, but as it got closer, the slope assisted and the putt swirled around the cup once and dropped.

"Nice," she said, tapping hers in easily. "We both two-putted from fifty feet."

I wondered about my silent plea. "Jen, do you pray?" I asked.

She gave me the same shy smile from the first day, the special smile she only shared on rare occasions, and only when we were alone. It made my heart thump.

You don't know how incredibly enchanting you are.

She came right up to me, letting go of her putter and gazing up at me with her pretty, sparkling green eyes. She said, "All the time, mostly about you, why?"

I had forgotten why. I simply stood there. Jen touched me, one hand holding mine, and the other on my chest. I couldn't stop an involuntary shiver, causing her to laugh.

"What's that from?" she asked.

"You touching me."

She smiled, a warm and friendly one. "Remember, when you said to think of something I like to relax?" I nodded. "Well, I like to think about you touching me. Remember when you did this for me?" She took my hand and put it against her stomach. "Yeah, it works."

Does touching her relax me? It does a bunch of things I like, but I'm not sure relaxing me is one of them.

"Dad's coming," she whispered, glancing past my shoulder and letting go of my hand. She picked up her putter and returned to her ball, addressed it, and sunk another long putt. I sank one about fifteen feet, half as long.

"Nice putting, both of you," he said. "You ready? How about a buck a hole?"

You want to play for money?

My question triggered an accompanying worse thought.

I don't have any money to pay for my round. I have always traded golf

210

balls for golf and played with Mr. Hernandez.

"Not fair, Dad," Jen whined, echoing my thoughts. "We're kids."

"I'll take you both on. Best ball against me."

What's best ball?

Jen read my mind. "After the tee shots, we both hit from the shot with the best lie until we reach the green. Once we reach the green, after the first putt, we each use our own lie. On the fairway, we have to agree on where to take the shots before we hit."

When I nodded in understanding, she added, "You're on, Dad."

"I didn't pay," I whispered to Jen.

She gave me a nose scrunch and whispered back, "Dad's treat."

I had never played golf with groups both in front and behind. Mr. Hernandez and I were always the last group for the day, and usually well after anyone else.

As we arrived at the first tee, a man drove up in a cart. It already had Mr. Carling's clubs on the back. Jen easily added hers, showing she had ridden in golf carts before.

They would ride and I would walk, which was fine, although I had never walked before. I had only played golf with Mr. Hernandez and he always used a cart. Since they didn't rent carts to kids, and Mr. Carling couldn't drive both, it left me with my feet.

Mr. Carling hit first, well down the fairway. The group behind applauded.

My nervousness showed; I doffed one thirty yards and onto the ladies' tee. No applause, but I did hear a, "Give him a mulligan."

Mr. Carling shook his head. "No free shots. It's already two to one."

Jen hit one right down the middle from the ladies' tee, and threw my ball at me. I managed to catch it and not appear to look even worse to the group following.

Away they rode off together in their cart, while I trailed behind with my clubs. To keep up, I needed to walk faster and to start ahead of them. On the plus side, they waited for me each time and not once said, "Hurry up." Jen even walked with me when our best lie was behind Mr. Carling. Still, with golf, lawns, and running, I felt tired after the first hole.

We lost the first two holes, but won the third, a par three, when Jen sunk a long birdie putt off my first good drive. We lost the fourth. Next was my golf ball patch hole. The group behind caught up while we waited, as the group in front failed to land any of their tee shots on the fairway. More balls for me to pick up later.

Mr. Carling hit first with a five wood, bouncing it right across the pond and into my golf ball patch.

I calmly used a seven iron and put it right past the last tree before the corner. "Nice shot." The people waiting behind us seemed impressed with me for the first time.

Jen didn't even bother to hit. As usual, they went ahead in the cart and I caught up in time to watch Mr. Carling take a drop and whack it into the end tree, where it shot up into the air, landed in front of him, and rolled to his feet. Although well behind me, he waved for me to hit next.

My shot went hard, but failed to get any air.

"Snaked it!" Jen yelled, sitting in her dad's card behind me.

I watched it bounce up the fairway, and, to my utter surprise, it rolled right onto the green. Mr. Carling got into the cart and pulled up next to me.

"Aren't you going to hit?" I asked.

"No point. I'm one hundred and seventy yards out, lying three." He pointed at the flag. "You are lying two, and what, thirty feet from the cup? Jenni isn't going to three-putt."

She didn't even hit from my spot. They roared ahead and by the time I reached the green, she had already sunk it for another birdie.

She walked back down the cart path to meet me.

"Nice putt," I said, trying not to sound negative, despite my continuous lagging behind.

"Had to sink it," she said, smiling. "Couldn't waste your two fab shots."

We high-fived and bumped heads.

"What was that?" Jen's dad asked, while waiting on the next tee.

"We're too young to kiss, so we bump heads instead," Jen said with a smirk.

Jen, no. Not to your dad.

Mr. Carling simply smiled and shook his head, and we played on. He never quite recovered from his bad hits on my golf ball hole and began slicing his shots. I gained confidence, stayed in the fairway, walked faster, and we won by three holes, more from Jen's putting than anything else we did. He fished out his wallet and paused. "Jenni, how about I buy lunch instead? You, too, Jon."

I thought of my lunch waiting in Dr. Canfield's garage and the time I needed. "Let's find Mr. Hernandez," Jen suggested, making the decision easy.

She found him behind the pro shop, filling range ball buckets from the bin where they dumped my golf ball patch finds after cleaning and striping them.

"Hi, Mel. Dad challenged us to best ball, and we won, Jon's hitting, and my putting."

"Hey, you do well, alright," he said, waving a bucket full. "Jon's contribution." He swished his hand over the bin. "Always use some more, Jon."

"We're having lunch. Can you join us?" Jen asked.

"Sure, why not? I only work here for fun." Back in the pro shop, the

To Face The World

head pro agreed, waving him to go with us.

Mr. Carling led us into the coffee shop. Mr. Hernandez followed with Jen. He spoke closer to her, but I could still hear. "You and Jon are together now. See I told you, these things work out if you let them."

At least for another week, maybe.

He turned to me, "How well do the clubs work? Are they okay?"

"Better than okay. Thanks, Mr. Hernandez."

"When your track season is over, we play, maybe all of us."

Mr. Hernandez kept our lunch light and happy with his stories of golfing in the old days and of his great-grandchildren. Mr. Carling had little to say. I wondered why he'd invited me. Finally, his chance came when we watched Mr. Hernandez and Jen snoop through the golf shirts in the pro shop.

"You have been spending a lot of time with Jenni. You've made her the happiest I have ever seen her. You do realize this has caused issues in the past, but it is all behind us now. Jenni hasn't had the easiest life. It doesn't help when we leave her on her own far too much. Since she has you for a friend, she doesn't mind now. Elise and I want you to continue to spend as much time as you can with her, and not only with her running. Thanks, and keep this to yourself."

Now I'm confused. Don't all parents want to monitor their daughters' social lives, set restrictions or at least guidelines? Am I to believe you have given me open season with Jen? Is it reverse psychology? What about her? Does she have any say? If I keep it to myself as you request, I can't discuss it with her. At least I have a clue to why you keep thanking me.

I had to get going if we were going to have time to run. When Jen held up a shirt for me, I shook my head. "Time for me to go."

Remembering my manners, I added, "Thanks, Mr. Carling, for the golf and the lunch." After all, I hadn't paid for anything.

"Thanks for letting us win," Jen added.

"Nothing is too good for my little girl," he replied.

Does he mean the golf, the lunch, me, all three, or something else entirely?

At the door, I watched Jen holding up shirts for her dad, laying them against his chest. Mr. Hernandez, acting as the decider, nodded or shook his head. Mr. Carling let them have their fun; maybe he would even let them talk him into buying one. He didn't seem like an uncaring father.

I felt a pendulum swinging back and forth in the way Jen's parents treated her, like the one Poe wrote about coming down on its victim. "Inch by inch -- line by line -- with a descent only appreciable at intervals that seemed ages -- down and still down it came!" I wondered if I could keep Jen away from their swishes and save both of us.

I changed into my sweats and tried to finish Dr. Canfield's yard in record time. I still took nearly three hours. I couldn't help but try to do a good job; his neighbor watched me. As Dr. Canfield would be back in a

213

John C. Pelkey

few days, his yard had to look great. I left my clubs, uneaten lunch, and the golf clothes in Dr. Canfield's garage. I would have to get them later. I ran to Mr. Dunlap's.

Jen came out on the steps and bounced her golf ball while I worked, but she waited until I cleaned up before coming over. "Dad said not to disturb you while you work since you are on Mr. Dunlap's clock."

"I get paid by the job, not the hour. Mr. Dunlap paid me and left."

"Why didn't you say so? I would have come over and helped."

"You would do yards?"

Somehow, I don't see you on your hands and knees, weeding.

"If you can, why can't I?"

Realizing I might be wrong, I said, "Dr. Canfield's neighbor wants me to take care of his yard. If I taught you how to do some of the work, we could finish both yards in the time it takes me to do one. Or close anyway. Maybe when school gets out."

"Sure, I've never made money doing anything."

I headed across the street to her house. "Where are you going?" she asked.

"Shouldn't you tell your parents you're leaving?"

"Mom's not back yet and Dad is in his study on a conference call, not to be disturbed. Watching you was my treat."

I can see me watching you as being a treat, but not the reverse.

She broke into a jog and I followed suit, catching up and keeping my mouth shut.

We ran to the end of the block. Jen slowed to a walk. "What did my dad want to tell you?"

"So you noticed."

"Well, he didn't exactly disguise his effort, did he?" she muttered.

"I guess he didn't. He thanked me for making you happy and spending time with you while he and your mom are out."

So much for keeping it to myself.

"Make me happy? Do you think you make me happy?" Her accompanying glare didn't signal happy.

"I don't know."

Right now, obviously, I'm not.

"I know when I'm with you, I'm happy."

"Jon, people can't make each other happy. It is something either you are or you aren't. When it comes to relating to kids, my parents weren't happy before and they aren't happy now. Besides, if they were happy, they would have had more than one of me, like your parents did."

"Maybe they couldn't."

"Of course they couldn't. Mom made Dad get fixed to be sure."

"They told you? My parents hardly ever mention sex, and never when it involves them."

For my quality question, Jen returned a quality stare. The

214

To Face The World

conversation attempt over, we walked the rest of the way. I didn't know how much energy I had left and didn't want to waste any.

At the track, we practiced timing. We were rusty, I was slow, and it took several tries to make the needed corrections. Once on track, Jen wanted to run by herself.

"You deserve a break. You walked and carried your clubs while I rode. Plus you did yards. You don't need the practice as much as I do. So stand in the middle of the field and yell the times."

I yelled and cheered while she ran a lap and joined her when she walked a half lap. The times were okay, but not great. During the fourth lap, I noticed Mr. Carling sitting in the stands and stopped Jen a half lap early. I wondered how long he had been there. She appeared tense and ready to quit. I wanted to find a shirt.

"Don't mind me; I'm here to watch, so go ahead!" her dad yelled, waving us to continue.

"I don't want him to watch," she muttered.

"Jen, you need to run under pressure. Let's try two more laps with him watching." My logic prevailed. We relaxed for a while, walking around and stretching a little.

"If I'm going to do this, I'm running at race speed," she insisted, a complete attitude reverse. "Give me the exact half-lap times."

Fine with me. You're the one running.

I waved as I started my watch. She was off like a rocket.

Jen matched the time for one and a half laps, and blew out the final half lap. I barely beat her back running across the field. She finished in 2:11 for 800 meters, well under her school record, and six seconds faster than my best time. More important, she wasn't even breathing hard.

She had run 800 meters four times in competition; I had only run it in practice. Didn't matter. I couldn't excuse my way out of admitting it; Jen was incredibly fast. She had run the last 200 meters in twenty-seven seconds, also faster than the girls' school record.

"How fast was I?" she asked, still breathing in her rhythm, and looking less tired than I felt.

When I told her, she added, "I think I can run faster, but it's not the whole distance. Do you think I can run two more laps as fast?"

I shivered in excitement or something. Based on her ease of keeping the seventy-second lap times for two laps after hours of practice, it made the same pace for four laps appear within her reach. Even without a closing kick, the time of 4:40 floated in my head, not a dream anymore. Nobody in our world could run 1600 meters as fast as Jen, including me.

"Tomorrow, we can try four laps and see." With only had one more individual day before Friday's race, I wanted to make it count.

She came close, and we bumped and fived.

Mr. Carling joined us. He was about to say something when the clouds, which had been sitting around all day threatening us, finally

215

John C. Pelkey

decided to let go. We ran to his car with him. It was the Z for two.

I headed for the shelter of the school, but Jen caught me. "Come on," she said. She towed me to the car, threw our sweats on the back shelf, pushed me in, and settled herself on top. Mr. Carling didn't say anything. Now I touched Jen with no shirt on, the seatbelt pulling her tight against me.

"Where to?" he asked.

"I left my stuff at Dr. Canfield's. Including my clubs."

"They'll fit in the back. What was Jenni's time?" When I told him, Mr. Carling smiled his politically-correct, baby-kissing best.

"Jenni, what school records do you have?"

"The 100, 800, and 1600. Maybe Jon's on Friday."

"I'm impressed. You are taking this seriously, both of you. I have an idea. Since the rain is going to continue tomorrow, you could practice at my club in the city. We have a huge bubble keeping everything warm and dry. What do you say?"

The thought of riding twenty miles with Jen on my lap instead of two appealed to me. However, it was up to her. I thought of how tense she was, trying to run with her father present.

"Are you going to watch?" she asked.

"From afar, way up on a balcony. You won't even notice me."

Jen smiled, indicating she thought it would make him far enough away. "Okay, Dad, if Jon's folks agree."

I could only hope. However, they had given me my nine days, my first line of defense if they wanted to say no.

At Dr. Canfield's house, Jen put her sweats on while I loaded my stuff in the back of the car. I had to take out my clubs to fit the bag and wondered how Mr. Carling had fit both of theirs. I felt stiff from sitting in the car directly after our practice. It was still exciting to have Jen sit on me again.

Every time we touch, it seems like the first time. Every time we let go, I hurt a little, wondering if we will ever touch again. Do you feel the same way?

I studied her, inches from my face, her hands holding my left hand in her lap, absently drawing circles in my palm.

We arrived at my house too soon. She climbed out, and we clasped hands and bumped heads for a second. She jumped back in and I retrieved my clubs. I watched them drive away, Jen's hand on the window, fingers apart. The little hurt got bigger, and I realized I was getting soaked. Rex wolfed from her doghouse as I went by on the way to the kitchen door. Not only was she a selective watchdog, but a fair weather one.

"Well, you do exist," Dave said for a greeting. "We wondered if you had moved out."

He had popcorn going in the microwave while everyone prepared to watch a movie Cindy had rented. Beth, playing Miss Moody, slouched

216

To Face The World

in a corner of the family room, but had a bowl ready for the popcorn. Cindy waved from the couch. Dad and Mom had disappeared.

"They went out, can you believe it? Your dinner is in the fridge. You can nuke it in the microwave." Dave's ideas on cooking were limited to boiling water and the microwave. Anything else was out of his range.

I ate my dinner, watched a few minutes of the movie, tried to cheer Beth up, and drifted upstairs to take a shower, trying to fight the fatigue. Before I forgot, I put 800 on my calendar in big numbers and 2:11 inside the top loop to the eight and the two zeroes.

The shower felt good, getting to stand there and let the warm water put me to sleep. Except the phone rang. Since no one bothered me, I took my time, drying my hair and brushing my teeth. Even buzzed some peach fuzz off with Dave's shaver, something I had to do about once a week.

Stepping out of the bath in my nice, fluffy robe, I almost crashed into Beth.

"Guess who's on the phone?" she asked.

"Your new boyfriend?"

"It's Jenni. Don't be a snot while I'm trying to be nice to you. After all, I kept her occupied for what, ten minutes, while you were primping. You can even take it in my room."

She started down the steps. Her saying, "Jon?" stopped me halfway to her bedroom. She leaned on the railing, with only her head visible.

"Jenni had a boyfriend before you. He sat in church with her and walked her home, well, almost home because he was afraid of her mom. Last year he graduated and went back east to college. She said he was a bit of a dweeb." Beth smiled, almost laughing. "Now I know why she likes you."

Ha, ha.

Beth dropped the smile and continued. "I know I've made a fuss about you being with her all the time, but I've decided to stop. I think Jenni is sweet. I know how much she likes you. No more fuss. Just wanted you to know."

Finished, she disappeared. Before I reached for the phone, I decided to pretend Beth hadn't talked to me. Jen had never mentioned anyone, and I wasn't about to bring up her past right after Beth saying how much she liked me.

As I picked up the phone and said hello, I heard a "Bye, Jenni" and a click from the kitchen. Other than the "dweeb" comparison, Beth had been nice, even with her revelation.

"Dad and Mom are on the phone with Grandpa," Jen said. "Dad's in the kitchen and Mom's in their bedroom. They told me I had to stay in my room, but they didn't say I couldn't call you. Something's happening. I hope it is about my aunt and not about me."

"Can you hear anything?" I asked.

John C. Pelkey

"Not without getting much closer. If they don't want me to know, I don't get to know."

"You did well today," I offered.

"Yeah, maybe too well. As soon as I joined the track team, Dad lost interest in my running, except he was glad you came along so he could quit pretending to run 5Ks. Today, he was searching for some 5Ks for you and me to run this summer. He says we need to keep practicing so we don't lose our touch."

"What about your mom?"

"Mom worked all day today. I think she got it out of her system. She said she wasn't going back. Since she came back from visiting Grandpa, she doesn't say anything about me."

I thought about Jen's rendition of her mom on autopilot. At least she hadn't crashed yet.

"Can you go with me to Dad's club tomorrow?" Jen asked.

"I don't know. My parents aren't home. I'll call you if I can't. Otherwise I'll come over as soon as we get home from church."

"You don't have to walk here. Dad said he would pick you up at 1:30 since you live on the way to the freeway. They have showers, so bring something to wear after."

I thought about fancy clubs, where the men had to wear ties. "Does it have to be formal?" I asked.

"No, just shorts, okay, not your PE shorts."

"Formal shorts."

"Yeah, I'll wear format shorts, too."

I had a pair of tennis shorts, a Christmas present from Mom's sister I had never worn because they had been too large. Maybe now they weren't.

"Okay, shorts. Anything else I should know?"

Jen went silent for a bit, then added, "Dad said it was okay if we bumped heads. He even told Mom. She smiled and said, 'Fine.' Scary."

I tried to suppress a yawn, at least the noise part. Too much to my day. I didn't want her to think she was boring me.

"Jon, why did you ask me if I prayed? Do you pray?"

Now I'm awake. When I asked you if you prayed on putting green, and you put your hand on my chest and gazed up at me, I shivered. I still shiver. You need an answer.

"I don't pray as much as I should. Probably not as much as you."

"When I was little, I prayed when I was alone, so I prayed a lot. It helped me through the lonely times. I prayed for someone to care about me. My prayer came true. First, I had Grandpa and Grandma to care about me; now I have you. Plus if things work out, I'll have Lisa, too."

She sounded so hopeful; I didn't want to burst it. I tried a safe question. "When do you see your grandparents?"

"Don't know. Dad and Mom don't share plans. Maybe this

218

summer."

So much for safe. The thought of Jen going away for a while, maybe the whole summer... I pushed it from my mind.

My family is such a part of my life, now larger with Cindy added. Mom has a sister, Dad has a brother, and they both have families. I can't imagine spending my life with only Mom and Dad. We don't always agree on things, but life sure would be empty without Dave and Beth. The others I don't see much.

"I didn't have any other relatives; didn't have close friends either, not for a long time, until you." Jen paused, but it wasn't for me to say something, so I waited for her to continue.

"Jon? You still there?"

"You have more. I can feel it. I'm waiting."

"Really, you can feel it? I do have more." Jen paused again, but only for a second.

"I have spent most of my life alone. Since all I had was me, I learned to get along pretty well with myself. When I first met you, I didn't want to be alone anymore. I wanted to be with you."

"Why did you come back to my locker the second day, after you had moved out of your locker?"

"To see you. You were so gallant. I knew your arm hurt."

"Why did you leave?"

"Everything I said sounded stupid. You were wonderful when you asked me my name. I was too chicken to talk to you. I had to ask a zillion people to find out anything about you because no one knew who you were."

Sounds about right.

"Now, everyone knows who you are."

So Cindy says.

"I hear movement. They must be finished getting their new directions. Mom's about to walk by." She whispered the last part.

After about ten seconds, I heard, "Jenni?" in the distance. They had to have yelled it for me to hear it on the phone.

"Yes, mother?" she replied.

Up closer, "We need you to come out here in the living room."

"Go," I said, and she was gone.

Chapter Twenty-Four

After a restless night, I gave up sleeping and went for a Sunday morning walk in the forest leading up to The Notch, even convincing Rex to come along. With the evergreen trees less wet to walk under in the rain, we did fine, except for dodging around the spring growth already crowding my trails. Another item on my list of things to do during summer vacation.

Feeling better, even without knowing what happened to Jen, I found Cindy making breakfast. Although I could feel some tension between us, I decided to help by dishing up pears for everyone, with the option of peanut butter or cottage cheese.

"Peanut butter?" she asked, watching me plop a glob in my bowl.

"Yum," I replied after a mouthful. I took Cindy's spoon, cut off a snippet of peanut butter, and added a pear chunk. "Try it."

She tried it. "Great for you," she said, shaking her head. She caught my eyes. "You aren't still mad, are you?"

"If I am, I promise to keep it a secret." I gave Cindy a toothy smile to show I was teasing. Her smile back ended our mini feud.

Dad and Mom must have had a good time out Saturday night, as they were the last ones up. Their smiles verified my conclusion. They didn't act as bumpy-butt as Dr. and Mrs. Canfield, but they still liked each other. They needed a hot tub. Except we would all be in it.

Church went fine. I remembered to smile and wave again. This time nothing happened, so I guessed last week had been a fluke.

Parents don't punish the kids for smiling in church. Not this week.

After Sunday dinner, Mom, Dave, Cindy, and Beth filled the kitchen table with wedding invitation samples. Mom planned to print the invitations in her shop. Dad watched a baseball game in the family room, actually not working on his equipment for a change.

As the family room was too far from the front door, and with the four of them buried in an invitation debate, I settled myself outside with my track bag, watching the sky. The rain had stopped, the clouds resting a minute before their next water fight. I hoped for the Z, but didn't expect it. Yesterday's rain was only reason we shared the front seat.

The sky gazing ended with, "Jon, telephone." A phone call meant her dad wasn't coming, and I watched my daydreams of Z riding float away. With everyone noisy in the kitchen, Mom let me take Jen's call in her bedroom.

"Hi Coach. In case you don't already know this, in a few minutes, some strangers will be wanting to pick you up, not Dad. He's too busy."

To Face The World

Too busy? Doing what? If he is too busy, why ask us to do anything?

The "Coach" part had completely blown by me.

Jen answered my thoughts. "He's lining up corporate sponsors. I think I'm becoming an event. Not an important one like Christmas, more like Circus Day. Dad's providing the clowns. If you don't want to go through this, tell them no. Even if I have to go, you don't."

"Corporate sponsors?" I asked. "What are you talking about?" I felt beyond confused. What Jen said didn't make any sense, other than she was unhappy.

"Okay, they aren't corporate sponsors. Dad said it in a joke. It's the reason they called me into the living last night. Some track experts are flying in to assess my potential. Dad's making it into a big deal."

Are they coaches? Personal trainers? Officials?

"What kind of experts?" I asked.

"I guess we'll find out."

"Are you going to be in this car when it shows?" I asked.

"No. They are coming from Seattle and you are closer to the freeway. They are picking you up first."

Who is picking me up?

"What about your mom?" I asked.

If she doesn't like you riding on the bus, she won't like you riding with strangers.

"Mom disappeared this morning before I got up. She's staying with her sister for a while, another part of the conversation."

"Are they okay?" I asked, wondering about her "Stepford Wife" remark.

"Dad seems happy," she replied. "At least he did when I left for church this morning, when he still planned to drive us. Since now he's not, I don't know. Maybe he has more marching orders."

I could feel the tension in Jen's voice when she added, "Are you going do this or what?"

I resisted the urge to ask her what she wanted me to do. She appeared to be doing likewise.

When I didn't answer, she said, "Do what you think you should, Coach," and hung up.

Coach.

Too late, I realized she had said it twice.

Do they think I'm her coach? Am I supposed to make them think I can coach?

I decided to search for help.

While I was on the phone, my family must have picked an invitation, because a discarded pile of samples on the table was the only indication they had been in the kitchen. In the family room, Dad had fallen asleep, leaving me alone with me for decision-making.

Back outside, I watched a huge, silver-colored car approach on

221

John C. Pelkey

Notch Hill Road, stop in front of our driveway, and slowly turn in. I recognized it as a Lincoln Town Car from seeing them on TV. It had to be the first time one entered our driveway.

A woman, barely more than girl even from my point of view, hopped out from the front passenger side. "Jon Perone?" she asked.

"Uh, yeah. Who are you?"

"I'm Connie. I'm here to pick you up."

"You work for Mr. Carling?" I asked.

"Well, not exactly. I work for Mr. Martin, who has detained Mr. Carling, so I'm filling in."

Mr. Martin. Grandpa Martin to Jen. Rich, nasty. Rewards those who mind. Bumps off those who don't. Yeah, I want to do this.

As most of the car had tinted windows, I couldn't see anyone in the back seat. The front seat had a driver. More like a piece of rock chiseled into the shape of a man, barely fitting. If he and the car collided, he would probably win.

"Where's Jenni?" I asked, even though I knew the answer.

"Mr. Carling said it would be better if I picked you up first. He didn't want Jenni getting into an unknown vehicle without a friendly face, you."

What about me getting into an unknown vehicle without a friendly face?

Caught in indecision, I studied the women. She was quite attractive; *knock out* described it better. Tall, red hair long and flowing everywhere, angelic face. Although she wore a modest blouse and blazer with slacks, she had enough shape to make Mrs. Carling jealous. Perfect example of Beth's trophy wife ideal.

Realizing I needed help, or at least some encouragement, she stepped closer. "Jon," she said. "I know I'm unexpected. I'm not in the abduction business. I'm more in the concierge business. How about we drive to the Carlings and you can decide there?"

She held out her hand. I didn't know whether to shake it or take it.

"Please come for Jenni," she added. "She has to do this, with or without you. We need you for support. Please, Jon."

Although Connie didn't appear to be the threatening type, the "with or without" came across as one. The message, "Get in the car or say goodbye to your coaching career," rang inside my head.

"Hello?" rang outside my head. Dad joined me on the porch.

Reinforcements.

"Mr. Perone?" Connie asked.

"I'm Jon's dad."

"Hi, I'm Connie Drayton. Mr. Carling has arranged for Jon and Jenni to work out at a sports complex in Seattle. He has to make further arrangements, so my assignment is to escort Jon there. With your approval, we are picking up Jon first."

"They pay you to escort kids?" Dad asked, with a somewhat

disbelieving sound.

"Among other things, yes sir."

"You knew about this, Jon?" Dad directed his question to me.

"Yes, I knew. Jenni warned -- um -- Jenni told me what to expect."

"Wow, escort service, Jon, just to practice. I guess I will have to watch you run on Friday."

Dad, so much for you being a decision-making influence.

Connie opened the back door, and I climbed in, hearing a chorus of voices in my head telling me not to. I ignored them. If Jen would have to go with or without me, my choice was no choice. I dropped the window and waved goodbye to Dad, who still seemed a bit stunned.

The chauffeur drove meticulously, no wasted motion. Connie introduced him as Tony. I thought of the tiger on Dave's favorite breakfast cereal. He would be closer to Tony the Elephant. It didn't have quite the same ring. Maybe Tony the Rock.

He wore a suit straining to hold itself together. The shirt had to be two feet around at the neck, or better put, what passed as the space between the shoulders and his head. Without looking, he grunted hello.

To make some effort at conversation, I asked, "You work for Jenni's grandfather. What's he like?"

"I don't exactly know," she replied. "I've never met him. Tony has. What do you think, Tony?"

"Not something to discuss," Tony muttered, successfully killing the conversation.

In Jen's driveway, they both turned to face me. Neither spoke. Connie had a *please go get her* implore, Tony more of a *go get her or die* glare. I took it as my cue.

Before I knocked, Jen opened the door. "Et tu, Brute?" she spat.

"Connie said I could decide--"

"Who's Connie?" she asked, cutting me off.

"She's in the car with Tony."

"You agreed to this?" She peered around me at the car.

"I--"

"Fine." Jen slammed the door behind her. "Just don't touch me."

Tony stepped out and held the door for her. He was more than half way between six and seven feet tall and about the same distance around, with maybe one percent body fat. He had to be careful to remember to unlock the car doors before opening them, because he probably couldn't tell the difference.

We sat on opposite sides of the back seat, about a half mile apart. During the twenty mile ride, Tony didn't break a single a law, complete stops, no speeding, proper signaling, everything. Someone should film him for driver's training. I wondered if he ever got mad.

Carefully looking sideways, I studied Jen. She wore a new pair of sweats with a tight fit. They showed she was a girl, instead of an

John C. Pelkey

undefined area with a head, hands, and feet. My math teacher would like Jen as an example of his undefined areas.

"Jon, describe an undefined area."

"Jenni, in her sweat shirt."

"Excellent, Jon, you get an A."

Not today, though. Today she had defined her area, as well as the space around her.

Despite my best effort not to stare, Jen noticed. "What are you looking at?" she growled.

I decided watching the freeway on ramps and off ramps was a better idea.

She played with several buttons on the door handle, trying them all, until one button revealed a solid partition between the front seat and us. Without hesitation, she pressed it. The front seat occupants didn't say anything.

The second the partition closed, she popped out of her seatbelt and crashed into me, catching me completely by surprise. Without a clue of what else to do, I held on.

"Jon," she whispered in my ear, "I'm so scared."

You're scared? What about me?

After several minutes, I dislodged her and pushed her back far enough to see her face.

"Jen, what is going on?"

"I don't want to become a piece of meat. This isn't why I run."

You think you're becoming a piece of meat. Are things more clear or less clear?

"Dad said my beloved grandfather has decided to take charge of my training. He has sent some experts out to review and assess my potential. Dad wanted to keep things informal, but we can see how well that went."

"What do they want with me?" I asked.

"You are the one who taught me how to run. They want to see you, too. How well you train and manage me, Coach."

"Why do you keep calling me Coach?"

"Because they think you are my coach. Otherwise, they wouldn't have invited you."

"If I look good, I get to keep the job?" I asked.

"Maybe. If I look good, you look good. If I look bad, you look bad. I don't know what will happen if we look good, but I do know what will happen if we don't. To have a chance to keep running together, we have to look good."

"No pressure," I muttered.

Jen smiled for the first time. "From the running perspective, not so much. Dad said if I can break five minutes for 1600 meters, they would be impressed. Remember, five minutes is way better than my school

224

record."

For the first time since I saw the car, I almost relaxed. Once she learned to breathe properly, Jen could break five minutes, with or without me. However, besides me, only she knew.

She searched for a seatbelt in the middle, and not finding one, slid back to the other side. "In case you are wondering, I can't only run well; I have to look good, too. So I get to be a girl today. Do you like it?"

"You look defined... uh... refined." *Oops.*

"You said it right the first time."

Jen went back to checking out the buttons, but didn't try any. "I'm sorry I hung up on you," she said, biting her lip. "I'm sorrier I told you not to touch me. I didn't mean it, honest. I should never say what I don't mean."

Again, I thought of Poe's work. I had read it in fifth grade, when Beth had it for an assignment and wanted me to read the ending, because she was too scared.

Only now, I am too scared. Somebody needs to read this ending for me, and not tell me if it is a bad one.

"Did you see Lisa?" I asked, trying to think of something to distract us. It worked.

"We sat together in church today, with Fred and Martha in my spot. We sang, too. Lisa can sing, probably better than I can. I helped her with the service."

Jen smiled, her warm, friendly smile, thinking about it. Having another person in her life had to mean a lot. Even with a tiny part jealous, I smiled, too.

"Pastor Kamorkov wants her to enroll in the adult Sunday School class. She's too old for the kids' classes. Maybe I can enroll, too. All it means is I would go to church an hour earlier."

"She's doing okay?"

"Think so. Dad said I had to leave right after church today, so we didn't get to visit by ourselves. Instead, I got to sit in an empty house for an hour, waiting for his phone call. On Monday, Lisa and I, we're meeting before school to talk, you, too."

Jen searched my face, checking to see if I was okay with her plan. We couldn't reach to bump heads and high five, so we settled for air fives.

Tony exited the freeway. In front of us loomed the sports complex with a huge bubble roof. I had seen it before from the freeway. I never dreamed I would go there. It even had underground parking, so we didn't get wet.

He stopped in front of the underground club entrance and hopped out to open the door for Jen. I thought she was going to beat him to it, but instead she sat and waited. I wasn't about to wait for Connie and managed my own door.

John C. Pelkey

Do rich people ever get into trouble for opening their own doors?

Once inside, Connie checked us in with a single word, "Martin." A woman dressed in a revealing body suit escorted us down a wide, carpeted hallway to adjoining locker room doors. After pointing toward the men's side, she and Jen disappeared into the women's side.

I cautiously snooped around the men's locker room, which seemed more like a hotel lobby. Carpet covered the floor, a contrast to the cement floors at school. The showers were all private, with dressing rooms in front. The attendant took my bag, gave me a towel, and shooed me out the door into the bubble. Jen was already there with the woman.

The bubble appeared larger when looking from the inside. Portable tennis courts filled the middle, with an artificial soccer field underneath. The track, also artificial, ran around the tennis courts. Bleachers lined part of the track, with jumping and throwing areas behind them. On our end, the bubble connected to the building about thirty feet above us. A restaurant, with a balcony inside the bubble, overlooked everything.

"Some of the fastest times in the city have been clocked on this surface." The woman gave me a fancy stopwatch. "Enjoy."

We warmed up by walking around the track. I counted about a hundred people in the bubble. The tennis courts were full. A man and a woman led twenty rather flabby older people in a fitness routine. Some people jogged around the track, but kept to the outside. It seemed Connie's key word had reserved the three inside lanes for us. The jumping and throwing areas were empty. The restaurant balcony was half-full, mostly people visiting. I checked for Mr. Carling, but didn't see him.

Connie appeared up in the balcony. She waved, but we didn't. I couldn't see Tony right away, but after a few minutes he appeared by the men's locker room door. He was easy to spot, as he dwarfed those going in and out, who all gave him some space.

"Come on, let's get going," Jen said, glancing up at the balcony. "Do whatever you had planned for today."

After our warm up, we ditched our sweats. The bubble was hot enough, like a tropical setting with the rain beating against the bubble. Jen skipped counting my chest hairs, but she did smile. I noticed she wore much less to run in than ever before, but not the crop top and bikini panties the professionals wore. Maybe wearing less would improve her times.

I began with intervals, running a half lap at race speed, walking the other half. As soon as we finished the first one, Jen touched my sleeve. "Can I share something with you?" she asked.

"Sure."

"Well, I'm trying something new."

I waited, still walking. She waited, too. "Okay," I said, finally. "What?"

226

To Face The World

"Breathing."

I waited some more. Jen waited some more, too, her face sending unreadable messages. This time I won.

"You said to breathe two in, two out, so I have been. However, since I'm smaller than you are, I think I need less air with each breath, but breaths more often, because my lungs are smaller."

I out-waited her again, barely. She expected me to say something, but I didn't know what.

"I'm switching to smaller breaths and a quicker pace."

"Have you tried it?"

"Not here, but I'll try it now if it is okay with you."

"Sure." I was completely lost because what she said and what she didn't say seemed far removed from each other. "What's wrong, Jen?"

"You didn't think of it."

"So?"

"I thought you would be sore if I did something you didn't think of." She searched my eyes, questioning, but I didn't know the question. She finally said it. "You have thought of everything so far."

Have I?

"Jen, this is about you. You know you better than I do. I wouldn't have thought of it. It's good you experiment. I don't know which exact pattern suits you best."

"You sure?"

"Beyond sure." I nodded until I got her nodding with me. "Let's try it."

Before we began the next interval, Jen jump-kissed me on the mouth, catching me completely unprepared, and left me behind. With so many people in the bubble, somebody must have seen her. Didn't matter if they did or not, Tony saw her.

After eight laps of intervals, followed by four times around at a ninety-second pace, we rested, slurping some water provided by the suddenly-appearing, snarky-dressed attendant.

"Nice for appearances, but not to run in." Jen said. To my unspoken question, she added, "No support. Even what little I have needs support."

She caught me checking her out. "Padded sports bra. Puts back what it takes away and makes me appear normal. Probably doesn't help me run better, but it makes me feel better."

Makes me feel better, too.

To get us refocused, I asked, "Your breathing change, does it work?"

"Yeah, seems to. I need to run faster to be sure." She caught me for a bump and five. "I'm still not used to you being you. I keep expecting you to want to be in control. Everyone else does."

Jen let go and pointed. A group of men had entered the balcony, all in suits. Connie got up and greeted them, then made her way back to her seat next to the railing. Mr. Carling appeared in the center of the group, and even from a distance, I could see all conversation revolved around him. Without touching her, I could feel Jen's tension.

After a couple of minutes of watching us walk, Mr. Carling yelled, "Jon!" over the railing, getting my attention.

Jen gave me a blank stare. "Must be time for the performance," she whispered. "He's paging you, not me. You're up, Coach."

I walked to a point under the balcony where he waited. Connie stood next to him, touching him due to a small press of people crowding the railing around them. "You guys done warming up?" he asked. "Connie says you've been practicing for over an hour. I hope you didn't wear Jenni out."

I could hear some snickering at his supposed joke. I wanted to tell him to come down and run four ninety-second laps after eight laps of intervals, but held my tongue. After all, he hadn't been there to watch.

"Everyone is getting restless, Jon. Have Jenni run something for time, like you did yesterday."

Two minutes and they're restless?

Jen joined me, her face scrunched. "Well," she said, standing with her back to the balcony, "I guess we should give him his money's worth. He brought a big enough audience."

I felt nervous inside, but kept it there. "Okay, yesterday you ran 800 meters at a seventy-second pace, did fine, and said you could go longer. Let's try the same pace for 1600 meters."

You haven't run four laps at a seventy-second pace, so this s a risk, but trying it here in practice is better than in a real race.

She nodded in agreement to my thoughts and walked back to the track, swinging her arms. This was it, the event she said they wanted, to showcase Jen with my training, what little I did.

"Mr. Carling, Jenni is going to run 1600 meters with a target of 4:40. I'll be timing her for the half laps to assist with her pace."

I could hear more snickering from the crowd, as if saying, "This we have to see."

"How are you going to get through?" Jen asked when I joined her. She pointed. I would have to run through three tennis courts.

The players in the nearest court were picking up their equipment. I opened both middle doors to their court and swished my hand back and forth. They waved and walked away. As the middle court was empty, I made my way to the third court, with two men in reasonable shape smashing the ball back and forth at each other. They stopped to see what I wanted.

"My friend Jenni," I waved at her through three sets of bars, "is running 1600 meters for the men in the balcony. To help her, I want to time the half laps. May I run across your court?"

Both men looked in Jen's direction. The man on the right could see

To Face The World

well enough and said, "She's a little girl. How fast do you think she's going to do this?"

"Our target time is 4:40."

"For 1600 meters? A girl? You mean 5:40."

"No, I mean 4:40, really. You can watch if you don't believe me."

"This I got to see," said the man on the left.

"I can't run that fast," the man on the right retorted, "and no little girl can outrun me. If I can race her, you can have the court."

They followed me through the empty courts back to Jen. "This guy wants to race you," I said, pointing.

She shrugged. Not what I expected. She didn't seem to care one way or the other.

"Remember to move aside when I lap you," he said.

Now she showed a little more interest. She tried to appear bored, but her eyes gave her away.

As they stood ready, I checked the courts again to be certain they were empty. Not only were the three I needed empty, so were the rest. Everyone had lined up along the track to watch. So had the new exercise group. The people on the balcony now completely lined the railing.

We got ready. I stood thirty feet in front, indicating I would drop my hand to start. I was certain ten stopwatches came out on the balcony. I tried to appear as professional as possible, starting them and the watch at the same time.

Jen opening burst left the man surprised as he passed me, lagging behind for the first twenty meters. She settled into her pace and he settled on passing her. I remembered my role and took off across the courts, barely beating them.

He crossed in less than thirty seconds, Jen three seconds behind. I got an almost imperceptible nod, but nothing else. She focused on the race, not on me.

They stayed the same distance apart, but their attitudes changed. He went from smug, to confident, to concerned, and, by the halfway point of the third lap, to desperate. She looked more and more like a wolf running down an antelope, and he looked more and more like the antelope. He didn't help his cause by wasting energy glancing back twice a lap.

He was a second ahead, and she was a second behind at the end of three laps, two seconds apart. Even as I sprinted across for the last split time, I could see her closing. She passed him coming off the first turn of the fourth lap, and crossed right on time, flashing me a quick "V" but nothing else to show any emotion. Still focused.

In contrast, he oozed out anger. Underneath his cold glare, I could see his tiny wheels turning with, *No little girl is going to finish ahead of me*.

While running back for the last time, I watched as he almost passed her before the final turn, but hesitated. Now he would have to wait it out. Coming off the turn into the stretch, Jen exploded, and the race part of the race ended. I got a hint of a smile, but nothing more as she crossed the finish. The man stumbled across about five seconds later, give or take.

The stopwatch said 4:35. Jen ran faster than my best 1500-meter time for her 1600 meters, and eighteen seconds faster than my school record. She ran the last 200 meters in thirty seconds after averaging exactly thirty-five seconds for seven 200s. Her dad had hoped for less than five minutes; I had hoped for 4:40. Neither mattered. She was beyond both of us.

The man plopped on the artificial turf next to the tennis courts, gasping. His tennis partner brought him a consoling drink, which he half sipped and half poured on himself. Jen looked much better, and after resting her arms on her knees for a few seconds, she began her warm down walk.

Facing the balcony, I tried not to gloat, but could hear it in my voice. "Jenni beat the target; I show 4:35. The guy nudged 4:40." No one snickered now.

One of the suits spoke up. "I timed her in 4:22 something for 1500 meters. With the way she blew out those last fifty meters, it could easily be less."

Another asked, "How old is she?"

"She'll be fourteen next month," Mr. Carling said, jumping in ahead of me.

Conversation stopped. The group of men stood around, staring at each other, then at me.

"She's thirteen?" the first suit sputtered. "After seeing her run, I thought maybe she was little for her age. Ralph, you're right; she's world class."

He stared down at me. "What's your name, kid? You her coach? How long have you been coaching her? What was her time when you started?" The barrage ended.

"Jon Perone. I'm more of a trainer than a coach. This is our third week running together. We were both in the fives in March."

"Does she have an 800-meter time?" he asked.

When I said, "2:11," I could see the smile dripping off his face. "Ralph, you could have a Junior Olympics double winner standing right in front of us."

Nodding, they all did it together, as if they kept time to some music.

The first suit turned back to me. "Hey, Jon Perone, you're doing a good job. You're no slouch running. I watched you cross those courts."

"Jon has the school record for 1600 meters," Mr. Carling added, reinforcing the comment.

"Yeah, the record Jenni annihilated just now."

She trotted over, looking like she had completely recovered. "Come

To Face The World

on," she said, pulling on me. "You sprinted and stopped, sprinted and stopped; you have to warm down or you'll get stiff and cramped."

As we walked away, the second suit yelled, "Tell the rabbit, good job."

"What?" Helped up by his tennis partner, the newly-labeled rabbit hobbled toward us. "I ain't nobody's rabbit."

"What's a rabbit?" his tennis partner asked.

"Stuff it," the rabbit man barked.

"You." He pointed at me. "You're the kid who hunts golf balls. You supply the range balls for my dad's golf course. You're Melvin's friend."

I had met Mr. Marek a couple times, once to thank him for the golf bag. However, I had never noticed his son.

He held out his hand for me to shake. "I'm Jeff Marek. This is Lenny."

Lenny waved.

"Jon Perone," I said. "She's Jenni Carling."

Jen waved, too.

"Who's Melvin," Lenny asked.

"Melvin, the short geez who relieved you of fifty dollars in that putting contest."

Lenny nodded, the light coming on. "Oh, yeah. Now I remember."

Sounds like something Mr. Hernandez could do.

"I want a rematch," Jeff muttered. "You kids run 5Ks?"

I shook my head; Jen nodded.

"Close enough. This summer. We'll find you. We know where Jon hangs out."

"Isn't getting beat once enough?" Lenny asked as they moseyed back to their tennis court.

We walked the length of the straight stretch and back. "Did Jeff help?" I asked.

"I don't know. I started fast so to rattle him, and I slowed to make him pass on the turn. I might have run faster had I stayed ahead and made him work harder at it. Or I might have used up everything and completely blown it."

Her comment forced out a conclusion.

I have no idea what you are capable of achieving. You did this after running for an hour. What can you do running fresh?

Jen said, "What?" and flashed me a questioning smile, indicating she wanted to know my thoughts.

"You're fast," was all I said.

After congratulating Mr. Carling, the suits filed out. He yelled, "Thanks, Jon. See you sometime tonight, Jenni. You rocked them." He pumped his fist, turned away, and joined the last two suits leaving, slapping both on the back. After a quick word to Connie at the door, he guided her through ahead of him and disappeared, leaving Jen to stare

John C. Pelkey

up at an empty balcony.

To Face The World

Chapter Twenty-Five

I could see Jen's disappointment, as she blew out a long sigh and stared at the ground. She hadn't attempted to argue with her dad. Besides me, I had never heard her argue with anyone about anything. After years of arguing with my brother, sister, parents, and everybody else in my life, this was a revelation.

I fetched our sweats while she practiced being a statue, with shallow breathing and no focus.

This is rock time, me being the rock. Not the time to be anxious or uncertain. I want to be more than someone to help you set running records; I want to be someone in your life you can count on all the time, someone grounded, as you appear to be drifting.

I tapped her arm, holding out her warm up jacket. Wordlessly, she returned from wherever she had gone in her mind and let me help her slip it on.

When I handed her the running pants, she asked, "Aren't you going to help me with them, too?"

Carefully choosing my words, I caught her eyes and said, "I have no idea how."

Watching me closely, a crooked smile plastered on her face, she pulled them on.

Rather than watch her dress inches in front of me, I thought about turning away, but the thought didn't generate any action.

I prepped for some smart remark for my staring at her, but none came. Instead, I got silence, along with clear confusion on her face; she had no idea of what to do next.

"Come here," I said, catching myself totally by surprise.

Further surprise, she came without hesitation. We did the softest head bump and high five ever recorded, and the longest.

"Thanks," she whispered.

Tony had disappeared, but Connie beckoned from the women's locker room door. "Come on, you two. Show's over. You need to shower so we can go. Tony's bringing up the car to take you home."

Jen left me, and trotted to and through the door.

When I didn't follow, still amused by my own thoughts, Connie said, "Come on, Jon." Maybe she thought I would prefer to stay at a club I didn't belong to, with people I didn't know, and situated over twenty miles from home. I glanced around for the last time, and gave up my rich-person moment.

Inside the locker room, I wondered how to get my bag back, but it

John C. Pelkey

appeared with the attendant. He gave me another towel, along with a dinky soap and shampoo, like from a motel room. He even opened a curtain, motioned me through, and closed it behind me. At least he didn't expect to wash and dry me.

After I finished, the attendant escorted me back to the garage door, where Connie waited. As I had taken at least twenty minutes, she must have been standing there the entire time. Through the door, I could see the car also sitting. I wondered how much of their time they spent waiting.

"You could read a book," I said, getting a confused expression back. "To give you something to do while you wait."

"Sometimes, I read," she said, nodding in understanding. "Tony reads, too."

I wondered how big the pictures were in the books Tony read, but decided it wasn't a nice thing to think.

Jen came out in a green shirt and matching shorts, both tailored and fitting quite nicely. I had to fight to keep my air sucking silent. With her hair dried and combed, she was a knockout. I got the image of a rich girl at a country club, drinking tea on the terrace between tennis matches.

She appeared to return the appraisal. "Nice shorts, but you need a better top."

I almost said something stupid, referring to me, not her.

She caught my hesitation, but not the reason, and added, "I know, if I didn't wear something fake like this, I'd need a better top, too."

"Jen!" I snapped, a bit too loud.

She cringed, almost as if I had hit her.

"Sorry," I said. "I didn't mean to scare you."

"Don't be," she said. "I deserved it."

"I don't like it when you put yourself down. I think you look great, your size included. Now and otherwise."

"I'm little otherwise. You like little?" she asked.

"I like you. All of you. It doesn't matter what size you come in."

She tried to smile, whispered, "Thanks," and added. "Then I like your shirt."

Fortunately, Connie had gone through the door when Jen first appeared, and missed our disagreement. She popped back through, "Something wrong?" she asked, clearly indicating she was asking Jen.

"Nothing we can't fix," Jen said.

I could feel her irritation as we followed Connie. Tony, of course, held her door, but Connie let me open my own door. I got the feeling there was a message somewhere, conveyed through the difference in door service, but I didn't know what it was.

The return trip began as a match to the arriving trip, the partition still up and Jen back to the other side corner. No conversation, but a sense of uneasiness, like something I had eaten not agreeing with me.

234

To Face The World

To keep my mind off worse things, I considered her hesitation with telling me her breathing change, which apparently worked quite well. I couldn't think of anything I had said or done to cause her to hesitate. Then the "worse things" part I had attempted to ignore came roaring back into my head.

Jen, you ran four laps today at an overall pace faster than you ran three weeks ago when you couldn't finish three laps. The only difference attributable to me was you learned how to breathe and to pace yourself. I have no idea how close you are to reaching your potential, or if I help or hold you back. What more can I teach you? What more can you accomplish if you have real trainers and coaches?

My uneasiness inspired stomachache found itself on its way downhill to a gut wrench. Her family could hire a coach, as they had hired Connie and Tony.

Is that going to happen now?

My leg must have decided we needed a diversion. I felt a cramp in my calf and stuck my leg out straight, the huge space in the back seat giving me plenty of room. Jen quickly understood my problem, flipped off her seatbelt, and moved next to me.

"Can I help?"

"Right there." I had to point; I couldn't lean forward to rub it.

She found the cramp at once and gave it a squeeze.

"Yeow!"

She massaged it with both hands, softer than her initial effort. After a while, my calf recovered, but Jen continued. She was quite good at it. When she finished, she didn't move back, but sat next to me without a seat belt.

"Where did you learn to massage cramps?" I asked.

"The nursing home I visit on Wednesdays. Some of the old people get cramps. I learned how to get them out."

She took my hand and massaged it, making me feel warm and fuzzy inside. Jen massaging my hand relaxed her, too, maybe more than me. When she moved back to her seatbelt, I let her keep my hand. We had to reach, but we could hold hands across the space between us.

"Car needs a middle seat belt?" I ventured, still wondering where it went.

"I'll remember to include better seat belts in the evaluation," she quipped, showing a tiny bit of smile. "They probably hid it so we couldn't sit close."

When we left the freeway, Jen lowered the partition. "Please take Jon home first," she instructed Tony. Without an acknowledgement, he drove to Notch Hill Road.

At the bottom, I asked him to stop. "You don't have to drive all the way. I had a cramp and it would help to walk it out."

"That's what the commotion was," Connie said, flashing a smile. The

John C. Pelkey

partition must not have blocked out my yell.

When Tony turned onto Notch Hill Road and stopped, I climbed out carefully. I could feel the twinge from slightly bending my knee. To everyone's surprise, Jen hopped out, too, and trotted over to my side of the car.

"Miss Carling, we can allow Mr. Perone to depart here. For you, our instructions are to return you to your home." Connie accompanied her direction with her best, *get in the car,* smile.

"I'm going to make certain Jon gets home. Plus there's no one at my house."

"Miss Carling!" Tony spoke for the second time. "Get in the car."

"My house is locked. Do you have a key?" Jen gave them a stare down, daring either of them to have one. When neither replied, she added, "So your plan is to dump me off and let me sit on my doorstep in the rain?"

"We assumed you would have a key," Connie mumbled, a bit deflated.

"I don't have my purse, and I don't keep a key in my bag."

"We don't think..." Connie stopped talking, probably realizing how lame she sounded.

Jen pounced. "You don't think. Exactly. You've brought me a half mile from home. Unless you expect to sit in driveway with me, waiting for my dad, please consider this close enough."

Connie gave it one last try. "I'm not sure--"

"You're dismissed!" Jen showed a bravery and resolve I could only wonder about.

So much for you not arguing with anyone but me.

Without another word, and as carefully as ever, Tony backed the car onto the empty lot. As he glanced our way, I could see what had to be a smile. Even with two of them, and one at three times her size, they were no match. If Mr. Martin was as tough as everyone described him, maybe Tony thought, *Chip off the old block.*

"I can't believe you did that," I said, as we walked up Notch Hill Road, me carrying both bags.

"What?" she snarled. "I dismissed the help."

"You have access to a key--"

"Which you know about because I trust you. No way do they get to know."

Which I almost gave away by blurting it out. Congratulations, Jon, on keeping your mouth shut.

"I wish I knew what my grandfather thinks he is doing for me. After almost fourteen years of nothing, now he's in charge? Like it makes me what, his new favorite toy?"

I didn't know what, and kept my mouth shut, again.

"My dad, he's like a politician in the middle of a campaign. I can't

236

To Face The World

wait for the TV ad. Mom, with one visit with Grandpa, she goes from, 'Don't do anything' to, 'Have a nice life.' She doesn't even call."

We walked along in silence. Finally, I took her hand. She didn't seem happy with me, so I tried to let go. However, she didn't want me to. Instead, she took my hand and draped it over her shoulder, covering it with her outside hand. She slipped her other hand around my waist, hooking her thumb inside the top of my shorts, and leaned against my chest.

The warm feeling came flowing back, all over. In contrast, I could sense the tension go out of her like the air slowly leaking out of a balloon. Even in the rain, we took forever to walk to my house.

At the end of our driveway, I stopped and faced her, dropping the bags. She silently questioned my action, staring up at me with clear uncertainty in her face.

"Are you okay?" I asked.

"You're asking if I'm okay?" She spun around, as if searching for the answer in front or behind us. "There's no one else here," she said.

After a few seconds, she produced a real smile, not even a fake teeth one. "When you're here and no one else is here, I'm always okay, or at least I'm in route. So yeah, I'm okay. You?"

"I guess. I'm a little concerned."

"About?"

"The future. Like five days could be it. The future appears glum from my side. Who knows what's happening on your side."

"What are you talking about?" Her confusion showed, complete with a nose scrunch.

"Dad said he thinks I'm too young to have a regular girlfriend. I talked him into letting us be until the meet Friday, not to interrupt your training. Then he decides."

Jen replaced her confusion with a hardened-eye grim. "How long have you known this?"

"Wednesday. I didn't want to ruin it."

I feel like I just admitted telling a lie.

"Well, Mr. Not-Ruin-It, why are you telling me this now?" she snapped.

"Because it doesn't matter anymore," I snapped back. "Dad thought we were goofing off, and the running was our excuse. I wanted him to wait to decide until your run Friday to prove I'm serious; we're serious, hoping he would change his mind. Before today, I worried about failure. Today it went the other way. Today, you ran against a man way faster than I am and you blew him away."

"You are worried because you think I'm faster than you are?"

If I am, I'm not about to admit it.

"I'm worried about the suits who came with your dad."

"Suits? That's how I thought of them, too. What about the suits?"

John C. Pelkey

"Now they've seen how fast you are. World-class runners don't have kids for coaches. They have suits."

Jen laughed, catching me off guard. "World class runners. Ha. Not this world-class runner, if even. Jon, I'm where I'm at because of you. We're a package deal. They want world class, choke, they get both of us, not me alone. I didn't run without you, I'm not running without you, and I won't run without you. Don't you get it, Jon? You're the reason I run!"

"What?" I stood there, feeling like a complete brick brain.

Jen huffed out some air, walked about ten paces up Notch Hill Road, spun, and faced me. "I love you." She tossed it at me like a rock from thirty feet away. "You are the reason I run, not the suits. They are not part of this, part of us." Jen smiled at me as if she had solved the equation for pi.

"I love you, too, bunches," I said.

She stomped her foot, but cracked a smile at my first ever use of her favorite word. "You aren't getting it. You already ran, way before me. I knew I was fast, but it didn't matter until I found out you liked to run. The only reason I took up running and got my dad involved in 5Ks was my hope to see you. For two stinking years."

Two stinking years?

It was like she had spit it at me.

"Can we do this closer than thirty feet apart?" I asked.

Jen trotted back to about five feet apart.

Close enough.

"Okay," she said, "prove me wrong."

"No difference," I said, nodding my head while she shook hers.

"Sure, I like to run, since fourth grade when the principal called me a runner. Before you, run was all I did. I didn't try to compete, to get better. Even though I said it, if you hadn't turned out for track, I wouldn't have. Maybe I'm the reason you run, but your role is every bit as important. You're the reason I try. It means we each race because of and for each other."

Following some hidden cue, we collided, right there in the middle of Notch Hill Road in the rain. I picked her up, and she wrapped her legs around my waist. This made everything awkward, as I had to focus on holding her, not falling down, and worse, looking up at her. Ignoring everything, I kissed her, and not one of the little kid kisses we'd done once or twice. This one was a full-blown, down and dirty, mega kiss, from my feet up to my lips and through her lips down to her feet. Whole-body participation, a full-meal-deal kiss.

Yeah!

Several wobbles later, when I stopped, she slowly unwrapped her legs and slipped down, holding my shirt with both hands, gasping. I felt I had finished a marathon, in first place, of course. Ecstatic and exhausted, equally.

To Face The World

"The 1600-meter record," she whispered against my chest. "Whatever it is. If you promise to keep kissing me, I promise to go get it."

Still holding me, she backed up. "Jon, if you promise to keep kissing me, you have to be there, with me. Promise."

"I promise both. If I promise both, you have to promise both, too."

"Then we both promise both. We'll be there with each other. For each other."

"And?" I asked, leaning toward her until we were inches apart.

"Lots of kissing and other stuff. Promise." We nodded together.

Unexpected, instead of more kissing and hugging, she let go and we shook hands.

"Deal," I said.

"Deal," Jen said back.

As we turned into my driveway, we went back to holding hands. My cramped leg had recovered enough for us to skip and we did. Rex, hearing our noise, left her precious doghouse long enough to bark hello from the shelter of our front porch.

Jen stopped short of going in the house. "Do you think your folks will mind?"

"No, Mom said you were welcome anytime, and we still have five days."

"Along with our promises," Jen added.

Although the kitchen door was unlocked, no one was home, only a note from Beth on the refrigerator: I had a little trouble reading it because my glasses were all wet.

> *Jon, we have gone out to find pizza. It takes all of us to decide what to get. Will bring your favorite. Be back by six. Unless we eat it there.*
>
> *DMDC & Me*

"We're all wet?" I announced, as if it could be a disputed conclusion.

"It's what happens when we walk in the rain. You didn't notice?"

"I think I did. I'm so used to it, I didn't consider... you."

Jen shook her wet hair, generating a hint. "I think you did a good job of considering me. We have a half hour wait. Could we get a little drier and warmer before we go back outside?"

I considered suggesting our sweats, but remembered Jen's anti-smell remark. Instead, I trotted upstairs to get her something warmer to wear, and chucked my shirt for a sweatshirt while I was at it. For Jen, I grabbed a thick, plaid flannel shirt from my clothes pile.

"You changed your shirt," she said. "I was trying to get used to you in a shirt. I'm already used to you in a sweatshirt."

"Dry sweatshirt," I said, "and a dry shirt for you, if this works." I handed it to her.

John C. Pelkey

She felt the fabric and sniffed it. "Soft, warm, and fluffy, thanks," she said.

I went into the bathroom for a towel, picking two from the linen closet and swiping my hair with one. When I turned around, Jen stood right in front of me, buttoning the last two buttons of my shirt. She must have changed while following me. It was way too big, the tails hanging past her shorts and the sleeves scrunched up. As I stood with a towel wadded in my hand, she turned around.

"See what you can do?" she asked over her shoulder.

I wrapped the towel around her hair, gently pressing it. Better than swishing it across her head. I was able to get her hair less wet, but not less snarled, which it was from the rain, and probably even more so from my improvised drying attempt.

I took Mom's comb, with a silent promise to wash it after, and worked on her hair, my first ever girl-hair comb. She stood perfectly still, letting me towel-dry and comb her hair. In the beginning, I couldn't comb it through a couple of snags, but once I got the concept down of being slow and careful, I did okay working them out with my fingers.

It took a long time to get every strand to mind, but in the end, they all were much dryer and even more obedient. When I had none left to fight, I ran my fingers through her hair from her forehead to her neck, and then down her back.

I found caressing a spot right above her left ear sent a shiver through her. At first, I avoided it, but my fingers snuck over for another go with the same result. The third time, she slipped away, but came right back.

"Okay, it tickles," she said, laughing.

"Fun tickle or irritate tickle?" I asked.

"Fun, no, irritate, no, not the way you think. I should be able to ignore it."

I wasn't certain what Jen's conflict was, but I did understand she had one. I fished with, "Why would you want to ignore it?"

She spun back around. "You're right. Why would I?"

I continued the finger massage, but went three passes before finding the right spot again. This time, along with the shiver, I got a soft moan and a slight motion, like a shrug.

When I finished, she leaned against me, holding up her hands, buried in the sleeves. I reached around and rolled up the sleeves, squishing her in the process.

"Jon," she said, gazing sideways up at me, while pulling my arms tighter around her. "Please don't take this the wrong way or read anything into it, but what you did with my hair was every bit as wonderful as your kiss."

I wasn't going to take it the wrong way, but I was going to store it for future reference. I liked what it did to her.

240

To Face The World

Jen hoisted her bag, stuffed in her wet shirt, and headed for back door, but, seeing the invitations on the table, stopped and picked one up, waving it at me.

"Dave and Cindy's wedding," I said.

"When? Am I invited? Can I come?" She looked so hopeful, I couldn't even think no, although I had no real say in such matters.

"The wedding is June thirtieth. Sure you can come; you can even sit in the front with me."

"Really? Thanks."

She jump-kissed me again and disappeared through the door. This time I was more prepared, but still not fast enough to grab her. Probably a good thing.

Outside, Jen sat on the bench next to Rex's doghouse. Rex came out and laid her head on Jen's knee, whining in pleasure over getting her ears scratched. "Aren't you in the wedding?" she asked, as I sat down next to her. "I mean, you are the brother of the groom."

"Dave has lots of football friends. I'm sure they'll be his wedding guys. Besides, it isn't a big wedding. I don't know if Cindy's family will even attend. They didn't part on good terms."

"Cindy seems easy to know. She's always nice; she smiles and talks to me. Hard to believe some people don't like her. You do, don't you?"

Loaded question. It isn't so much if I like her, but how.

"She's okay. She makes me nervous, kind of."

Jen stopped petting Rex, who took it as a cue to return to her doghouse, lying down with an *oof* dog sound. Jen studied me, concern and uncertainty fighting for control of her face. "Kind of what?"

"Like she wants something from me."

There, the whole truth and nothing but the truth, so help me God.

Jen smiled, about as opposite a reaction as I thought I'd get. She caught my eyes. "I thought you would make something up, but you didn't. You are so brave."

Jen rewarded me with a kiss, which, somehow I managed to sit through without moving. Already, she was keeping her promise.

She moved back and said, "I see the same from her. Oh, not for me; I mean for you."

I felt her kiss falling to the porch. "Why me? Dave's a hunk and I'm not."

"Being a hunk isn't necessarily a solution to a girl's dreams," she said.

"You don't see Dave?"

"Well, more the opposite. Dave ignores me for the most part, like he doesn't see me. Cindy sees you."

"How do you think Cindy sees me?" I asked, trying to hide a sudden irritation.

Jen scooted next to me and offered a hand for me to hold. "I like

John C. Pelkey

Cindy," she said, each word carefully spoken. "She loves Dave, but she sees you as an opportunity."

"Jen!" I yelled. I wanted to let go, but she did her vice thing.

"Listen. You spoke the truth; I can, too. I'm not jealous or mad. Besides, she isn't going to do anything about it. She likes me, too."

Excellent redirect, counselor.

It worked, too, as. I calmed down. For a second.

"What about us being together?" she asked. "Why do your parents mind?"

Loaded subject. Tread carefully, Jon.

"Dad and Mom have a rule about dating, for me it means not being alone with a girl on a date until I turn sixteen."

"Like with me right now?"

"It has more to do with going to movies or places in a car, dating stuff. Beth for example, they didn't allow her to be alone in a car with a guy. Dave didn't date alone until he could drive. Neither of them have had someone to work with toward a goal, like we have. On Friday, when you set a new record, maybe Dad will realize I'm serious about running with you and he'll reconsider. So I hope."

She let go and stood up. "Finding us sitting here together isn't going to help our cause."

I caught her hand and pulled slightly, but enough to signal my intention. She sat back down, first against me, then away. I pulled her back.

"What if?" she asked.

"We can hear them coming up the driveway long before they can see us around the corner of the porch. Besides, we are outside and not inside. What are we going to do, stand out in the rain to prove it?"

"It would have worked an hour ago," Jen said. I thought she would move, but she stayed against me and made herself comfortable for a minute or two, then sat up. "What would you do if I wasn't here?"

"Probably read. Study my homework, except I finished it. I don't watch TV much."

"I finished mine, too, and I don't watch TV at all."

A sudden inspiration, I popped up. "Be right back."

"What are you going to do?" Jen asked.

"Get a book."

"Bring me one, too?"

I fished around in the living room bookcase, wondering what to read. Thinking of the books Jen had, I grabbed two contemporary novels. As I turned to go, an old hardcover book, with a dust jacket covered in plastic, caught my eye. I set both books down and pulled it out. *Diana*, a novel by R. F. Delderfield. I checked to see how old it was. Copyright 1960, making it historical fiction.

I hadn't opened it before, as it was ancient, and for some reason to

242

To Face The World

my mom, precious. Still, she never said I couldn't read it.

On the dust jacket I read, "John Leigh fell in love twice, and for life, on the same October afternoon -- the afternoon of his fifteenth birthday."

Wow! My age in six months. Close enough.

A woman, much older than fifteen, graced the cover. With red hair, redder lips, and with a completely smug expression, she glared down on the reader with disdain.

I hoped it wasn't a May-December romance, or, since he was fifteen, more like a March-August romance. Grabbing Mom's afghan, I trotted back outside.

"One book?" she asked as I sat at the end of the bench. "What are you going to do?"

"I'm going to read it."

"What am I going to do?"

"You're going to listen."

Jen's frown sprinted into a question, and moseyed on into a smile. "You are going to read it out loud? To me?"

"Yup. Get comfy." I handed her the afghan.

She did, spinning around and fluffing it over her legs. She commandeered my right hand to join hers in her lap as she snuggled against me with her feet up on the bench, leaving me with my left hand to hold the book and to turn pages.

I didn't mind; this was far higher up the cozy meter than when she leaned against my shoulder while we did our homework. Knowing Jen didn't mind how much of her nestled against how much of me, long term, meant so much more than simply being with her. Staying outside had its upside; no way would we attempt this inside.

Thus, from my lips, by thine, I read.

Although easier than *Romeo and Juliet*, which I read with Beth when she studied it, reading aloud became an instant challenge, as I muffed three words in the first sentence and two more in the second. Starting over, I got the hang of it on my second attempt and we drifted into an adventure of words flowing out of the old English countryside.

After a fight, a rescue, and excessive description, I rested at the end of chapter one.

"Well," Jen said, hugging my arm, "Do you think you're John Leigh and I'm Diana?" She flashed me a sneaky smile over her shoulder. "Did you set this up on purpose?"

"Right. I made it rain, chased my family away, subconsciously convinced you to get out of the car and come home with me, and, to top it off, I picked out a book I'd never opened before, knowing we were captured inside."

"Oh, guess not." She turned to face me, letting go of my arm, which landed against her seat. She ignored it and smiled. "Jon, this is incredible."

John C. Pelkey

When I gave her my best, *Huh?* look, she continued. "Reading aloud to me. While holding me. Like this." She spun around, grabbed my arm back, and pulled it against her top with both her hands, giving me an instant, warm sensation.

"Continue," she demanded, seemingly happy in our new and even more cuddly positions.

"My arm?"

"Oh, sorry. Change sides?"

I moved to the other end of the bench and we reassumed our positions, including her moving my arm across her top and holding it.

Cindy would love this. Now, Jen wears my clothes, and she wears me.

"I like this shirt, how the fabric feels against me," she said. "I like how you feel against me, too." She kissed my arm and squished herself with it.

The book, Jon, focus. Ignore the feeling where your arm's touching her.

I gave myself ten seconds to enjoy the sensations of softness and tension, which strayed well beyond the warm, cozy feeling I already had from holding her so close. Then I did it; I refocused.

On to chapter two.

"You know you are John Leigh, hopeless romantic," she added, "but I am not Emerald Diana Gayelorde-Sutton, or any such self-indulged snob. I do care about what you do when I'm not around."

"I am not lanky," I muttered in denial, remembering John Leigh's description of himself.

Half way through chapter three and much closer to seven-thirty, we could hear a car in the driveway. Jen popped up, slid to the other side of the bench, wrapped the afghan around herself, and scrunched her knees up under her chin, facing me. "Don't stop?" she pleaded.

Dad, Mom, Dave, Cindy, and Beth found us outside with the rain, facing each other on the bench, and with me reading and Jen listening. Completely innocent, us.

"What are you doing?" Dave demanded.

"Whatever it is, you are loud enough," Cindy said. "We could hear you from the car."

"So can the horses." Beth pointed. Both horses stood at the fence closest to us, out in the rain and leaning over the railing, as if straining to catch every word.

"*Diana,*" Mom added when she saw the book, a smile crossing her face.

"You were reading it aloud?" Dad asked. Coming last with a single pizza box and a six-pack of root beer, he completed the conversation.

"I guess you stayed there to eat the pizza," I deduced.

"Since it is way past seven, good guess, Sherlock," Beth said, smiling to show she was teasing. To Jen, she said, "I hope you like pepperoni and olives."

To Face The World

As the rest, even Dad, returned to addressing the invitations covering the kitchen table, we ate the pizza in the dining room. Jen had one piece, leaving me the other three. I did split the last one with her, but ended up eating half of her half.

As I downed the last of my root beer, Jen said, "Dad has to be finished playing host to the suits by now. I should go home."

It wasn't loud, but before I could respond, Cindy appeared. "Jenni, I'll drive you," she offered. "I have something to ask you."

As I walked Jen to Dad's car, she fingered her collar and asked, "Your shirt, do you want it back?"

"Keep it and stay comfy," I said, handing her the bag.

Getting a warm smile with thanks and a promise to see me at the bus, we ended with our bump and five before they drove away.

Sigh. One minute we're in the dining room, eating pizza; the next minute I'm standing alone out in the rain.

The second I stepped back into the house, Mom hustled Dad and me into the living room. They sat in the love seat. I folded Mom's afghan, and put it back on the couch, another great stall technique.

"Dad let you get into a car with strangers," Mom said, leading off the adults-to-kid discussion. She didn't say it as an accusation, but I could smell one.

Dad jumped to my side, even before I had a side. "Em, it wasn't like Jon didn't know they were coming, and besides, they asked."

"Rapists and kidnappers asking politely first makes it okay?"

"It was an expensive car," he muttered. "They would have had to be rich rapists and kidnappers."

"It didn't even have a middle seat belt in the back," I added, to help Dad and further confuse Mom.

"Do you think I care about the car and the seat belts?" Mom snapped. She pointed at me and said, "Next time, you don't get into a car with strangers."

To Dad, she added, "And you don't let him."

"Next time, I will know them, Connie and Tony."

"Who?" Mom asked.

"Connie and Tony, they work with Mr. Carling. Tony drove; Connie talked. We went to his fitness club, a great place to run, with an outdoor track under a bubble. Upper, upper crust. Nice track, too. Jenni set a new state record for girls, running 1600 meters."

"So?" Mom said, clearly not on team Jon Perone, boy trainer.

"So, Mom. Jenni, for 1600 meters, she has the fastest time for a girl ever recorded in this state." Not satisfied, I gave it another, "Ever!" for emphasis.

Mom glared at Dad. "Ever," he repeated, smiling.

"The point I'm trying to make is this, Mom. If I hadn't gone with her, it wouldn't have happened."

245

John C. Pelkey

After a heavy sigh, Mom said, "Go clean up your mess," and the kid survived again. They never even mentioned Jen wearing my shirt.

While picking up, as I finished her root beer, Dave wandered in. He took the can, added it to the pile in the pizza box, set it back on the table, and pointed to the living room. All four actions were like the first time for him, and I felt like I had missed a cue or something.

Without a word, he walked across the entry and disappeared around the staircase. Not knowing what else to do, I followed. He sat in the love seat Dad and Mom had vacated, and pointed at the couch. I sat. I wondered what kind of problem he had with me.

"Cindy said I should have already done this, so here goes. You know I'm not good at this kind of stuff."

Good at what kind of stuff?

"Jon, I'm getting married next month. Except you, everyone's helped plan the wedding. Now you need to work on your part."

I must have made a face, because he laughed, something rare with only the two of us. "Yeah, you. I want you to be my best man." He stopped and erased the air. "No, I did it wrong. LB... I mean, little brother... no, Jon, yeah... Please, I'm asking you, Jon. Jon, will you be my best man? Please."

After being stunned for what probably seemed forever for Dave, even though he let me be and didn't say a word, my first coherent thought had nothing to do with his request.

I'm never going to get everything from today to fit on my calendar.

"Okay, Dave. I don't know exactly what it means, but yes."

I wonder if this is what it feels like for a girl to hear a proposal. No wonder girls seem in shock, especially if they don't see it coming.

"Why me?" I asked.

"Because you are more important to me than my buddies," he answered, sounding like he had rehearsed it. "Besides, I didn't know which lunkhead to ask." He hadn't rehearsed the second part.

Dave waved. Beth, who had been hovering out of my life of sight, joined us, sitting on the couch next to me. "We are in this together, Jon Boy, because Cindy asked me to be her maid of honor."

"Congratulations?"

"Tell him the rest," Dave said.

"While we were eating pizza, Dad told us about his concern with Jenni and you. When he got to the part about him considering the need to split you up, Cindy spoke up for you. She even cried a little."

"And," Dave said.

"Okay. I cried a little, too."

"Not that part." Dave waved his hands, indicating more. "Come on, Beth."

"Well, it was important for Jon to know." When Dave continued to wave his hands, Beth waved hers back, both of them laughing.

246

To Face The World

"Cindy," Beth said, refocusing. "Right now, she is asking Jenni to be a bridesmaid. So Dad has to let you two stay together. Well, at least until the wedding."

She snickered at the face I must have made, sitting there still in shock. "You didn't hurt your cause one bit with your porch thing, reading Mom's favorite novel out loud to Jenni and my horses. So obvious, but I'll bet you melted both of them. That was genius."

Genius, maybe, but it had never even crossed my mind. It was simply something we could do together.

Cindy came back an hour later, and seemed quite happy. "We visited while she waited for her dad. Nice house. We mostly talked about you, and no, you don't get to know. Mr. Carling thanked us, and he said how much he appreciates our whole family's support for Jenni. Oh, the most important part, Jenni agreed to be a bridesmaid. Now, if we can find her a nice guy for an escort." She added, "I'm joking," when I cringed.

Better to find an escort for Beth and let him be best man. Wait a minute. No way am I going to give up something so special. Dave had asked me, with my name and a please.

I tried to think of a new symbol to put on my calendar. Something to cover the events of the day, riding my first chauffeured car, setting Jen's record, kissing lots, combing her hair, reading while cuddled together, and becoming a best man.

Funny, but in reference to Jen, the rain kiss was major wow, but the hair comb was more personal and the cuddling much more intimate. Who knew?

I drew two hearts to represent Dave and me, and wove in a Cindy heart for Dave and a Jen heart for me. Adding Jen's new time summed it up.

My bedtime prayer was a thank you to God for being alive and for having Jen to help me focus on what was important. At the end, I carefully crafted a request for encouragement to Dave and Cindy, and last, I threw in a plea for Beth to find someone.

Despite the adverse situation, hers more than mine, I formed a vision of us for longer than the track season. With classes and studying together, choir, running, and yard work, we had a large variety of things to share. My new and much wider horizon painted a wonderful picture, but also a scary picture, full of unknowns, with the New York suit people lurking in the background -- poised and waiting.

John C. Pelkey

Chapter Twenty-Six

Monday morning brought back our routines, capped with the anticipation of Jen's run. Only four days away, it seemed like months. So much had happened in a single week. So much could happen. With a legion of issues competing in my brain for prominence, I left to meet Jen at the bus stop. She arrived before me, but I did get a wave from her dad as he drove away.

We did our bump, which turned into a hug.

"Missed you last night," Jen said, scrunched tight against me.

"We never see each other at night," I countered, trying to figure out what she meant.

"I know," she said, letting go of everything but her smile. "That's why I miss you."

Jen, do I miss you at night? Well, yeah, but not with any expectation it could be different.

Before I could respond, she changed the channel. "Mom called Dad right after Cindy left and before I could grill him about the suits. He disappeared into the bedroom and didn't come out. Coward. He was tight-lipped this morning. I think he and Mom got into another fight." Jen shrugged, the smile gone for now.

To get us onto another track, I blurted out, "Dave asked me to be his best man." This brought her smile back.

"Oh, yeah. Cindy asked me to be a bridesmaid. I didn't think I was important to her, but she said it was more for the future than the past. You and me, we both get to dress up and polish our manners."

"Like in a tux?" I asked.

"Of course like in a tux," Jen replied. "Did you think you could wear your warm up suit?"

"You will have to wear a pretty dress, too."

"No. You wear a tux, and I'll wear my warm up suit. It is fancy enough."

She shuffled her feet and studied the ground before facing me. "It does have pockets," she said, maybe a twinge of guilt clouding the smile, "but they are all hidden inside, including the one with a key."

Jen, you lied. What bothers me isn't your lying to adults, especially irritating ones, but how good you are at it. I don't lie much, not because I don't want to sometimes, but because I can't pull it off nearly as well as you can.

My internal struggled showed, as Jen caught my hands. "Jon, I don't lie to you, ever. Not true. I know I keep things from you, but I don't tell you anything I know isn't true."

248

To Face The World

I considered her comment. My family didn't have significant enough issues to need to cover them with lies to survive. Jen lived in a different world, one where she had learned to say and do certain things to get through the day.

To give her some leeway, I said. "Tell me what you can, when you can. Leave out what you can't. I'm not going to make a demand."

Easy to say, as I don't even know what demand to make.

I saw the expression again, gratitude. It came from her eyes, always locked on me anyway, but also from her mouth, the way she held her lips together.

One more issue conquered, of sorts, we shared a kiss and another hug, right on the corner in front of the whole world, or at least the row of houses across the street.

Does anybody watch? Doesn't matter. I don't know anyone who lives across the street.

With the kiss still fresh, we stayed in smile mode for the bus ride to school, Jen trying to educate me on all the parts of a tux, removable buttons, a bow tie she knew how to tie, and a thing to cover my belt, even if I wore suspenders. I wondered how she knew; most likely, her father wore them.

As we stepped off the bus, Lisa greeted us with a copy of the school paper. "One for my cuz. One for my cuz's squeeze." She laughed at our faces. "Nobody else heard. If I can't tease family, who can I tease?"

We group hugged again, the three of us. "Read it and weep, I always do," Lisa said, quoting the Joan Wilder character from a movie I liked.

The headline read, "Jon and Jenni, stars on and off the field." She had written the article quite well, highlighting both of us. Her article began with our common 1600-meter records and hinted about the chance of a new record happening in the next track meet.

She moved into our outside-school activities. My church choir and City Youth Board participation, my fledgling lawn care business, Jen's Wednesday evenings visiting a rest home on my choir practice night. Only we both missed last time, or at least I did.

Something else I didn't know. Jen was political. On an occasional Saturday morning, she worked as a volunteer for a local conservative representative, opening mail and stuffing envelopes. It smelled of her father's influence. Unlike her, I wasn't political, but I knew Dad and Mom didn't vote for him.

Lisa was considerably better at journalism than I would have given her credit. She had none of the, *Oh, I'm so cute and dumb and everybody knows it,* wiggle in her article. She had left us out as a couple, and my involvement in catching the burglar, to my relief. Lisa the writer was so much different from all the misconceptions of the guys in the locker room, myself included.

"This is great, Lisa. You write good."

"You write well." Lisa corrected me with a smile. "Thanks, you guys were good subjects."

She laughed as I wrinkled my nose at her proper use of the word I purposely flubbed. Another similarity, I deduced, remembering the last person who wanted to correct my grammar. Jen and Lisa were grammar police.

Lisa caught Tom and Trish at the entrance and gave them each a copy.

"Well, how did it go?" I asked, as they read it. "You guys get into any trouble?" They both popped up with the most innocent, *Who, us?* responses to my question.

"We had a great time," Trish said, with Tom nodding agreement. "We went hiking in the rain and saw a bear. Mom and Dad didn't let us out of their sight, though. They said since Tom was such a gentleman, we could camp again this summer."

They beamed happy thoughts to each other from inches apart, before they caught themselves almost in a kiss. Off they went to class, Lisa with them.

Jen stayed quiet and thoughtful as I walked her to her first class. We didn't hold hands like Tom and Trish, but she did run her finger over my hand as we said goodbye in front of her classroom door, sending happy shivers up my arm.

Small things make a difference.

The Monday school announcements generally were boring, nondescript stuff about getting fees paid by a deadline or if some part of the school was broken and out of bounds until fixed. Not this Monday.

"For all interested parties, the final track and field meet with North Valley Middle School has been rescheduled from Friday to Thursday, to allow for the full opportunity of Labor Day Weekend."

Normally, it would not have been a big deal, and wasn't' until it sunk in.

My four days left with Jen have instantly shrunk to three, along with Dad rearranging his schedule to take Friday afternoon off now also shot.

I went into an immediate internal meltdown.

I heard a vague, "What's wrong," from Ed across the aisle, and had to bring myself back.

"They killed a day of practice. I want to be ready for Rafer and I need it."

"That's all?" he asked.

No, but that's all you are going to get.

*****

The after-school track practice got weird. The coach seemed more

To Face The World

anxiety-ridden than normal, and not from the lost practice day. "We're going to restructure Thursday's events," he said, waving a schedule. He went around the group with assignments. When he came to me, I got my first clue of the extent of his concern. "Jon, I need you in a race besides the 1600, something you can get us a point for."

"What about my jumps?" I asked. I had scored in every meet so far.

"They have three guys jumping five and a half feet or better, and have swept the high jump all season. Maybe Jim can get us a point there; maybe he can't. I'm not going to waste an opportunity if you can get us points somewhere else."

I checked the schedule. The 800 was too close to the 1600 and Rafer Washington. I needed to try something shorter I could conquer with three days' practice. Jen, facing me, held up two fingers. "How about 200 meters?" I asked.

"Okay, he said. Your goal is Ed and you, one and two."

"About time you practiced eating my dust," Ed said.

"For the 1600..." The coach cringed.

"I can beat Rafer."

"He set a new school record last Friday, and it is five seconds faster than yours."

"Then I'll set a new record."

"Don't foul it up, Jon. We need at least a second."

I knew track was a team sport, but I wasn't about to give up my race, and the opportunity to at least try to beat Jen's time. Still, I didn't like the way I sounded, boastful, even to myself.

The coach saved Jen for last. I guessed she fit what saving the best for last meant. "I want you to run a third race; maybe you can get us more points."

"What about the 1600?" she asked.

"Their best runner is over ten seconds slower than your record. You should be rested enough after the 800 to still win it."

Instant shock. Jen had been skipping the 800, giving Marianne a chance to win and letting a mousy seventh grader named Sandi get the opportunity to score points.

"May I run the 100 and 200? Then I'll be more rested for the 1600."

The coach considered this. "They have three good 100-meter runners. How about running the 200 and the 400?"

"If I run the 100, they can't sweep," Jen countered. "I win; we begin the meet ahead."

I did my absolute best to cover my, *What did you say?* reaction. Jen had simply said she could beat anyone on the other team. It wasn't boasting or idle chatter.

What is it? Confidence. I have confidence. Why does her confidence sound so much better?

We had talked about running, not confidence. Although I had often

251

John C. Pelkey

told her how fast she was, this was the first time she admitted it. Somehow, without my help, she had found hers. More so, she could articulate it without boasting, something I struggled with internally.

How can I learn to present confidence?

The coach's face echoed my thoughts. He checked his schedule, and then checked Jen. "You sound like you think you can win both of them. You have only run one of them once."

"Yeah, and I set a school record. I want to lower it."

Confidence. Simply show it, no frills, no boasts, no, "Eat my dust." Simply state the facts; Jen can. I need more practice.

While I forged an internal struggle, all tense, Jen seemed as relaxed as ever, confidence flowing out. The coach considered her reasoning, almost said something, shook his head, and shrugged.

"Okay," he said, to my relief. "You can run the 100 and the 200, as long as you win at least one of them."

"It isn't only winning," Jen said, a smirk overwhelming her face. "It's whose time I can beat."

Coach Harris seemed confused until he saw me.

I snapped, "You're on," to Jen before he could comment on his own. Maybe I could do confidence, too, without the boasting part, as long as it wasn't for more than ten seconds.

Coach Harris pointed at Jen. "You're running against the girls." Back to me, "You're running against the boys."

"But they aren't the real competition." We said it in unison, even without practicing.

I needed to rethink this new confidence-sharing thing. Despite my own concerns about showing off, sounding confident was cool.

When the coach moved on, instead of joining our separate practice groups, we broke the established routine to work together. I began with 200-meter intervals at thirty-five seconds, walking 200 meters, and each time cutting down two seconds. When we ran a perfectly-timed match of twenty-nine seconds on the fourth interval, Coach Harris caught us.

"How did you do it?" he asked.

"Timing," I answered, waving my watch. "We run fast enough to knock two seconds off each time. It helps us build up to race speed."

"No," he said, waving his hands back and forth as if to erase my response. "Not the timing. You two running together. I came to tell you to separate. Jenni needs to work with the girls and you with the boys. But when I watched you. You were both in a dead sprint, and yet, start to finish, you stayed exactly even for the entire... How did you do it?"

"We've been practicing. Since we run the same speed, it's not hard." I wasn't going to lie, but I hoped it didn't get us into trouble. The school had no rules about kids running together, but the coach could have his own set, unpublished.

"Ed!" he yelled. Ed was across the track working with the other

To Face The World

short distance runners. He trotted over. The coach caught his shoulder and said, "Ed, educate Jon and Jenni on how to run 200 meters."

"Sure, coach." Ed's smile reinforced his, "eat my dust," comment earlier.

No way. Not without a fight.

As we set up the blocks, Ed took the outside. He muttered, "Come on, pretty face. I'd say, 'Let's see what you got,' but I won't be seeing either of you until after it's over."

Confidence or boasting? I decided it was boasting.

Jen, in the middle, seemed more irritated with the face comment than his challenge. She moved over to my lane. "Obviously, he's referring to you, so you run next to him."

"Hey," Ed protested as we swapped, "the second lane's the best. I was giving you a chance by taking the outside."

"Outside is fine with me," Jen countered. "Catch me." She stepped in front of him and adjusted the block to fit her.

The Jen and Ed swap put her ahead in the staggers, me still in the middle. The coach didn't say anything until he got the automatic timer set. "I don't want to see twenty-sevens on the clock," he said, pointing at it. I didn't know if he referred to Ed, Jen, me, or to all of us. Jen had run a twenty-seven second 200 to finish her 800 on Saturday. He wasn't going to see one from her.

On the coach's go signal, Jen shot out of the blocks. I hadn't done much block-start practice and my lack of skill didn't help my cause. Ed caught me before the turn finished and I took up residence in third place. It was almost worth it watching Jen blow us away. Somewhere along the way, my competitive gear snuck in and I didn't let Ed go. I had to make up two meters in the last fifty, and barely managed it before we crossed.

Ed had almost caught Jen, but when she floored it for the last twenty meters, I could see some space growing behind her as we finished.

Ed didn't stop, but continued in a slow run around the track. Jen's face clouded as she watched him go.

"It wasn't his best race." I said, between air gasps. "He wanted to wait for the finish to blow by you."

"I know," Jen said, less gasping, more grim. "So I waited, too."

My heart pounded, wanting out. Although 200 meters was a tough sprint, and I wasn't used to it, Ed was. For the final meters when we all ran our fastest, as I caught him, she pulled away. Worse, or better -- I didn't know which -- she knew she could. If I wanted to continue this, I didn't merely need to train her, I needed to train me.

"I guess I needed a better instructor for you two," the coach said. "Why did you two stop training with your proper distance groups?"

"They aren't fast enough," I replied.

"I suppose now you don't think Ed is either."

John C. Pelkey

The glare accompanying his remark caught me by surprise. We watched him trot off to console Ed. Yes, he and Ed had misplaced confidence, but it wasn't wrong to win.

There were politics in track, as in everything else in life. It wasn't always so obvious. Instead of praising Jen for her victory, almost all the runners avoided her, and, by association, me, as if we had contracted something contagious. Even the coach seemed perturbed. However, his sudden one-on-one care and feeding of Ed's ego kept him occupied and freed us from everything except some not so smart remarks, even from her friend Marianne.

"Ignore them," Jen said, easier for her than for me, and we continued to work together, unencumbered by anyone or anything. This was nice, because with her dad now watching her each night, the morning bus ride and track practice were the only times I saw her.

*****

The next morning, she seemed troubled, perhaps by her family situation, and she wanted me for my presence more than for my voice. After my greeting, she touched my mouth with her finger for silence and simply leaned against me, waiting for the bus and while on the bus. Although she could go for hours with me not saying a word, I didn't have such an easy time. My mind flowed with an endless list of topics to share, discuss, and ask for her opinion.

To make things tougher, when her dad showed up for practice, he wasn't alone. Connie sat with him and Tony played shadow next to the stairs, probably chauffeuring the suits who came with him.

"Mom's still gone," she said on Wednesday morning, the only words she spoke.

During practice, she focused on running, listening to my directions and plans, and ignoring everything and everyone else. My time with Jen was both plus and minus, time alone with her being the plus, and too quiet and too short being the minus.

My other social moment, lunch at our table, had taken a downturn, even with Lisa bubbling over on everyone. Ed and Dan sat on the opposite end, trying to participate with the group and at the same time ignore me.

During Wednesday's lunch, Trish confronted Ed with, "What's your problem? Jenni caught you goofing off and beat you. You know the solution, don't you?"

"Which is?" Ed asked.

"Duh. Run faster. Jenni would be stupid to run slower so you can win."

He said nothing to Trish, not with Tom watching. To me, he said, "No mercy, tomorrow."

254

To Face The World

"None expected," I returned. I thought about adding something juicy to stir the soup, but sometimes Dave's advice could apply to guys, too. I left all comments in the keep-my-mouth-shut drawer.

*****

The team's continuing tension spilled into Wednesday's practice, where we became a slew of running icebergs, cold to each other and floating around in our own world. Everyone worked hard, but no one had much to say.

The coach, instead of rallying the troops, acted more tense than we did. He kept shaking his head, rubbing his eyes, and groaning, as if we had already lost. He carefully went over everyone's assignments again, even after he had done so on Monday and Tuesday.

When he got to the 200-meter race, he pulled me aside. "Jon, you have the 1600 to win for us. You guys could finish one, two for the 200. I don't think you have noticed, but Ed has been chaffing for his chance to shine, and this is it. If he has a chance, help him take it."

If I had heard it repeated from someone, I would have called them a liar, would have thought it, anyway. This, however, was straight from the coach to me. Run slow and throw the race for Ed.

"Did you tell Jenni, too?" I asked, trying not to boil over.

"I don't need to. Ed can beat any time Jenni puts up." He made it sound irrefutable.

I let it go. If Ed could beat her time, he could beat me.

"Perone," he said, with irritation showing instead of anxiety, "you don't worry about Jenni. You focus on Rafer Washington. Beat him."

When he set his clipboard down to talk to someone else, I noticed the North Valley 200-meter times. They had two runners faster than anything Ed had run, one by almost a half second.

Coach, you're delusional.

He finished his latest revisions and pep talk with Jen, again, as he did last time.

"Jenni, I should have thought of this before I let you talk me into what races to run. Think of it this way. You have the opportunity for something truly rare. I know you have only practiced this with the relay team, but I want you to run 400 meters instead of the 100. If you win it, you can coast in the 1600. You already have the school records for the 100, 800, and 1600. Running the 200 and 400 will give you the opportunity for a sweep. You could own the right side of the record board, every single race. If we are ahead, you won't even have to run the 1600."

Jen's face remained blank, but the rest of her resembled a mountain about to explode. Even though her hands weren't in fists, her knuckles had turned white. She appeared locked into tense mode. I needed to do

255

John C. Pelkey

something before she did.

"Coach, please, let Jenni run the 1600."

"Why should I, Mr. Perone? Furthermore, why should I listen to you? Didn't we--?"

"Sunday, Jenni ran 1600 meters in 4:35."

Cutting him off only fueled his anger. "Jon, will you stop? This is serious. Sure, Jenni can run, she has some fast times to prove it, but, come on, 4:35? I don't need fabrications."

"We ran on a track in Seattle, the sports complex under the bubble. Her dad had some suits from New York in the balcony timing her. The same suits are now sitting in the stands." I pointed.

Following my finger, his face went from anger to uncertainty to disbelief. After a long stare at the group watching, he appeared to add dread. "She can't run 1600 meters in 4:35," he muttered. "No one her age can." At the same time he said this, he wrote something on his clipboard.

"It's why they're here, Coach, to watch her run. The record is 4:34, set in 1986. She wants to break it." If Jen could sound confident without boasting, I could, as long as it wasn't about me.

"You're talking about the high school record, way beyond anything... She's not even in high school." He stopped, gave the stands another look, and glared at me. "Who's coaching her?"

"I am. For the past three weekends. It isn't against school rules for us to run together on weekends. I checked."

The coach glazed over, as if I had informed him of something terrible, like someone had run over his dog. "Four... thirty... five," came out, slowly.

He faced Jen, who he should have been talking to all along, not me. "Tell you what. You run the 100 and the 200, you skip the relay -- we can let Sandi run it -- and you can have your shot. As much as I want my track team to own all the school records, having a national record? Yeah, I can live with it."

He left us, and the kids scattered, carefully avoiding Jen, who, judging from the glare from her eyes, was about ready to explode. "Why are you fighting my battles for me?" she demanded, her hand pushing against my chest.

I had no idea what to say, but I had to say something, something good. I looked her straight in the eye, not flinching despite her fuming, opened my mouth, and let go with, "Because you are worth fighting for."

She began a rebuttal, probably already rehearsed, but caught herself when what I said registered on her face. She opened her mouth, closed it, opened it again, and said, "Wow." Her thank you smile provided enough warmth to get me through the rest of the day.

*****

256

To Face The World

In my room, I drew a pair of boxing gloves on my calendar. I practiced a dozen times on paper first, so I could tell they were gloves and not donuts. I smiled to myself about my situation.

Despite everything, including the challenges and uncertainties of running, right now, maybe you're thinking about missing me to match my thinking about missing you. All in all, you are worth fighting for.

Chapter Twenty-Seven

Thursday morning finally came. I hadn't slept well Wednesday night, but the excitement of what could happen overcame the weight of the previous day's tension. Today would be our most important day so far, running wise. The sun smiled a greeting as it popped out from behind Notch Hill, warming up the bird choir in the trees around our house as I went out to feed Rex, the cats, the cows, and Beth's neglected horses. For once, Mother Nature was on our side.

I knocked out twenty chin-ups without pausing, but doubted I could ever do thirty again unless inspiration hit me in the form of Jen watching. Still, twenty twice a day was routine now.

While feeding the horses, I heard a warning growl from Rex, who checked the barn door. The cats went through a second of concern, but food came first, so they ignored the door opening. I thought of Beth, out to give her horses their mandatory five minutes, but instead, Dad appeared.

Skipping good morning, he launched in with, "Are you feeding Beth's horses?"

"If I'm going to feed Rex, the cats, and the cows, adding horses isn't a big deal."

What's wrong, Dad?

"About the horses. Beth wants a car, so I told her the horses have to go first. Jenni is the only one I've seen riding them this month."

I found myself petting Janet, who nickered a thank you. More than leaning over the fence to listen to me read aloud, the horses wanted attention.

Attention, I can do. Petting them, yes; riding them, no.

Dad headed for the door, but I couldn't imagine he came out to talk about horses. When he turned back, I knew whatever he had to say was about to happen.

"Jon, I might not be able to watch you run this afternoon. We have a tricky section today, pushing the pipe under an intersection, almost one hundred feet between openings. We have to begin and end today, and any complications will drag things out. I rented an extra backhoe so I can dig and bury each side at the same time. If it goes perfect, it is a six-hour job. But as you know, seldom does anything go perfect."

I thought of a dozen things to say, all about me, but settled for the only one I could think of about Dad. "If it doesn't work out for you, Lisa is writing an article for the paper. Tomorrow, you can read about how well we ran."

To Face The World

"Your school paper doesn't come out tomorrow." Dad's confused expression revealed his issues with talking to me; something he exhibited in any conversation more important than about food.

"It's in the Aurora Valley News. Mrs. Koffman got her a guest slot in Friday's paper."

"Two papers in the same week. You've been busy."

I wanted to jump up and click my heels, or something.

The upside, you read Lisa's article. The downside, if my cause needs help, you missing the final meet won't help.

"I'll do my best not to miss it."

"Jenni runs last, probably well after four. If it takes eight hours..." I stopped. Somehow, the second I mentioned Jen, Dad morphed into a defensive parental unit position, his face scrunched in irritation.

"I'm not coming just to see Jenni," he growled.

"I run right before she does, but her run counts, not mine." I wasn't about to let it go.

However, Dad was. "Let me clear up something. If you think my showing up, or not showing up, is going to influence my decision about Jenni and you, it isn't."

I tried to read Dad, hoping his face could give away something, but it didn't, which was why he could always beat me at chess. From his appearance, I could never tell if he thought he was winning or losing. Right now, I appeared to be the one losing.

"We'll talk after your meet. You need to focus on beating Rafer Washington."

Dad had read about him. His encouraging me in track was also something new.

Flush from my ability to be zero influence on my Dad, I set off to meet the bus, cresting the last rise in time to watch Mr. Carling drive away for the fourth time in a week.

"How does your dad time it so well?" I asked her after our morning bump and five.

"He doesn't time it. He stays until he hears you coming. He doesn't want me to wait for the bus alone."

I walked up the road and back, listening to myself. I wasn't a super sleuth, but I didn't make enough noise for people to hear me when I was out of sight. Mr. Carling had x-ray hearing.

While on the bus, I thought of talking to Jen about what my dad had said, but dropped it. Although our relationship was like finding a shiny new penny, it also had more issues than my entire piggy bank, the lack of a future being the big one. Tough enough for it to dominate my thoughts. She had enough thoughts going on and didn't need me throwing rocks at them. Besides, her leaning against me on the bus felt nice, even if it could be for the last time.

Lisa met us at the bus door, wanting another group hug. So did

John C. Pelkey

about one hundred other kids, and, circling the school sign, we executed a massive shuffle-hug, which quickly fell apart into laughter. If nothing else, almost everyone in the school was pumped.

Although we had to attend class, even the teachers were too excited to ask for much. We got a lecture from each of them on good sportsmanship, the importance of trying over winning, and an admonition to annihilate North Valley.

A rally preempted last period choir, so we jammed into the gym together. Banners and pictures covered the walls and spilled into the hallways. The rally was full of spirit, including our fight song, which we repeated until Mr. Koffman reeled us in. Coach Harris introduced the track team one by one to rousing cheers. He introduced me as the guy who was going to make mincemeat of Rafer Washington. The school gave me a loud cheer. Jen, he introduced last to a louder cheer. It helped when he mentioned a record or two might fall.

The students had been making chants for the different team members. "Drop the bomb, Tom," morphed into, "You can win, Jim," on to, "Ed and Dan, fast as you can," and other yells, ending with, "Jon and Jenni, beat them plenty."

As the track team left, Mr. Koffman cornered me. "Hold up, Jon."

Captain Phillips and Officer Thompson joined us on the stage, with Dr. Canfield bringing up the rear. In front of everyone, they had to say something about the burglary. Captain Phillips made a speech, Officer Thompson put a ribbon around my neck, and somebody gave the mike to Dr. Canfield. Remembering his previous conversations, this made me nervous.

Dr. Canfield addressed everyone. "Jon, the Mrs. and I want to share our appreciation to you for your service, both to our yard and to our fortunes. Now we got through the boring part, let's get to the important part. You guys go out and whip them varmints from the north end, ya hear?" For his effort, he got a cheer.

Mr. Koffman handed me the mike, indicating he expected me to give an acceptance speech. Since I had no idea what to talk about in reference to the burglar, and I wasn't about to tell anyone I only went to Dr. Canfield's house to get away from Lisa, I focused on the meet.

"You can come to the meet and see records fall, or you can read about it in Lisa's articles, in the Aurora Valley News tomorrow or in the school paper next week. Better if you do all three." Silence; they all waited for some punch line I failed to deliver. "See you all after school. Be there, or don't be there."

Satisfied I had messed it up sufficiently, I handed the mike back to Mr. Koffman, who immediately went into something else.

Adults. They think they invented awkward, not us kids.

I felt so much relief when they let me go.

"Oh, my hero," Alyssa loudly announced as we exited the gym.

To Face The World

Before I could think of a reply, Jim covered for me with "Shut up, Alyssa. You never did anything important."

Jen and I traded raised eyebrows.

Jim, my archrival, defending me? Or is it something else?

"He likes her, doesn't he?" she whispered.

"Or he doesn't like her," I replied, mostly to myself. It dawned on me; for some kids our age, they were pretty much the same thing.

When we stopped at the girls' locker room door, Jen fingered the medal tied to the ribbon around my neck. "Pretty cool," she said.

"Here," I said, taking it off. "You can wear it. Better than the ribbons we win for running."

"I like my ribbons. I pinned them on my wall. What do you do with yours?"

"Nothing. They're still in my locker."

"I'll keep it for now, but it should go on your wall. I'll find a spot. For your ribbons, too."

Fine with me. You can decorate my walls all you want. More photos will be a good start.

"Remember three weeks ago?" she asked. "I wanted so badly to beat you. Now maybe I do, maybe I don't. The record isn't important to me anymore. Being with you is. This sounds dumb."

"Jen, it's not dumb. Break my record. Somebody else will break it eventually, anyway. Better to be you. Let's go get them."

As she disappeared into the girls' locker room, I thought of a place for the ribbons.

You can staple them to my calendar next to my drawings. As long as I get to watch.

When they announced the boys' 100-meter race, the first event, I scrutinized Coach Davison's event list while listening to his pep talk. Like Coach Harris, the North Valley coach had restructured their entries. Both coaches had kids with no previous race times competing and had shuffled out kids with mediocre times.

The adults seem more focused on winning-or-else than the kids are.

Jen won the 100 meters, the first girls' event, and our girls began five to four instead of zero to nine when they took second and third. She had to eclipse her school record to win. The North Valley team was miffed; they had expected us to hand them an opening sweep for both the girls and boys. Every other school had.

The announcer flashed her name and time on the scoreboard. "The 100-meter race winner, Jennifer Carling, has set another school record and a league best this year."

I had to admit, 12:23 was impressive. I would be happy to be as good.

I finished third in the long jump, barely beating out their second guy. With a second and third, Jim and I still got our team some points.

John C. Pelkey

We lost the 1600-meter relay, but I couldn't have saved us, even if I'd run it. Their guys were fast, all four. Ed and Dan didn't stand a chance, much less me. I wondered if one of their runners was Rafer. Unlike the individual running events, they simply announced the winner as North Valley, so I didn't know.

The 200-meter race came next. I had practiced block-starts all week, but still wasn't a rocket. Jen was a rocket and had beaten everyone in block practice.

Ed, with the season's third best time, ran in the third lane. With no previous 200-meter time, I ran in the sixth. With the staggered starts, if I finished first, I wouldn't even see anyone else. Not likely. More likely, I would see all of them on their way by.

As I adjusted my block, I heard Jen's voice, "Jon!" I saw her standing with the girls' 200-meter group. "Beat me," she said. "Dare you."

Since she wouldn't run until after I finished, I countered with, "Since I run first; you'll have to beat me!" I got a nose scrunch with the smile.

Dan, in the lane next to me, muttered, "It's probably you against me for fifth."

Ed left his spot for a second and joined me. "If you win, no hard feelings," he said, reaching out to shake my hand. The three North Valley guys started laughing. They were still laughing right up to the, "Ready!"

Bang!

I almost flinched, but managed to push instead, one of my better efforts, but still a meager start. I decided to go all out for the entire race, not save anything, and see where it took me. I was almost through the curve before I saw another runner, over in the first row. Soon, I could see two more; at least Ed was one of them.

What to do when running your fastest and guys are passing you? Run faster.

I shortened my stride, pumped harder, and put everything I had in the last twenty meters. I felt my legs go to lead, but crossed with the proper lean and everything.

The winning time popped up on the clock: 25:94. Lane one, not my lane. It was slow, compared to his best time, but still good enough. The rest of the times between us began with twenty-six. Lane two came up fourth, lane three, third. Sorry, Ed. At least he got us a point. Lane four came up sixth, lane five, fifth. Dan got his wish, fifth place. It sunk in the same time as the board indicated second place in lane six at 26:00.

The announcer confirmed it with, "Second place, Jon Perone, South Valley."

Me. I beat Ed, despite the coach's instruction. Instead of one, two, we were two, three. Except I finished on the wrong side of Ed, ahead instead of behind.

"Hey, Jon," Ed said. "Nice run. Lane six is the toughest. You could have won in my lane."

262

To Face The World

We shook hands again, seemingly a weird thing to do for kids. Dan added a back pat.

I guess it means our feud is over.

When Ed insisted we turn and wave to the crowd, I got a surprise. Dave, Cindy, Beth, Mom, and Dad all sat in a row next to Pastor Kamorkov.

My dad had come to watch me run for the first time. Not Dave in football, but me in track.

Seeing you here, regardless of his verdict, is as good as a win. At least it is right now. If you decide against us, I'll feel differently.

More important, being here means your pipe connection went perfect, or you left it. Not much chance of the second option. Since you're here, how you got here doesn't matter.

If you saw Jen's first race, you have to know I'm serious, especially with her setting a new record. If she can get another one, my case will be complete. I don't want to think of you as a judge, but for their kids, parents are judges.

When I waved, Beth curved her hand back and forth, mimicking a parade wave, and pointed at me, wanting me to copy it. Since I was on display, I copied her parade wave to please her.

I noticed Mr. Carling several rows behind them, sitting with Connie and several other suits, all dressed way too fancy for a middle school track meet. They looked like the suits who watched us on Sunday and during the week.

I felt the tension rise inside me. "Not now," I said out loud, to Ed's questioning frown. "Parade wave." I showed him. "It's dumb."

"Your girlfriend's up," he muttered in response.

Across the field for her 200-meter race, Jen adjusted the lane six starting blocks I used. She also didn't have a previous time.

Too late to get to there before the start, I moved to the finish line on the side closest to her lane. Ed and I were only a few hundredths of a second apart, so if she beat Ed, she would probably beat me, too. Although I had never run 200 meters outside practice, this had been my fastest time ever. I wondered what was fast enough for Jen. Even if she only came close, it would be a huge victory for her.

Take care of her, I prayed, catching myself and wondering if it was the right thing to do.

Bang!

Jen shot out, short strides, pumping hard as if she was at the finish instead of the start. Even with the curve, it didn't appear the others had gained on her. She kept the lead to the straight stretch, flying right at me. When I didn't think she could run any faster, with twenty meters to go, she found another gear, the same as she had in practice when racing Ed and me. *Whoosh.* No one was even close. She should have run in our race. I watched the clock. Anything beginning with twenty-six would be a school record.

263

John C. Pelkey

When the twenty-five popped up, the crowd in the stands lit up with a common, "Oh!" The two zeroes after the twenty-five didn't register at first. They looked like eyeballs staring at me. When they did register, they came as a shock wave. Jen had not only beaten me; she had crushed me along with the rest of the boys, like a football score of fifty to nothing.

In the stands, I watched Connie give Mr. Carling a hug. The other suits slapped his hands. Old guys high-fiving seemed dumb, but I wasn't about to tell anyone. Besides, Connie's hug bothered me more. It wasn't a hug like one I would give to Mom; more like one I would hope Jen would give me.

Ed, standing next to me, asked, "What are you putting in her drinks?" before shaking his head and walking away.

Although elated with Jen's win, inside I felt almost the same way. In missing first place in my race by six hundredths of a second, I was close. No part of Jen blowing us out by a whole second could we consider close.

I watched the suits conferring, and coming to some common conclusion.

Consensus is what they call it. Whatever they need from Jen, they now have, and they have it before her most important race.

Chapter Twenty-Eight

After walking the rest of the straight stretch, Jen trotted back to meet me, not even looking as exhausted as I still felt. "Beat you," she said.

I waved at the suits. "Made them happy."

"I don't care about them," she snapped in reply. "I care about you. What you need to do to get your second back. If you could learn to break faster, maybe you could."

Leave it to you to find something positive to say.

"I think it's going to take more than starting blocks."

"So what? I still love you, even if you are slow." She had a wicked grin to go with her quip.

We had some time before our final races. Since we weren't supposed to visit people in the stands, I stepped off the track and walked around on the outside, taking Jen's hand.

"Your dad's here," she said.

"Yeah, like for the first time ever."

"Is it to decide about us?"

"If it is, you setting two new school records should help."

Or not.

She smiled and nudged me. "I never thought of it. Running to save us works. All we have left is to find Beth a boyfriend?"

Not likely to happen in the next hour or two. I wonder if it is the most critical part. To be honest, I wish Beth could find a nice boyfriend. She seems so lonely, like I used to feel.

Holding hands wasn't enough. Jen slipped my arm over her shoulder and her arm around me, giving me the support she needed from just finishing the race. We were the most intimate we had been in front of anyone, but I didn't care. In case Dad decided against us, I wanted us to have a last time close together.

"This works," she said. "We need to relax. You need to relax, so you can get me back in the 1600. You don't use a starting block, so it should make us more even."

"Jon! Jenni!" Beth's voice. We pivoted together to look.

Beth, Dave, and Cindy were doing a wave, going back and forth. It gained momentum when Dad and Mom joined them, more so when Pastor Kamorkov added his considerable size. Next to him, an older kid contributed, maybe his son. Hard to tell as he did not resemble Pastor Kamorkov, but appeared to be much closer to my size.

Some of the others in the stands continued growing the wave, but I noticed none of those with Mr. Carling participated. He did give us

John C. Pelkey

thumbs up, and Connie waved.

"Did you see Connie's hug?" Jen asked, as we wandered along next to the backstretch. "I wonder if Dad's fooling around again."

"Again?" I asked. "Wasn't Lisa's mom, if even, years ago? Has he..."

No way could I finish the sentence without messing it up. Jen often indicated her parents in various states of being unhappy with each other, and her mom had left with no explanation except staying with Lisa's mom. I thought it was for support, but maybe not. Connie wasn't in any way inferior in the sizzle department. She did have a better disposition, which could be more attributable to her being in Grandpa Martin's employment than any other reason.

Jen studied them across the track, as we had wandered to the far side. "I think Dad has always fooled around. Mom thinking he cheats might be what they fight about."

"Are they fighting now?" I asked.

"Now, no, not with each other. Mom staying with Aunt Renee is something Grandpa insisted. They argue with him as much."

"Tell me why you think what you think." I was vaguely precise.

"Dad's always travels a lot, and even when he's home, he works late. Worse, he always seems to have someone young and cute as an assistant, even though, as he says, he doesn't supervise anyone. I wonder if it's what Mom did when they met."

"You think you mom was his assistant?" I asked. This was new territory, and I wanted her to continue.

We stopped, and she glanced up at me. "You doing an interview?" she asked.

"Maybe. If I am, I promise not to tell anyone."

She accepted my promise, and we continued walking, but not like before. For the moment, she had forgotten about me and had gone somewhere else. I thought she had dropped the subject, but she continued talking, while gazing into the distance.

"I was born June first, which means I must have begun about September first, probably in Miami where they go on Labor Day Weekend to celebrate each year. I saw their wedding certificate once. They married three months later, on New Year's Eve in Las Vegas. I'm the result of them fooling around, maybe while on some assignment Dad had. The reason they took so long to get married could be because Mom was married to someone else."

It was the most Jen had ever mentioned about her parents' past. Although she continued to hold on, I could feel the change, the tension creeping into her shoulder.

"Jen, how do you know?" I asked.

"On the wedding certificate, the name she signed. It was Elise Marie Gartner, not Martin, or Carling. I'm not certain Carling is Mom's real last name."

266

To Face The World

I thought of how surprised I was by Dave's request for me to be his best man. This was far more a surprise, a scary surprise. We walked in silence as I tried to absorb the conversation.

"Have you talked to them about it?" I asked.

"You're kidding, aren't you? No. You are the only person I've told." Her eyes, catching mine for an instant, further scared me. I could see something beyond concern. Fear.

Cindy, you're right. No one is better at keeping secrets than Jen is.

I needed to direct both of us back to track, especially me. "We need to focus. Everything you said, it's all about them. Today is all about us, well, more like all about you."

Jen smiled, a small crack in the tension. "It's about you, too. If I win, you win. You got me here."

We stopped to watch the girl's 400-meter race, which meant we had missed the boys, even while walking next to the track. It was a bit more than a minute race and done. North Valley took first. Jen's friend Marianne came in last.

"Same as the boys." So she had noticed, even if I hadn't.

"Was Rafer in it?" I asked.

"Yeah, he won. You didn't hear the announcement?"

"I was focused on something else."

She switched sides with me, so when I faced her, I faced the track, too. "Now you can watch the track and I'll watch you," she said.

I checked out the stands, where my family still sat together, intact, despite my contribution of less than thirty seconds to their day. I wondered what they thought of us walking around together. More specifically, what Dad thought. He had to realize there was more to us, even with running together as our chief motivation and focus. Would understanding us make things better or worse?

I could tell Dad we need to relax before our final run, and walking with Jen is good for relaxing, even if the subject matter isn't. Like anyone would believe me?

Beth pointed at us and initiated another parade wave. Everyone joined in, even the guy sitting next to Pastor Kamorkov. Jen turned and watched them, too. We waved it back.

"Who's the guy on the end?" I asked. Since he appeared to be with Pastor Kamorkov, maybe she knew.

She stopped and faced face me, her smile melting the tension. "He's Pastor Kamorkov's son. I can introduce him to you after the meet."

I could see there was more to this than she was ready to talk about.

Another secret?

"Let's go," she said. She turned to go back the way we had come.

"Jen," I said, catching her hand and stopping her. "It's faster if we keep going." We had walked all the way to the far turn.

"Oh, yeah," she said. "Good thing one of us pays attention."

John C. Pelkey

Ha, ha.

We had a half hour before our final run. Our team didn't seem to be doing so well, as the announcer kept saying, "North Valley, North Valley, North Valley," especially for the girls.

Lisa caught us. "Jenni, you set two records today, and Jon, you were right when you said I should be here. I get exclusive interviews, okay?"

It's not like you have any competition.

Since we had time, Lisa asked Jen questions while I checked coach Davison's score sheet. The field events listed Tom at the top for his throws, but Jim didn't creep past third for his other two jumps. So much for getting a highlight in Lisa's article.

Lisa's interview with me ended with an admonition. "If Jenni sets a record in the 1600, you should, too. It doesn't have to be as fast as hers."

"If I'm going to beat Rafer, I'll have to set a record."

"Good, I'll be right back after I interview Tom. He cleaned up on the tosses."

I had never thought of the javelin, shot, and discus as tosses. "They are called throws."

Lisa scratched on her pad, "Throws, not tosses. Got it. Why doesn't Trish throw the javelin? She can toss it back almost as far as Tom can throw it."

She snickered in recognition of her brilliant play on words, and I rewarded her with an eye roll.

To answer her question about Trish, I didn't know. As a track manager, Trish had to go through the same process as the competitors did. She had to be in shape as she could easily carry Tom's gear. Still, the only reason she participated at all was because Tom did.

Lisa gave me a quick hug and trotted backwards. "Win, so I can write about it. Jon and Jenni, swept them plenty."

Lisa hugging me seems less threatening than Connie hugging Mr. Carling. Mrs. Carling is already about fifteen years younger than he is. Doesn't she already qualify as a trophy wife? How young do they have to be? Why do I care?

I knew what bugged me. Lisa hugged and stopped. Connie lingered and leaned, seemingly reluctant to let go, even after Mr. Carling did. From far away, I could still sense it. She wanted more. Of course, I could be completely wrong.

Jen joined me in time to watch the girls' 800 finish. North Valley easily took the first and second places, with the third up for grabs until Sandi put on enough speed to squeak by their third runner. Marianne, the fastest 800-meter runner when Jen skipped, didn't compete. The girl subbing for her finished last.

"I think the girls are losing, even if you boys aren't," Jen muttered, before running over to congratulate Sandi. I joined her and gave Sandi a five, adding, "Good race."

"It's my tenth point," she said, beaming. "Now I letter."

268

To Face The World

"Congratulations." I gave her another five.

Marianne's situation became apparent when she hobbled up to the group, her ankle wrapped. "Congratulations on earning my point. Coach shouldn't have made me run the 400. Didn't finish then and can't run now." She headed toward the stands, having satisfactorily dampened everyone.

"She needed one more point, too," Jen muttered.

It showed how much I paid attention. I had no idea who needed points to letter, for either the girls or the boys. Ed had won the 200 at least twice so he had enough points. Winning all three throws today, Tom had earned enough points in this match alone. He had in every other match, except last week. Jim also had enough after the first meet. Dan, I didn't know. A couple of relay wins, some third places, they had to be enough.

Coach Harris gathered the team together. "Well, the boys are three points ahead. We can win of Jon beats Rafer and tie if he doesn't. The girls are too far behind. With two events left, we need ten points. We would have to place first in the javelin and in the 1600 to win the meet. Right now, they are sweeping the javelin and our two girls have no more throws."

I thought about Lisa's comment. Even if it made no difference, I decided to try it anyway. "There's time left, isn't there?" I asked.

The coach replied with, "Ten minutes maybe. Why?"

"Lisa wanted to know why Trish doesn't throw the javelin. She's been tossing Tom's back to him in practice all season."

"She's only a manager. She hasn't completed enough practices." He suddenly reversed himself. "You said she's been throwing in practice all season? If you're correct, she has way more than enough."

Watching him sprint away, I realized the coach must have run something in track, even if his claim to fame was in the pole vault.

We moved toward the throwing area. The javelin runway began right next to the track's far turn, but they threw facing away, barely visible from the stands. Since no one was running, we watched from the track.

The coach had Lisa, Tom, and Trish in a huddle, Lisa writing madly. When they broke, Tom handed Trish his javelin. She got ready and threw a warm up, short of the three North Valley markers lining the side of the throwing area. The second warm up landed closer; the judge placed her flag almost even with the third place marker

"I'm plenty warm already," Trish said. "I'm not going to throw it any farther."

"Of course not," Tom said. "But you are throwing my 800 kilogram practice javelins. You only have to throw a 600 kilogram javelin in competition."

"What? All this time, I didn't think I was good enough because I've

John C. Pelkey

been practicing with a heavier javelin and comparing it to the girl's distances. Why didn't you tell me?"

"I didn't think it mattered."

Tom handed Trish another javelin, not from his bag. I thought she was going to hit him with it, but when the timing judge said, "You have two minutes to make a qualifying throw," she ran and chucked it.

We watched it land beyond the first place marker, the distance judge giving Trish almost half a meter. It was all for naught when the line judge waved a red flag, indicating a scratch.

Tom handed her another one. "Last one, twinkle toes," he said. "This one has to count because you won't have time for another throw."

"I can't throw it now," Trish said. "I'm not mad enough anymore."

They locked in a stare down. "Toss the dumb spear, cave girl," Tom muttered.

"Thirty seconds," the timing judge announced.

"Fine," Trish said, breaking eye contact. She readied herself, shot up the run, and let fly, this time from a bit short of the foul line.

Even as we watched it, the line judge waved his green flag. However far it went, it would be a good throw.

As it landed, the North Valley coach charged over. "What's going on? This competition is over."

The timing judge snapped his watch and faced the coach. "Yes, it is." He turned to the announcer's box above the stands, waved, and talked into his radio. "The javelin competition is closed."

"Wait a minute. They had a late entry. My girls still had more throws."

"Yes, you did. Which you passed on, remember? Per the rules, I warned you three times."

"But we had won."

"Maybe you still won."

The distance judge marked the throw and threw his hands palm up. "It appears we have a tie," he announced.

The North Valley girls complained, but Trish danced circles around Tom. "What are you doing?" he asked, spinning around to keep facing her.

"Twinkle toes," she replied.

As the timing judge walked away, the North Valley coach caught his arm, instantly letting go. "Give us five more minutes," the coach said. "One more throw each."

"What you want is called cheating," the timing judge said. "I don't cheat, even of both teams agree."

He talked into his radio. "The javelin competition is closed. I'm awarding North Valley five points, for a first place tie and a third place. I'm awarding South Valley four points for a first place tie."

As the North Valley coach stomped off with his assistants, and our

To Face The World

team surrounded Trish with cheering, our coach caught Jen and me. "You two love birds ready to focus again?" he asked. As we weren't even holding hands, he must have been watching us walking around after our last races.

"All we needed was an inch," the coach mumbled. "Why didn't I notice Trish before?"

Attention to detail, coach. Lisa is quite good at it.

"About the record, Jenni, go for it, all out. You setting another record will remind North Valley we didn't go down without a fight. The girls aren't going to win. Even when you beat their top girl, we will be one point short, and we've no one else ready to run."

With all his angst over the meet, the coach had simply fretted himself into a corner, throwing the girls into races where they did not place. I checked Coach Davison's sheet. The top North Valley girl's time was close to Jen's current record and well ahead of any other South Valley girl's time. The best we could hope for was third, and only if we could find someone.

Coach Davison sat on the warm up bench and waved for us to join him. We went through every girl on the team. Marianne had a race left, but hobbling through it wasn't going to work, as North Valley had two solid runners and probably would line up a third. Sandi was the only girl left with a 1600-meter time under six minutes. Jen put her finger on Sandi's name.

"Sandi Ashburn," he said to the Coach Harris. "She's it."

"We can't ask her to run," the Coach Harris said. "The 800 finished only a few minutes ago. She can't even compete without a twenty minute break."

"It's been at least ten minutes," I said, waving at the official clock on the scoreboard. "The boys run first and they haven't called us yet. Between the two races, we should be able to stall out a few more minutes."

While the coaches conferred, Jen also conferred with me, sending me a question with her eyes. I nodded and pointed. Sandi was part of the group congratulating Trish.

Jen ran to get her, Coach Davison following, as they had come to the same conclusion we had, to my relief.

Coach Harris took the break to steer me around the track. I didn't know what to expect, but it wasn't what I got. "Jon," he said, "About the Ed discussion, you did the right thing."

"I did?" I asked.

"Yeah, you ignored me. Sometimes I get a little too concerned."

Or you show a little too much in the favoritism mode. On the good side, your sweating over Ed freed Jen and me all week. However, you should have noticed Trish way before now.

Not knowing my thoughts, he shrugged and continued with, "Are

John C. Pelkey

you going to be okay if Jenni beats you and your record? How about if Rafer beats you?"

"Rafer isn't going to beat me, and if Jen breaks my record, I'm okay about it. I helped get her into this."

"Well, if nothing else, you two have done well, exceptional. Think about it, two school records in one day already, and one of them a league best. So, congratulations and no hard feelings."

Shaking off Coach Harris's weirdness, I answered first call by trotting to the prep area for the 1600-meter run and checking in with the meet official. Jen had already checked in, and I watched her and Coach Davison give Sandi a pep talk. When a third girl joined the two from North Valley, I knew their coach wasn't taking any chances.

With a few minutes to go, I finished warming up by myself, as my 1600-meter teammates were still on the outs. Two North Valley runners warmed up with us. I wondered which one was Rafer. I was about to ask, when someone behind me yelled, "Hey, which one of you white boys is Jonny Per-Ronny?"

Chapter Twenty-Nine

A black guy from North Valley, who had been warming up with the 1600-meter girls, left them and headed toward our group. I remembered him running by during the 400-meter race, so I must have been paying some attention. I almost raised my hand, like if I wanted him to call on me in class, but forced myself to wave instead. "It's Perone," I said, providing him the correct pronunciation. "I'm him."

"Gotcha," he said, smirking.

"Gotcha?" I asked.

"Come on. It's trash talk. All in fun, of course. Gets us motivated and relaxed. You seem a little tense."

I was a little tense, but not about racing Rafer. I should have been; Rafer's time was better than mine. I remembered Ed's comment.

"Okay. Eat my dust."

Rafer groaned. "You are the absolute most lame trash talker ever."

"Gotcha."

He broke into a smile. "Subtle. Hey, you're better at this than I thought."

Rafer was my height, the only thing we had in common. He had a barrel for a chest, broad shoulders, narrow waist, big seat, huge thighs, skinny calves, and hands the size of baseball mitts. I had him beat in the calves. When I looked closer, I saw it. He had an earring.

He continued playing his "Gotcha" game. "You have to remember," he said, his eyes dancing with his smile.

It was a bite, but I didn't care. "Remember what?"

"To move to the outside when I lap you."

It was lame, too, but I didn't think Rafer was trying to be mean. "Can you run this in 4:40?" I asked.

"Yeah, my last time was 4:48, the time you have to beat. Your ponderously slow 4:53 won't cut it in my race."

"No, not 4:48, 4:40. I need a 4:40 pace from you for the first three laps so I can keep up with Jenni Carling's time."

"You want me to be your rabbit?" I could see his demeanor taking a dive from friendly to somewhere else.

"Gotcha."

"Oh, man," he said, laughing. "You learn real fast."

Rafer, between me and me, I do want you to be my rabbit.

"Jenni Carling, I watched her run today. She is very fast, roadrunner fast. My girl's the coyote in her race. Jenni's going to blow her away. But if we get second and third, the girls still win."

John C. Pelkey

"Your girl. You have a girl?"

He waved his hands. "Don't say it. I surrender. Hey, it's okay, man. No sweat. Next fall, we're going to be teammates for four years, unless you go to one of those fancy, uppity schools. One race doesn't matter, unless you win."

He put up his hand for some bump and slap routine he thought I would know, but didn't. Realizing this, he smiled and put out his hand. I wasn't up on his handshake, so he did it the old-fashioned way. "Gotta live with the white man all around, gotta know how to shake their way." At least he didn't say, "Gotcha."

"You win anything today?" he asked.

"Third in the long jump and second in the 200. I skipped the relay."

"How come?"

"Save myself for you."

"I usually run the 400 and 800, but the only guys I've competed against are on my team. I've been entering the 1600 to get ready to race you. I skipped the relay, too. I took the 400, but in the high jump, your guy nudged me out of third."

Good for Jim. Winning the meet depends on inches and seconds, and an occasional nudge in our favor doesn't hurt.

"You want to meet someone?" he asked.

"Like your girl?" I asked back.

"Yeah, like my girl. I do have one, you know?" He waved at the North Valley 1600-meter girls grouped with Jen and Sandi. A tall, dark, and good-looking girl waved back. They moved toward each other and I tagged along with Rafer.

"Jon, meet MaLinda DeClines. She's my girl."

We touched hands. Hers was soft, but colder than mine.

"You're with Ralph, right?" I nodded toward Refer.

MaLinda dropped my hand in instant anger. "So what if the newspaper got his name wrong. It happened weeks ago."

Something flashed on her face, and she spun to face Rafer. "Raf," she said, pushing a finger into his chest. "You been playing Gotcha again?"

"Not so well," he responded, locking in eye to eye with her. "I'm down three to two."

"I hope you played nice. Remember, not everyone knows you as well as I do."

"I must be playing nice," Rafer said, defending himself. "I'm losing."

They locked eyes, the same way Tom and Trish did; only here they both smiled.

I don't lock eyes at some off the chart intensity level with Jen, do I?

The answer came roaring back. *Yes, you do.*

"You want to meet my girlfriend?" I asked.

"Yeah," MaLinda said, breaking eye contact. "Rafer should meet Jenni. She and I were talking. Jon, she thinks you can beat Rafer, She *knows* she can beat him."

Rafer caught MaLinda's hand. "Whoa, girl. You listening to--"

"Gotcha," she said.

"Girls are so mean," he muttered. "Never play Gotcha with a girl."

They were fun to watch. In an instant, MaLinda had diverted Rafer from love to bluster.

I motioned to Jen. She hesitated at first, and then came.

"Jenni, this is Rafer."

I waited for some kind of "Gotcha" remark, but instead, Rafer held out his hand, as he had done for me. When Jen touched it for a second, he let go and jumped around, fanning his hand and blowing in it. "Girl," he said to her, "you are so hot."

As soon as it sunk in, he shot MaLinda and me with his index fingers, and blew on each one, pretending he had won a gunfight. "Double Gotcha," he said. "Twice the points."

"Do I even want to be seen with you?" MaLinda asked. "Come on, Jenni." As they walked away, she turned and fluffed her fingers at Rafer. He had a smile twice as wide as his face.

"Isn't she something?" he asked.

She is something, including her ability to melt you. I thought I had it bad. MaLinda has you reeled in and ready for the frying pan.

"Your girl," he said, walking to the starting line with me. "We know she can run. Question is, can you?" As I was about to say something, he kicked in with a final, "Gotcha."

Rafer, you won the "Gotcha's." Now, I need to win the race.

The announcer called us to line up. I found I felt relaxed, despite the importance of the race and the other events happening around us. Rafer had accomplished his mission, or at least helped.

With the best time, he stood on the inside. I stood next to him. The rest could start farther out or behind us. The two other North Valley runners lined up on my right, the one next to me rather close.

I wondered about jostling, a means to help their lead runner. It hadn't happened to me yet. The starter stepped out and spaced us, giving me a couple more inches. I wanted to thank him, but managed to stay quiet and focused.

Bang!

Rafer took off fast at the beginning. I had to abandon my race plan to keep up and ditch the two on my outside. I gave him a one-meter lead and managed to stay close. The rest of the group fell in behind on the first corner.

Once on the backstretch, the second fastest North Valley runner caught me and tried to pass. It wasn't hard to figure out his plan. He would pass, cut in front, and slow down, like in car racing. I sped up so he would have to pass Rafer, too, almost climbing up the back of Rafer's legs. The North Valley runner didn't give up, closed in, and, bam, bam,

John C. Pelkey

he bumped me hard twice with his elbow.

I tried not to get angry or panic and break stride, which was what they wanted. I weighed my choices. I could keep fighting the second North Valley runner, or let him cut and pass both of them. Either way, I wasted valuable energy.

Rafer, even with your teasing, you didn't strike me as someone who would do this. Did I ever misjudge you. Makes me the fish in the frying pan.

Another runner appeared on his right, one of my teammates who had been ignoring me all week. Before the North Valley runner could react, my teammate tried to cut in front of him. They collided, and both went down, almost taking me with them. I managed to stay upright, but had to break stride to jump a leg, giving Rafer about a five-meter lead.

We stayed in the same positions through the first turn of the second lap. I could feel the tension of the incident impacting my race. Not getting enough air, I fought a wave of fatigue, with the race less than half over. I thought of Jen's suggestion, breathe with a faster rhythm, and switched. Nothing to lose at this point.

On the backstretch, I passed the two runners standing next to the track, both yelling. A race official approached them, holding up a red flag.

Disqualified. More tension I don't need. At least Rafer has to wonder what's going on. Since I don't see any reaction, maybe he already knows. Did their coach plan it? My coach didn't say anything about bad running manners. Or about fights.

Half way through the third lap, my legs got the same lead feeling I felt near the end of the 200. My lungs were fine, Jen's breathing method helped, but I had no remedy for tired legs. Still, I wasn't about to quit. I could always get second, giving us a tie. All I had to do was finish the race.

No. I didn't come this far to finish second. I came to win. Nobody who cheats is going to beat me. Rafer Washington, I won't let you win this without a fight.

I focused on my boxing glove drawing and ignored my leg messages.

By the beginning of the fourth lap, I had lost track of the time and missed the clock, but had to make my move. Fighting off the lead feeling, I caught Rafer after the first turn and burst past. If I didn't collapse, he would have to pass me on the outside before the far turn or wait until the final stretch. I was hurting more, as my sides joined my legs. I felt like one of those airline movies, where as soon as the pilot fixes on problem, another one starts beeping.

Then, like lightening, something struck.

Even though they feel like lead, my legs, they still work.

I almost laughed out loud.

Yes!

276

To Face The World

I came out of the final turn at full blast, short strides, leaning forward, breathing fine. I used roadrunner thoughts to block out everything else. I kept it going and didn't look back until after I crossed.

Rafer was well behind. He must have lost it when I passed him. He ran hard to about a foot beyond the finish, and stopped.

"Jon, my new friend," he gasped, copying my position, bent over with his hands on his knees. "I'm going back to the 400... You can have this race... You must have set a new record... Both of us maybe... At least I made you run."

A new record? Yeah, but how much of a new record?

The clock showed my time, 4:30. Despite the altercation, racing Rafer had scared twenty-three seconds off my school record time. Second place showed 4:39. Rafer had knocked nine seconds of his school record.

"Congratulations," he said, still smiling between the gasps.

Memories of what had happened flooded back, and I watched my smile fall onto the track. "Yeah, I won. No thanks to your teammate. He played bump and run on the first lap. I thought we had switched to football."

"What are you talking about?" Rafer asked, his smile fading.

"Right. You didn't see your teammate on the sidelines?"

"Yeah, I did." His smile disappeared completely, landing next to mine. "What happened? Your face..." He pointed at something.

"Your teammate tried to take me out. My teammate sacrificed himself and took them both out. It gave you five meters, but I still won."

Rafer didn't hear the last part. He had left me, trotting toward his coach, still engaged in a discussion with my coach. They both waved their arms and pointed in my direction.

I almost followed him, but decided not to participate.

I hadn't done anything during the race except run, find an elbow in my face twice, and jump over a flailing leg. Still, their coach could try to pin the blame on me. My contribution to an argument will only seal my guilt, even if I don't have any. Opening my mouth when I shouldn't can only come back to bite me.

I sent another *thank you* to Dave, and searched for my saving teammate. He and the North Valley runner were walking out of the first turn, still in a heated discussion. Despite my aching sides and legs, I trotted up to them.

"Thanks," I said to my teammate, not caring if I interrupted their argument, and ignoring the North Valley runner. "He was trying to do to me what you did to him."

"Wait a minute now. I ran a clean race. You bumped me, too."

"I bumped you? Yeah, right. My lip jumped out and bumped your elbow. A clean race doesn't involve your elbow in my face and you know it, so save your crap for someone else."

Wow. I sound meaner than I ever had before. I didn't even know I could.

John C. Pelkey

Before he could form an appropriate response, I followed up with, "Did your coach tell you to take me out? Did you sacrifice your chance to finish so your team can win?"

His bluster faded, and he stared at the ground, shuffling his feet. "I didn't want to."

I'd heard enough. Fresh with my own head of steam and ignoring my aching legs and sides, I ran back up the track toward the coaches. I was more than ready to make a bad situation worse.

I almost made it, but at the starting line, MaLinda stepped in front of me. "Jon, what happened in your race? Rafer is over there yelling at our coach. Jenni and I were watching, and suddenly she split. She didn't wait for the race to finish." MaLinda pointed toward the end of the stands. "She's up there. What's going on?"

Instead of prepping for her race, Jen had left the track to engage in an animated discussion with three people. Looking closer, they appeared to be her mother, a police officer, and Captain Phillips. Mr. Carling had left his seat, trying to reach them by crossing the stands full of people.

Why didn't Mrs. Carling come with Mr. Carling? What is going on?

Forgetting the coaches, I shoved my tired body into gear and raced Mr. Carling. I arrived well ahead of him by running in front of the stands instead of forcing my way through the crowd. Mrs. Carling continued to scream at the officer and pointed toward her husband. Jen, silent now, had plopped down onto a bench, seething. When I glanced around, even the coaches had stopped their fight to watch.

When I approached, the three combatants turned to face me. If not careful, I would become the fourth. "Hi, Mrs. Carling," I said.

I turned to Jen. "Jenni, your race is like right now."

Jen's anger disappeared when she looked up, replaced with concern. "Jon, your face."

When she jumped up and reached toward me, Mrs. Carling blurted out, "Don't you touch him, Jenni; he's bleeding."

The officer had been holding Mrs. Carling's arm. When some recognition hit him, he let go and backed away.

Captain Phillips took over. "Jon, is this Mrs. Carling?" he asked.

"Jenni's mom. Yes."

"You are certain his is not Lisa's mom, Renee Martin."

Jen's eyes caught mine, indicating she wanted me to react in a certain way. I almost asked her what, but instead nodded. "No, she's not Ms. Martin."

"How can you tell?"

Now I know what Jen tried to say. How can I tell?

I tried to remember Ms. Martin in the car.

She had appeared tired and old. Why?

Then I knew why. "Even though they may appear identical, without makeup on, Lisa's mom has more wrinkles."

To Face The World

Jen cringed, the police officer smiled, and Mrs. Carling spouted something. Captain Phillips brought everything to a halt with a sharp commend of, "Silence!" Adding, "Please," as an afterthought, didn't soften it any.

"Jon, you are sure?" he asked.

I was more tired, hurt, and angry than sure. Otherwise, I wouldn't have lashed out with, "If you don't believe me, you can take your medal back."

Captain Phillips acted as if I had tried to punch him. "Mrs. Carling, our mistake. When you weren't with your husband, we..."

Mr. Carling squeezed around an obese man, almost knocking him down. In a complete huff, he demanded, "What is going on here?"

Before anyone else could speak, Mrs. Carling said, "So, you are back at it again, aren't you?" to Mr. Carling. "Now I know why you want to keep me away. You and my father are planning something. What is it this time? I saw your redheaded slut cuddling up with you. Is she your reward for obedience?"

"She-she's my assistant," Mr. Carling said, stammering. "She works for your father."

"You seem to be forgetting something important, Ralph, darling. I was your assistant once. I worked for my father. Remember, dear?" She stomped forward, forcing him back. "I was your reward. I know what's in the job description. Don't you even pretend..." Mrs. Carling ground down to a halt.

Mr. Carling pulled Mrs. Carling away from everyone to talk to her alone. Not whispering, but not loud enough for me to hear. Mrs. Carling, I could hear. She repeated one word for everything Mr. Carling said.

"No!"

I noticed the officer and Captain Phillips had moved away and engaged in their own discussion behind the stands.

I caught Jen's hand and tugged on her. "What is everyone fighting about?" I asked.

She stood, but let go and watched her parents. I thought she had missed my question, but she spoke, like someone in a dream sequence.

"They thought Mom was Renee, and if so, her being here violated her court order to stay away from Lisa. The officer said he followed her from Renee's hotel. They didn't believe me when I told them Mom was staying with Renee."

She turned to face me. "I'm her daughter and they didn't believe me."

I could feel the anger. She wasn't anywhere near ready to run a race. Everything we had worked for came crashing down in my mind.

"Jen?"

She softened her glare, which had been going right through me. "Good job, convincing them. Thanks." She took my hands, squeezing

279

John C. Pelkey

them. "More wrinkles?" she added, almost smiling.

"Sorry," I mouthed back, as I tried to steer her toward the race, one tiny glimpse of hope still prevailing.

Mrs. Carling caught me tugging Jen. "Where are you going?" she demanded.

"Jenni has a race--"

"No, Jon," Jen said, tugging back. "It's too late."

"No, it's not too late," I countered, pointing toward the coaches. "They're still fighting about the last race."

If Mrs. Carling was going to interfere, she lost her opportunity when Mr. Carling spun between her and us and said, "Let Jenni go. She needs to run this race."

"She doesn't need to do anything!" Mrs. Carling shouted from behind him. "You need her to run this race. You and those--"

She stopped when she found Mr. Carling's hand covering her mouth. I thought she would bite him, but she didn't.

"Jon," Mr. Carling directed over his shoulder. "Take Jenni to her race, now. Please."

I didn't need any more encouragement, but after going forward a few feet, we couldn't move. The two situations had captured everyone in the stands for an audience, all caught up in the altercations. They stood frozen in front of their seats and in the aisles, swinging back and forth to watch both the Carlings and the coaches. There were too many of them.

"Are you okay?" I asked, as we waited for a space in the crowd.

"About what? My mom accusing Dad of something? Daily routine." She almost smiled, far calmer than I felt. "At least I'm not bleeding."

We still hadn't broken free when Dave and Cindy appeared, trailed by Dad.

"Need some help?" Dave asked.

"Jenni's race is next."

Dave and Dad ran interference in front of us while Cindy took up the position of rear guard. In formation, we left the Carlings in their standoff. Unfortunately, we didn't move fast enough. I heard Mr. Carling shout, "I'm not sleeping with her." Mrs. Carling followed with, "You're not sleeping with me, either."

I expected to feel some reaction from Jen through her hand, but got nothing. Maybe she had tuned them out.

"Nice running, son," Dad said as we cleared the stands and stepped down to the track. "Glad I came."

"Yeah," echoed Dave. "Who said track wasn't a contact sport?"

At the bottom of the steps, Cindy pulled a tissue from her purse and waved it at me. "You're bleeding," she said, in case I didn't already know.

Before I could grab it, Jen did, and wet it with her tongue. As soft as possible, she dabbed my lip and my chin, which now decided to inform me how much it hurt. As I touched it on the right side, I realized my lower lip was about twice the size as my upper lip. To complicate things, I felt a bruise forming below my lip.

"You'll have to kiss her with the other side," Dave said, to a bump from Cindy.

"Go," Dad ordered.

As we headed toward the starting line, I asked, "Jen, why doesn't your mom want you to run?"

"I don't know. She didn't want me to run, then she did, and now she doesn't. Maybe it's because Dad does. Or maybe it's because Grandpa does. He's the reason for Connie and the suits. Dad does whatever Grandpa wants and Mom doesn't."

I searched all around. I couldn't see Jen's parents, and noticed two of the suits had left.

"Your parents, they're gone."

"Duh. They'll go somewhere and fight each other to a standstill. Then they'll call Grandpa and complain about each other until he threatens them. Takes about three hours. After he gives out their daily orders, they'll go home. Somewhere along the way, they might remember I exist. If I'm home, they will ignore me and go to their bedroom to make up. If I'm not home, when they remember me, they'll try to think of where I am and with whom. Somehow, they will find me, take me home, and then ignore me and go in their bedroom to make up."

I could feel the pain in her voice and in her words. Her shoulders sagged, weighted down by the strain of her crazy parents. As we walked across the track, I couldn't stop myself. "Jen, you can skip--"

"No, Jon, you got me here now; don't give up. With them, today is another normal day. Dad and Mom, they have constant issues. I don't want to think about their issues. I want to run."

I noticed MaLinda and Sandi a few feet away, trying not to listen. Some people next to the starting line yelled at me to get me off the track. I waved in recognition and backed up.

"I can't call out the splits," I said. "You have to read the lap times on the scoreboard."

"Doesn't matter. I'll count. I've practiced."

I let it go. "Remember to breathe."

"In three, out three."

She shook herself and began her warm up, stepping backward toward the starting line and keeping eye contact. "I'm okay. I can do this. You can do something, too. Find Lisa. Please." She blew me a kiss and flashed her teeth for a smile. "See you in four minutes and thirty-five seconds."

Certain my smile looked like I had picked it up off the track, I dusted it off and wore it anyway. I tried to think of a prayer, like I had before Jen's 200, but nothing brilliant came. Anger and prayer didn't mix, at least not for me.

John C. Pelkey

Why do her parents have to try so hard to become complete screw-ups on Jen's breakout day? I want to punch both, or at least yell at them.

Back at the railing, I felt a hand on my shoulder, one of the missing suits. "Danks, mon, for 'sisting Miz Carling."

His accent was on the heavy side, but I understood him. I also noticed he stood exactly even with the starting line and held an electronic device. Even with the electronic clock, he was going to time her.

He noticed me staring at it. "Et coptzures z start, z lap, on z finish. Iz hondy."

I spotted the other suit on the far curve, standing next to the track, and holding a similar device. They waved to each other.

"Z 1600 iz for z school. Z 1500 iz for z world. You 'member diz, Coach."

The suits don't care about Jen's 1600-meter time. They want the shorter 1500-meter time. Why?

"Iz bleeding," he said, pointing at my lip.

"Yeah, I know. Here, track's becoming a contact sport." I dabbed at it with Cindy's tissue.

"Iz very boud, fighting. Not a gud thing. To win race, you do well."

"Thanks."

So you noticed more than Jen. Yeah, you did. You called me, "Coach."

"Naw, Miz Carling, she do batter."

"Hope so."

I do hope so, despite what it means.

Chapter Thirty

"Clear the track," came from the announcer's box.

I left the suit to his work and found a spot at the railing about twenty meters past the starting line. Jen noticed, but I didn't wave. She didn't need me bothering her.

The race official came next. "Take your positions."

Jen took her place on the inside, with MaLinda next to her and Sandi on the outside. The two other North Valley girls lined up behind them. No time to finish her warm-up. She shook her hands out and nodded, as did Malinda, Sandi, and the two girls in the back.

I tried to help her get ready by conveying final race preparation thoughts.

"Runners, ready your mark!"

One last shake.

"Set!"

Lean forward.

Bang!

Jen let MaLinda take the lead as if part of an unknown plan. Sandi passed both of them before the turn, and she increased the pace when MaLinda and Jen decided to keep tight with her. This separated the three in the front from the two in the back. As they came off the first turn, I wanted to yell, "Faster, Jenni," but saved it. If she couldn't hear her parents screaming from twenty feet away, she couldn't hear me.

"Jon, I need to talk to you."

I turned around. Coach Harris stood behind me, Rafer off to one side. They didn't seem to be together.

"Can't it wait?" I asked, trying to turn back to watch.

"No, we need to discuss this now."

I tried to send Jen one last race thought, gave up, and faced him.

Right now, there's nothing more important than Jen's race. Of all people, you should know.

"Did you bump the North Valley runner?" he asked.

"Did I bump him?" Anger boiled over, quick, and deadly. "Of all the stupid..."

I caught myself. The anger and the pain on my face had ganged up against me. Although I tried to stop, it still came. "What does it matter?" I shouted at him.

"You don't talk back to me. North Valley has filed a protest. They want you disqualified."

"Yeah, Coach, I bumped him, twice. Once with my lip and once

John C. Pelkey

with my chin. See?" I pointed at my lip, which reinforced my self-accusation by bleeding again. "If you check out his elbow, you might find my teeth marks. Then you can accuse me of biting him, too."

Coach Harris examined my face, touching the bruise. He drew a wince despite my best effort to ignore his plodding fingers. "After the race, where did you go? Why didn't you say something? I would never have agreed to the disqualification had I known."

"You agreed to disqualify me?" I forgave myself for yelling at him, before and right now. He hadn't even checked first.

"Jenni Carling is running the race of her life, which you should be watching, which I should be watching!"

Calm down. You aren't helping Jen by freaking out.

Instead of continuing to scream at him, I quieted down and said, "Coach, their guy hit me on purpose. When I asked him why he did it, he said he didn't want to. Somebody made him hit me."

Another man stepped around the coach. The yellow ID hanging from a ribbon around his neck indicated he was the meet marshal. He examined my face, handed me a clean tissue, and turned toward the third man now present, the North Valley coach.

"I've seen enough evidence," he said, pointing at my face. "South Valley, I am reinstating your runner. North Valley, I'm denying your protest. Furthermore, if he is correct, and you instructed your runner to strike an opponent, I may have to disqualify your team."

The shock of what he said stunned everyone into silence, even Coach Harris. I had to say something. "Sir, please, don't pick on the team. They don't have any choice. Don't ruin it for them and us. We're just kids. This is our lives."

The marshal rubbed his chin. While he was considering my request, I had enough time to notice where the runners were. As they came around the corner, Jen had passed MaLinda, but not Sandi, and the second lap lead-time went well past what she needed. Sandi was trying, but too slow.

2:24

2:25

2:26

Sandy crossed, Jen right behind her. Half way, 800 meters down, 800 meters to go. The clock kept ticking.

2:28.

2:29

2:30

I wanted to sit down and cry. Jen would have to run the second 800 meters in two minutes, seven seconds, to catch the record. She would have to run faster than her school record. Still, she was so far ahead of MaLinda and the other two North Valley runners, she could trot the final distance and win. Then, when Sandi wore herself out and gave up

284

To Face The World

somewhere between now and the finish, they would beat us by a point.

Sandi came wide off the corner, and Jen picked up the pace and passed her. When Sandi's running turned into jogging, I thought she might stop. Somehow, she kept going.

The gap between them increased. Jen had to know how slow her time was, and how unsurmountable the record had become.

The marshal tapped me on the shoulder. "You show good sportsmanship, wanting to give them a chance."

Done with me, he waved the other men forward. "North Valley, let's go talk to your runner. South Valley, you come, too. I want to get to the bottom of this right now."

As they walked away, Rafer caught me. "Jon, I'm sorry. I won't blame you if you don't believe me, but I didn't know. Maybe I talk trash, but I don't ever cheat. Ever. Cheating is not what being a Christian is about."

"What did you say?" I asked. Rafer's admission came from left field.

"I don't cheat. I'm a Christian, Jon. You can't hide cheating from God."

I had all sorts of things I wanted to say, but what I managed was, "Rafer, I believe you."

For my small admission, I got a huge smile reward. "You and me, we have to be buds. There aren't enough of us around."

Despite everything, I couldn't help but smile back. Rafer had a way of making other issues seem less important.

Meanwhile, unlike me, the clock ignored everything else and kept ticking away.

3:22

3:23

3:24

Jen came around the corner, now alone. Trish passed Sandi, still on the backstretch. Although Sandi had sacrificed herself to be the rabbit, her time was too slow. To finish ahead of the 4:34 record, Jen needed to have crossed already.

3:32

3:33

3:34

Jen crossed at 3:35. I managed a, "Go, Jen!" as loud as I could get it. If she heard it, she had to know it was from me.

Her third lap was sixty-eight seconds. She would have to run the final 400 meters in less than sixty seconds to capture the girl's record. After everything else, the voice inside me proclaimed, *Not a chance.*

We watched MaLinda fly by at the end of her third lap. She didn't look, but she wigged her fingers. Rafer's smile got even wider. Priorities. Rafer and MaLinda knew theirs.

I heard a gasp from the stands, and searched for Jen.

John C. Pelkey

Did she fall? No, she didn't.

The gasp was for something else. As she entered the final turn, she was flying.

"Nobody can run that fast," Rafer said, his mouth propped open. "I can't. You can't. Even God can't."

God. I found myself praying, *Please don't let her fall; please don't let her fall.*

"What are you doing?" Rafer asked, as I must have been moving my mouth.

I couldn't think of how to explain, so I kept silent.

"It's okay," he said. "I do it, too."

Sandi appeared around the corner, with a few feet separating her from the two other North Valley runners. She ran in obvious pain, pushing an elbow against her side with each stride, but at the same time, she didn't give up.

The race officials waved the final three runners to the outside as Jen shot into the final stretch, and she passed all three.

The clock kept ticking, as if it was sprinting, too, trying to fend off Jen at the finish.

4:29.

4:30.

4:31.

The clock lost as Jen was across.

4:32

4:33

4:34

Beyond all comprehension, she had beaten the record by three seconds.

My fantastic girlfriend creature person has done this. She, Jennifer Carling, in less than one month, she has gone from not finishing a race to being the fastest girl ever. Ever! More important, she likes me, loves me. Me!

The warm and euphoric rush of incredible feelings attacked and completely overwhelmed me, and I let it.

Her time didn't appear, as if even the clock couldn't believe it. The announcer came on. "Folks, bear with us. We have two hand-held timers on the track. We need to verify everything first."

Rafer pushed me toward the track. "Come on, Jon. Your girl won, big time won. Go congratulate her."

As I approached the stairs, I watched an official question the suit I had visited with at the finish line. After a quick check, he turned and gave thumbs up to the announcer's booth. The screen lit up with "Jennifer Carling wins the1600-meter run in 4:31:76."

As I approached her on the track, Jen stood bent over in lane five, hands on her knees. The second she saw me, she was up and in my arms, spinning us around.

To Face The World

"I did it; we did it," she said between gasps as I put her down. We moseyed along the track in the outside lane. Jen practiced her breathing and let me practice holding her up.

"The scoreboard... says 4:31... Three seconds... Yes... You are the best... coach, ever, and the best... boyfriend... Thank you, Jon."

In front of the stands, in front of my parents, in front of Mrs. Koffman at the railing ten feet away with her camera clicking, in front of our whole world, Jen kissed me, more of a lip nuzzle on the left side of my mouth.

You remembered my lip.

I kissed her back, using both sides of both lips, although it hurt.

Sometimes I just have to do it and suffer the consequences.

"Jennifer Carling, I love you," I whispered to her ear, right in the middle of a hug. "No matter what happens."

Jen slipped back, enough to capture my eyes with hers, while still hanging on. "Jon Perone, I love you. Nothing is ever going to change my heart."

We turned toward the stands, and Mrs. Koffman's camera, arms around each other. Jen waved, but I didn't. The waving part was her moment, but the holding on to each other was our moment. We were giving notice.

Together, we are ready to face the world.

John C. Pelkey

Epilogue

July 28, 1996

At the Atlanta games, the women's 3000-meter run continues; Dad, Mom, and I watch. The only sound is Cindy breathing into the phone. The American establishes herself in front and away from the pack through the second lap. The race turns into a waiting game. The camera focuses back and forth between her and Trina, trying to develop a strategy by just showing the runners. Trina lets the pack pull her along, but appears concerned about being so far behind so early. Bob and Jim forget for a minute they are announcing and watch with everyone else.

Rex introduces some howling to go with the barking, and Dad waves at me to let her out. I give myself a couple of breaths, drop the phone, sprint around the corner into the kitchen, throw the door open, and yell, "Out, Rex!" She doesn't need me to tell her twice. I fly back.

"Nobody said or did anything in the five seconds you were gone," Dad informs me.

Back on the phone, Cindy says, "I heard that. What's Rex doing in the house?"

"Barking, same as she does outside."

The third lap repeats the second. I check the sound on the TV. *Yeah, it works.* It's like everyone in the running world is holding their breath. I notice I still am.

Finally Jim speaks. "Our girl looks good so far."

Our girl... My girl... once. Even now, years apart, my soul mate and the love of my life. Yes, she looks good so far.

Although only to the TV, I yell encouragement. "Go, Jen, go!"

The American continues to glide along well in front, smiling as if she heard me.

Still over four laps to go. Can she win this?

Even as I whisper, "Of course, she can," I know the answer.

Only time will tell.

A Time for Icebergs -- Coming June 2015

About John C. Pelkey

John Pelkey wrote his first short story in fourth grade. His teacher was so impressed; she bound it and placed it in the library for other students to check out for book reports. Thirty-two years later, he started writing again, when one of his co-workers asked him to explain what it was like to be a Christian. His stories feature young people in first love romantic situations. *To Face the World* is his fourth novel. John is a retired financial manager with the State of Washington and a graduate of The Evergreen State College, with a degree in psychology. He lives in West Puget Sound with his wife Cheryl, five fluff dogs, and Nellie the cat.

Made in the USA
Charleston, SC
24 June 2015